Praise for *USA TODAY* bestselling author Julie Miller

"[The hero is] exactly what the doctor ordered."
—*RT Book Reviews* on *KCPD Protector*

"Picture perfect."
—*RT Book Reviews* on *Yuletide Protector*, Top Pick

"Talk about fogged windows."
—*Dear Author* on *Out of Control*

"With its equal measure of romance (fifteen year age gap isn't much!; besides, Jillian and Michael are simply meant to be together) and suspense (with the added chills of a quasi-thriller embodied by Jillian's twisted "Loverboy" stalker), tight plot, great pacing and wonderful characters this story is a definite keeper and highly recommended by this satisfied reader."
—*Goodreads* on *Takedown*

"An exciting romantic suspense thriller with a thinking alpha male hero and an appealing heroine."
—[illegible] on *KCPD Protector*

Julie Miller is an award-winning *USA TODAY* bestselling author of breathtaking romantic suspense—with a National Readers' Choice Award and a Daphne du Maurier Award, among other prizes. She has also earned an *RT Book Reviews* Career Achievement Award. For a complete list of her books, monthly newsletter and more, go to juliemiller.org.

Be sure to look for more books by Julie Miller in Harlequin Intrigue—the ultimate destination for edge-of-your-seat intrigue and fearless romance. There are six new Harlequin Intrigue titles available every month. Check one out today!

USA TODAY Bestselling Author

Julie Miller

HEROES OF S.W.A.T.

Recycling programs
for this product may
not exist in your area.

ISBN-13: 978-0-373-60976-5

Heroes of S.W.A.T.

This edition published by arrangement with Harlequin Books S.A.

For questions and comments about the quality of this book, please contact us at CustomerService@Harlequin.com.

Printed in U.S.A.

CONTENTS

PRIVATE S.W.A.T. TAKEOVER

For the Greyhound Museum in Atchison, Kansas. What a pleasure to meet "The Talented Mr. Ripley," a retired champion greyhound, and his two female companions, who greeted us at the door, kept us company as we toured the facility and insisted that we pet them.

Thanks to the friendly docents and dog owners who made the visit an unexpected yet marvelous addition to last summer's vacation. And thank you to every person with a kind heart and a conscience who rescues unwanted, discarded and neglected animals and gives them a loving home.

PROLOGUE

April

"...'TIS I'LL BE HERE in sunlight or in shadow. Oh Danny Boy, Oh Danny Boy..."

Officer Holden Kincaid had learned three things from his father—how to sing like an Irish tenor, how to shoot straight and how to be a man.

He'd never learned how he was supposed to deal with losing the father he idolized to two bullets. He'd never learned how he was supposed to help his mother stop weeping those silent tears that twisted him inside out. He'd never learned why good men had to die while bastards like the ones who'd kidnapped, beaten and murdered Deputy Commissioner John Kincaid could cozy up someplace safe and warm while Holden buried his father in the cold, hard ground.

The lyrics flowed, surprisingly rich and full from his throat and chest, while he sought out his fractured family. Thank God his brother, Atticus, was here to sit with their mother and hold her up throughout this long, arduous day. Though he was the hardest one to shake of all the Kincaids, Atticus was hurting, too. Holden noted the way his unflappable older brother sat, with his hand over his badge and heart, revealing a chink in his stoic armor.

He looked farther back and spotted Sawyer standing just outside the tent, getting soaked. The tallest of all the Kincaid brothers, Sawyer might be hanging back so as not to block anyone's view of the graveside ceremony. Judging by the way he kept shifting from foot to foot, though, it was more likely he was scanning the crowd of mourners, sizing everyone up as a potential suspect. Holden could understand that. He was about to crawl out of his own skin because he was so antsy to do something about the injustice of their father's murder.

But Susan Kincaid had asked him to sing. Had asked him to honor his father with John Kincaid's favorite song. He'd suck up his own grief and anger, and do whatever he had to do to bring their mother some measure of peace and comfort.

Speaking of comfort, where the hell was Edward? Holden's oldest brother should be here, too, no matter what the reclusive master detective was dealing with. Yeah, he knew that there were a couple of heartwrenching reasons why Mount Washington Cemetery was the last place Edward might want to be. But after losing the husband she'd loved for more than thirty-seven years, all her sons gathered around her might be the one thing that could bring a smile back to their mother's face. For her sake, if not his own, Edward Kincaid needed to be with the family.

Holden finished the song, as quietly as a prayer, and blinking away his own tears as he pulled his KCPD hat from beneath his arm and placed it over his light brown hair, he turned to the flag-draped casket to salute his father. The steady drumbeat of rain on the green awning over the burial site punctuated the ensuing silence like a death knell. Holden didn't even remember moving, but next thing he knew, he was seated beside his mother, warming her chilled fingers in his grasp. The Commissioner of Police completed the eulogy and the twenty-one gun salute resonated through every bone in his body.

And then it was done.

Or was it all just beginning?

"Holden?" Atticus asked him to take his place at their mother's side. Instead of telling him the reason, he nodded toward a copse of trees about thirty yards up the sloping hill.

Son of a gun. Edward had shown up, after all. He wasn't wearing his KCPD dress uniform like the rest of them, but even from this distance Holden could tell he'd cleaned up, and, hopefully, sobered up to pay his respects to their father.

Holden was twenty-eight years old and he still had the urge to charge up that hill and swallow Edward up in a bear hug. But he'd let wiser heads prevail. Namely, Atticus. Charging and hugging would probably send Ed running in the opposite direction just as fast as his cane and gimpy leg would allow.

With his extensive training in Special Weapons and Tactics, Holden understood that teamwork usually got the job done better than any one man's heroic gesture. Tamping down his own desire to take action, Holden slid into the role required of him on this particular mission. He drew his mother's hand into the crook of his arm. "I'll stick with her."

As Atticus picked up an umbrella and went to talk with Edward, Susan Kincaid's grip shifted. "You did a beautiful job, sweetie."

"Glad to do it, Mom. I know Dad loved that song. He

taught it to me on one of our camping trips. Scared all the fish away with our singing. All the brothers, too."

He heard a bit of a laugh. Good. Maybe not.

He easily supported her weight as she wrapped her arm more tightly through his and leaned her cheek against his shoulder. As he looked down at the crown of her dark brown hair, he noticed gray sprinkled through the rich sable color. Hell. He hadn't noticed those before. He'd bet good money the sudden sign of aging hadn't been there a week ago when he'd stopped over for a family dinner—while his father had still been alive.

An unexpected rage at the collateral damage the senseless murder had spawned exploded through every cell in his body. John Kincaid's killer hadn't just stolen his life. The killer had left a big hole in the leadership of the Kansas City Police Department, and an even bigger hole in the hearts of the Kincaid family.

Somebody had to pay for all that.

But with the same kind of deep breath that iced his nerves before he pulled the trigger to shoot, Holden buried his anger. Instead of lashing out, he leaned over and pressed a kiss to the crown of Susan's hair. "I love you, Mom."

She hugged the triangular folded flag tight to her chest and nodded, rubbing her cheek against his sleeve. The sniffle he heard was the only indicator of sadness she revealed. Her brown eyes were bright and shining when she looked up at him and shared a serene smile. "I love you, too, sweetie." Then she settled in at his side, holding her chin up at a proud angle his father would have admired. "Walk me to the car?"

"You bet."

They were all the way down to the road when a man in an expensive black suit stopped them. “Su?”

“Bill.”

Holden adjusted the umbrella to keep his mother covered as William Caldwell, his father’s best friend since their fraternity days at college, bent down to exchange a hug. The laugh lines alongside his mouth had deepened into grooves, emphasizing his silvering hair and indicating another casualty of John Kincaid’s death.

“Holden.” As Bill pulled away, he reached for Holden’s hand. “I can’t tell either of you how sad, and how angry, this makes me.” Releasing them both, he straightened his own black umbrella over his head. “I’m making a sizable donation to the KCPD Benevolence Fund in John’s name, but if there’s anything more personal I can do…anything…ever…”

Bill Caldwell ran his multinational technology company as smoothly as he’d told B.S. stories around the campfire on the many hunting and fishing trips he’d taken with the Kincaids over the years. But today he seemed to be at a loss for words.

Susan squeezed his hand, rescuing him from his overwhelming emotions. “Come to the house, Bill. We’re having an informal potluck dinner. Nothing fancy. I just want to be surrounded by everyone who loved John. I want to celebrate what a good, wonderful man he was.”

Bill squeezed back and leaned in to kiss her cheek. “I’ll be there.”

Holden settled his mother into the back of the black limousine they’d ridden in to the cemetery. After tucking a blanket over her damp legs and finding a box of tissues to set beside her, he closed the door and circled the long vehicle to greet Atticus as he walked up the asphalt road. Alone.

Holden's temper flared again. "Where the hell is Edward?" His long strides took him away from the limo. "You went to talk to him. What did he say?"

As usual, Atticus didn't ruffle. "I talked to him. As tough as this is on us, you have to know it's probably harder for him to be here. His wife and daughter aren't that far from where—"

"I know he's hurting," Holden snapped. "But Mom wants to see him. He can't be such a selfish son of a bitch that he'd cause her pain, can he?"

"Get off your high horse. Sawyer's with him—bringing him around to avoid the crowd. Ed won't let Mom down."

"You don't have to defend me, Atticus." Edward and Sawyer walked out of the woods to the limo. "Got your boxers in a knot, baby brother?"

The rain whipped his face as Holden spun around. Edward's dark hair and beard had been trimmed short—a vast improvement over the shaggy caveman look he'd sported a couple of weeks ago, the last time Holden had dropped by his place to try to annoy him out of his drunken grief. Yet there was something dark and sad about his pale gray eyes that wiped away Holden's temper.

He noted the scar cutting through Edward's beard, and the way he seemed to lean heavily on his cane as he approached. Edward had been through more than any man should have to endure, and Holden was immediately contrite about any doubts he'd had about his oldest brother's loyalty to the family.

"Hell." It wasn't much to offer in the way of sympathy, but Holden walked the distance between them and wrapped Edward up in a tight hug. "I miss you."

At first, Edward's shoulders stiffened at the contact. Then one arm closed around Holden's back and squeezed with a familiar strength. But just as quickly as the bond was affirmed, Ed was pushing him away. "Get off me, kid." He inclined his head toward the limo. "Is Mom inside?"

"Yeah."

Edward swiped the rain from his face and looked at Holden, then beyond to Sawyer and Atticus. The four brothers hadn't been united like this for a long time. But the unspoken sentiment between them felt as strong as ever. "This ain't right."

After Edward climbed into the backseat for a few minutes alone with their mother, Holden closed the door and straightened, standing guard to ensure their privacy. Sawyer rested his forearms on the roof of the limo on the opposite side, looking first to Atticus beside him, and then across the top to Holden. "We're gonna get whoever did this, right?"

"Right," Atticus said before turning away to scan the departing crowd and keep everyone else away from the private family meeting.

Holden took the same vow. "Amen."

CHAPTER ONE

October

Oh God. In her sleep, Liza Parrish rolled over and tried to wake herself up. It was happening again. And she couldn't stop it.

"Shh, baby. Shush."

Liza closed her hand around the dog's muzzle and hunched down closer beside him in his hiding spot in the shadowy alley. The fact that he didn't protest the silencing touch was evidence of just how close to starvation this furry bag of skin and bones was.

He was lucky she'd come here after classes and work tonight, following up on a call to the shelter about an emaciated stray wandering the dock area that neither the county's Animal Control Unit nor the Humane Society had been able to catch. She'd get him back to the vet's office where she was interning—feed him a little bit of food and water, run some tests to make sure he wasn't infected with heartworm or some other debilitating disease, give him some love and a bath, and maybe just save his life.

But who was going to save her*?*

She hoped the dog was the only one who could hear her heart thumping over the whoosh of the Missouri River, surging past only a few yards away.

Trying to calm herself so the dog wouldn't panic and give away their position, Liza blinked the dampness of the foggy night from her eyelashes. If only she could blink away the stench of wet dog and old garbage just as easily. If only she could blink herself to safety.

Her leg muscles were beginning to cramp in protest against just how long she'd been curled up with the knee-high terrier mix, hiding behind the trash cans and plastic bags that smelled as if they could have been left in this alley off the river docks ever since the warehouses on either side had closed. She was tired, aching, chilled to the bone—and scared out of her mind.

But she wasn't about to move.

Hearing two gunshots from the other side of the brick wall she huddled against did that to a woman.

Watching the two men waiting in the black car parked only ten, maybe twenty feet from her hiding space also kept her rooted to the spot. Her jeans were soaking up whatever oily grime filled the puddle where she crouched. The only warmth she could generate were the hot tears stinging her eyes and trickling down her cheeks.

Was this what it had been like for her parents and for Shasta? Endlessly waiting for death to find her. Fighting back the terror that churned her stomach into an acid bath. Driving herself crazy trying to decide whether, if she was discovered, it was smarter to fight or run for her life.

She felt her parents' terror. Felt her pet's confusion as he valiantly tried to protect them. Felt their senseless loss all over again.

Two gunshots.

Death.

And she had a ringside seat.

The dog squirmed in her arms and Liza absently began to stroke his belly, feeling each and every rib. "Shh, baby." She mouthed the words. She wasn't the only witness to this crime.

Eyewitness.

Almost of their own volition—maybe it was a subconscious survival streak kicking in—her eyes began to take note of the details around her.

Black car. Big model. Missouri plate B*? Or was that an 8? Oh hell. She couldn't make out the number without moving.*

But she could see the men inside. She had a clear look at the driver, at least. He was a muscular albino man, with hair as shockingly white as the tattoos twining around his arms and neck were boldly colored. In the passenger seat beside him sat a black man. He was so tall that his face was hidden by the shadows near the roof of the car's interior. She could tell he was built like a lineman because he was having a devil of a time finding room enough to maneuver himself into his suit jacket.

The size of the black man was frightening enough, but the albino looked crazy scary, like he'd beat the crap out of anyone who stared crosswise at him.

She was staring now. Stop it!

Liza closed her eyes and turned away. She could note any damn detail she wanted, but if those crazy colorless eyes spotted her, she was certain there'd be no chance to tell anyone what she'd seen.

The gunshots had rent the air only a couple of minutes ago, but it felt like hours had passed before she heard the next sound. The sticky, raspy grind of metal on metal as someone opened the front door of the warehouse and closed it with an ominous clank behind him. At the sharp bite of heels against the pavement, she opened her eyes again. The black man was getting out of the car with an umbrella, opening the back door.

"No, Liza. Don't look." It was almost as if she could hear her mother's voice inside her head, warning her to turn away from the eyes of a killer. "It'll hurt too much."

"But I need to see," she argued, feeling the tears welling up and clogging her sinuses again. "It's the only way I'll be free of this nightmare."

"Don't look, sweetie. Don't look."

"I have to."

Liza squinted hard, catching sight of the back of a pinstriped suit climbing into the backseat of the car.

"No!" She threw her head back. She'd missed him. She hadn't seen the man who'd fired the gunshots.

The next several minutes passed by in a timeless blur. The car drove away. She'd seen fogged up windows, and a face through the glass. But it had been too vague. Too fast.

She didn't know what the third man looked like.

As she had dreamed so many times before, what happened next was as unclear as the mist off the river that filled the air. But Liza was inside the warehouse now, cradling the weightless black and tan dog in her arms, creeping through the shadows.

If there were gunshots, if there were killers, then there must be…

"Oh, my God."

Liza had no free hand to stifle her shock or the pitying sob that followed.

In the circle of harsh lamplight cast by the bare bulb hanging over the abandoned office door was a man. Lying in a spreading pool of blood beside an overturned chair, his broken, bruised body had been laid out in a mock expression of reverence. His twisted fingers were folded over his stomach. The jogging suit he wore had been zipped to the neck, and the sleeve had been used to wipe the blood from his face.

"Stay with me, baby." She set the dog on the floor, keeping one foot on the leash she'd looped around his neck in case he should find the energy to try to run from her again. Although she was in grad school learning how to treat animals, not humans, she knelt beside the man's carefully arranged body and placed two shaking fingers to the side of his neck. She already knew he was dead.

"Remember." Liza heard the voice inside her head. Not her own. Not her mother's. "Remember."

"I'm trying."

Barely able to see through her tears, Liza pulled her cell phone from her pocket and turned it on. She punched in 9-1-1. "I need to report a murder."

"Remember."

"Shut up." She tried to silence the voice in her head. She wasn't on the phone anymore. She was kneeling beside the body, reaching out to him.

The dead man's eyes popped open.

Liza screamed. She tried to scoot away. "No!"

His bloody hand caught hers in an ice-cold grip and he jerked his face right up to hers. "Remember!"

"No-o-o!" Liza's own screams woke her from her nightmare. She thrashed her way up to a sitting position. Panting hard, she was barely able to catch her breath.

And though she felt the haunting chill of her cursed dreams deep in her soul, she was burning up.

"What the hell? What…"

She became aware of wiping her hands frantically, and then she stilled.

On the very next breath she snatched up the pen and notepad from her bedside table, just as she had been trained to do. Write down every detail she remembered from her dream before the memories eluded her. *Dead body. Cold hand.*

"Remember," she pleaded aloud. Before the body. There were gunshots. She put pen to paper. "Dead man. Two shots." And…and…

Blank.

"Damn it!" Liza hurled the pen and pad across the room into a darkness as lonely and pervasive as the shadows locked up inside her mind.

A low-pitched woof and a damp nuzzle against her hand reminded her she wasn't alone. She was home. She was safe. She flipped on the lamp beside her bed and with the light, her senses returned.

Three sets of eyes stared at her.

She could almost smile. Almost. "Sorry, gang."

The warm, wet touch on her fingers was a dog's nose. She quickly scooped the black and tan terrier mix into her lap and hugged him, scratching his flanks as she rocked back and forth. Liza couldn't feel a single rib on him now. "Good boy, Bruiser. Thanks for taking care of Mama. I'm sorry she scared you."

Not for the first time Liza wondered if the scrappy little survivor remembered that night more clearly than her own fog of a memory allowed her to. She traced the soft white stripe at the top of his head. "I wish you could tell me what we saw. Then we could make this all go away."

But she and her little guardian weren't alone. The nightmare might have chilled her on the inside, but her legs were toasty warm, caught beneath a couple of quilts and the lazy sprawl of her fawn-colored greyhound, Cruiser. "So I woke you, too, huh?"

Cruiser outweighed Bruiser by a good sixty pounds, and could easily outrun him, but a guard dog she was not. She was the cuddler, the comforter, the pretty princess who preferred to offer the warmth of her body rather than her concern. Liza reached down and stroked the dog's sleek, muscular belly as she rolled onto her back. "I know you're worried, too, deep down inside. I wish I could be as serene and content as you."

And then, of course, there was the furry monster by the door. Yukon's dark eyes reflected the light with something like contempt at the disruption of his sleep. Despite weeks of training and all the patience she could muster, the silvery gray malamute had yet to warm up to her. No amount of coaxing, not even a treat, could lure him to join her in bed with the other dogs. He didn't even mooch when she cooked in the kitchen. Yukon tolerated the rest of the household. He accepted the food and shelter she offered and ran or roller-bladed with her anytime she asked. She always got the feeling that he was looking for a chance to escape—to run and keep on running away from the prison he temporarily called home. No way was Yukon ever going to thank her for rescuing him from being euthanized by an owner who couldn't handle such a big, athletic dog. No way did he care that she'd been scared, trapped in a nightmare she'd relived time and again these past six months. No way was he going to offer one bit of his strength to make her feel any better. She spotted the crumpled notepad lying just a few feet away from him against the wall. "Nothing personal, big guy," she said. "Sorry I woke you."

Liza checked the clock. Four a.m. She'd worked the late shift at the vet clinic and had her applied microbiology review in another four hours. She should try to get some more sleep.

But she was wide awake in the middle of the night. She had no family to call, no arms to turn to for comfort. She was isolated by the very nightmare she desperately needed to share with someone who could help her complete the memories and then get them out of her head. But the KCPD and a restraining order from the D.A.'s office—to keep her identity out of the press—prevented her from talking to anyone but the police and her therapist about the gruesome crime she'd witnessed. She was alone, with no one but her three dogs for company.

She glanced over at Yukon, who was resting his muzzle on his outstretched paws again. *He* understood isolation. "But you like it better than I do, big guy."

With sleep out of the question and class still hours away, Liza shoved Cruiser aside and kicked off the covers. "Move it, princess."

Knowing she'd have extra fur and body heat to keep her warm, Liza kept the house cool at night. The October chill that hung in the air shivered across her skin as her bare feet touched the wood floor beside her bed. Instead of complaining, she let the coolness rouse her even further. After a few deep breaths, she stepped into her slippers and pulled on her robe as she walked past Yukon and headed for the kitchen.

The usual parade followed, with Bruiser right on her heels and Cruiser padding behind at a more leisurely pace. Yukon deigned to rise and come out of the bedroom, only to lie down outside the kitchen doorway. Liza brewed a pot of green tea, ignored her fatigue and pulled out her pharmacology text. She read her next assignment until the first rays of sunlight peeked through the curtains above the kitchen sink.

It was 7 a.m. Late enough to politely make the call she'd been ready to make since the nightmare woke her.

The male voice on the other end of the line cleared the sleep from his throat before answering. "This is Dr. Jameson."

Great. She'd still gotten him out of bed. Now her therapist would think she'd had some kind of breakthrough. But all she had was the same familiar nightmare she wished would go away.

Combing her fingers through the boyish wisps of her copper-red hair, Liza apologized. "I'm sorry to wake you, Doctor. This is Liza Parrish. I think I'm…" She swallowed the hesitation. There was no thinking about this. *Just say it and get on with it, already.* "I want to try the hypnotherapy you suggested. I need to get the memory of that cop's murder out of my head."

"CAN SHE TELL ME anything new or not?" The burly blond detective named Kevin Grove addressed the question across his desk to Dr. Trent Jameson rather than to her.

The gray-haired psychologist answered for her as well. "Possibly. Though she seems to be juxtaposing her parents' deaths with your crime scene, there were certainly a few more details in the account she shared with me this morning. She's certain there were two gunshots now. And that the victim's body had been arranged in a way that indicates the killer—or someone who was on the scene with the killer—cared about him."

"Uh-huh." Grove frowned, looking as skeptical as Liza felt.

Dr. Jameson continued. "I realize those are clues your forensic team can piece together as well. But I tell you, the clarity of her memory is improving. I believe we've reached the point where I can put her under and guide her memories toward a particular fact."

"You can do that? You can pick a specific memory out of her head?" Grove asked.

"It's a new technique I've been working on for several months with some success." Jameson blew out a long sigh, as though defending his expertise was a tedious subject. "I believe questioning Liza while she's in a suggestive state could tap into those memories she's either blocked or forgotten."

"You want to hypnotize her here." Detective Grove still wasn't up to speed on the idea of hypnotherapy. Or else, that doubt in his tone meant he understood just fine what Dr. Jameson was proposing—he just didn't think it was a worthwhile idea.

Liza squirmed in her chair. Surrendering her thoughts and memories to a professional therapist was risky enough. To do it in front of an audience felt a whole lot like standing up on a firing range and letting the entire world take a potshot at her.

But she had to try. This was about more than clearing her head of the nightmares that plagued what little sleep she did get and left her exhausted. She owed something to John Kincaid, the dead man she'd found in the warehouse. Six years ago, witnesses had come forward to help convict the thieves who'd murdered her family in a home invasion. Liza had been away at college, working on her undergraduate degree, the night her parents and pet were murdered. She hadn't been there to fight to protect her family. Or to see anything useful she could testify to at their killers' trial.

But she could testify for John Kincaid. If she could remember.

Helping another victim find justice was the only way she could help her late parents.

Twisting her gloves in her hands, Liza distracted herself from the uneasy task that lay ahead of her by counting the dog hairs clinging to the sleeves of her blue fleece jacket.

"The setting isn't ideal." Dr. Jameson gestured around the busy precinct office with an artistic swirl of his fingers. "But I'm skilled enough to perform my work anywhere I'm needed. A little privacy would be nice, though."

Detective Grove pushed his chair back and stood. "A little privacy sounds good. We can use one of the interview rooms."

Divided up into a maze of desks and cubicle walls, the detectives' division of the Fourth Precinct building was buzzing with indecipherable conversations among uniformed and plain-clothes investigators and the technicians and support staff who worked with them. Liza felt a bit like a rat in a maze herself as she got up and followed Dr. Jameson's fatherly figure and Grove—the bulldog-faced detective who'd interviewed her before in conjunction with the Kincaid murder case.

Liza tucked her gloves into her pockets as they zigzagged between desks. While Dr. Jameson discussed their late morning session with the detective, she couldn't help but compare the two men. Both were eager to tap into the secrets locked inside her brain. But while Detective Grove wasn't concerned with how her memories got tangled up, her therapist seemed to think he could use the painful experience of her parents' deaths to tap into her hazy memory of John Kincaid's murder, and draw out the information that he believed was hiding in a well-protected corner of her mind.

It felt odd to be discussed as though she were a walking, talking clinical experiment instead of a human being with ears and feelings.

About as odd as it felt to be watched by the tall, tawny-haired hotshot standing beside a black-haired man with glasses at the farthest desk.

Liza's first instinct was to politely look away. The two men were obviously sharing a conversation, and the parade through the desks had probably just caught his attention for a moment. But the moment passed and she could feel him still watching her. Liza turned his way again, then nearly tripped over her own feet as she stuttered to a halt. "Impossible," she gasped.

Remember. An imaginary hand from her nightmare grabbed hers and she flinched.

She was being watched by a ghost.

Closing her eyes and shaking the imagined sensation from her fingers, she purged the foolish notion from her head. Her brain was tired and playing tricks on her. Ghosts, shmosts. They weren't real. Taking a deep breath, her streak of self-preservation that had seen her through the most difficult times of her life kicked in, giving her the impetus to mask her shock before opening her eyes and moving on.

Man. Ghost.

Reality. Memory.

She snuck another peek as the man lowered his head to resume his conversation. *See? You twit. Get a grip.*

The similarities were there, yes. But that honey-brown hair wasn't streaked with gray.

The square jaw was whole. Not bruised and broken.

The eyes were blue as cobalt. Piercing. Very much alive.

Liza circled behind a carpeted cubicle wall. No way could Captain Hotshot be the same man she'd found murdered on that warehouse floor. She was going nuts, plain and simple. Agreeing to interrogation under hypnosis was a very bad idea. She should go home. Go back to work. Go for a run with her dogs. Anything normal. Anything physical. Anything that would stop the fear and confusion, and get her life back to its fast-paced, sleep-deprived, business-as-usual state.

But when she cleared the wall, Liza was forced to pause again as a pair of uniformed officers escorted a young man wearing baggy pants to a desk and handcuffed him to a chair. Determined to convince her brain that she'd only imagined Kincaid's ghost across the room, Liza used those few camouflaged seconds to study the man who'd spooked her.

The badge hanging from a chain around his neck marked him as a police officer. Yet, unlike the detectives wearing suits and ties or the patrol officers wearing their standard blue uniforms, this man was dressed in black from neck to toe. Black turtleneck. Black gun and holster at his hip. Black pants tucked into what looked like black army boots. And a black flak vest that bore two rows of white letters—*KCPD* and *S.W.A.T.*

Mask the spiky crop of hair with a knit cap and add stripes of eye black beneath his eyes, and she'd think he was ready to launch some kind of covert attack.

Against *her,* judging by the way his gaze darted back to her the instant her path cleared and she took a step.

That nosy son of a... Red-haired temper flamed through her veins, and Liza tilted her chin and hurried after Jameson and Grove.

So Captain Hotshot was a tough guy. One of those S.W.A.T. cops who defused bombs and calmed riots and shot rifles at bad guys from a mile away. He probably hunted for fun—had trophies of innocent deer and hapless pheasants mounted on his walls at home.

Tough guys didn't scare her.

The detective with glasses standing beside him kept talking, but the man in black continued to watch her. Suspecting her own scrutiny might have intensified his, Liza resolutely focused her gaze on the back of Jameson's silvery head and wished the path from Grove's desk to the interview room was straighter and shorter.

She felt the tough guy turn his conversation back to the man beside him, but the instant she snuck a glance over to make sure his fascination with her had waned, he blinked. And when those clear blue eyes opened again, they locked on to hers across the sea of desks and detectives. What the hell? Liza's pulse rate kicked up a notch. Without looking away, he lowered his head to say something to the other man. Were they talking about her?

Liza broke eye contact as she neared his position. A distinct feminine awareness hummed beneath the surge of temper. But both energies fizzled as an all-too-familiar panic crept in. Maybe she had more than her sanity to worry about. Did he recognize her? Did he know why she was here? Dr. Jameson and Detective Grove had reached the hallway leading to the interview rooms. Another few steps and she'd be there as well.

Two more steps. One more glance.

Enough.

"What?" she exclaimed, turning and taking a step toward the armed man, realizing too late that he was several inches taller and a heck of a lot broader up close than he'd been with the length of the room between them. But guts and bravado spurred her past the unnerving observation. "Do I have lunch in my teeth? You think I'm some kind of circus sideshow? Why are you staring at me?"

Without batting an eye or missing a beat, he grinned. "You started it."

"I did not." *Snappy, Liza.*

"Holden… We need to walk away." The caution from the detective beside him went unheeded.

Tough Guy faced her, looking as calm and bemused as she was fired up. When a man was armed for battle and built like a fort, he probably didn't feel the need to lose his cool. "Maybe I'm just admiring the view."

Liza scoffed at the flirtatious remark. Right. Like her freckles and attitude had turned his head. "And maybe you're just full of it."

An elbow in the arm from the man standing beside him made the tough guy raise his hands in surrender. "My apologies. Can't help it if I've got a thing for redheads."

"Uh-huh." Liza hadn't expected the apology. Didn't trust it. Wasn't quite sure how to handle it, either.

She nearly jumped out of her skin when she felt a hand at her elbow. She calmed her reaction before it reached her face and looked up into Dr. Jameson's indulgent expression. "Liza? It's not the time for chatting. I want to pursue this while the dream is fresh. Come along."

"Who's chatting?" Liza grumbled. Grateful for the opportunity to escape, she allowed Detective Grove to usher her into a room stuffed with a conference table and chairs. Before the door closed behind her, she gave one last look over her shoulder. The tough guy with the smooth lines and eerily familiar countenance was still watching her. Her reaction to his intense scrutiny was still sparking through her veins. Something about those probing blue eyes was as spellbinding as it was unnerving. Turning away from his inexplicable fascination and determined to dismiss her own, Liza let the door close behind her.

"Who was that man staring at me? I'm sure I've never met him, but he looked…familiar."

Detective Grove glanced toward the door as if her ghost had followed them into the room. "The big guy in the S.W.A.T. vest?" As if anyone else had zeroed in on her through the midday crowd like that. "That's Holden Kincaid."

Liza sank into the nearest chair. "As in Deputy Commissioner John Kincaid?"

"Yeah."

That explained the resemblance. *A thing for redheads, my ass.*

So much for anonymity. If she could figure out who

he was, then he had probably identified her as well—the woman who'd reputedly witnessed John Kincaid's murder. Behind that smart-alecky charm, he was probably wondering why the hell she hadn't come forward with the entire story and fingered the killer already.

She'd get right on that. Just as soon as she could remember.

"Holden Kincaid, um…how is he related to the man who was killed?"

Grove spread open the case file at the end of the table. He could make that bulldog face of his look pretty grim when he wanted to. "He's John's youngest son. And you need to stay away from him."

CHAPTER TWO

"GOT HIM." HOLDEN KINCAID framed the target in the crosshairs of his rifle scope, blinking once to make sure his vision was clear.

Clear like crystal.

His mind and body followed suit, blocking out any distraction that might interfere with the execution of the task at hand. The crisp October air lost its chill. The rough friction of the roofing tiles against the brace of his elbows and thighs vanished. Emotions were put on hold as months of training calmed the beat of his pulse.

Every observation was now made with cold-eyed detachment. From his vantage point atop the neighbor's roof across the alley, he could look right over the privacy fence into Delores Mabry's trashed kitchen. There was a cloudy spot on the window glass, a greasy hand print from the last time the perp had looked out into the back yard. But the smudge didn't mask the gray-haired woman cowering behind a chair against the refrigerator. The window's curtains hung wide open, indicating the target hadn't given much thought to how the police would react to this hostage situation. Holden's target was big enough to make this a relatively easy shot—if his orders had been to shoot to kill.

But as the pudgy stomach in the bright white T-shirt

passed by the window again, Holden knew there would be nothing *easy* about this shot.

Al Mabry was armed. He was moving. And the poor SOB probably had no clue to the danger his delusional state had put his mother, himself, and a dozen cops into. Going off his meds did that to a schizophrenic. Mabry was ill. Suicidal. If possible, KCPD wanted to end this standoff with everyone alive. But if Mabry decided to obey the voices in his head and suddenly start shooting up more than the living room furniture, then Holden's orders would change and a life would end.

No emotions allowed.

Static crackled across Holden's helmet radio and Lieutenant Mike Cutler, his S.W.A.T. team leader and scene commander, came online. "You can take that shot?"

Holden rolled his shoulders and neck, easing the last bit of tension from his body before going still in his prone position. "Yes, sir."

"Molloy, can you confirm?"

Dominic Molloy, Holden's lookout, backup and best friend, adjusted his position on the roof beside Holden and peered through his binoculars. "I wouldn't want to take it. But I'm not the big guy." Holden sensed, rather than saw, the teasing grin around the steady chomp of Dom's gum. "The hostage is on the floor," continued Molloy. "Scared out of her mind, maybe, but she doesn't appear to be harmed. Mabry's pacing the kitchen with his gun to his head. Hasn't pointed it at Mama yet. He does lower the weapon when he stops to drink his coffee."

Mabry had ordered his mother to brew a fresh pot earlier. After spending the better part of the past night on this call, Holden longed for some hot coffee himself. Or a hot breakfast. Or a hot… No. He couldn't afford to feel anything right now. *Focus.*

"The perp's routine hasn't varied for the last forty minutes," Holden reported. "The next sip he takes, I could drop him. I think I can even neutralize the gun."

"You think?"

Cutler's skepticism didn't rattle Holden. "Not a problem, sir. My shot is clear."

Dom chuckled beside him. "I see what you're planning." He raised his voice for Cutler and their teammates to hear. "I can confirm. Kincaid can take the shot."

"We've been messin' with this drama long enough," Cutler rumbled. "There's no way to reason with him and I don't want this to escalate." If Mike Cutler couldn't talk a hostage down from his crazy place, then no one could.

Holden was ready to take the next step. "Do you want me to take the shot, sir?"

"Let's get him back in the psych ward. Remember, incapacitate him and we'll take it from there. He hasn't hurt anything but the furniture yet. I'd like to keep it that way." Lieutenant Cutler's tone was concise and commanding—a trait that had always inspired Holden's own confidence. "Assault team ready to move in?"

"Yes, sir." The responses echoed from both the front and rear ground locations.

"You have clearance, Kincaid. Assault team—on my go."

Dom patted the top of Holden's helmet. "You're up, big guy. Do it."

Shoulder? Knee? Either shot would take Mabry

down. Funny how the man who'd murdered Holden's father six months ago had shared the same skills with a gun. One neat shot to the forehead, one to the heart. Clean. Precise. Deadly.

Hell. Where had that thought come from? *Get out of my head.* But the comparison lingered, forcing Holden to think his way through it before he could purge the ill-timed distraction.

The killer had used a hand gun, not a high-powered rifle like the one Holden cradled in his grip. He'd been a good forty yards closer than Holden was to this shot. The victim had been his dad, not a stranger. Had John Kincaid pleaded for his life? Had he held his head high in stoic silence at the end? Had he known death was coming?

Al Mabry didn't know.

Holden's heart quickened with each detail, beating harder against his chest, pumping a familiar rage and sorrow into his veins.

The man who'd killed his father had taken a perverse pleasure in torturing him before pulling the trigger. Holden was a better man than that. Mabry wouldn't die. And if he had to die, he wouldn't suffer. This was his job. Lieutenant Cutler's S.W.A.T. team was here to save the damn day.

"Get out of my head," he muttered, willing his training to retake control of his emotions.

"What's that, buddy?" Dom asked.

This is my job.

"Taking the shot." Holden iced his nerves, stilled his breath, framed the target in his sights and squeezed the trigger.

Boom.

Holden's shoulder absorbed the kick of the rifle. Glass shattered and Al Mabry screamed.

"Go!" Cutler's order echoed through his helmet.

Crimson bloomed on the perp's hand as the gun sailed across the kitchen. Holden quickly lined up a second shot to the perp's left temple in case things went south. But before Al Mabry could fully understand that he'd been shot, Holden's teammates had battered down the door and rushed the mentally disturbed young man. Jones and Delgado had Mabry facedown on the floor with his hands cuffed behind his back, the gun secured, before Holden allowed himself another blink.

The hate and sorrow were buried. The ice remained. Closing his eyes, Holden finally allowed himself to breathe.

"All clear, big guy." Dom sat up beside him. His boots grated on the gravel roof as he stowed his gear into the various compartments of his uniform. With the flat of his hand, he reached over and slapped Holden's helmet. "Hey. Cutler gave us the 'all clear.' I guess there's a reason why they call you the best. You *were* aiming for the gun, right?"

Even more than the chatter of commands and replies zinging from the radio in his helmet, Dom's gibe reminded Holden that he needed to get moving.

Striving for the same detachment from his work that Dominic Molloy seemed to enjoy, Holden rolled over, splayed his hand in Molloy's face and pushed him away. He could give as good as he got. "Jealous, much?"

"You wish." Dom's eyes sparkled with humor. "I could have made that shot if I wanted to. But it's my job to watch your backside."

Holden secured his rifle and picked up the tripod as

he pushed to his feet and made his way toward the ladder at the front edge of the roof. "Then enjoy the view. Last man down buys the beer."

Once on the ground, they shed their helmets and locked their equipment in the back of the black S.W.A.T. van. Combing his fingers through the sweat-dampened spikes of his hair, Holden crossed down to the street to join Rafael Delgado and Joseph Jones, Jr.—Triple J or Trip, as he liked to be called.

He held up his hand to urge the gathering crowd of curiosity-seekers off the street while the others guided the ambulance carrying Al Mabry through. Lieutenant Cutler followed right behind, signaling the EMTs when they were clear to take off. Cutler joined the team as they gathered at the van. The lieutenant congratulated them on a successful mission, reminded them to write their reports. Then he shook Holden's hand and pulled him aside. "Nice shooting, Kincaid."

The October morning had enough bite in it to create a cloud between them when Holden released a long, weary breath. Winter was going to be damp and cold—and early—this year in Kansas City. "Thanks, Lieutenant."

"We'll get Mabry to the hospital to stitch up his hand and have him evaluated. But he'll be all right."

Holden propped his hands at his hips and nodded toward the house. "Take his mother, too. You said she had a history of high blood pressure. Being taken hostage by her own son can't be good for her health."

"Don't worry. She's on the ambulance, too. We'll let her decompress, then take her statement at the hospital. I want you to do the same."

"Go to the hospital?" Other than being hungry as a

bear and needing to take a whiz, Holden was in fine shape.

"Decompress. You're wound up tighter than a cork in a champagne bottle. You've been on duty twenty-four hours, standing watch while we tried to talk Mabry off the ceiling for the last eight." Cutler pulled off his KCPD ball cap and smoothed his hand over his salt-and-pepper hair before tugging the cap back into place. "Your dad would be proud of you today. By wounding Al Mabry, you probably saved his life. And his mother's. He was an innocent man, a sick man, but I know you were prepared to make a kill shot."

"Just doing my job, Lieutenant. I turn off thinking about anything," he lied, "and take the shot you tell me to."

"Uh-huh." There was something in Cutler's sharp, dark eyes that saw more than Holden wanted. So he scuffed the steel toe of his boot on the pavement and looked down to watch a tiny pebble fly against the curb—until Cutler's words demanded his attention. "Think about this, Kincaid. Before you report for your next shift, I want to hear that you got drunk, got laid or got checked out by the departmental psychologist. I know this has been a tough year for you, and this was a tough scene to work. Go home. Go out. Go to the doc. But take care of yourself."

"Yes, sir."

Dominic materialized at Holden's shoulder, his wise-ass grin firmly in place. "Aren't you gonna order me to go get some tail, too, sir?"

"That'd just be feeding the fire."

Trip and Delgado joined the circle, laughing out loud at Cutler's deadpan reply.

"Ha. Ha." Dom slapped Holden on the shoulder. "C'mon, big guy. We'll check out the action at the Shamrock after we clean up and get a bite to eat. Drinks are on me." He turned to Trip and Delgado. "You comin'?"

"You're gonna pry open that tight wallet of yours?" Trip's lazy drawl mocked him with awestruck humor. "This I gotta see."

"Lieutenant?" Dom looked up at their commander. "You're welcome to join us."

"I'll pass this time. My son has a football game tonight. I'll check in with you guys day after tomorrow. Don't forget those reports."

A chorus of "yes, sir's" quickly changed into a noisy conversation about the new lady bartender at the Shamrock and whether she had any sisters she'd like to introduce to them. Delgado climbed in behind the wheel and started the van while the rest of the team buckled themselves in. Holden had found the woman pretty enough the last time they'd gone to the Shamrock, but for some reason he was having a hard time remembering what she looked like.

He must be off his game big time, to let his feelings about his father's murder distract him from his work—and his play time—and to let them distract him enough that Lieutenant Cutler had noticed.

He'd been through all the grief counseling, and had been cleared by the department's psychologist to return to duty four months ago. He hadn't lied to Cutler or the psychologist about his and his three brothers' determination to see their father's killer brought to justice. Even though they weren't allowed to work the case because of a conflict of interest, Holden, Atticus, Sawyer and

Edward had all found ways to keep tabs on the stalled-out investigation.

Atticus and his fiancée, Brooke Hansford, had uncovered evidence about a covert organization named Z Group that had operated in eastern Europe before the breakup of the Soviet Union. Before becoming a cop at KCPD, their father had worked with Brooke's late parents in Z Group as a liaison from Army intelligence. Something that had happened to a double agent all those years ago in a foreign country had gotten John Kincaid killed.

His brother Sawyer and his pregnant wife, Melissa, had dealt with an offshoot of Z Group soon after their father's funeral. But one of the thugs hired by the group had had a personal vendetta against Melissa. He'd terrorized her and kidnapped their young son. Despite the opportunity to blow open the murder investigation, Sawyer had done what any husband would have—he protected his family. John Kincaid would have done the same—any of Holden's brothers would have—so there was no blame there. Now, Melissa and their child were safe, but anyone who could tell them anything had been driven into hiding or killed.

And yesterday morning, while Atticus had been reporting on the trip he and Brooke had taken to Sarajevo to visit her parents' graves—only to discover that it wasn't her mother's body that had been buried in that casket nearly thirty years ago—Holden had run smack dab into Liza Parrish. A name he wasn't supposed to know. A woman he wasn't supposed to meet.

The lone witness to his father's murder.

Yeah. He was a little distracted.

A lot distracted.

Liza Parrish could make the scattered pieces of this whole jigsaw puzzle fall into place. His father's killer would be brought to trial and the Kincaid family could finally find peace.

So why wasn't she talking? Why wasn't she telling the detectives assigned to the investigation everything she knew?

And why the hell couldn't he remember what the sexy bartender looked like, the one who'd slipped him her number at the Shamrock, when he had no trouble whatsoever picturing freckles and copper hair, a sweet, round bottom and an attitude that wouldn't quit?

As much as his father's murder challenged his ability to focus on his work, little Miss Liza with the sass and curves—and answers—kept nagging at him like an itch he couldn't scratch. If he couldn't get his head together, he'd be a bigger danger to his team than the bad guys they were trained to neutralize.

Cutler realized that.

"Yo, big guy." Dom smacked him on the shoulder, pulling Holden from his thoughts. "I said whoever got Josie's number first would have to buy the second round of drinks tonight. You in?"

Josie. Right. That was the bartender's name. Yet it was hard to razz his buddies about the fact he already had her number, when he couldn't even recall the color of her hair.

But copper-red? Short—almost boyishly cropped and sexy as hell? *That* he could remember.

He was so screwed. Faking a lightheartedness he didn't feel, Holden fixed a grin on his face and turned to Dom. "You're on."

It was a hollow victory. But right now he'd take whatever victory he could get.

HOLDEN'S LONG STRIDES ate up the pavement as he ran the abandoned Union Pacific railroad bed. It had been reclaimed as part of an exercise trail along Rock Creek, near the Kansas City suburb of Fairmount, and would make for a scenic run in the daylight, with the red, gold and orange leaves of the old maples and oaks rising along the hills to his left and flattening out to the residential streets to his right.

Pulling back the cuff of his sweatshirt, he pushed the button for light on his watch and checked the time. At 11:27 p.m., however, the deserted path was gray and shadowed beneath the cool moonlight. Still, it was a good place to get away from the traffic and crowd near his downtown apartment without venturing too far from the amenities of the city.

Hanging out with his buddies at the Shamrock hadn't provided the cure Lieutenant Cutler had prescribed. Al Mabry was fine and full of remorse now that he was back with his doctors at the Odd Fellows Psychiatric Hospital. His mother, Delores, was resting comfortably at Truman Medical Center for a night of routine observation. No one had been seriously hurt. Holden had made a good shot. They should all be celebrating.

But the beer and noise had given him a headache. The greasy food had been tasty enough, but it had sat like a rock in his stomach. As for the women? Well, when doing a little flirting began to feel like a polite chore he had to perform, Holden knew he needed to get out of there.

With the honest excuse of a long day and a longer

night before that dragging him down, he shook Dominic's hand, warned Delgado and Trip to keep an eye on him, and left. Instead of heading home, though, he found himself at his Fourth Precinct police locker, changing into his gray sweats and running shoes. After a brief chat with his brother, Atticus, who was there to pick up Brooke for a late dinner after a meeting with her boss, precinct commander Mitch Taylor, Holden pulled on his black KCPD stocking cap and headed across town.

Sleep might have been a wiser choice, but Holden was more inclined to get his blood and adrenaline pumping, and cleanse himself of this restless apprehension from the inside out.

Normally, he was content to work out in the precinct's gym or run the streets near his apartment. But tonight, he needed something fresh and different to shake him out of this funk. The brisk dampness in the air would clear his head, while every turn on the route would reveal something new to pique his interest.

And if the path just happened to lead him past the address where Liza Parrish lived, then that could be excused as coincidence. The houses were close to the road, but set far enough apart to almost give the feeling of living out in the country. Probably at one time in Kansas City's history, this had been farmland, but with expansion and annexations, the neighborhood was inevitably being transformed into suburbia. As he passed a quarter mile of grass and trees, he realized how this must seem like a different world from the downtown animal clinic where Liza worked an internship through the University of Missouri College of Veterinary Medicine.

"Are you looking up what I think you are?" Atticus

had caught Holden sitting at a computer in one of the darkened precinct offices. Leading his fiancée by the hand, he'd entered the room before Holden was even aware of his presence.

Brooke peeked around Atticus's shoulder with a wry smile. "Sorry. We were on our way to the car when I mentioned that I'd seen you here. He figured out the rest."

His smarty-pants older brother never missed a trick, so there was no sense in lying to him. Holden folded the print-out he'd made and shut down the computer. "Yeah. I checked out the public information available on Liza Parrish. Brooke just told me where to find it on the computer."

"You helped him?" Shaking his head, Atticus turned to Brooke. "Honey, we talked about this. As much as it galls me to sit on the sidelines, we have to let Grove and his men run their investigation."

Brooke adjusted her glasses on her nose and softened her expression into a smile that always seemed to turn his brother's suave control into mush. "That's not what you said this summer, when we were on a hunt to decipher the clues your father left me. You were certainly involved in the investigation then."

"Yeah, well, we both know what kind of danger that 'investigation' put you in. I don't want to see anyone else get hurt."

She laid a calming hand on Atticus's arm. "All I did was show Holden a shortcut to the public access files on the computer. So he wouldn't accidentally trigger any security protocol that might alert Grove or anyone else to his search."

Holden circled around the desk and draped an arm

around her shoulders. "I knew if I had a computer question, Brooke was the source to go to. I didn't mean to get her into trouble."

As their father's former secretary, Brooke had been a friend for so long that she felt like family. Holden had been more than pleased to see that Atticus had opened up his heart and put an engagement ring on her finger to make that familial feeling into the real thing. So he wasn't about to let his leggy buddy here accept any of his brother's blame.

But Atticus wasn't angry, nor was he looking to place blame. His pale gray eyes reflected concern and an admiration for Brooke's talents that went far beyond her computer skills.

"Brains as well as beauty, eh?" He pulled Brooke from Holden's hug and curled her under his possessive arm. After pressing a kiss to Brooke's temple, Atticus gave Holden a look as serious as any he'd ever seen. "Just be careful, little brother. Don't get caught sticking your nose where it doesn't belong." He guided Brooke to the door, then paused to glance over his shoulder. "And if you find out anything, give me a call."

Holden grinned. Yeah, Mr. Serious was not only crazy in love but as determined as he was to find the whole truth about their father's murder. "Will do."

So now he was here with his brother's blessing, running his third mile, wondering why the hell he'd thought checking out Liza Parrish's place would give him any sense of peace. He was working up a sweat and getting irritated with himself because no matter how hard he pushed his body, his thoughts kept coming back to the freckle-faced witness who could make or break the investigation.

At least Holden wasn't as alone in this misguided late night jaunt as he'd first thought. Someone else was out on foot, either walking the streets a couple blocks over or biking or running the path ahead of him, closer to the houses. One by one, he could hear dogs barking at the intruder passing their territory.

Holden's senses pricked up a notch to a mild alert. This wasn't a dangerous part of town, but it was pretty remote for a woman who lived alone to reside in. Surely, Liza Parrish wouldn't be out for a stroll at this time of night. The woman did possess some common sense, didn't she? Of course, her preliminary deposition to KCPD said she'd been chasing after a stray near the docks in the warehouse district where his father had been murdered. Late at night. And that was definitely a dangerous part of town. Maybe he should hold off on the common sense assessment until…

Another bark pierced the night, turning his attention back to the houses. It was something yippy, aggressive, much closer than the other sounds had been. Holden's wariness sharpened the way it did when a call came in for the S.W.A.T. team. Maybe it'd be worth a detour through one of the yards to the nearest street to find out what was putting all those mutts on alert.

Lengthening his stride, Holden veered toward the next access point and rounded the corner, straight into the path of a fast-moving pack. "Ah, hell!"

The woman holding on to that pack gave a curse as pithy as his own, a fact which amused him for all of two seconds before he realized she was zigging when she should have zagged. Between his bulk, the momentum of the three dogs, the tangle of leashes and the speed of her roller blades, the collision was inevitable.

"Look out!" Holden threw his arms out to catch her.

The smallest of the dogs darted between his legs. The greyhound leaped and the big malamute just kept running.

"Yukon!" the woman shouted as her helmet smacked into Holden's shoulder.

Recognition was as surprising as it was irrelevant. A leash jerked around Holden's ankles, cinching his legs and abruptly tripping his feet. "Hold on!"

He snaked his arms around the redhead's waist and twisted, dodging the dogs and taking the brunt of their fall as they went down hard. Holden landed on his back with Liza Parrish sprawled across his chest.

"What the hell…? You?" Liza froze above him. The sounds of panting dogs and her accusation filled the air. Her eyes caught the moonlight and reflected like silver coins. But there was more fire than cold metal in their expression as surprise quickly changed into indignation. Bracing one fist against his shoulder, she pushed herself up. "Are you following me?"

"I…damn." Holden sat up as best he could with a nylon lead looped around his neck as she clambered backward onto his thighs. He loosened the cord and pulled it over his head. "I ran *into* you, Sherlock—I didn't run up behind you. Nobody's following anybody. Watch it," he added as a skate came dangerously close to the promised land in her struggle to extricate herself from his lap. "Ow!" That was because of the malamute, still eager to run, dragging them both off the curb.

"Yukon, no! Stop! Catch his leash!" Liza had lost her grip on the leads in their tumble, and the biggest dog took a shot at freedom.

Holden lunged for the disappearing strap. "Got

it." The big dog nearly pulled Holden's arm from its socket, but Holden tugged back. "Whoa!" With the sudden jerk on his lead, the gray and white malamute halted, turned. His dark, nearly black eyes seemed to tell Holden exactly what he could do with his command. "Is he friendly?"

"Not much."

Great, thought Holden. "Yukon. Sit." The malamute needed a minute to think about it.

"Sit!" Holden gave the leash a slight jerk. He was feeling bruised and off-kilter and slightly less amused by this situation than he might have been on any normal day with any other woman sitting in his lap.

The dog shook his silver fur, then curled his bushy tail around his backside and eased back onto his haunches.

"Sorry." The fringe of Liza's coppery hair was barely visible beneath the rim of her helmet as she adjusted it on her head. Then she slid onto her kneepads beside him and tried to untangle the leashes that bound their legs together. "He doesn't warm up to people easily, but as far as I know, he doesn't bite. Bruiser's the one who'll nip—"

A miniature German Shepherd-looking terrier thing jumped, barking, onto Holden's thigh and stretched as close to Holden's face as his ensnared leash allowed. He recognized the yipping bark from earlier. "Um…"

"Bruiser. Sit." Liza snapped her fingers and pointed, and the black and tan spitfire moved back to the pavement and obeyed.

"Sweet." He admired her authority over the dog. Not counting the tan greyhound who was sniffing his stocking cap, the canines seemed to be under control. Holden joined the quest to untangle themselves, but a closer inspection revealed the pale cast beneath the freckles on Liza's cheeks. "Are you hurt?"

She shook her head. "That's what the helmet and pads are for." She spun around on her knees to untangle the red leash that had wound around his ankles. "Are you?"

"I'm fine." In fact, he barely noticed the ache in his shoulder and hip. Sheathed in fitted black running pants, her firmly rounded bottom bounced in front of him. Holden politely looked away—for a second or two. Heck, he was a healthy young male, and she was definitely a healthy young female. *Holden Kincaid.* He shifted uncomfortably as his mother's voice reminded him of her expectations about how a lady should be treated. Ogling wasn't on the list. Ignoring the improper heat simmering in his veins, Holden turned his attention to the greyhound who insisted on being petted. He stroked her smooth, warm flank. "I guess the dogs are okay, too? Are these guys all yours?"

Liza glanced up long enough to visually inspect each creature. "I'm sure they're fine." She continued to work quickly, almost frantically, to extricate herself and the dogs. When Holden reached down to help, she snatched her fingers away to attack a different tangle.

In another few moments they were free. Holden pulled his feet beneath him and stood while she looped the handle of each leash around her wrist. He took her arm to help her stand. But as soon as she was upright, she shrugged off his touch, nearly toppling herself again. "Easy," he murmured.

She skated backward far enough to put her beyond his well-intentioned reach. When she was firmly balanced on her wheels, she tilted her chin and glared. Her puff of breath clouded the air between them. "What are you doing here? I'm not supposed to be talking to you."

"Well, it's a little late for that." But she clearly wasn't one for sarcasm, so he turned to more serious matters, and gestured up and down the empty path. "You should find an indoor track if you want to run at night."

She pulled the dogs between them and straightened their leads. "And who would allow these three to join me? They need their exercise, too."

"Then how about running in the daylight? Even with the dogs to protect you—" not that the greyhound nuzzling his hand was any great deterrent, "—this path is isolated enough to make it a dangerous place to run at night."

"You're here," she argued.

"It takes a few more guts to go after someone my size than yours." She was above-average height, and the wheels on her skates put her at eye-level with his chin. But there was still something distinctly feminine and vulnerable about her slender curves and youthful freckles that could catch a determined predator's eye. "Any woman should take the proper precautions."

Her eyes darted to the side as she seemed to consider his advice. But there was nothing but bold bravado in her expression when she tipped her chin to meet his gaze again. "You're John Kincaid's son. Do you know who I am?"

"Yeah." There was no sense lying about what she must have already guessed. "I'm Holden Kincaid and you're Liza Parrish." He extended his hand to complete the introduction.

She didn't take it. Instead, she wound the three

leashes around her palm and tested their snug fit. "You're not here by accident, are you. Detective Grove and the D.A. want to keep my face and name out of the papers—keep me as anonymous as possible. How did you find me?"

"I'm a cop."

"You shouldn't be here. I shouldn't be talking to you."

"So you keep saying." Propping his hands at his hips, Holden leaned in a fraction. "But my brothers and I intend to find out the truth about what happened to our father. A gag order isn't going to keep us from knowing that you're the key witness. What story are you telling Grove? Did you see who killed my father?"

"I can't answer those questions."

Maybe assertive cop mode wasn't the best approach here. He reached down and scratched behind the ears of the willing greyhound, suspecting the dogs might be the way to gain her trust. "What's her name?"

"Cruiser." The confident voice hesitated, as though suspicious of the new tactic. "She's a rescue hound. She used to race. They're all rescue dogs. The little guy's Bruiser and the big guy is Yukon."

Though the terrier mix seemed to be watching the interchange between mistress and stranger intently, the malamute faced away from them, looking poised and eager to continue their run. Holden said, "I know it's scary to come forward to work with the police, especially when there's a murder involved. But we have teams in place who can protect you. KCPD and the D.A.'s office won't let anyone hurt you. Just tell Grove the truth. He'll make the arrangements to put you in a safe house if you're worried about some kind of retaliation." He looked up from petting his new friend and offered Liza a gentle plea. "This case has been dragging on forever. The longer it takes to solve it, the less likely it is that we will."

The conversation seemed to rattle her independent attitude. Her silvery gaze blinked, fell to his chest, wandered off into the shadows. The abrasive woman who'd avoided his touch and given him lip was now avoiding eye contact and backing away. "I really can't help you. I mean, I want to, but—I don't think I can help you."

"You don't have to break protocol and talk to me," Holden reassured her, "but please be completely honest with Detective Grove. Tomorrow. As soon as you can."

"I need to be going." She turned away, clicked her tongue at the dogs. "Good night, Mr. Kincaid."

"It's Holden." But she was already skating ahead with her dogs, crouching slightly and holding on as the two bigger dogs pulled her down the path. Little Bruiser jogged along behind. In less than a minute she was out of sight beyond the trees and shadows.

Holden tipped his face to the moon, cursing his dumb luck and dumber idea for coming here in the first place. So he'd said his piece to Liza Parrish—gotten that much frustration out of his system. Instead of speeding the process, he'd probably terrorized the woman into being even more afraid of sharing everything she knew with the police.

He took a few moments to stretch before resuming his run. A few moments to realize that her scent clung to his shirt, citrusy and fresh, with a tinge of antiseptic thrown in. Feminine. Clean. It only intensified his improper fascination with the woman.

He gave himself a mocking thumbs-up. "Way to get her out of your head, Kincaid."

He'd better make that appointment with the department shrink because he didn't feel like getting drunk and when he was off his clear-headed game like this, he had no business getting laid.

Looking around the maze of shadows and moonlight, Holden forced himself to think like a cop. Things had quieted down in the neighborhood now that Liza and her pack had passed through. But the exercise path was still deserted. It was still nearly midnight. Even if she wasn't a murder witness, this wasn't the safest route for a lone woman to take.

Holden inhaled a deep breath and turned around. Keeping his distance so she didn't know he was following, he jogged after Liza and her dogs, keeping a watchful eye out. That's all his family needed—to have something freaky happen to the eccentric, albeit finely built, redhead who could identify his father's killer.

CHAPTER THREE

"BRUISER, YOU MOOCH—get your nose off the counter. Brownies aren't for dogs." Without pausing to let Liza remove his leash, her furry soul mate had trotted straight into the kitchen to inspect the pan she'd left out on the counter to cool. Liza locked the door behind her and sat on the Hide-a-bench in the front hallway to remove her skates. "Besides, they're mine."

Chocolate was a good antidote for a stressful day, and she'd been craving the sweet stuff more than usual lately. If she thought Bruiser's short legs could handle it, she'd add another mile to their nightly run to make up for the indulgence. As it was, she'd better watch how many "antidotes" she baked after dinner or the stress would start to show on her hips.

But she'd start watching tomorrow. After the week she'd been having—too little sleep, too much work, therapy sessions that left her agitated, embarrassed and more uncertain than ever that she could recall anything useful about John Kincaid's murder, plus two run-ins with John's overbuilt, in-her-face and under-her-skin son—she deserved a double-sized brownie tonight.

Liza lifted the top of the bench seat and dropped her inline skates, helmet and pads into the storage compartment inside. She finger-combed her hair back into its wispy layers and whistled for the dogs. Bruiser and

Cruiser showed up right away to let her unhook their leashes and reward them with a treat. “I’m feeding myself first, Yukon, if you don’t come when I call you.” She whistled again. “Here, boy. Yukon, come.”

He barely acknowledged her from his spot on the couch.

“Fine. We’re eating without you.” She padded to the kitchen in her stockinged feet, shedding her jacket and hanging it over the back of a kitchen chair as she went. Then she opened a cabinet and reached for a plate to serve herself a brownie. “Ouch.”

Drawing her arm back for a closer inspection, Liza cradled her elbow and slowly twisted it from side to side. How could she have missed hurting herself? She must have jarred her funny bone pretty good in her tumble with Kincaid. Though she’d like to credit the endorphins released during that final mile of her run for masking the injury, she had a feeling her preoccupation with Officer Kincaid was the real culprit that had kept her from feeling any pain until now.

How embarrassing, crashing into a man she wasn’t even supposed to meet. Pressing her body against his from chest to toe. Noticing things.

Even in those few short moments they were tangled together on the pavement, she’d noticed he was A) incredibly warm, despite the temperature’s drop into the 30s; B) built like an Olympic swimmer—long and solid and packed with muscle, hinting that he probably enjoyed sports and working out as much as she did; and C) he had the most beautiful eyelashes she’d ever seen on a man. Light brown, long and framing piercing blue eyes.

“Stop it.” Liza chomped a bit of brownie that was too big for her mouth, determined to take note of every sweet, chewy detail of her snack rather than wasting another moment thinking about Holden Kincaid. "He's just a man," she muttered around the mouthful.

A man who happened to bear a discomfiting resemblance to the murder victim who haunted her dreams.

"Yeah. There's no bad omen about that, is there." She swallowed her sarcasm along with her brownie. "C'mon, guys."

After tossing a couple of rawhide chews down to Bruiser and Cruiser, and tucking one into Yukon's dish, Liza poured herself a glass of milk. With the glass in one hand and a plate of chocolate therapy in the other, she joined the dogs in the living room. She didn't bother turning on a light or picking up the remote. There wasn't much on TV she wanted to watch at this time of night, and sitting with her three best friends—make that two friends and a maybe, as Yukon hopped down when she tried to join him on the couch—would help her unwind so that she'd have a shot at five or six hours of uninterrupted sleep.

Yukon ambled off to the kitchen to enjoy his rawhide in solitude while Cruiser curled up on the cushion beside Liza and Bruiser stretched out at her feet. The quiet was soothing, her body replete from exercise and fresh air. Once the initial sugar rush wore off, the chocolate and milk and late night should make her sleepy.

With her eyes adjusted to the interior darkness, she could see the sparse practicality of her furnishings. One woman didn't need a lot, especially when she spent the majority of her time at work or in class. And with three dogs of her own, and others she fostered from time to time living here, she didn't want a lot of good furniture around that could be turned into dog beds, or a house filled with sentimental knickknacks that might be accidentally broken by a wagging tail.

Still, the darkness revealed the loneliness of her existence. She'd put most of her parents' belongings into storage after their deaths—or had given them away to relatives and charities. As a college student, she'd lived in a small apartment with no space for such things, but mainly, as an orphaned nineteen-year-old, she hadn't wanted reminders of all that had been taken from her.

The one family photo she kept on her bookshelf looked mighty lonely. Maybe after six years, she was ready to face her past on a day-to-day basis without breaking into tears or clenching her fists in anger. She should unpack one of the embroidered pillows her mother had made, or put one of her father's bowling trophies out beside the photo so that the picture wouldn't seem so lonesome. So that *she* wouldn't feel so lonesome.

Almost as if she could read her thoughts, Cruiser nudged her head into Liza's lap and demanded she be petted. Liza smiled and obliged, smoothing her hand along the graying muzzle and stroking the dog's streamlined head. "How can I be lonely with you guys here?"

Talking to dogs and missing her parents—yeah, the darkness revealed an awful lot.

Including the tall black SUV parked across the street.

A faint blip of awareness nudged its way into Liza's brain. "What the…?"

Suddenly, the stench of garbage and an icy dampness chilling her skin were as real to her as they'd been on that April night down by the Missouri River when two gunshots had rent the air. Almost as if she was plunging down into a black hole, reality deserted her and she found herself alone in a dark alley, with only fear and death and a starving dog for company. Everything around her was black—the wall in front of her. No, not a wall. A car. A big black—

Bruiser's high-pitched bark yanked her firmly back into the reality of the late October night. Cruiser jumped off the couch and joined the smaller dog at the front window, offering a token bark of her own. A deliveryman coming to the door was usually the only thing that got them this excited.

"Hush, you two," Liza chided as she climbed to her feet. "You'll wake the neighbors."

Yukon beat her to the window to check out the commotion. Pushing aside the dog and pulling back the sheer curtain, Liza peered out at the vehicle. Any shiver of unease was overshadowed by the three-dog alarm going off in her house. Wait a minute. Was that...? Her gaze zeroed in on the oversized man sitting behind the wheel. Surely he wouldn't...

Liza's nerve endings hummed with awareness, waking her senses. She leaned forward. There were a million black cars in the world. Nothing particularly profound about this one except... There was definitely someone in that car. Not her neighbor's car. Not her neighbor. "Oh, my God."

The shadows beyond the circle of light cast by the nearest streetlamp kept her from making out a face. But the bulk of the man's shoulders looked familiar. There was no exhaust coming from the back of the car, so the engine wasn't running. He was just sitting there. Watching. Big man. Too close. Paying too much attention to her and her house.

"The nerve of that guy." She was already striding toward the front door. "Just leave me alone, already."

Trusting her temper would keep her warm, and that telling off the nosy cop wouldn't take two seconds, Liza unlocked the door and stepped outside. The moisture collecting on the concrete of her front step soaked into her socks but didn't stop her.

"Hey! Kincaid!" She marched down the sidewalk, pointing her finger at the tinted glass and silhouetted driver inside. "For the last time, quit following me. You know damn well we're not supposed to have contact. You're going to get yourself in trouble." She reached the street and angled her approach, heading straight for the car. "Besides, you've got my dogs all fired up and I don't want a complaint—"

All of a sudden, the headlights came on, flashing the high beams into her eyes. "Hey! Damn it, Kincaid!"

She threw her arms up in front of her face, shielding her eyes. The next curse out of her mouth died when she heard the engine turn over and rev up on all cylinders. "Kincaid...?"

The grinding pitch of rubber tires spinning against asphalt screeched in her ears.

Not good.

By the time the tires found traction, Liza was already running, diving toward the curb as the SUV barreled toward her. She hit the grass and slid, feeling the wind of the speeding car whip past her, and the cold muck of the damp ground seeping into her clothes.

"You son of a bitch." That was no accident. He had to have seen her. He was a cop, for Pete's sake. Whatever happened to "serve and protect"? Liza pushed up on her hands and knees. "Kincaid!" She stood as the

SUV spun around the corner, kicking up gravel and speeding out of sight. “You son of a—”

“Liza!”

Footsteps pounded the pavement behind her. A hand grabbed her arm. She yelped, spun around. Saw a ghost.

“Are you hurt?”

She shook her head, squeezing her eyes shut against the ball bearings rolling around inside her skull. “How did you…?”

“You okay?” She blinked her eyes open. Kincaid was still there. Tall. Broad. Close. He glanced over the top of her head, then behind him, looking in every direction before zeroing in on her. “I saw that idiot peel out of here. Not that you’re a whole lot smarter for running out in front of him—”

“I don’t understand….” The ground rushed up beneath her.

“You’re *not* okay.”

Strong arms caught her as she sank to the curb. Long fingers pushed her head forward between her knees, and massaged the back of her neck until the faintness passed.

As Liza regained her senses, the dark asphalt dusted with bits of gravel came into focus. She became aware of the warmth springing from her neck and circulating out into her stiff limbs. She marveled at the size of the big running shoe lined up beside her narrower, muddy sock.

She was sitting outside on a damp autumn night next to Holden Kincaid. And she was squeezing his big, sturdy hand between hers as though it was the only lifeline to keep her from drowning in a swirling pool of nightmares.

The comfort she should have taken from that hand ended as soon as the realization was made.

"Remember!"

Suddenly, in her mind's eye, she was clutching a bony corpse's hand. The touch was cold and dead, not warm and full of life. *"Remember."*

Liza jerked her hand away. "If only I could," she murmured, rubbing away at the imagined chill that remained.

"If only you could what?"

Why was she so certain she'd recognized that big man? That stranger? She didn't know him. Didn't know that car. Didn't know enough about anything anymore to properly protect herself.

The massage at her nape went still. "Liza. Talk to me. What just happened?"

Even at a whisper, the timbre of his voice was deep and resonant, and utterly soothing.

She pointed her thumb toward the intersection where the SUV had turned. "I thought you were stalking me."

"What?"

"I was so certain that was you." Liza lifted her chin and looked Holden in the eye. She touched her fingertips to the prickly stubble shading his jaw, reassuring herself that he was real. That he was here. That she wasn't crazy. The heat of remorse warmed her cheeks and she curled her fingers into her palm. He was real enough, and she'd been completely unfair to be so suspicious of his intentions. "I'm sorry."

"Besides the fact that I drive a red Mustang parked three miles from here, I'm not in the habit of running down women in the middle of the street."

"Only on the exercise path."

A slow smile eased the grave intensity from his face. "Good one. But, for the record, you and your pack ran into me."

She felt herself smiling back. "We tend to go wherever Yukon wants."

"I can imagine."

Liza shivered. She hugged her arms across her middle, unsure whether the chill came from the cold seeping in through her soggy clothes or her mind recalling just how close she'd come to being roadkill. "Why would someone do that? Was that road rage for yelling at him?"

"I got a plate number, so I'll call it in, see if we can pick him up." Holden stood, towering over her huddled position. "Could be nothing personal at all, just a dangerous drunk who shouldn't be behind the wheel tonight. I'll take care of it."

He'd take care of it? What? No. She handled her problems her own self. That was just the way she operated. Still, the concise, confident words were reassuring, even if spoken by this Montague she wasn't supposed to be talking to. "Thank you."

"Can you stand?"

Liza nodded. When he reached down to take her hand, she avoided it and the disturbing nightmare his tight grip conjured, drawing herself up onto her own two feet. But when he flattened his palm at the small of her back, checking up and down the street before escorting her across, Liza didn't pull away.

She'd grown halfway accustomed to his casual yet protective touch by the time they reached her front door. But as guilty as she felt about believing he'd purposely meant to harass or hurt her, she wasn't prepared to invite him inside to make amends.

"Why are you still here?"

He pointed to his chest. "Cop, remember? Besides, my mom says I should always walk the lady to her door, no matter what the night was like."

"If tonight was a date, it'd rank as pretty lousy, wouldn't it?"

"It wouldn't have been all bad. I mean, considering neither one of us had to be rushed to the hospital…."

She laughed before she could stop herself, but quickly fell silent. After all, this *wasn't* a date. "I meant, why are you even at my house? In my neighborhood? We parted ways twenty minutes ago."

He nodded, shifting his supporting hand to her arm to guide her up onto the front step before releasing her. "I ran to the end of the path and was on my way back when I heard somebody cursing my name. Pretty loudly, I might add."

Liza cringed before turning around to face him. "Sorry about that. I saw the big silhouette of a man in the car, remembered how you were watching me at the police station yesterday—"

"I told you I was admiring the view."

Standing on the step above him, her eyes looked straight into his. She couldn't tell if the dark blue irises were being mischievous or sincere, but she could say that either possibility intrigued her. "Right. You have a thing for redheads. I still don't believe that line."

Definitely mischievous. "Why were you staring at *me?*"

Because you remind me of a dead guy?

That sobering thought put the brakes on the inexplicable desire to continue sparring with the man. She wasn't so starved for human interaction or rattled by nearly getting run over that she'd let her sarcasm go to that place. "You remind me of…" *Your father.* What was she doing? Inhaling a deep, cleansing breath, Liza fixed the coolest, most reserved expression she could muster onto her face. "You remind me of someone I met once. Thanks for your help, but this is awkward. Detective Grove said I shouldn't have contact with your family, in case this goes to trial and I have to testify—"

"This *will* go to trial." His friendly, amused expression disappeared behind a mask that was all cop, all man, all business—and frankly, a little scary. "Anything you can do to help Grove find Dad's killer, and build the case against him—I *need* you to do that. My brothers and mom—and me, too—we need your help. Please tell Grove exactly what you saw so that we can move on this investigation. If you're afraid of some kind of retribution from the killer, KCPD has safe-houses. We can protect you."

So that was why he was here. Why he'd picked her out of the crowd and watched her at the police station. Why he was being charming and attentive now. Why he was ignoring Detective Grove's recommendation and having this face-to-face conversation with her.

Save the day. Name the killer. Fix their broken lives.

No pressure. No guilt.

The chocolate brownie burned like acid in her stomach.

No memory? No damn way she could help him.

Liza withdrew, both literally and figuratively, reaching behind her for the doorknob. "I'd better go in, and get into a hot shower before all these bumps and bruises take hold. I'm sorry I thought that driver was you. I know you're one of the good guys."

"Please, Liza." He stepped forward, she backed away.

Understanding his pain and frustration, she tried to summon an apologetic smile, but failed. "I'm so sorry for your loss. Good night, Kincaid."

His hands fisted at his sides, and the effort it took to hold himself still and stop pushing the issue emanated from him in waves. "Good night, Parrish."

She stood there in the open doorway, clutching the knob behind her, wanting to reach out to the sorrow tempered by confusion etched on his face. Wanting to say something, but fairly certain that nothing she could explain about amnesia or her own losses or good intentions would give him comfort.

He must have misread her silence. "I'm not moving until I hear you lock the door on the other side."

"Oh." Embarrassed that she couldn't seem to separate what she *should* do from what that lonely nugget of need inside her *wanted* to do, Liza turned and went inside, closing the door behind her and bolting it. There was no sense prolonging their goodbyes or wanting anything besides to be left alone.

Suddenly drained of energy, Liza leaned against the door's sturdy support. "You are a piece of work, Liza Parrish. Not only do you not help the man, but you probably made him feel even worse."

Of course, after that encounter with Holden Kincaid, she wasn't feeling real whippy, either.

For several seconds, she stood there, her palms and forehead pressed against the wood. But then she caught a glimpse of movement through her front window and breathed out a resigned sigh when she saw Holden jogging down the sidewalk and disappearing into the night.

A warm, furry body brushed up against her legs, eliciting a smile and reminding Liza she wasn't completely alone. When she didn't immediately respond, Cruiser butted her nose beneath Liza's hand.

"What is it, girl?" Liza scratched the dog's ears as she pulled away from the door. The aging greyhound sat in Liza's path, twisting back one ear and staring up with her soft brown eyes. "No, I am not going to invite him inside for comfort food. And he's not that hot. We're like Romeo and Juliet—I'm not allowed to like him."

Cruiser turned and heeled beside her as Liza went into the kitchen to freshen their water for the night. Liza could almost imagine the dog communicating with her.

"Okay, so maybe he *is* hot, if you go for that square-jawed, clever, buttinsky type." Liza set the last dish on the floor and realized Bruiser had joined them—probably to see if there was anything new to eat in his dish. But Liza imagined he was giving her the same knowing look. "So he needs me to rescue him. I can't."

The greyhound cocked her head to one side while the terrier trotted forward, both responding to Liza's voice. "Don't look at me like that. Dogs, I can help. But Kincaid? His family?" She tapped the side of her head. "I'm kind of useless to them right now."

Great. Now Yukon appeared at the kitchen archway, checking to see what the discussion was all about. "Not you, too."

He walked his legs out in front of him and lay down. Like the others, his eyes and ears were attuned to every word. "We do not need a man in our lives—especially that one. I'll do what I can, but you have to forget that you ever met him." Liza frowned down at her three canine consciences. "I have to forget him, too."

MR. SMITH HUNG BACK in the doorway, one hand tucked casually into the slacks pocket of his Prada suit. He was content to observe and evaluate until summoned. The older woman who'd called him away from his extended stay in the Cayman Islands strutted across the office toward the boss. He'd done work for both of them in the past, and had been paid handsomely for his expertise. He had no loyalty one way or the other, but he intended to end up on the winning side should this reunion not go well.

This was the first time in a long while that both of the big players in Z Group were together in the same room. Mr. Smith waited for the nostalgia to kick in. Once, their team had worked to maintain the status quo between hemispheres during the Cold War. Later, Z Group had infiltrated Communist Europe and helped pave the way for democracy. Those had been important times. It hadn't been all about the money back then.

Now, a generation of patriots had become movers and shakers in the world. Profiteers. The government had officially closed Z Group's covert operations when the Cold War had ended. But these two had seen an opportunity. With operatives in place, a market for arms and technology at the ready and secrecy assured, it had been a cakewalk to turn their talents into cash.

Would this East meets West meeting be a joining of forces? Or a clash of titans?

They greeted each other with smiles and traded hugs.

Nothing. But then, Mr. Smith didn't do misty-eyed and sentimental.

He'd stand back and watch these two take their trip down memory lane, and silently place a bet as to which one of them really had the power these days, and would garner his loyalty.

"How did you get in?"

The older woman, looking as if she were poured into her expensive suit, laughed. "Your assistant believes I'm interviewing for the public relations position you advertised."

"I can't believe you're here." The boss gestured to a seat across the desk. "Are you sure it's safe to be in the United States again? What if someone recognizes you?"

"It's been thirty years since any of my old friends have seen me. Not even my own family would recognize me. No one knows who I am."

"John Kincaid did."

She smiled. It was as beautiful and cold as Mr. Smith remembered. "Yes, but who is he going to tell?"

Refusing to be baited, the boss unhooked the top button of his Armani jacket and sat. That one was a cool customer, too. As far as Mr. Smith could tell, this pissing match was dead even.

Instead of taking her seat, the woman leisurely circled the posh office, casually stroking her fingers behind the boss's crisp collar, then moving on to inspect photos and awards. "This is nice. I see you've done very well for yourself."

"I've earned it."

Mr. Smith pulled back his sleeve and checked the time. His gold Rolex stood out in sharp contrast against his dark skin. He wasn't worried about the time, or even nervous about the silence. Inspecting his nice things was just something he liked to do.

"Weren't my communiqués clear?" The boss sitting at the desk broke the quiet first, indicating a defensiveness that tipped the balance of power to the curvy woman's favor. "I told you I've taken care of anyone who could possibly find out that Z Group still exists. James McBride, Laura Zook, Charlie Rogers, Leroy Maynard—"

"That's a lot of dead bodies in a short period of time."

"No one can trace the deaths back to me. I handled it like you did things in the old days. I recruited the talent I needed from prison to carry out each mission, and then eliminated them." The boss's blue-eyed gaze crossed the room to where Mr. Smith stood. "Or, I used people I can completely trust."

The woman's red lips curved with a sardonic laugh. "And who might that be, darling?"

Hands curled into fists, the boss rose behind the desk. "I've fooled the FBI and the local constabulary for months now. They have no idea that I'm connected to any of those crimes—or that you even exist."

"Overconfidence makes you foolish." Now the claws were coming out. "When John Kincaid's own son comes to Europe and starts digging up graves and running DNA tests, then that makes me think you're not getting the job done here."

"I gave *your* son, Tony Fierro, the job of finding out exactly what Atticus Kincaid and that mousy woman he now thinks he wants to marry knew about us. Tony screwed up and became the problem himself. I had to silence him as well."

If he was given to laughter, Mr. Smith would have guffawed at the irony. *He'd* been given the task of silencing Fierro. But apparently, Mommie Dearest felt no grief.

"Is there any wonder why I never claimed Tony as my own? He was eager to please, yes, but incompetent. It shows *your* incompetence to rely on him." She waved her red-tipped nails toward the door. "That's why I called in Mr. Smith."

That was his cue to come all the way into the room. He pulled the manila envelope from beneath his arm and strode to the desk, looking down at both the woman he currently answered to, and the boss who'd paid for his services just a few short months ago.

"For what purpose? You can't kill Atticus Kincaid or any of his brothers. You'll have the whole of KCPD breathing down our necks, scrutinizing their every contact, every old girlfriend, every high-school buddy. I've had a profitable arrangement with the police department for several years now. I don't want to jeopardize that."

"Don't be so dramatic." The older woman finally sat, crossing her long legs and nodding to Mr. Smith to continue. "There's a simpler solution. Mr. Smith has already uncovered some information that you were unable to. Report."

Mr. Smith set the dossier of ten names on the desk top and pushed it across to the boss. "I've located the last of the Friedman Animal Clinic employees. Their addresses and phone numbers are there, as well as photographs so I can identify them on sight."

Sitting to peruse the file, the boss thumbed through the pages. "And we're certain the Friedman clinic is the one that was called to pick up that stray mutt the night we took care of John Kincaid?"

Mr. Smith nodded. His deep, theatrically-trained

voice resonated through the office. “They’re a private practice, not a public service unit. Unless there’s a criminal action involved, beyond the initial phone call record and the health evaluation on the dog, they don’t keep detailed reports after six months. So it’s not clear who responded to the call. Only that one of their employees *was* in the dock area that night.”

“My contacts at KCPD mentioned a possible witness. But if anyone came forward, their information must not have been enough to make an arrest.” The boss closed the file and leaned back. “All three of us were there at that warehouse that night. It’s been six months and the three of us are still here, still free. I haven’t even been questioned. The witness must be unreliable, of no consequence.”

The older woman laughed, but there was no humor. “Do you really want to risk that? According to your reports, Sawyer Kincaid was the first to discover there was a larger conspiracy involved in his father’s murder—that it wasn’t just a crime against a cop. Allowing that was your first mistake.”

“I wanted to kill John outright,” the boss argued. “You’re the one who made it personal.”

Ignoring the accusation, the older woman continued. “The information his brother, Atticus, uncovered could expose our entire operation—*if* he had a name or face to link it to.”

The boss was no fool. “And this witness of yours might be able to provide that name or face, and give them a case.” Mr. Smith felt the boss’s scrutiny, felt the understanding that *he* was the final option who would make this entire mess go away. “And how, exactly, do you intend to narrow down the list of clinic employees and find out which one of them saw us that night?"

"Process of elimination. I intend to spice things up a bit. We'll see who the police work the hardest to protect. And that," concluded the woman, "will be our witness."

Mr. Smith nodded. "Within twenty-four hours of identification, that witness will be dead."

"No trace?" asked the boss.

The question was insulting. "I never leave a trace."

The boss grinned from ear to ear as though a giant weight had been lifted. "I like *dead.*"

CHAPTER FOUR

"CAN YOU HEAR my voice, Liza?"

"Yes." Her voice was a drowsy murmur. The pillow behind her head was soft, the strains of New Age music filtering through her ears even softer.

"Tell me, what do you see?"

Blackness. Liza's hands fisted in the pillow she clutched over her stomach as a slight panic speared her.

"Shh. Easy, Liza. Don't be frightened. I'm right here with you." The scents of lavender and vanilla teased her nose. Some drowsy part of her mind suspected that Dr. Jameson had lit another one of those mood candles that, like the soft music and silk mask blocking the light, were meant to relax her. "Do you remember the eye mask you're wearing?" She nodded. "That's the blackness you see. Let it go and look further inside."

Liza pictured the black mask she wore and then shut it away in an imaginary box, the same way her therapist had instructed her to dismiss the other sensory objects in the room. As her initial panic subsided, she drifted back to that floaty place in her mind where sight and sound, taste and touch had no meaning.

"Now you're relaxed." Just when she thought she might actually fall asleep, the scent in the room changed, stinging her nose. The sweet smells became something dank and moldy, and suddenly she was back at the docks along the Missouri River, on one dark, fateful night when her life had changed.

Liza tensed, hearing the lap of the current against the dock pylons and rocky banks. She was moving through shadows, feeling the damp, uneven pavement of the rundown area beneath her running shoes as she searched each alley with her flashlight.

Directed dreaming, according to Dr. Jameson's research. He was stimulating her senses while in a suggestive state, guiding her mind toward a specific memory.

"Are you there, Liza?" Jameson asked quietly. "Do you see the warehouse?"

She nodded. "I hear him. Just a soft whimper. He doesn't come when I whistle. He doesn't bark." There. Two small orbs reflecting her light from beneath a Dumpster. "I see him. He's skin and bones. He's not getting up. He must be so afraid. Here, boy." She made a kissing sound twice with her lips. "Come here."

"Never mind the dog. The dog is fine. He's safe with you now." Yes. Bruiser recovered. He was fit and sassy and ruling the roost at her house. The doctor paused to let her shuffle the information in her mind and settle back into that relaxed, suggestive state. "After you found the dog that night, what happened?"

"I heard the explosion. Two explosions. Bruiser was so starved and dehydrated that he didn't even jump at the sound."

"Forget the damn dog." The slight edge in Dr. Jameson's voice crept into her consciousness. "Those were gunshots, Liza. What did you do when you heard the gunshots?"

"I hid." She flattened her back against the rough brick wall, crouching down behind a pile of stinky garbage bags. "I'm hugging the dog close and muzzling him with my hand so he doesn't make any noise. The pavement is wet."

"Are you afraid?"

"Yes."

"Why are you afraid?"

"I don't want them to see me."

"Who are you hiding from?"

"The men in the car." Where had the car come from? When did the men drive up? Her head was working in funny ways, skipping over chunks of time. Or maybe these were the only fragments she could remember.

"Can you see the car?"

"It's black. Big."

"I want you to move closer, Liza. Slide along the wall and get a better look. Be very quiet."

Obeying the command, she peeked through the narrow gaps between the plastic garbage bags.

"Do you see the car more clearly now?"

"Yes."

"What kind of car is it?"

"Big."

"Look closer. Do you see a logo? A word that tells you what kind of car it is?"

She squinted and leaned in. "There's a logo on the front grill. A circle with three flags or shields… Wait. It's a black Buick."

A shiver shook Liza on the couch as a black SUV very like the one that had nearly squished her on the road last night took shape in her mind. So powerful. So fast. So deadly.

"You're all right, Liza. No one can see you." Jameson wanted her to relax. "What does the license plate read?"

With the mix of memories, doors were slamming shut in her mind. "I can't see it."

"Take a deep breath and look again."

She shoved against one of the doors that was trying to close. "It's white. No, blue. It's white with a blue design on it."

"What do the letters say? The numbers? Look carefully."

Her knees felt scraped and wet as she scooted closer to the garbage. She lowered her gaze to the license plate. But a blinding pain flashed behind her eyes, as though she were looking straight into a pair of headlights. "I can't. I can't."

"Breathe deeply. In through your nose, out through your mouth." By the time she pulled back from the lights, that door in her memory had locked shut. But the questions were still coming. "Is anyone inside the car?"

"Two men."

"A white man and a black man?"

She'd been to this place before. Seen these men. Told this story. Why did she have to go back? "Yes."

"Is anyone else in the car with them?"

"Someone's getting in."

"Who?"

There was another flash of pain, another roadblock. "I don't know."

"What does he look like?"

"I can't see."

"Move closer. Take your time. Look harder."

"No. They'll hurt me if they see me. They'll hurt the dog if they find us." Fear, not clarity, snuck into her memories. Her head throbbed as she grew more agitated. The shadowy docks became an empty, blood-stained living room. She flashed back to the speeding SUV and diving for the curb. "The dog will try to protect me. They'll shoot him. I have to hide."

"They can't see you. Or the dog. Tell me about the man getting into the car."

"No." She was fidgeting, afraid, trapped in a blend of nightmares. Someone climbing into the back of the vehicle at the docks. A police officer in her parents' home, asking her to identify her slain parents and dog. Speeding cars. Seeing ghosts. Holden Kincaid on her front step, looking so like his father, demanding her help. "No!"

"Liza." Her mother's voice. Gentle. Calming. Something to cling to when she was afraid.

"Mom?"

Liza felt a jarring touch on her hand and snatched it away. "Your mother's not there, Liza. Stay with me. Stay in the alley. Tell me what you see."

"Stay away, sweetie. It isn't safe."

"Mom? I have to help. I want to help."

"Damn it. I've lost her." Trent Jameson wasn't talking to her anymore. He used a sharper, clipped tone to speak into his tape recorder. "Subject is reverting back to earlier memory. May look into drug trials to keep her in relaxed, focused state."

"Dr. Jameson?" She called to him, reaching for a steadying hand to guide her through the chaos in her head.

"Relax." The sonorous monotone had returned. "Go back to the quiet place. Tell me who is getting in the car, Liza."

But in her mind, the car was gone. The foggy windows and faceless figures inside had gone with it.

New images were battering her now. She was inside the warehouse, kneeling beside the dead body, watching the pool of blood expand beneath the man's head. "He's dead."

"Go back to the car, Liza."

"Stay back, sweetie. It isn't safe."

"I need you. Good night, Parrish." Holden Kincaid's strong arms and soothing voice dissipated almost as soon as they appeared.

Then she was reaching down to feel John Kincaid's pulse. His skin was cold and clammy and still. Tears burned in her eyes at the cruelty of his death. His face was so familiar. But the square jaw was discolored. Broken. "I want to help you," she cried. "I'm trying."

"Liza. I need you to go back to the men in the car."

"Stay away. It isn't safe."

"I'm sorry I couldn't help you, Mom. I'm sorry I wasn't there to keep you and Dad safe."

"Liza—"

"It isn't safe."

"I need you."

"I have to help. I have to remember."

"Yes. Remember. Tell me about—"

The dead man grabbed her hand. *"Remember!"*

Liza screamed herself fully awake. She tore off her mask and sat up, wincing as even the dim light from candles and behind drawn shades seared her sensitive eyes. Her head ached, and she felt disoriented.

Feeling like an abject failure because her mind refused to cooperate, she picked up the pillow that had rolled to the floor and set it back on the couch in an apologetic need to straighten out the literal and figurative mess she had made. "I'm sorry."

Dr. Jameson didn't look up from his notes for several moments. When he did, his rueful smile made him appear gravely disappointed—or maybe that was pity. "Headache?"

Liza massaged her temples, feeling sick to her stomach, from the intense pain. "Nasty one."

"I told you to let me wake you up slowly. The jump from a hypnotic state to waking consciousness is too abrupt."

That was more fatherly rebuke than sympathetic support. "But it's so frightening. So frustrating." Liza stopped the massage that wasn't helping anyway. "Did I remember anything new?"

"You confirmed the make of the car you saw that night. A Buick. But then you skipped to discovering the body. And you revisited your parents' murders again."

"I heard my mother's voice. She told me to 'stay away.' From the gruesome sight of John Kincaid's body, I guess." Not that the warning had worked. Why couldn't she forget *that* most heartbreaking part of the crime she'd witnessed?

Even though she'd like to talk a little more, her session time was apparently over. Dr. Jameson was checking the calendar on his phone. "I'm more convinced than ever that the memories are there. That you did see something significant that night, but that you're blocking it. When I asked about the license plate, you mentioned a door closing."

"The car door?"

"The door blocking that memory. And the memory of what the men inside the car looked like. I believe we're on the brink of discovery—of breaking this wide open."

She wished his optimism was contagious. "I want to review the transcript from this session, organize my thoughts, then try this again tomorrow."

"Tomorrow?"

He punched in numbers with his stylus. "Are you free?"

She had school, had a job, had a life. But mostly, she needed time to regroup from this raw, vulnerable feeling. "I was hoping to have a few days off to relax. This is scary for me. I mean, I want to know, but then, I'm afraid to know."

"I can cancel my lunch appointment if that's the only time you're free."

This was the place for therapy, not sympathy, apparently. "I can't take a break?"

"I don't want you to regress any. We are right on the edge of a breakthrough. I can feel it."

She wished she could. "I really think I need the time to—"

"I know your nightmares torment you, Liza. And you believe that if you could just remember everything the police want you to that you could put it out of your mind." It was a cruel reminder, but the doctor softened it by pulling her to her feet and wrapping an arm around her shoulders as he walked her toward his office door. "It's the searching for answers, for closure, that keeps the nightmares coming back. You know I'm your best chance at unlocking those hidden places inside your head. The longer you delay, the longer the nightmares will continue. Do you want that?"

"Of course not." Feeling uncharacteristically drained of fight, Liza grabbed her backpack. "Between my morning seminar and work at the clinic tomorrow afternoon, I'll stop by."

"I'll see you at noon?"

"Sure." He opened the door for her and she headed out, feeling a little jittery—like she'd been up studying all night for exams and was subsisting on caffeine rather than sleep. "Dr. Jameson? Be honest. Am I getting any better? Do you think I'll ever remember everything?"

"Hypnosis isn't an exact science, dear. But we're making such good progress, I'm hopeful that yes, we'll eventually unlock all of those memories inside your head." He stopped at the outer door and finally gave her the reassurance of an indulgent smile. "At the very least, I promise that I'll make the nightmares go away."

Liza appreciated the sentiment. But as she walked to the elevators at the end of the hall, she could only think of one thing. She didn't have to be asleep to be haunted by nightmares. And until she could remember who'd killed John Kincaid, she doubted Dr. Jameson's claim was a promise he could keep.

"WHAT DO YOU MEAN, weird things are happening?" Liza held the bull terrier still on top of the clinic's metal examination table while her friend, vet tech Anita Logan, swabbed a medicated ointment over the dog's skin rash.

"That's it, Marvin. Good boy." Anita praised the dog for his calm behavior. Already a good-natured animal, he seemed grateful for the soothing relief that a bath, tests and medicine had given him. As Anita stooped down to tend to a patch on the dog's belly, she continued. "I'm just sayin'. Lots of unusual things have been happenin' to the people who work here. My granny would say we're under a bad star."

Liza frowned. "Define 'lots.'"

"All done." Anita pulled a pen from her lab coat pocket and jotted the name and application time on the dog's chart. "Well, there was you and that crazy SUV driver you told me about. Dr. Friedman said someone egged her car last night. Then, this morning, Reynaldo came in and said somebody had vandalized his mailbox last night—shot it all up. He and his family were all at Wednesday church services, so no one was hurt. But still..."

"That's a relief no one was injured." Liza set Marvin on the floor, looped a lead around his neck and headed for the kennel area in the back room.

"And this morning..." Anita pitched her trash and followed, waiting until they were alone in the back to finish. "This morning, I could swear this guy was following me."

Liza opened one of the lower cages and put Marvin inside before removing the lead and closing the cage door. "Didn't you take the bus?"

"You know I did. I can't afford parking *and* gas these days." Anita was playing with the black lab mix in the cage next to Marvin's. The flawless caramel skin at her forehead was creased with a frown. "That's just it. I saw this man on the bus—somebody new, not from the neighborhood. I caught him staring at me more than once."

"Maybe he was hitting on you."

"If he was, he's not my type. He was a *big* brother. Shaved head, goatee."

The man sitting behind the wheel of that SUV last night had been big. But no, what kind of connection could there be between Anita's story and Scary Man with the headlights? Liza managed to keep the frisson of foreboding that crawled through her veins out of her voice. "That doesn't sound too bad. Did he say something crude? Was he wearing a wedding ring?"

Anita pulled her fingers away from the dog and shook her head. "I didn't want to look that close. He just stared. Never said a word, never smiled. It creeped me out. Especially when he got off at the same stop."

"He followed you to the clinic? He didn't try to accost you, did he?"

"No. He came right up behind me, like he wanted to try something, but he walked on past. And Liza, girl—this is the really weird part—when I went to Snow's Barbecue for lunch, I swear I saw him standing across the street, watching me again."

"You're sure it was the same man?"

Anita's dramatic shiver rippled from head to toe. "Girl, you don't forget that kind of scary. It was him."

Liza's life had grown disturbing enough over the past six months without hearing that her friends were being victimized as well. She reached out to rub a supportive hand up and down Anita's arm. "Do you think you need to call the police?"

Anita snorted. "And tell them what?"

Detective Grove had asked plenty of questions about what she'd seen at that warehouse, so Liza knew the routine. "Give them a description. Tell them where he got on the bus and where he got off. That you saw him again at the restaurant. Tell them he scared you."

"They don't arrest a man for lookin' tough."

"No, but if his description fits some other crime—or if they can link him to the same kind of report from other women—KCPD would want to know that."

Holden Kincaid, Kevin Grove and the rest of KCPD would love to have such a detailed description about a possible suspect. They'd be more pleased with the accuracy of Anita's description and would probably have more patience with her than they did with Liza's vague report.

A little bit of the headache that had throbbed for an hour after leaving her lunchtime session with Dr. Jameson began to rap at her temples.

"You all right, girl?" Anita's concern startled Liza, and she wondered how long she'd stood there, trapped inside her own thoughts.

Liza combed her fingers through her hair, mussing up the copper fringe and buying herself a moment to summon a reassuring smile. "I've just got a bit of a headache, I guess. Probably another manifestation of your granny's 'bad star.'"

"Maybe." Anita accepted the excuse, even if her light brown eyes showed that she didn't believe it. She opened the door to the main room and pointed toward the reception area. "Linda keeps some ibuprofen in her desk. Why don't you take a couple and find an empty room to lie down in for a few minutes. I know you're burning the candle at both ends."

Liza eyed the stack of treatment charts on the counter that Dr. Friedman had asked her to review. "I've got work to do."

Anita took her by the shoulders and nudged her toward the front desk. "Granny may be superstitious, but I'm not. I'm tired of all this craziness, but a headache I can deal with. Now go take care of yourself. We can manage without you for ten minutes back here."

"Are you sure?"

"Go."

Smiling her thanks, Liza wove her way through the examination tables and lab counters to the front room. Liza spotted their receptionist, Linda, through the front windows, huddled in her jacket and smoking a cigarette with one of their community volunteers. Trading a wave to let the receptionist know she'd was borrowing her desk for a few minutes, Liza sat behind the counter and opened the desk's main drawer. "Let's see. Ibuprofen, ibuprofen…"

As she rummaged her way through the drawer, the telephone rang. Linda was still in the middle of an animated conversation outside, so before the phone ended its second ring, Liza picked it up and answered. "Friedman Animal Clinic."

"Get out of the building."

The voice was so low that Liza questioned whether she had heard right. "Excuse me?"

"Get out of the building."

An icy finger touched the nape of her neck and pricked goose bumps across her skin beneath her sweater and lab coat. "Who is this?"

"Get out."

"Why?"

"There's a bomb."

HOLDEN LIFTED HIS father's ten-speed bicycle off the ceiling hooks in the garage and handed it down the ladder to Bill Caldwell. "Got it?"

"I've got it."

The tires were flat and the rubber around the rims sticky from years of disuse. Still, they handled the old bike as reverently as a newborn baby—because it had been John's.

"Where do you want it, Su?" Bill asked, squeezing between Holden's mother and a stack of boxes she'd packed with some of her late husband's clothes. "With the boxes you're donating to the church for their Christmas bazaar? Or in the back of my truck to go to the city mission?"

Susan tucked a sable-colored strand of hair back into her ponytail and pointed to the corner of the garage. "There'll be some child who wants a bike for Christmas, and after the men's group fixes it up, it'll make a perfect gift."

Holden looked down from his perch and watched Bill dip his head to kiss Susan. "Spoken like a true mother. John would be pleased to see a little boy putting this bike to good use again."

"I think so, too."

Interesting. Was his mother blushing? Bill Caldwell seemed to be stealing several pecks on the cheek or lips lately. More than he'd done when Holden's father was still alive. It wasn't uncommon for Caldwell to greet Susan with a kiss. After all, John Kincaid had often given a friendly hug or kiss to Bill's late wife, Erin, when they met. But now there was something subtly different about their interaction that made Holden want to trade places with Bill and put a little hands-off distance between the two sixty-year-olds.

Not that he begrudged his parents' generation the right to be attracted to someone. His mother and Bill had a lot in common beyond their ties to Holden's father. Susan Kincaid was a smart, loving, beautiful woman, and Bill Caldwell—with those distinguished silver sideburns and a multinational technology business that he'd built from the ground up—was probably a pretty good catch himself. If their friendship evolved into something more, Holden couldn't stop it.

He just didn't have to like how quickly the new relationship seemed to be progressing. How could they move on to something new when his father's murder hadn't even been solved yet?

He shook off the uncharitable feelings and turned to straighten a box of books. "What are you, eight or twenty-eight?" he chided himself. Bill and his mother had both lost their very best friend. Who was he to fault them for being drawn together now that they were both alone?

He hoped when *he* was older he would have the right woman by his side to keep things interesting.

Hmm. Did copper-red hair turn gray, silver or white when it aged?

"Oh hell." Holden nearly tipped the ladder as that random thought caught him by surprise. He thought he'd put Liza Parrish firmly out of his mind. Maybe he'd better climb down before he hurt himself.

While Holden descended and put away the ladder, he discovered that his thoughts would go where they wanted to go. Back to Liza.

This afternoon's irritability probably had something to do with the sweet, round bottom that had tumbled into his lap last night. Dogs and bruises aside, he'd been very much aware of curves and warmth, and the way the moonlight reflected in her silvery eyes and made them sparkle. Her lips were a natural shade of peach, adorned with nothing but lip balm. They moved with a fascinating agility when she argued, which was often. And despite his nobler instincts, he'd wondered if her lips would be equally agile if silenced with a kiss.

Beyond the unexpected sexual attraction he felt toward KCPD's prime witness, he'd been thrown even further off his game twenty minutes later when he'd gotten a glimpse of the frightened, vulnerable woman lurking beneath that tough-chick facade. Liza Parrish had no problem standing up and fighting for herself, but once the adrenaline of fear and bravado had worn off, she'd collapsed into his arms and clung to his hand like a woman who needed him. That unspoken request had tapped into something far deeper inside him than the simmering mix of frustration and desire that had kept him awake late into the morning hours.

He'd finally been able to fall asleep. But then he'd been plagued by a variety of erotic dreams that involved rolling around on the ground, heated kisses and finding out whether those freckles that dusted her cheeks covered the rest of her body as well.

Yeah, right. He had no business judging his mother's taste in a new partner, when he seemed to have made an unplanned and ill-advised choice himself. Liza Parrish was forbidden fruit. He couldn't afford to be tempted. Finding the truth about his father's murder—finding peace—might depend on his ability to keep his distance from her.

"Do you need me to move anything else for you, Mom?" Susan Kincaid had invited him to stop by when she was done teaching her high-school English classes. Beyond the opportunity to check on her, which he and his brothers did frequently, Holden had willingly agreed to trade a little muscle for one of her home-cooked meals. "If not, maybe I can get some of those leaves raked up in the yard before dinner."

"Are you sure?" She came over to pat him on the stomach, then stretched up on tiptoe to kiss his jaw. "My intention was to fatten you up a bit on my pot roast and spend some quality time with you, not work you like a slave-driver."

"I don't mind, Mom." Holden grinned and dipped his head to kiss his mother's cheek. "I'm more than happy to work for your pot roast."

He heard the crunch of tires on the driveway and spotted a familiar, if rarely seen, beat-up green Jeep Cherokee pull in, even before Bill Caldwell announced its arrival. "I'll be damned." He closed the back of his truck and went to greet Holden's oldest brother, Edward. "Look what the cat dragged in. How're you doin', son?"

Edward climbed out of the Jeep, his worn jeans and black sweater a familiar uniform of late. Edward considered questions like "How are you?" or "How do you feel?" to be rhetorical, and never answered them. But he did shake Bill's hand. "It's been a long time, Bill."

"Edward." Susan hurried ahead of Holden, her arms outstretched as she pushed past Bill and wrapped Edward up in a tight maternal hug. "Oh, sweetie, it's so good to see you."

He bent his head and hugged her back, hanging on just long enough for Holden to join the group. He extended a hand behind her back and straightened. "Little brother. Mooching a free meal?"

Holden grasped his hand, relieved to feel the strength in his brother's grip. "I'm earning my keep."

Susan pulled away, studying her reclusive son from head to toe. "Let me look at you."

Holden took the same opportunity to assess Edward's ongoing recovery from the tragedy that had not only wrecked his body, but had destroyed his soul. Edward hadn't shaved for a day or so, and the dark stubble made a smattering of scars along his jawline stick out like brands. Though a smile would be hard to come by, there were no circles beneath his eyes and his color was a healthy tan, indicating he was continuing to stay sober. He didn't reach inside the Jeep for his thick, walnut cane until he was ready to close the door. Was it Holden's imagination, or was Edward's limp even less pronounced than when he'd last seen him three weeks ago?

Outwardly, at least, John Kincaid's firstborn was on the mend.

"You look good, son." Susan's gentle smile had healing powers that even Edward wasn't immune to. "I wasn't sure you'd come, but I'm so glad you're here."

Edward leaned in to accept her kiss. "I smelled your pot roast a mile away, Mom."

Susan reached for Holden's hand and pulled him forward. "Holden, will you help your brother unload his truck? He's got some things he wants to move out of his house. I said I'd put them in with my church donations."

"Sure." He gestured to the back of the Jeep. "Lead on, Macduff."

While her oldest and youngest sons moved to the rear of Edward's vehicle, Susan linked her arm through Bill Caldwell's and led him back inside the garage. "You come with me to the kitchen and toss together a salad while I get the roast and veggies out of the slow cooker. I have to set another place for dinner."

After Edward opened the back hatch, Holden reached inside for a pile of clothes, still on their hangers in plastic bags from the dry cleaners. Holden hesitated for a second before scooping up the first armful. These were Cara's things. Edward's late wife had been petite and curvy, a dynamo of a woman who'd left a successful career in business to become a full-time mother. Her colorful, classy tastes were reflected in the stylish suits and dresses.

It must have been hell for Edward to finally empty his wife's closet. Holden picked up the entire stack and carried them for his brother. No need to ask why Edward wanted to get rid of them.

He carried in a box of jeans and casual clothes, and a little girl's bike that had never been ridden.

Holden tried to distract his brother from the painful parade of memories. He talked about Chiefs football, and Atticus's trip to Sarajevo with Brooke. He mentioned how it felt to be working under Mitch Taylor, the new precinct commander who now oversaw the Fourth, and how he often asked about Edward and when he planned to return to his work as an investigator. He even asked a curious question of his own. "So, what do you think about Mom and Bill getting to be such good friends?"

"We'll see."

Conversation with Edward was a minimalist thing, so Holden didn't push for answers.

Until he saw in the backseat the open box he was supposed to carry in next. A shaggy blond head with sweet blue eyes blipped into Holden's memory and twisted his heart. He'd often volunteered to assist Edward in coaching his niece's track and kickball teams.

He stopped Edward on his way to the garage. "These are Melinda's things. Her Special Olympics participation medals, some artwork from school. Christmas decorations. You're not getting rid of these, are you?"

"I don't need you to be my conscience, little brother."

"I'm talking common sense. Even Mom isn't getting rid of all of Dad's things." Holden knew he was treading on mighty thin ice here. But somebody needed to say this. "You can't just erase your wife and child from your life, Ed. What if you get to the time when you've moved on, and you could treasure some of these sentimental items but you've given them away to strangers? Wouldn't you feel the loss all over again?"

"Move on?" Edward turned away from the box and leaned on his cane with both hands, seeming to need its support now more than he had a minute ago. "Every damn day it's a chore to get up in the morning. And when I do I figure that means I'm moving on the way that grief counselor told me to. I try to stay busy. I've fixed up the house. I fixed the damn Jeep. And I think I'm doing okay, that I'm gonna make it." Edward turned, and Holden saw a look of such bleak pain in his brother's eyes, that he backed up half a step. Edward limped forward. "But then I go up into the attic to get a storm window, or I open a storage closet in the basement and I run across something of Cara's or Melinda's, and I'm back on that Christmas Eve morning. It's a matter of survival, Holden." His cane punctuated his sentence on the concrete beside Holden's foot. "They have to go."

Well, hell. Holden could get all tough and in-your-face, too. But it was harder just to listen, and to love. He reached into the box and pulled out a hand-sewn rag doll ornament with plastic eyes glued crookedly on its face. An odd present to give a man like Edward Kincaid, but because his daughter had made it herself, Edward had loved it. "You're not giving *this* to some stranger."

Edward swiped his hand across his jaw, taking all trace of emotion with it. He tapped his cane against the box. "It all goes."

Because he wasn't about to lie to his brother, Holden simply nodded. He set the doll ornament back into the box, then carried it into the garage—setting it well away from the boxes that were going to the church. He'd tell his mom later. *She'd* want to keep the sentimental things. If Edward did want them one day, she'd be more than happy to give them back.

After a few minutes of silence Edward's mood seemed to come back into the tolerable range, and Holden offered a suggestion. "You know, if you're looking for something to do to stay busy, come work out with me at the gym. I've found that physical exertion has been a pretty fair antidote to deal with losing Dad. And staying healthy's always a good thing."

With his Jeep now empty, Edward locked it up. "I'll think about it."

Holden slowed his pace to walk side by side into the garage. "You could always go back to work. Maybe get your private investigator's license if the badge doesn't suit you anymore. You could help Sawyer and Atticus and me find the man who killed Dad and broke Mom's heart. If the four of us worked together as a team, we could get that bastard."

"I thought that investigation was off-limits to Kincaids. I know Sawyer uncovered some circumstantial evidence that the lab has, and Atticus has been nosing around in Dad's journals, looking at his work with Z Group before Dad became a cop. But they've turned all that over to the police." Those piercing gray eyes could still do a knowing big-brother look. "You're a sharpshooter, not an investigator. So what are you up to?"

Holden shoved his hands into the pockets of his jeans before he answered. "I, uh, went and had a chat with a witness who was there that night."

Edward's hand on his arm stopped him. "You're kidding, right?"

"I just wanted to know why she won't open up about what she saw, and give us some kind of break on the case."

"She?"

"Liza Parrish." He skipped the description of freckles and curves and keeping him up at night. "She's scared of something. Or someone. I saw a car nearly run her down last night. I don't know if it's connected. I ran the plates and it came up a rental car. Maybe if we could assign a bodyguard to make her feel safe, then she'd feel it was okay to open up and talk."

"You think she's in danger?" Despite the fact his gun and badge were packed up in a drawer somewhere, Edward still thought like a cop. "Did you notify the OIC of your suspicions?"

The OIC—Officer in Charge of the investigation—Kevin Grove, would have his hide if he knew Holden had already made personal contact—lots of contact—with the witness. "You think I should?"

"Hell, yes. If she can break open Dad's case, we want her in one piece." Edward frowned at Holden's uncharacteristic silence. "Is there something more going on here? Did something else happen between you and that woman?"

The phone on Holden's belt vibrated, saving him from having to answer.

He flipped open his phone, recognized Lieutenant Cutler's number. "Lieutenant? What's up?"

Mike Cutler's clipped tone confirmed that this was no social call. "We've got a situation in the 1100 block of South Broadway. Someone called in a bomb threat to the Friedman Animal Clinic."

When he'd done his research on Liza Parrish, he'd found out that she was working an internship at that same clinic. Cars gunning for her in the middle of the street? Bomb threats? He wouldn't buy any coincidence theory.

The instinct to get to Liza jolted through his limbs. But he wasn't supposed to know about her. He wasn't supposed to care whether or not she was safe. He grit his teeth and ignored the distracting impulses. "That's bomb squad's department."

"Not when we've got a perp in the building across the street firing shots into the crowd of evacuees, onlookers and official vehicles."

Holden swore. "Any casualties?"

"Not yet. But we're up, big guy. Is your head back in the game yet? We need to do a sweep of the building across the street."

Holden put his hand over the phone and looked at Edward. “Will you stay with Mom? Tell her I’m gone?”

He nodded. “Go save the day, little brother.”

Pulling his keys from his pocket and dashing toward his Mustang, Holden put the phone back to his ear. “I’m on my way.”

CHAPTER FIVE

"CLEAR!"

After Dominic Molloy gave him the signal, Holden turned the corner around the last of the air-conditioning units. Leading with his Glock, he checked between the exhaust vents and outer wall. With no shooter in sight, he announced it was safe for Dom to proceed. "Clear!"

Holden watched his partner's back while Dom peered over the edge of the building. "Clear! The next building's roof is eight stories below us. If the shooter had jumped, I'd see a body."

It was probably safe to breathe easier now, but both men had been trained not to drop their guard until they were back at the van stowing their gear. Holden had one last wall to check. With the sunset at his back, he followed his own shadow to the front side of the building and looked over the edge to the street below. South Broadway was a four-lane street with bus lanes, parking and sidewalks on either side. No way would the shooter have risked a jump like that unless he thought he could fly. "Clear!"

He nodded to Dominic.

With an answering nod, Dom lowered his weapon and tapped the microphone inside his helmet to broadcast to their entire unit. "Roof's clear, lieutenant. The perp must have gotten out with the last of the tenants when we evacuated."

"Understood. I'm waiting to hear from Trip and Delgado in the basement."

Holden lowered his Glock, noting how easy it would be to shatter the animal clinic's front window from this position. The shooter had, too. Hitting a target inside the ground-level clinic would be impossible from this height, but anything on the street would be fair game.

A man with a high-powered rifle would be untouchable this high up unless they had a chopper. Holden touched his black-gloved fingers to the ledge near a trio of powder burns where the shooter had rested his rifle. But he'd policed his brass like a pro. There were no casings on the roof, not so much as a gum wrapper to give any indication of the terror that had rained down just a half hour earlier.

"This guy's good," Holden reported.

Dominic walked up beside him. "Yeah, well, if he's so damn good, why didn't he hit anybody? Not that I'm askin' for trouble, but there were civilians, cops, EMTs, reporters all on the street before we got the area completely closed off. How come all he hit was a window, a bus and a couple of traffic lights?"

Holden crouched down and put himself in the shooter's position. Even now, as uniformed officers kept bystanders and reporters more than a block away, he could adjust the angle of the weapon and make a difficult but doable shot and take out the driver of the television news van and two traffic cops.

"What are you thinkin', big guy?"

"That our shooter hit exactly what he aimed at."

Dominic chomped his gum and frowned. "So what's

the point of calling in a fake bomb to get all these targets on the street, and then miss them on purpose?"

"That's what I'd like to know." Had he been gunning for someone in particular? Like a mouthy redhead with fear in her eyes? "Maybe he didn't spot his intended target so he fired wildly to throw us off track."

"Or maybe he just wanted to throw a scare into somebody."

Holden glanced down at his buddy. Dom's off-the-cuff intuition was usually amazingly accurate. And bad guys *did* like to scare witnesses who might testify against them. Holden was already backing toward the roof entrance. "Did we clear the clinic across the street?"

"Bomb squad did." Dom followed behind him. "Our shooter's long gone."

"Basement's clear." Lieutenant Cutler's voice sounded inside their helmets, ending Holden's intent to run across the street and find Liza. He still had work to do. "Report back to 517. I want to take this room apart before we turn it over to the lab guys."

"On our way."

The secondary location where the bomb threat call had been made from wasn't an apartment so much as a bunch of empty rooms—rented for the week and paid for in cash. There was a card table, a folding chair and a telephone, and not a damn clue as to the perp's identity.

Dominic snickered at the name scrawled inside the building manager's registry. "You honestly think our perp's name was Johann Hart?"

Holden was leaning against the window frame, watching as a team of crime scene investigators ducked beneath the yellow tape marking off the animal clinic.

Uniformed officers were also beginning to let some of the clinic workers back in, assuming that was who the four men and women in the white lab coats were.

Like the others on his S.W.A.T. team, he'd removed his helmet and holstered his gun, standing down from full alert. They now wore their ball caps and some pretty conflicted expressions over a dangerous suspect who'd escaped them.

Razzing from the others drew Holden's focus back into the room as Dominic waved a copy of the registration page in the air. "Hello? Johann, John. A hart's a deer, a doe's a deer. John Doe?"

Trip shook his head. "How long did it take you to think that one up?"

"This guy's a ghost," Delgado griped. "We'll never find him."

"Focus, people," Cutler ordered. "Our shooter's in the wind. Unless we dig up a gun in this apartment, I'm going to assume he smuggled the weapon out somehow, and that he's armed and dangerous."

A shock of copper-red caught Holden's attention as Liza ducked beneath the tape to hurry after the other clinic workers. Ah, hell. Not only was that hair as good as a neon sign to aim at, even through the lengthening twilight shadows, but he'd spotted a television reporter and her cameraman pleading with one of the officers to let her in to the crime scene.

Holden was going to jump out of his skin if he couldn't do something about the train wreck he saw coming. "May I be excused from the search, sir?"

Cutler's blue eyes narrowed, no doubt assessing the unusual request. "Is there a problem?"

"I need to take care of something."

The lieutenant deliberated for a few seconds, then dismissed him. "Go. If you see something, you get on the horn and call it in."

"Yes, sir."

HOLDEN SKIPPED THE elevator and took the stairs two at a time down to the street. He pushed open the front doors in time to see TV reporter Hayley Resnick and her cameraman being pushed back out of the clinic by a testy female CSI. When the reporter stuck her microphone in the CSI's face and asked her to comment on the situation, the tall brunette turned and followed Holden into the building.

"Just stay clear of the bullet holes in the front desk and counter," she warned, hurrying past him. "The back of the building is clear, but I've got my people pulling a couple of slugs here."

Deciding that a response was neither wanted nor necessary, Holden headed toward the back where he could hear several voices—including Liza's. His boots crunched over the glass on the floor, but as the CSI had indicated, it appeared that all the damage was relegated to the very front of the clinic.

"…not bringing the dogs back here tonight, are we?"

"No. We'll leave them in the Sterling and Wyandotte shelters for tonight. Anita, make sure we have the charts for the acute cases."

Holden followed the voices through a swinging door into a lab and examination area. An older woman was directing her staff. "I already have Liza securing the pharmacy. I'm not going to risk any break-ins tonight. Reynaldo, I need you to…"

With an acknowledging salute, Holden left them to

their work and pushed open the door marked "Pharmacy." He shouldn't have breathed a sigh of relief when he saw Liza's heart-shaped bottom wiggling in the air as she bent over an open cooler, but he did.

She popped up, startled by the sound. Her pale cheeks were flushed when she spun around. "Kincaid? You're not supposed to be here."

Though she held her defiant chin high, the tension on her face made her mouth stiff, her eyes a dull battleship gray.

Holden never paused, never broke stride. He walked straight across the room, pulled off his black S.W.A.T. cap and plopped it onto her head, tugging it securely over the short wisps of her hair.

"Red hair makes an easy target."

He wasn't the only one breathing a sigh of relief. A smile suited those pretty lips better than that tough survivor frown had. "Is it wrong to say I'm glad to see you?"

"I hope not. Because the feeling's mutual." His answering smile faded when he reached out to touch the nick on her cheek with the tip of his finger. "Are you hurt?"

He could have sworn her skin trembled beneath his touch, but she pulled away so quickly he couldn't be sure.

"We all have little cuts and bumps." She went back to pulling bottles of pills and liquids off the shelves and packing them into the cooler. "We were still evacuating the last of the big dogs onto the transport truck when that crazy man—I mean, I'm assuming it was a man—shot out the main window. But the EMTs checked us out. There were no serious injuries."

"Did you see the shooter?"

She paused for a moment, then made a sound that wasn't quite a laugh. "Not this time."

Her skin had gone pale beneath its dusting of freckles as she stretched up to get a second cooler off the top of the medicine cabinet. Holden moved in behind her, easily reaching over her head to retrieve the cooler. "Let me."

As she rocked back onto her heels, she butted up against Holden's chest. He heard a sharp catch of breath—maybe it was Liza's, maybe it was his own. He was instantly aware of a chest-to-groin heat that seared through his flak vest and clothes. He should have retreated. Instead, he propped the cooler against the wall with one hand and pulled her close to ease any lingering doubts he might have that she was unharmed.

But Liza had a saner notion of propriety and protocol. With an unnecessary apology, she ducked beneath his arm and scooted away to open a refrigerator door. Holden set the smaller cooler on top of the first one, and stepped aside to let her fill it with vials from the fridge.

"I *did* take the phone call when the bomb threat came in. That was definitely a man's voice. It was low-pitched and resonant, like yours, but…" she paused with her fist resting on the top shelf "…cold. Like there was no emotion there whatsoever."

She pulled the last of the meds out and nudged the door shut with her hip, suddenly energized, suddenly apologizing.

"Your voice isn't like that at all. It has a warmth to it. It can be annoying, but, that's usually *what* you're saying. When it's soft, the tone of it is almost…soothing." She was that close to being dead and she was worried about hurting *his* feelings? The lurch in Holden's stomach felt a lot more personal than the idea of losing a link to his father's murder.

"This guy sounded like Shakespeare-meets-the-Terminator, but you could be a—"

"It's all right, Parrish." He caught her jaw beneath his palm, stopping the rambling apology—and the deeper sense of fear and uncertainty she was revealing. He stroked his thumb across the point of her chin. "It's all right."

Her eyes sparkled with some unnamed emotion. "Is it? I've seen so much violence, I can't… How do you handle it?"

He needed her to be out of this place. Now. He needed Liza somewhere safe.

"Come on." The instant Liza closed the top cooler, he pushed it into her hands. Then he picked up the larger one. "Where do these go?"

"Dr. Friedman parked her van in the back. This way."

He followed her down a hallway lined with kennels to the back door. But he stopped her before she could open it.

"Wait." He stacked the coolers on the floor and reached for the Velcro straps at either side of his black flak vest.

"What are you doing?" He pulled the vest over his head and dropped it over hers in one smooth motion. "Kincaid?"

He straightened his cap on her head and reached around her to secure the straps over her white lab coat. "There's a guy with a gun out there, remember?"

She ripped open a strap in protest. "But it's okay for you to get shot?"

"I wasn't the target." He covered her hand and latched the strap.

Whether his words or his touch bothered her, he couldn't tell. But she quickly pulled away and picked up her cooler. "You think he was shooting at me? Putting all these innocent animals and people into danger because of me?"

"It's too soon to tell." She swam in his vest, like a little girl playing dress-up in her daddy's clothes. But to Holden's mind, it was a good fit. "Silencing or scaring a murder witness so that she won't testify? Wouldn't be the first time." Holden opened the door and headed into the alley. "Stay close."

She followed right on his heels, opening the back of the van and showing him where to store the medical supplies. "I heard at least six shots. That guy wasn't shooting at me. Other than the front window, he never came close. Unless he's a lousy shot."

"He wasn't."

"How do you know?"

He slammed the van shut and turned on her. "Because *I'm* a sharpshooter. I saw his setup. I saw the shots he could take and the ones he did take. He's trained. Military, cop, hit man, I don't know. If he wanted you dead right now, you would be. This is some game he's playing, and I'm not going to take the chance that *you're* the one he wants in the middle of it."

She propped her hands at her hips, squaring off against him. "Because I need to stay alive to testify against your father's killer?"

"Because you need to stay alive, period."

"Look, we hardly know each other. What right—?"

It was a bright light, not a gunshot that stopped the debate. "Doctor?"

Liza squinted and turned toward the television camera. "Me? Not quite yet. But Dr. Friedman's inside if you need a vet."

Holden took Liza's arm and pulled her behind him, putting his body between her and the blond reporter. "Get that camera out of here."

"I'm Hayley Resnick, Channel 4 News. Could I ask you some questions?" With a strength of will that belied her movie-star pretty face, she darted to one side and focused her plea on Liza. "Miss? Were you a victim of the bomb threat? Can you tell us anything about why someone would target these defenseless animals or someone who works here?"

Holden felt Liza's response in the clench of her fists at the back of his shirt. "You think this is about the animals?" she whispered.

"No, I don't. Hey!" Holden adjusted his stance, pushing Hayley back and giving her cameraman the high sign to kill the light and stop rolling the film. "This isn't a good time for an interview."

But Hayley kept pushing. "So this is personal? Have you received threats before?"

"I'm supposed to remain anonymous," Liza spoke against his shoulder. "Detective Grove promised."

Holden stretched his arms behind him, hugging Liza to his back and turning to keep her hidden. "There are others who can give you better information about today's events, Ms. Resnick. I suggest you try elsewhere."

The reporter shifted her attention to Holden, gracing him with a practiced smile. "You're Atticus's brother, aren't you?"

"I know who you are, too, lady. And you're trouble, according to A." He threw his arm around Liza and tucked her to his side to walk her out of the alley. Hayley had once dated his brother, then taken advantage of his connections at KCPD to further her career. Oh yeah, Atticus was a lot better off marrying a class act like Brooke than this conniving piece of work. Hayley Resnick needed to get out of Holden's face. "Ms. Parrish has no comment."

Leaving the stymied reporter behind them, Holden hurried Liza around the corner to the side street where the S.W.A.T. van was parked. He opened the back doors and lifted her onto the back bumper. "Get inside."

Liza paced off the length of the narrow passage between their gear and weapons cache while Holden closed the doors behind them. "I'm tired of being bombarded with questions," she raged. "From KCPD. From my therapist. From you, and now that woman. I can't answer every damn one of them. I'm tired, I'm tired, I'm tired."

"Hey. Hey." Holden caught her flailing arms and pulled her to his chest, holding her tight until the tantrum and frustration had worked their way through her system. With a weary huff of breath, Liza finally relaxed, turning her cheek into his shoulder and leaning against him. The hard plates of the flak vest masked the curves of her figure. But there was plenty of woman to hold on to as she nestled her head beneath his chin. He cupped the back of her head with one hand and slid the other down to the swell of her hips.

Holden feathered his fingers through the silky fringe of hair beneath the cap she wore, breathing in the citrus-like scent of her shampoo and the sharper, medicinal smells that clung to her clothes. He whispered apologies for adding to the barrage of questions that weighed with such pressure on her. Her breathing evened out as he continued to talk, and she snuggled against his throat. "Nobody's going to hurt you in here. Nobody's going to ask you to do anything. You're safe now. It's quiet here. Quiet and safe."

His own erratic pulse and turbulent thoughts had calmed during these few moments of tender stillness. But when she pulled back to free her arms and wind them around his waist and move even closer, his heart rate shifted into a higher gear. The vest was cold and stiff against his chest and stomach, but farther down, where their hips and thighs touched, they were generating an amazing heat. It was impossible not to imagine the conflagration that full-on body contact with this woman would feel like.

"I'm not supposed to like you, Kincaid," she whispered against his collar. "I'm not supposed to even know you."

"I know."

"Did you ever read *Romeo and Juliet?*"

He laughed, and he thought he could feel her cheek plump with a smile. "My mom's an English teacher. Where do you think I got a name like Holden Caulfield Kincaid?"

"Seriously?" She tipped her head back to meet his gaze.

"My brothers are Edward Rochester, Thomas Sawyer and Atticus Finch Kincaid. So yeah, I get that I'm a Montague and you're a Capulet." He released one hand just long enough to pull his S.W.A.T. cap off her head so he could read her expression in the van's shaded interior. "I also get that I like you, too."

Liza's fresh, angelic face—momentarily free of attitude or suspicion—was smiling. "Thanks for the rescue, Romeo."

Those peachy lips were parted in anticipation, and, like a hungry man, Holden couldn't resist. He leaned in, brushed his lips against hers. Her taste was sweeter than he'd imagined. And when she lifted onto her toes to press her lips more firmly against his, the spark of that first kiss was hotter than any embrace he'd ever shared with a woman.

Holden tangled his fingers into that sassy, silky hair and pulled her even closer. Moaning with surprise and absolute approval, he traced the seam of her lips with his tongue and ventured inside to deepen the kiss.

The scrape of metal on metal jarred Holden from the unexpected pleasure of that kiss, reminding him that nothing could come of it—that he was only guaranteeing trouble for them both if something *should* come of it. The outside handle on the van turned, and Liza froze. Holden released her and reluctantly retreated as the back door opened.

Kevin Grove's bulky frame and disgruntled mood filled the opening. Lieutenant Cutler, Dominic and the rest of his team were gathered behind the detective, looking up at them with everything from reproach to amusement. Grove looked from Holden to Liza and back to Holden again. "This isn't what I think it is, is it, Kincaid?"

Feeling more than a little disgruntled himself at the interruption—and at allowing the situation to get so personal in the first place, Holden couldn't keep the sarcasm out of his reply. “If you mean securing the witness? Keeping her away from the press? Then, yeah, that’s exactly what I’m doing.”

“That’s why you…?” Liza’s voice faded away and an invisible armor thicker than the S.W.A.T. vest she wore lodged into place. Her hair fanned out in a sexy disarray, as though a man’s hands had been in it. But she quickly smoothed each spike back into place. “Thank you for your concern, Officer Kincaid.”

“Parrish—”

But she was already pushing him aside and reaching for Grove’s hand to help her down from the van. “Mr. Kincaid helped me evade a reporter in the alley behind the clinic. But I’m sure she’s gone by now. I’d better get back inside to help pack up supplies.”

Holden instinctively moved forward when Grove didn’t release Liza’s hand. “I can’t allow you to go back in there, ma’am,” said the gruff detective.

“But I have to help out. We have to get the clinic cleaned tonight, or it won’t be safe to bring the animals—”

“No, ma’am.” Grove cut her off. “You’re done working for today. Lieutenant Cutler? I need your team to escort Ms. Parrish to the back of my car.”

Holden jumped down from the van. With a gentle tug on her arm, Grove released her, but she shook off Holden’s touch as well. Well, hell. She could misread his motivations and be pissed off at him all she wanted, but Holden wasn’t going to let Grove order her around as though she was a suspect instead of a victim. “She didn’t do anything wrong. She’s not responsible for any of this.”

"I'm taking her downtown until we can confirm this wasn't an attempt on her life."

"Is that what you think?"

Grove ignored Liza's question and mirrored Holden's defensive stance. "I'm just like you, Kincaid. I'm trying to keep her safe. Do you have a problem with that?"

Holden held his gaze for as long as he could before the lieutenant could call him on it. "No, sir."

"Good. Cutler?" Grove pushed Liza into the triangle formed by Dom, Trip and Delgado, then jogged ahead to clear the path to his vehicle.

Lieutenant Cutler was only slightly more sympathetic. "Keep it together, big guy. You're no use to me if you're not thinking straight. You're no use to her, either." He tapped the center of Holden's chest. "Now put on a spare vest and let's get Ms. Parrish downtown."

CHAPTER SIX

MR. SMITH SAT in his room at the historic Raphael Hotel at the south edge of the Plaza, miles away from the fun he'd had earlier this evening. With the extra pillows plumped at his back, and the cabernet sauvignon breathing on the bedside table, he sorted through the names in his file.

He stopped on the picture of the pretty redhead whose bio said she was 25, but who looked ten years younger with that tomboy haircut and freckles.

Mr. Smith picked up the cell phone in his lap and punched in his employer's number. When the phone picked up, there was no greeting, just, "I have her. Liza Parrish. She's your witness."

"So your plan worked?"

"A S.W.A.T. team escorted her away from the scene." It was proof enough for him that he'd exposed the right woman. "Shall I take care of the situation?"

"Give me twenty-four hours to see if I can find out how much she's told anyone. I'm tired of loose ends on this project. If you don't hear from me by tomorrow night at this time, I'll expect you to eliminate her. All trace of her."

"WHAT DO YOU THINK THEY'RE talking about in there?" Holden sat on the corner of Atticus's desk at the Fourth

Precinct office, swirling cold coffee in the bottom of his plastic cup.

Atticus pulled off his glasses and swiveled in his chair to look at the conference room where Liza, Detective Grove, the assistant D.A., Lieutenant Cutler and almost a dozen other officers and civilians had gathered behind closed doors. "After three hours? I'm guessing they're talking strategy. Whether she's a witness who's important enough to warrant moving to a safe house. How viable the threat is against her, and what spin they're going to put on this with the media."

"She needed to be in protective custody six months ago."

Atticus loosened his tie and unbuttoned his collar, a sign of just how long this day had gone on. "I've gotten the sense all along that she's been reluctant to tell Grove everything she knows. Or maybe she just doesn't want to get involved."

A woman who rescued three dogs from the pound? Who wanted to go back inside a clinic where a bomb threat had been called in to help clean up the mess? A woman who charged across the street to confront a man she thought was following her? Who stretched up on tiptoe and deepened a forbidden kiss?

Liza Parrish wasn't afraid to get involved. Not that copper-haired spitfire. There had to be something else going on here. But what?

"Mom was good when you saw her?" Atticus asked.

"What? Yeah." The abrupt change in topic startled Holden from his thoughts. "She was having Uncle Bill over for dinner. Edward showed up, too."

"No kidding. How was he?"

"Sober. Healthy." Holden shrugged, suspecting that

this tangent in the conversation was his brother's efforts to distract him from worrying about Liza—and feeling guilty that she'd misread his interest in her as some kind of manipulation regarding their father's murder. But with nothing but a closed door to study, he went along with the conversation. "I picked a fight with Edward."

"Really? And how did that work out for you?"

Holden grinned. "Turned out to be kind of a good talk, I think. He was getting rid of Cara and Melinda's things, said he couldn't move on as long as they were around. I suggested he keep a few sentimental items—that he might want them back some day."

"You tried to stop him and he didn't slug you?"

"Not this time. I doubt I'm on his favorite brother list right now, but he stayed to have dinner with Mom and Bill when I got the call to the animal clinic."

A third voice, deep and rumbly, joined the discussion. "Maybe Ed's starting to heal a little bit." Their second oldest brother, Sawyer, came over from his desk where he'd been working at the computer. "At least he's keeping his head above water and coping with the real world—not like he was a year ago." He tossed a print-out onto Atticus's desk. "Take a look at this. I got a hit on that Trent Jameson guy Grove called in. He's a psychologist, known for his groundbreaking research into hypnotherapy."

Atticus picked up the print-out and photo. "Looks like we're in the wrong line of work, boys. Dr. Jameson earns upwards of $10,000 an hour to talk about his research."

Holden scanned the paper next, zeroing in on three lines near the bottom. "This says Dr. Jameson has been sued for malpractice twice in California."

Sawyer leaned across the desk and pointed out the next two lines. "One case was dismissed, the other settled out of court. Psychology isn't a finite science." Sawyer would know, as he continued to go to counseling sessions with his wife, who'd barely survived an abusive first marriage. "Sometimes, a patient has unrealistic expectations about what can be accomplished or how fast it can be done."

"And sometimes, the psychologist just doesn't get the job done." Holden dropped the paper and stood. He tossed his coffee cup into the trash and circled around to stand beside Sawyer—one of the few men in KCPD who stood even taller than he did. "Why the hell would you need a hypnotherapist on a police investigation? If he's there for Liza, anything she'd say under that kind of influence would be inadmissible in court."

Atticus, ever the voice of reason in the family, had a theory. "Could be he's just her regular therapist. We know she doesn't have any family—that they died during a home invasion down at the Lake of the Ozarks a few years back. That's public record. Maybe Jameson is who she calls when she needs a friend around."

Holden knew from their own limited investigation that Liza lived alone and had no parents. But he hadn't realized they'd been murdered. Earlier, at the clinic, she'd asked him how he dealt with all the violence in his line of work. She wasn't just talking about today's events, or even his father's murder. Maybe Liza had seen all the violence she could stand, and Dr. Jameson was helping her cope with that. Could be that, as much as she was willing to work with KCPD, it was just an extremely difficult task for her to get through.

Now all those people were in there, bombarding her with questions?

And she was alone with them?

"Um, where are you going?" Sawyer called after him.

Holden was already halfway to the conference room. He wanted to know if Liza was okay. If Trent Jameson was there to help her. He wanted to know if she'd accept his apology and let her know that, in a room full of Montagues, he was there for his lady Juliet.

He knocked on the door and heard a responding lull in the conversation on the other side. When the heated sounds picked up again as if his interruption was of no consequence, Holden raised his fist to knock again.

The door swung open and Kevin Grove answered. "What do you want? Didn't Cutler dismiss you?"

There were files out on the conference table, a city map had been pinned to the wall. A least three different conversations were going on at once.

"Kincaid?" Holden looked past Grove's shoulder and zeroed in on Liza's tight-lipped expression. Her eyes locked on to his.

"You okay?" Holden didn't know if he'd whispered or shouted.

But his words reached their target. Her slight nod would have been more convincing if her skin wasn't so pale and her hands weren't clenched into fists on top of the table. Dr. Jameson, who sat beside her, patted her arm, demanding her attention. She glanced at the doctor for a moment, then swung her gaze back to Holden.

"I'm sorry about all this."

Grove was the only one who heard his apology as he urged Holden back into the main room and closed the door behind him. "Sorry, pal, you're not invited to the party."

"What are you doing to her in there?"

"Go home." Grove's tone was sympathetic enough, but he wasn't budging from the doorway. "You've done your job with Miss Parrish. Now let me do mine."

For a split second, Holden debated whether he could shove the burly ogre aside. Given his current mood, he probably could get past him. But the thought of fighting his way through all the rest of the officers inside—as well as a little common sense and departmental protocol—made him think that walking away was a better choice. For now.

Ignoring the questions and unwanted advice from his brothers, Holden stalked down the hallway to the men's room. He took care of business then went to the sink to splash cold water on his face.

When he straightened, he looked into the mirror and saw he had company.

Kevin Grove turned on a spigot two sinks down and washed his hands.

Holden took his time drying his. This meeting wasn't a coincidence.

When Grove reached for the paper towels, he finally spoke. "Anything you want to tell me about you and Liza Parrish?" Holden wadded his towel and tossed it without answering. "Don't pretend you don't know her. I saw Hayley Resnick's news report. And I know what a bodyguard looks like."

"Liza needs one."

"It shouldn't be you." Grove pitched his trash and buttoned his suit jacket. "You two have history?"

About seventy-two hours' worth.

But the connection to Liza Parrish was there, and he wasn't going to deny it. "I want in. Even if I'm just the runner who delivers the pizza and bagels to the safe house you're sticking her in, I want to be on her protection detail."

Grove seemed to give his request real consideration. "I don't like it. But if you want to help, you may get your wish. Come with me."

Holden shrugged at his brothers' curious expressions as he followed Kevin Grove into the conference room. Some sort of decision must have been reached because folders were now closed, and at least one of the conversations he overheard was about a new truck someone was thinking about buying.

Grove waved Liza over, but she was already on her feet and hurrying around the table.

"Thank you." She beamed a smile up at him that elicited half a grin of his own.

But he was still missing something here. "Thank me for what?"

Liza pulled back the lab coat she still wore and reached into the front pocket of her jeans.

Grove started to fill in the blanks. "Miss Parrish won't even talk about cooperating with us until she knows her dogs are okay."

Well, hell.

She pulled a key ring from her pocket, then proceeded to remove what looked like a house key. "Bruiser, Cruiser and Yukon have been locked up in the house all day long. They need to be fed again, given fresh water and taken out for their run. Otherwise, I'm afraid they'll chew up my couch or leave some unexpected presents for me."

"That's what you want me to do? You want me to check on the damn dogs?"

Liza tucked the extra keys back in her jeans, looking a bit stunned by his response. She glanced up at Grove, then propped her hands at her hips and turned on the attitude. "Would you excuse us for a minute, detective?"

With a reluctant nod, Grove stepped aside and Liza nudged Holden out the door. He got around the corner into a secluded hallway before the attack started. "Look, Kincaid—those dogs are my family, and I'm responsible for them. I'm just asking you to do a favor."

Holden could go on the offensive, too. He backed her toward the wall. "I'm a trained special weapons and tactics officer. I've taken survivalist training and I know how a man like the guy who's after you thinks. And you want me to let your dogs out?" When he realized he was venting more frustrated emotion than coolheaded logic, he retreated a step and softened his voice to a more rational tone. "Is this some kind of punishment for kissing you?"

"No. I—"

"Because I wanted to. And if it wouldn't cost me my badge, I'd do it again."

"You want to kiss me again?"

"Like hell on fire."

The freckles vanished as a blush colored her cheeks. Her gaze fell to the center of his chest, possibly to the badge hanging on a chain there. "Could you really lose your job by getting involved with me?"

His chest expanded with a deep sigh. "I'd at least get a reprimand in my file. Maybe get a promotion delayed. But I didn't want you to get into trouble, either. I want you to be focused on your testimony and help find justice for my dad. And I want you to listen to the men who are in there trying to figure out how to protect you."

She reached out and touched his badge, gently, almost reverently. "You look just like your dad, you know. The first time I saw you—for a second, I thought I was looking at a ghost." She pulled her hand away. "You've been through so much already. I don't want to get you into trouble. I'm sorry. I won't bother asking you for the favor."

When she turned to walk away, Holden's heart nearly imploded inside his chest. He snatched her hand and pulled it back to his chest, splaying her fingers over his aching heart and holding them there.

Shakespeare wasn't the only one who could create a mess with an unwise but irresistible relationship. "Talk to me about the dogs."

"I need someone to take care of them." The warmth of her hand and the growing brightness of her smile seemed to have a healing effect on his ravaged conscience. "They know you. At least, out of all the choices in that room, you're the only one the dogs have met. Cruiser definitely has a crush on you. And Bruiser will like anybody who gives him treats. And Yukon, well… he needs someone with a strong will and a commanding voice in order to stay in line."

She paused unexpectedly, turning her head to the side. Holden tucked two fingers beneath her chin and turned her face back to his. "A commanding voice I can do. What else?"

"I need someone to understand what those dogs mean to me, Kincaid. I owe those three everything. They're the only thing I have in my life that I can always count on."

Holden looked down at those beseeching gray eyes that wanted so badly to trust. He released her hand and reached for the one that still held the key. He caught both the key and her fingers and held on tight. And he made a vow.

"No, they're not."

CHAPTER SEVEN

LIZA DECIDED THAT Kevin Grove was a lot nicer than his gruff demeanor first led her to believe. She wouldn't make the mistake of thinking he had changed his mind about needing her testimony to nail John Kincaid's killer—after all, he'd stationed police officers in unmarked vehicles at either end of her block, and had ordered two more on foot to patrol the wooded area behind her house. But she'd discovered that he could put that bulldog tenacity on hold and actually be a bit of a softy—for short periods of time, at any rate.

"All right," he groused, apparently satisfied with all the electronic sensors and listening devices he'd plugged into her telephone and set up around each door and window of her house. "I'm going out on the porch to uh, have a cigarette." His expression was far less amenable when he looked over at Holden, lounging against the kitchen sink. "You can have that long with her before I chase you out tonight."

"You don't smoke," Holden pointed out.

"Do you want me to step outside or not?"

"Enjoy your break, detective."

Once they were the last two people in the house, Liza pushed Bruiser's head off her lap and got up from the kitchen table to rinse the milk from her empty glass. Her brownies had been a hit with each of the security team members who'd come inside, and she pulled the now-empty baking dish off the counter and scooted Holden aside while she filled it with water to soak overnight.

While she'd been dutifully listening to every security precaution that Grove had insisted upon, Holden had been out on the exercise path with the three musketeers, as he'd dubbed her menagerie of pets. "So how did your evening go?"

"Great. Everyone's been run, fed, watered, and now they're settling down to sleep it off." He nodded toward Bruiser, who was still circling the table, looking for something edible fall to his level. "Except for Moochface over there. You'd think he'd be full by now."

Liza laughed, and the black and tan terrier mix took the sound as an invitation and trotted across the linoleum to join them. "This one's never full. Probably comes from living on the streets and eating food whenever and wherever he could find it."

Holden rinsed the empty glass he'd been drinking from and put it in the sink beside hers. "You said Bruiser's the dog you were rescuing the night you found Dad?"

She nodded. "Bruiser was skin and bones when I found him under a Dumpster in that alley. You could see every rib, each hip bone—his nails were overgrown and he could barely stand on his own when I picked him up." Liza smothered a sob at the sad irony of her situation. Details about the dog she could remember. But details about the gunshots and the men who'd killed Holden's father?

"Hey." A strong, gentle finger twisted through a wisp of hair at her temple and tucked it behind her ear. "Don't go there. Not tonight. You've had enough to deal with already today."

"Thank you."

"For what? Not pushing? Not tonight."

When he leaned in like that, she could see that Holden really did have long eyelashes. The beauty of them was so at odds with the ruggedly masculine angles of his face that it made noticing them feel like she'd discovered a secret about him. One that was hers alone to keep. "I'm sorry you've been reduced to dog-sitter, but trust me, from my perspective, you're the hero of the day."

"Just doin' my job, ma'am," he drawled in that soothing, warming pitch.

She tore her gaze away from his blue eyes and found herself staring, for the second time that night, at the brass and blue enamel badge that hung around his neck. He was a cop, just like his father. Just like each of his brothers, apparently. Watching Holden and his S.W.A.T. teammates work and joke with each other, seeing Detective Grove's diligence and the dedication of each of the officers who'd been in that conference room with her earlier tonight, she was beginning to understand that there was a brotherhood among the members of the KCPD that went beyond badges and bloodlines.

One of their own had been murdered. And they were all looking to her to give them the answers they needed to bring their brother's—or father's—killer to justice. The weight of that responsibility was daunting. But she vowed tonight, more than ever, that she would do whatever was necessary to restore her memories and give them the answers they—and she—needed.

But standing close to Holden like this, in the warmth

of her kitchen, with his fingers stroking gently at her temple, and his seductive voice calming her more effectively than any therapy or medication, Liza began to believe that she *would* remember what she needed to one day. With every breath of his clean, undoctored scent, made musky by the work of the day, Liza began to believe that she wasn't quite so alone in the world. As unbelievable as it seemed, in the short few days that she'd known Holden Kincaid, she was beginning to think that she might be falling in love with him. Could reality be working as quickly as Shakespearean fiction?

"You tired?" he asked, misreading her silence and pulling away.

"Exhausted." She summoned a smile to alleviate his concern. She was in no way, shape or form ready to admit to her thoughts. "But then I'm a grad student doing her internship, so I'm pretty much always tired."

"Then I'd better be saying good-night so you can get to bed. Make sure Grove sleeps on the couch, okay?"

"If the dogs let him." Not quite ready to let Holden's reassuring presence go, she started plucking short, tawny hairs off his black uniform shirt. "I can see from the evidence here that you were playing with Cruiser. I told you she's got a crush on you."

"Yeah, I've always been popular with the ladies." Liza arched an eyebrow at the macho bravado in his voice. "By the way, the little guy likes me, too."

Liza scooped up Bruiser and cradled the dog high in her arms, holding him so that he could rest his front paws on Holden's chest. "Do you like Kincaid, too, Bruiser?" In answer, the dog licked Holden's face. "Oh, yes, you do. Yes, you do."

"Easy, tough guy." Holden smiled wryly, grabbed the

dog's muzzle in a playful grip and pushed his tongue away. "Not exactly the kiss I was hoping for."

Laughing in a way she hadn't for a long time, Liza pulled Bruiser down to her hip and reached up to wipe the traces of the dog's lick off Holden's cheek. His eyes locked on to hers at the caress, and the piercing blue color warmed, warming her in turn. Sliding her hand around to the sandy-brown crop of hair above his starched collar, Liza pulled his head down to hers. *This* was the kiss she wanted him to have. The kiss she wanted to receive.

Holden's hands came up to frame her face and feather into her hair as his mouth opened, moist and deliberate, over hers. She parted her lips and his tongue swept in, as familiar and wonderful as if they'd kissed like this before. Liza whimpered at the delicious tingling that danced through her blood when she slid her tongue against his.

Making a basket with his fingers, Holden tilted her head back and closed the distance between them, plundering her mouth with a lazy thoroughness that made her breathing erratic and her breasts heavy with need. She stroked her palm over the sandpapery stubble at his jaw, then let her hand trail over the soft knit turtleneck at the column of his throat. He claimed everything she was willing to give, stamping his touch, his healing, his passion onto her eager mouth.

Liza's fingers slipped lower, hooking on a button and unfastening it. She slid her hand inside his shirt, rubbing her palm over the ridges of his sweater and squeezing her fingertips into the warmer bulge of muscle underneath.

Holden's hands were moving, too. He dragged them

down along her spine, creating a heated friction that warmed her from her skin to her core. When he reached her hips, his fingers spread downward, catching the curve of her bottom through her jeans and lifting her into his growing arousal. Pulling her closer. Kissing her harder.

An icy cold nose poked her chin, startling Liza. With a gasp, she drew away.

"Bruiser! Oh." A different kind of heat flooded her cheeks and left her feeling slightly unbalanced. She set the dog on the floor and sucked in a couple of deep breaths, trying to clear her head and ready an apology for spoiling the passionate moment. "Sorry about that." She shot her fingers through her hair and glared at the innocent pooch. "I can't believe I forgot we had company."

But Holden was smiling instead of complaining. "Don't apologize. I kind of lost track of where I was myself. That kiss was perfect." He touched her lips. They felt swollen and hot, and they chased after Holden's fingers as he grinned and pulled them away. "Perfect."

It was only when he reached up to rebutton his shirt that she saw his hands quaking with the same kind of tremors that seemed to be dissipating like aftershocks through her body. "I'd better go before Grove comes back in and arrests me for loitering."

Liza walked him to the front door. She could definitely see the dangers of things moving so quickly between them. Romeo and Juliet had acted impulsively on their ill-conceived passion, and look where it had gotten them. Still, Liza had felt more secure, more herself, more alive in these few hours she'd spent with Holden Kincaid than she'd felt since before her parents' deaths.

As heady as it was frightening, it wasn't a feeling she was eager to let go. "Will you be back tomorrow?"

"Nobody can keep me away." He stopped at the door and looked behind her to the furry trio making themselves comfortable on and around her couch. "After all, I promised the three musketeers that I'd take them for a run in the morning." His gaze came back to her upturned face. "And we'd hate to disappoint them."

"We sure would."

"Plus, if you're going to thank me like that every night..." He let the invitation, the promise, linger in the air.

He dipped his head and caught her mouth in a quick kiss—a graphic, vibrant, all-too-brief reminder of the passion they'd just shared. "Until tomorrow morning."

"Good night, Kincaid."

He knocked to signal Grove that he was coming out before opening the door.

"Good night... Liza."

"I AM NOT GOING without my dogs. Period. End of discussion."

Holden stood back like a fly on the wall while Kevin Grove and Lieutenant Cutler tried to argue with Liza about the benefits of moving her to a more secure safe house. He'd shown up at about seven in his sweats and running shoes to find Liza practically stomping around her kitchen, feeding the dogs and the cops breakfast and filling the dishwasher while zipping back to take periodic glances at a thick textbook which lay open on the table. Her hair was still damp from a shower and drying naturally into chunky wisps that she occasionally smoothed with her fingers.

The woman was a dynamo of energy, and Grove and Cutler didn't stand a chance.

"I thought you'd arranged everything so that I could stay here," she went on, jotting something from the text onto a note card and sticking it into the back pocket of her jeans.

Kevin Grove looked like he needed sleep more than he needed the mug of coffee he cradled in his hands. "That was before you told us about the car nearly running you down night before last. If someone has already IDed your house and is following you, then we'd like to throw him off the trail by putting you up someplace where he can't look up your address in a phone book."

She shooed Bruiser away from the open dishwasher, added soap to the dispenser and then started the machine. "I told you, I'm perfectly willing to cooperate as long as you move me someplace that can house them, too."

"The dogs complicate things." Cutler tried to explain one of the lessons of witness protection Holden had been taught. "They require going in and out—"

"*I* require going in and out."

"Three dogs would draw attention to the house. The idea is to blend in with the scenery so no one suspects what kind of operation is going on inside."

Holden scratched Cruiser's smooth head as the greyhound leaned against his leg and thrust her head into his hand. They could throw out logical appeals until they were blue in the face, but Holden was quickly learning that arguing with Liza Parrish with her mind made up was like arguing with a brick wall. Cutler and Grove should give up now. They had a better chance of being hit by lightning than of separating Liza from her pets.

"Why can't you just post more guards here at my house?" Liza picked up her backpack from beside her chair, closed the book and stuffed it inside.

"We have a budget to consider—"

"Would you stay put inside?"

"No." Liza zipped the bag shut and plopped it back on the floor. "I have classes to attend, a job to go to."

Cutler leaned back in his chair. "Not for a few days, you don't. You wouldn't want to put any of your classmates or coworkers at risk, do you?"

"No."

Holden straightened away from the wall as Liza sank into her chair at the table. Cutler had used a hostage negotiation technique on her, and it had worked. Liza was thinking about worst-case scenarios now, evaluating how her choices could affect the people she cared about.

"What about my appointments with Dr. Jameson?" With a little less zing in her voice, she turned her argument to Kevin Grove. "You said they were more important now than ever. I'm supposed to see him this morning."

"He can come here."

"Trent Jameson?" Sitting didn't last very long for Liza. She was up out of her chair, pacing the length of her kitchen as she continued. "Do you know what kind of convincing it took to get him to come down to the police station last night?"

Grove carried his coffee mug to the sink and rinsed it out. "Jameson is a citizen of the community who can do his public duty like the rest of us and work here for one day. The city will still pay him his basic fee, whether he does the job at his office or here."

"The city's paying Jameson ten thousand dollars to

counsel you?" The words were out before Holden could stop them. "What about the department's shrink that you told me to go to?"

Liza's arms slid around her waist in a self-comforting hug that he wished he could give her. Her gaze slid toward the corner of the room where Holden stood, but didn't quite reach his eyes. What the hell was going on here?

Lieutenant Cutler pushed away from the table and stood. "I recommended our psychologist to you because I just needed you to blow off some steam and focus. What I understand from our meeting last night is that Miss Parrish is part of some kind of research study." He glanced at Grove and Liza to verify his explanation. "Apparently, Dr. Jameson has developed a treatment program that works specifically with witnesses like her."

Liza nodded. But Holden still felt as though he was missing something when she continued to avoid eye contact. "Dr. Jameson wasn't particularly pleased with the results of my session at the precinct offices. He thinks I'll do better in the controlled space of his office," she said. "There would be too many people, too many distractions here."

"Fine," Grove agreed. "We'll escort you to Jameson's for your appointment."

"Before we go, can I go for a run with my dogs? I'm not used to sitting around so much. They aren't, either."

"Should I just paint a 'Shoot me' sign on your back?"

Holden moved forward. "You're out of line, Grove."

"Back off, Kincaid."

Cutler positioned himself between the two men. "Boys!"

Liza tried to be a little more reasonable. "Presidents of the United States have gone running with their Secret Service men. Why don't you all just come with me?"

"I'll go with her," Holden volunteered. Her pent-up energy pushed against the walls of the house. Like Cutler had told him, she needed to blow off some steam if KCPD wanted her to keep her head in the game. "Trip, Molloy and Delgado can come, too. We have to do daily fitness training, anyway. We could take care of both jobs at the same time."

Cutler nodded. "Fine."

"Cutler!" Kevin Grove's protest boomed through the house, startling Cruiser and sending her trotting out of the kitchen. "Miss Parrish is *my* responsibility. This is my—"

"The investigation may be yours. But security is my detail. She's fighting us on things the way they are, so if we give on this, we'll get more cooperation in return. I trained these men myself. I guarantee you they'll keep her safe." He turned and dismissed Holden with a nod. "I want her in a vest, and I want your team armed and hooked up to a radio at all times."

"Yes, sir."

Resisting the urge to gloat, Holden opened his phone and crossed into the living room to call Dominic and the others. After hanging up on Delgado a few minutes later, Holden tuned in to the hushed voices of the two men still arguing in the kitchen. Liza was still in her bedroom changing.

"If this doesn't pan out, I can't make my case. This better be worth the trouble we're going to for this witness."

"Is there any reason why it wouldn't be?" Cutler asked.

"I kept her name out of the press for as long as I could. Now that the world knows we've got a witness to John Kincaid's murder, the bastards behind his death will be closing in. The clock is ticking." Kevin Grove's curse drew Holden closer to the archway to eavesdrop. "I just hope she remembers what she needs to before they get through us and find her."

"They won't get through—"

"Remember what she needs to?" Holden had never been one to avoid a confrontation when something needed to be said. He stepped into the kitchen and demanded an explanation. "What does that mean?"

Grove scowled, looking even more like a bulldog than ever, then he laughed. "You mean with all the unsanctioned snooping you and your brothers have been doing for the past six months, you don't know?"

"Don't know what?"

"Your girlfriend didn't tell you?"

"Grove..."

"Allow me, detective."

Holden turned at Liza's voice.

She stood in the kitchen archway, pulling a navy blue sweatshirt down over her gray, fitted running suit. She tilted her chin up proudly, defensively—but the robust energy that had sparkled in her eyes a few minutes ago had vanished.

"I'm sorry, Kincaid. I want to help your family and KCPD, I really do." Something inside him sagged as her own deep sigh rounded her shoulders. But she never once lowered her gaze. "I suffer from traumatic amnesia. I remember finding Bruiser, and I remember finding your father. But what happened in between? All I know is I was afraid. I can't tell you who murdered your father...because I don't remember."

Liza jumped inside her skin as two gunshots exploded in the night.

"Relax. You're perfectly safe here." She wasn't sure she believed Dr. Jameson, but she tried to obey. "Breathe deeply, Liza. Return to your quiet place."

She hugged the pillow to her stomach and focused on her breathing.

Liza clutched the emaciated dog tightly in her arms and smelled the dank river. The sound of tires on the damp pavement drew her attention to the front of the alley. She muzzled the dog with her hand and crouched down low, flattening her back against the rough brick wall. Car doors slammed and she could hear men's voices. One of them laughed.

"Liza?" Dr. Jameson's voice filtered into her mind. "I need you to tell me what you're seeing. What you hear."

The spring night was damp this close to the river. The moisture of it clung to the dog's fur and intensified his sour smell. Thank goodness she'd parked far away, because the men wouldn't realize she was here. Of course, she hadn't known how far she'd have to go to track down this dog Anita had told her about. She hadn't known she'd be witnessing a murder.

"Liza." His tone was a little sharper now, less patient than the gentle voice that had lulled her into this sleepy state. "Can you hear my voice?"

She nodded. "I hear you."

"Good." The soft music in the room was replaced with the abrasive whine of a rusty metal door sliding open. Someone was coming out of the warehouse. Or was someone going in? She couldn't see. "Now I want to you move closer to the black car. Open the door in your mind and tell me what you see."

She pulled her mind back to the car, to the images she could barely see. "Two men. One has white hair and tattoos clear around his neck and down his arms. He isn't wearing a coat."

"Good. What does the other man look like?"

She peered through a gap between the plastic bags. The stench of the rotting garbage inside made her eyes tear up and her nose run.

"Tell me about the other man."

"He's—"

Liza's mind shuttered, as if someone had drawn a blindfold over her eyes. There was only blackness inside her head. "Doctor…?"

"Relax. Breathe deeply. In through your nose, out…"

Dr. Jameson's words got lost in the fog of her memory. Another voice—cold, heartless—shivered down her spine. *"Did you hear that?"*

The skinny dog could barely move, but he still had fight in him. His mournful whine vibrated through his body and echoed along the walls of the alley.

Fresh tears stung Liza's eyes, replacing the caustic irritation of the garbage with the shock of bone-deep fear. She stroked her fingers along the dog's empty, distended belly, desperately coaxing him into silence.

"Tell me about the other man, Liza. Who's there with you?"

"It's just a mutt." The tattooed man's voice was higher in pitch than the other man's. "I had a dog when

I was a kid. I lived in Yugoslavia back then. Hell, they don't even have Yugoslavia anymore. I miss that dog."

"I hate dogs."

The other man sounded vaguely familiar. But how could it? She'd never been to this part of Kansas City before. She didn't know these men.

"What is it, Liza?" Dr. Jameson kept pushing. "Tell me what you're seeing."

"From the sound of it, he'll be dead by morning."

"If someone hears it, they may call the police."

"Or the dog catcher." The tattooed man laughed. "Do they still have dog catchers?"

"If anyone comes, it could give us away before the boss is finished with the mission." There was a rasp and a click that Liza couldn't identify.

"What are you gonna do with that gun?"

"I'm going to track down that dog and shut him up."

Liza jerked as if she'd been slapped. Suddenly, she was in a different place. At a different time. "No. Please. I don't want to be here."

"From the look of things, the dog was probably trying to defend the place when they broke in." The police woman who'd called Liza home from college was trying to be kind.

"I'm sure Shasta barked at the intruders."

"Then I imagine they did it to shut her up. Before the neighbors could hear. She was the one alarm they couldn't shut off with a stolen key code."

So the thieves had shot her dog.

"No. Mom? Dad?" They'd killed her dog. Killed her parents. Liza was locked inside her head with the nightmare. The hot tears that leaked from beneath the silk eye mask were as real as the pain she felt. "I don't want to do this anymore." Was she speaking out loud? Was she dreaming? "Make it stop. Mom and Dad are dead. I don't want to see that again."

"Damn it, Liza. Go back to the alley."

Her jumbled up mind struggled to sort out the present and the past.

"Test subject is too agitated to remain in deep suggestive state." Dr. Jameson was talking into his recorder. "Drug therapy is only recourse left to pursue."

Her parents' deaths were in the past.

Men who would murder were in the past.

"Liza, I'm going to count to three and you will be awake. One…"

"I don't want to do this," she pleaded.

"Two…"

Drug therapy?

"Three."

Liza's eyes popped open beneath the mask. She ripped it off her face and squinted up at the ceiling, waiting for the ivy-print border to come into focus. When the rapid rise and fall of her chest evened out and she thought she could sit up without the room spinning around her head, she did. The headache wasn't as bad this time, just a dull twinge behind her eyes. But the fear and confusion were more disconcerting than ever. "Dr. Jameson, I don't think this is helping."

He looked up from the notes he'd been scribbling. "You're too impatient. You don't listen to me half the time. It's no wonder we can't make this work."

"I'm not taking drugs. I heard you say that. Even for the truth, I won't do it."

With a scoffing noise, he tossed off his reading glasses and went to his desk to turn on a lamp. "I'm only talking about a small dose of Sodium Pentothal to relax you."

"Truth serum?" Hadn't she already surrendered enough control of her mind to this man? She wasn't about to turn what was left of it over to some drug. "Like they use to get POWs to talk? No, thanks."

"You watch too much television."

"Not much at all, really." She grabbed her backpack and slung it over her shoulder as she stood up. Holden and two of the members of his S.W.A.T. team were waiting for her out in the reception area. A fourth member was parked out front in their armored van. It would be damn near impossible to talk them into taking her somewhere besides straight home, but she intended to try. Being locked up inside her home with Holden's brooding silences, now that he knew she wasn't able to help him solve his father's murder, after all, sounded about as appealing as Trent Jameson's plan to inject her with drugs. "I need some fresh air."

"Where do you think you're going?"

"We're done, right?" She gestured toward the closed shades at the window. "I need sunlight and the smell of the leaves on the ground. I can't be cooped up in here or inside my head for another minute."

Jameson moved fast for a man more than twice her age. When Liza opened his office door, he was suddenly there, reaching over her shoulder and slamming it shut. "What aren't you telling me?"

A momentary burst of fear stuttered through her next breath, but Liza quickly replaced the panic with her mouthy, street-savvy attitude. "We're done here."

"Liza?" Holden's voice was a distant call.

"We are done when I say we're done." Jameson

grasped her arm and spun her around, forcing her to read the disappointment and accusation etched on his face. "You've been fighting against me from our very first session. My therapeutic techniques have been proven successful by other patients. Why are you working against me?"

Liza shrugged off his touch and shrank against the door. "It's nothing personal. What the hell kind of doctor are you?"

"I'm the kind who gets results. When my patients cooperate."

There was some kind of commotion in the outer office.

"Liza?"

"Officer, I can't let you… He's with a patient."

"Step aside, lady."

Liza wished she was on the other side of this door to see it. "Well, I'm not one of your patients anymore."

Liza reached behind her to turn the knob, but Jameson slapped his hand against the wood beside her head. "*You* have no idea what you're up against, do you. Someone murdered someone else, and they think you know who they are—"

A familiar jolt of fear, just as powerful as anything she'd felt in that dark alley, made her heart pump faster. "I want out of here. Now."

"—and whether you ever remember them or not, they're going to want you dead."

"Liza!"

Jameson pulled her away from the door as the knob turned from the other side. The door flew open, tearing the wood beneath its hinges.

Liza saw the gun pointing at Dr. Jameson before she

felt the hand clamp down over her arm and drag her behind the wall of Holden's back. "Are you hurt?"

"No. But I want to leave. He wouldn't let me leave."

"We can fix that."

She was staring at a sea of black. No, she was surrounded by a shield of crisp black uniforms as the slow-talking Trip and raven-haired Dominic Molloy took up flanking positions a step behind Holden. Their guns weren't drawn, but they each rested their hand on the gun butt sticking out from their holsters. One kept an eye on the receptionist, the other had a hand on Holden's back, guiding him so he could back out of Jameson's office without taking his eye—or his gun—off the doctor.

Jameson seemed unimpressed with the efficient show of force. "You'll pay for this door, I'm assuming?"

"Go to hell."

Liza curled her fingers around Holden's belt, unsure whether she was holding on for her own safety or urging him to retreat. "Please, Kincaid."

Holden held his stance a moment longer before he turned in a fluid ripple of motion, took her by the arm again and steered her past the receptionist's desk toward the outer door and the elevators at the end of the hallway. "We're out of here. Dom, take point. Trip—"

"Don't worry, the doctor will stay right where he is."

Trip could block Jameson in his office, but he couldn't stop the therapist from calling after her. "I know your nightmares torment you, Liza. You think that if you could just remember everything the police want you to that you could put them out of your mind. It's that searching for answers, for closure, that keeps the nightmares coming back. You know I'm your best chance to unlock those hidden places inside your head.

You'll never find peace without me. You know that. You'll come back to me."

Every taunt was a cruel "I told you so" that hit its mark and left Liza clutching the rail at the back of the elevator and sagging against it.

"You shut the hell up, Doc," Holden ordered. "The lady's done with you."

Liza perked up at the protective anger in his tone as the door slid shut. She wanted Holden to turn around and take her into his arms, to let her feel—and not just hear—that he was still on her side, that his disappointment at her inability to help with the case hadn't completely eroded the connection growing between them. But he was snapping orders into the radio at this shoulder, ordering Delgado to have the van in place when they walked out the front doors.

He was cold and remote, like a machine, and seemed not at all interested in offering comfort to a woman who'd kept the truth from him and his family.

"What was that about?" Molloy asked, apparently less affected by the tension of the situation than Holden was.

"Desperation," Liza answered, when no one else spoke. "Maybe we can get Hayley Resnick to broadcast that my brain is mush and that there's no sense in the bad guys coming after me because I don't know who they are." The joke was lame and nobody laughed. The headache behind Liza's eyes deepened to a throb as tears burned in her sinuses and threatened to spill over again. Riding down seven floors, staring at the center of Holden's broad back, was cruelly symbolic of the bleak turn her life had taken. She'd ceased to be useful to him, but he was still determined to do his job, to protect her even though he now probably thought it was a waste of time. Maybe he even thought that the feelings he had for her were a waste of time. "I'm sorry, Kincaid. I really thought Dr. Jameson could help me remember."

"He's not interested in justice. From the look of things, Jameson was using you like a lab rat to further his own career." That almost musical warmth that she'd found so soothing in Holden's voice had returned, though he never turned around or relaxed his guarded posture. But at least he was talking to her again. That was a good thing, right? "You don't need to go back there."

"What if I can't remember on my own?"

"Then I guess I'll have to find another way to find who killed my father."

MR. SMITH TURNED OFF the tape recorder, pulled out the tape and crushed the plastic cassette in his leather-gloved fist. He tossed it on the floor next to Trent Jameson's body and pulled his cell phone from his belt.

He punched in his employer's number as he paged through Jameson's treatise on "Hypnotherapy Applications to Memory Recovery Technique." Looked like the good doctor was puffed up on his own ego and liked to hear himself talk. According to his research here, he'd had success with "Scent Triggers" and "Guided Recall" with some of his patients. But when it came to Liza Parrish…

His employer picked up the call.

"I don't think she knows enough to put us away," Mr. Smith reported.

"How certain are we that she'll never remember the details of the crime?"

Mr. Smith didn't need Jameson's therapy to remember the information he'd read in his files. "It's fifty-fifty. But chances are, since it's trauma and not injury-induced, she will, one day, remember. Could be tomorrow, could be when she's ninety-two." He closed the treatise and rose from behind Jameson's desk. "How do you want me to proceed?"

"Even when she's ninety-two, the statute of limitations won't have run out on Kincaid's murder. He was a thorn in my side for thirty years while he was alive. It's not fair that he should continue to haunt me now that he's dead."

Striding past the receptionist slumped over her desk, Mr. Smith turned out the lights and closed the door behind him. He pushed the button for the elevator and waited for a reply.

With a bastion of KCPD officers shadowing Liza Parrish 24/7 now, he needed to move quickly or this could get messy. He could handle messy, but clean and swift was so much easier.

"I need you to give me the order."

This time, his employer didn't hesitate.

"Kill her."

CHAPTER EIGHT

HOLDEN FINISHED TOWELING off and pulled on his shorts and camo pants before rummaging through the duffel bag. He felt out of place, like an intruder himself, showering in Liza's bathroom, with its blue border of Noah's ark and animals circling the ceiling, and a collection of plastic and ceramic animal pairs sitting on the shelves above the toilet and towel racks.

Probably not the most apt place to unpack the spare hunting clothes he kept in the back of his Mustang for impromptu weekend getaways. It was a habit he'd learned from his dad. There'd been hundreds of times growing up—and as a man—that he and his dad, one or all his brothers and often Bill Caldwell, had kissed Susan Kincaid goodbye and gone off to hunt or fish, or simply camp and enjoy the outdoors. The eyes of every cute little critter seemed to be watching him, judging him. At least he'd left his Bushmaster rifle stowed in the trunk.

He opened the velcro pocket where he'd stored his service Glock, and looped the holster onto his belt, along with his badge.

The irony of who he was, and who Liza seemed to be—his Montague to her Capulet—only added to the guilt he carried on his shoulders.

He had a thing for the copper-haired animal lover.

Maybe he'd let his lust for her impair his judgment. But hell, it was more than that; their connection had been sealed the first time their eyes met across the crowded precinct floor. He'd known something wasn't kosher about all the delays in KCPD's investigation into his father's murder. There had always been something suspicious about an alleged eyewitness whose identity was kept secret. Yet, if she was so valuable a lead, why were only sketchy details on the case being pursued?

Now he understood.

She'd lied to him, damn it. All right, so it was a lie of omission, but neglecting to mention her amnesia was a pretty big lie all the same. She wasn't the key to solving his father's murder, after all. There was no face she could describe or breakthrough clue she could provide. She couldn't tell KCPD any more about his father's murder than the dog she'd rescued that night.

He'd pinned all his hope on her—probably a damn foolish thing for a man his age to do. A trained cop, no less. After knowing her for only a few hours, he'd been so desperate to end the suffering and uncertainty his family was going through that he'd latched on to Liza Parrish as though she was some kind of avenging angel who, if he could just push the right buttons and keep her in one piece, would finally reveal the truth that could give his family closure. She was a scrappy fighter. She had the strength and drive to get the job done.

And he loved her for that.

After four short days, he loved her.

"Ain't that a kick in the pants," he chided his reflection in the fogged-up mirror, before pulling on a clean T-shirt and khaki green sweater.

How could he really love a woman who harbored big

secrets he knew nothing about? He was supposed to choose loyalty to his family over his own desires, right?

It had taken overhearing that bizarre, abusive therapy session with Trent Jameson for Holden to get off his pity pot and realize he still had a job to do. His emotions had gotten in the way of clear thinking again, just like they had on that Al Mabry shoot earlier in the week. No matter how conflicted he felt about Liza, nobody deserved to be put through that kind of hell. Nobody.

He just wasn't sure he knew how to get past the betrayal he felt—that he probably had no right to feel. Or maybe it was the disappointment in his own judgment. He didn't trust what might be in his heart any more than he trusted Liza right now.

His life had been a hell of a lot easier when he could ice over his feelings, stop second-guessing his decisions and just do what needed to be done. He missed his father tonight as much as he had the day of his funeral. John Kincaid would have known what to say, how to guide his youngest son through this. He'd probably tell him to grab his fishing pole, pack some food, and they'd go out into the country somewhere. Pitch a tent. Drop their lines in the water. Talk. Listen. And by the time they got back home, Holden would know what to do.

But his father wasn't here to guide him anymore.

Holden squashed the pain of all he had lost into an icy ball inside his chest and let it numb his confusion. He pulled on his socks and hiking boots, packed his muddy sweats in the bag and turned off the light before opening the door. At this time of night, even with the shades drawn, any interior light would give a perp outside a pretty good idea of where there was activity—and a possible target—inside the house.

He slung the duffel bag over his shoulder and walked out into the darkened living room. He'd stop in the kitchen one last time to fill the dogs' water bowls before he left through the side door to the driveway where he'd parked his Mustang. According to Cutler, his only job right now was to guard the dogs. It sucked at Holden's pride to be relegated to glorified dog-walker, but maybe it was the only job he was suited for until he could get his head screwed on straight again.

Kevin Grove was sitting in the lone chair in the living room, holding a flashlight and reading a book, when Holden walked in. Though he couldn't exactly claim that they'd become friends, they had developed a certain rapport that involved an acceptance of their differences, a little respect and a healthy dose of traded barbs.

Holden inclined his head toward the novel by Tolkien in Grove's hands. "Who knew a big lug like you could read. And it's not even a picture book. Impressive." He adjusted his duffel over his shoulder. "Thanks for letting me clean up."

The burly detective bookmarked his page and shut off the light. "I didn't want to spend any more time than I had to with a man who smelled like he'd run five miles through the mud with a pack of hounds."

"It's been a real pleasure spending some quality time with you, too, Grove." He paused as he walked past Liza's closed door; the ice hadn't numbed everything inside him yet. "She asleep?"

"Yeah. About as soon as you hit the shower, she called the dogs in and closed the door."

Gathering the troops around her for protection. Against a man who wanted her dead? Or against the cold shoulder he'd thrown up between them and couldn't seem to breach? "Well, good night."

"Hold up." Grove crossed through the shadows. "I got a phone call while you were in the shower." The fact that he had lowered his voice to little more than a whisper couldn't be good. "A nighttime cleaning crew found Trent Jameson and his secretary dead in his office. According to the M.E., Holly Masterson, they look like professional hits."

Only hours after Liza had been in that office herself? "Our killer's already closing in."

"Looks that way."

Holden's gaze slipped to Liza's door again. Even with armed guards inside and around the house, she seemed isolated. Alone in her room with no one but her dogs to cling to for comfort. No wonder she wouldn't leave them. The emotions he'd shunned tried to fight back. "What's the plan? I know you have one."

"I'm making arrangements to move Liza to a more secure location at first light. I want her in a closed apartment with restricted access. We'll kennel the dogs at the K-9 training facility."

Isolate her even more. "She won't go for that."

"No one's giving her a choice this time." Grove had always looked like a brawny wrestler, but as he propped his hands at his hips, Holden noted that his barrel chest was thicker than usual. He was wearing a flak vest under his jacket. Armed with a Glock at his waist and a spare piece at his ankle, he was prepped for battle. Expecting the worst. "I've been working on this case for six months. The answers to your father's murder are inside her head. I want the chance to recover those answers before your father's killer shuts them down permanently. In the meantime, until the extraction team comes at dawn, I'm looking for all the reinforcements I can get."

Holden dropped his bag at his feet. "I'll get my gear."

KEVIN GROVE WAS a snorer. No wonder, with that crooked nose that looked as though it had been busted up once or twice.

But that wasn't the sound that had snagged Holden's attention away from Grove's book that he'd picked up to read while the detective crashed on the couch for sixty minutes.

Holden hit the light button on his watch and checked the time. 2:14 a.m. Way too soon for the extraction team to arrive. The guards outside were either sitting in their cars staying warm, or farther off in the woods. The only sounds he should hear from them would come over the radio hooked to Grove's belt. And the noise he'd heard wasn't electronic.

There it was again.

A thud. Like a fist meeting a chin—only softer. The sound repeated. Again. And again.

Silently he stood, setting the book on the chair and unsnapping his Glock as he moved to the center of the room to pinpoint the source of the sound. There. He turned his ear toward Liza's bedroom door. Another thud.

Holden curled his fingers around his gun.

"Son of a…" His breath seeped out on half a curse and half a sigh of relief at the sound of tiny claws scratching the other side of Liza's door. "Damn dog."

He'd been poised and ready to strike. To shoot. To kill.

It was just a furry musketeer needing a bed of his own or a potty break.

"Cool your jets, Pee-Wee." Again, he breathed the words, unwilling to wake Grove or Liza, and hoping the dogs wouldn't wake them, either. But Bruiser must have already smelled his approach, and excitedly scratched at the door again. "I'm coming."

Thud. "Unh."

Dog? Or woman?

The sound repeated itself. *Not* the dog. Unless one of them had learned to speak. Actual words.

"Shh, baby. They'll hear."

"Parrish?" Holden opened the door. Bruiser jumped over his boot and trotted past him, heading straight for the kitchen. Holden began to push the door open farther, but hit a roadblock. He glanced down to see silver fur and an indifferent glance. "Yukon."

"Black Buick." Thud.

Ah, hell.

"Move." Yukon got up and ambled to the foot of the bed as Holden pushed his way into the room.

With his vision well-adjusted to the darkness of the house, Holden had no trouble identifying the sound now. Liza was thrashing in her bed, caught in the grip of a vicious nightmare. Her body shook. With her legs pinned beneath twisted covers and Cruiser's paws, the only thing that could move was the mattress itself. That explained the thud every time it knocked against the wall.

"Stay with me," she muttered, clutching her pillow to her stomach. "I'm trying. I'm trying."

"Liza?" The greyhound seemed frozen to the spot, either sitting on Liza to protect her mistress, or too stunned by the spasms that had disrupted her sleep to move. He shooed the dog out of the way. "Go on. Get down. I'll handle this."

Cruiser quickly obeyed, hopping down from the bed and spreading out on a pillow over in the corner.

"Liza," Holden repeated, picking up the hem of the quilt she had kicked to the floor, trying to untangle her legs without startling her awake. "Wake up, babe. It's just a bad dream." A thin sheen of perspiration dotted her skin and made a dark spot in the cleavage of her long-sleeve T-shirt. Holden eased himself onto the edge of the bed and stroked the back of his knuckles across her forehead, smoothing aside a damp fringe of copper. "It's okay, Liza. You'll be okay."

"…hate dogs. He'll shoot us. Hush…"

"Liza?" He moved his hand to her shoulder, and had to use a little muscle to hold on as she jerked. "Wake up."

Her ramblings now, her whimpers of anguish, weren't all that different from the terrified cries he'd heard coming from Trent Jameson's office during that last so-called therapy session. Was this muted suffering what her amnesia cost her? Or the aftermath of what those sessions did to her? How many times had she faced these night terrors?

No. How many times had she faced them alone?

The fist of hurt that had strangled his heart eased its grip. A lie of omission didn't seem like such a big stumbling block right now.

"Liza." He shook her. This needed to stop. "Wake up. Li—"

"No!" A fist flew at his chest. "No-o-o!"

She twisted from his grasp and sat up, fighting for her life, screaming.

"Sh, sh, sh." Holden easily absorbed the unconscious blows and quickly gathered her to his chest, pinning her arms between them and forcing her mouth against the pillow of his shoulder. "It's okay, babe, it's okay." He rocked back and forth, hugging her tight, muffling the last of her cries against his chest. "Hush now. I've got you."

"Kincaid!" The bedroom door flew open and Kevin Grove barged inside, his gun drawn—his eyes alert, his posture ready to fight.

Holden held up his hand, warning him off. "Easy."

"What the hell is going on in here?" Grove moved closer to the bed. Liza's jerk must have been as visible as the jolt he felt against his chest because Grove holstered his weapon and backed off a couple of steps. "I thought…we were under attack."

Holden wrapped his arm back around her. "Only inside her head."

"Nightmare?"

Holden nodded. He could feel the heat of her tears soaking through his sweater and the manic clutch of her fingers pinching into his skin underneath. "I've got it under control."

Liza was shaking, her breathing coming in shallow, erratic gasps. But she was finally awake, and coherent enough to apologize. "I'm sorry. I'm sorry I…woke you."

"That's okay, ma'am. Stress, I guess." Grove looked to Holden as he retreated to the door. "You got this?"

Holden nodded. As Grove closed the door behind him, Holden tunneled his fingers beneath the soft, sleep-matted fringe of hair at her nape. He massaged her gently there and rocked her back and forth. He wasn't a therapist. He didn't know what he was supposed to say or do. He just knew he wanted to make this better. "Easy, Parrish. Easy, girl. You're okay."

The stiffness of her muscles and the cold chill he could feel through her shirt and flannel pajama pants said otherwise. "I want to remember. I see the car, and the men… But every time I come close to a face, it all shuts down and all I can remember is being afraid." Her words were little more than a sob against his chest. "I'm tired of being afraid."

"I know you are. Don't think about it now. Don't think about anything at all." He held her tight, stroked her hair and continued to rock her in the darkness.

Her tears continued to fall. "I can't remember…"

"Shh." When the right words escaped him, he started humming a tune, a mournful lullaby in his throat. He dipped his head and pressed his lips to her temple and let the simple melody—one that his father had taught him long ago—be the only sound in the room.

The tears eventually stopped and the death-grip on his sweater began to relax. Minutes later, he guided her back to her pillows, smoothing her damp hair away from each freckle as he stood and pulled the sheet and quilts up to cover her.

Liza turned away and curled her legs up into a fetal position. Her eyes were closed. She wanted to sleep. But she was still shaking.

He couldn't put his own feelings to sleep, either.

With a shush of warning to the curious dogs, Holden sat back on the covers, and then lay down behind her. He slid one arm between her neck and pillow and curled the other one around her. He wrapped her up, fetal position and all, and pulled her into his body and warmth.

Resting his lips against her ear, he began to hum again, crooning a quiet tune. He held her like that, until the shaking stopped, until her muscles relaxed—and long after, until they both settled down into a deep, healing sleep.

BLESS THE TERRIERS of the world for always knowing when to sound the alarm.

Bruiser's frantic bark woke Holden an instant before a window in the front room shattered.

"Hell."

Holden looped his arm around Liza's waist and rolled to the floor. "Stay down!"

"Kincaid!" Grove cursed and fired his weapon. "Kincaid, get out here!"

Liza was wide awake and nightmare-free as she yanked away the covers still tangled with her legs. "What's happening?"

"Sounds like D-day." Holden trained his ears to identify the sounds. There was no answering report of gunshots, only the crash and smack of bullets decimating their targets inside the house. Their attacker was using a silencer or was one hell of a distance away. He palmed Liza's hip and pushed her toward her closet. "Stay close to the floor. Get your shoes on."

She nodded, then hustled across the hardwood as though she'd been to S.W.A.T. training herself. Some part of Holden grinned in admiration of that wiggling ass, but he willed the rest of him to ice over inside as he pulled his weapon and slid a bullet into the firing chamber.

"I'm comin' out, Grove!" The detective laid down a barrage of cover fire as Holden reached up to quickly turn the knob and then slide out into the living room. "What do we got?"

Grove was on the floor, using the overturned chair and coffee table as cover while he ejected his empty magazine and reloaded a fresh clip. "Shots fired on the house. At first I thought they came from the house across the street, but now I'm not sure. Every time I put my head up to pinpoint it, we get hit." He nodded toward Bruiser who bounded back and forth through the shattered glass from the door to the sofa and back, barking his fool head off the entire way. "That crazy dog heard it before I did. Damn good thing, too." He pointed toward the bullet hole ripped through the couch, just above where he'd been sleeping. He cocked his weapon. "I gotta get me a dog."

The radio on Grove's belt was buzzing with chatter. "I got nothing…from the east…our shooter's mobile… we could have more than one… Where's Molloy?"

Grove pulled the radio from his belt while Holden crawled for his own bag to pull on his flak vest and retrieve a spare. "Molloy, report!" Grove cursed at the static that answered. "Molloy! Hell. He was in the car at the north end of the street. Molloy!"

"What frequency you on?" Holden pulled out his radio and tried to reach his buddy who'd volunteered for the overtime assignment. "Dominic, this is Kincaid. Come in."

Another voice cleared the static. "He's hit, Kincaid, he's hit. Man down! Man down!"

"Son of a bitch!" Another ripple of bullets sprayed the wall above the couch. Bruiser barked. The other dogs had picked up the panic and added their voices. Holden fought like hell to keep his emotions turned off so he could focus. But his stomach was twisting into knots. His best friend. Damn it. "Dominic! I need a roll call right now!"

"This is Delgado. I'm with Molloy. He's gone."

Holden punched his fist through the drywall beside his head. Tears burned in his eyes, but he couldn't shed them.

"What's going on?" Liza's door swung open. She crawled from the bedroom with jeans and a sweater on as well as her running shoes, pulling the leashes of two dogs behind her. Still lying on the floor, she reached out toward Holden's split knuckle and the blood seeping through his fingers. "You're hurt. Kincaid?"

He snatched his hand away before she could touch him and shoved the vest at her instead. "Put this on."

Ignoring her concern, Holden rolled back to his radio. "Every man, check in."

The four surviving officers outside radioed in their location and situation, and the fact they'd lost sight of the shooter's position—if they'd ever really had it.

Grief and anger must have plugged his ears because Holden wasn't even aware of the silence until Liza asked, "Why has the shooting stopped?"

"Damn." A thin red beam of light reflected off the shards of glass on the floor and bounced up onto the ceiling. The bastard was finding his range, taking aim. "He's switched weapons. High-powered rifle!" Holden warned the others over the radio.

The first shot hit, blowing a hole the size of a cannonball in Liza's front wall. They ducked their heads as the wood splintered and plaster dust snowed down on them.

"Where's it coming from?" Holden tried to push himself up to follow the targeting laser back to its source.

But the instant he raised his head, the sofa behind him was rent in two by a second shot and he dove for the floor.

"Oh, my God." That was Liza.

He propped his gun at the top of the chair and fired blindly into the night. He needed his damn rifle. "You hit?"

"No." Another shot took out a lamp. The red dot of light bounced across the back wall. "Bruiser!"

Holden rolled onto his back to see a flash of brown and tan leaping at the sofa. Bruiser barked at the laser dot, chased it back and forth. The red dot zeroed in on a patch of reddish-tan fur and stopped.

"Don't shoot my dog!"

"Liza!"

They jumped at the same time. Liza grabbed the dog and Holden grabbed Liza. Wood and metal shrapnel followed them to the floor as the sofa exploded.

"Damn it, Liza! Are you crazy?"

"Aaaah! Damn!"

Holden climbed off of Liza and the dog to see Grove clutching his left shoulder. Blood poured through his fingers. "You hit bad?"

"It went through." But the sleeve of his jacket was quickly turning red. Holden reached for the med kit in his bag. "Forget it," Grove ordered. "Get out of here."

"I'm not leaving—"

"Get out of here! He's picking us off one by one. I'm not waiting until it's just the three of us left standing."

Liza ignored Grove's tough command and pulled out a wad of gauze. While another shot tore her bedroom door off its hinges, she ripped the gauze apart and crawled over to check his wound.

Holden pulled his helmet from his gear bag and propped it up on top of the chair. He wasn't leaving Grove to be a sitting duck. With his sharpshooter's rifle and scope stored in the gun locker of the S.W.A.T. van, his improvised counterattack was going to be pretty piecemeal. But he hoped it'd be effective enough to buy them at least a few seconds of time.

"Go for it," he whispered. *Sucker.* In the few seconds it took the laser dot to track the helmet, Holden braced his Glock atop the chair and centered his aim along the red light. And fired.

He saw a blur in the distant shadows, a chimera in the night. The attacker's simultaneous shot hit wide, spinning the helmet to the floor, but missing dead center. He'd hit the scope or rifle, if not the shooter himself. "Ha! You son of a bitch—that one's for Dom."

Holden slid back behind cover and reloaded while Liza pressed the gauze to the back of Grove's wound and the detective gritted his teeth and pressed the front.

"Okay, boys and girls. I'm bettin' my next paycheck he's got a whole damn arsenal out there with him. The bullets will start flying again any second. The time to bug out of here is now."

"This will only stanch it for a little while," Liza advised. "You need to get to a doctor."

"Yeah, I'll get right on that." Grove bit down on a groan. "You must have the memories of some pretty important people inside your head, ma'am."

"Maybe just some pretty crazy ones." Plucking Holden's bandana from his back pocket, she tied the makeshift bandage into place. "If I leave, he'll come after *me,* right? He'll stop shooting police officers and come after me?"

"Probably."

She turned brave, knowing eyes to Holden. "Then let's get out of here, Kincaid."

"I thought you'd never ask."

Grove agreed. "Get her away from here until we can regroup. Here." He pulled a pen from his pocket and wrote a phone number on Liza's pant leg. "Call me when you're someplace safe and we'll get a Plan B in motion. Are you up to protecting her on your own?"

Holden nodded. "We're going."

Grove got on his radio again. "Little Red is leaving in the Mustang in the side driveway. Let's give her cover. I repeat, Little Red is leaving."

Holden waited for one more look from Grove. "We're gonna get this son of a bitch who killed my dad and Molloy, and I hope the hell not you."

Kevin Grove laughed. "Yes, sir, we will." He nodded, then pulled himself up from behind the chair and started shooting. "Go!"

While Grove and the men outside fired almost continuously, and the sirens of KCPD backup sped toward the house, Holden snatched Liza by the back waistband of her jeans and hauled her along beside him.

He grabbed his duffel bag. She grabbed three leashes.

He had them out the side door, behind the cover of his open car door, and stuffed inside his car before the first wave of backup skidded to a halt in front of the house. A terrier, malamute and a greyhound took up a lot of space inside a little Mustang, but Holden shoved them into the backseat, pushed Liza down to the floor, and started the engine. He laid several feet of black rubber on the driveway before the spinning wheels found traction and he spun around the corner and into the night.

For the first few minutes, Holden just floored it, putting the spinning lights and shouted commands and shot-up house as far behind them as he could. He passed two ambulances that were no doubt enroute. His head had such tunnel vision that he could no longer hear the sirens. No longer hear himself even praying that Grove would survive and Molloy's death could be reversed—and that the brave woman clinging to the seat and dashboard and flying up into the air with every bump and curve might one day feel even half of the soul-deep connection that was pounding at him to keep her in his life.

There was only escape. Only speed. Only driving as fast and far as he could and hitting the open road of the highway.

Until he felt the warm hand branding his thigh. Squeezing him. Demanding his attention.

"Holden!" Liza's voice pierced the single-minded fog around his mind. She'd already called to him twice. "Holden, can you hear me?"

He blinked, clamped down on the emotions and shoved them aside before his eyes opened again. Bruiser was on the floorboards now and Liza had climbed into her seat. Thankfully, her head was still down. Yukon's puffy head was silhouetted in the rearview mirror.

"Are you okay?" he asked. "Maybe you should buckle up."

"No." She pointed to the back window. Her skin looked so pale, her hair so bright…

The dog was *silhouetted* in the rearview mirror.

"How the hell…?"

The high-beam lights of the car behind them were closing in fast.

"Get the phone off my belt. Call 9-1-1. Tell them an officer is in a high-speed pursuit on Highway 291, heading south. The shooter is no longer at Grove's location." She leaned over the center console, pushed Cruiser's curious nose aside and retrieved the phone. "Tell them officer needs assistance and that suspect is armed and dangerous. Give them my plate number." She dialed the number and recited the information as he gave it to her. "Tell dispatch the suspect's car is probably—"

"—a black Buick SUV."

Holden squinted against the blinding reflection in his mirrors. "You can see that?"

"From the other night. And…" He shifted his gaze to the firm tilt of her chin. "I remember. Parts of it. The tattooed man was driving a black Buick SUV that night. If the killers have used the same make of vehicle twice already…"

Holden nodded. "Tell Dispatch. And tell them to send backup fast."

Holden was flying down the curving interstate highway at well over ninety miles per hour. But the vehicle behind him was gaining on him fast enough that he could make out the individual headlights now. On a black vehicle. "How the hell does this guy—?"

The first shot hit a rear taillight and Cruiser leaped into the front seat. "Damn!"

Holden swerved as the big dog caught his shoulder.

"Easy, girl. It's all right."

He righted the car but nearly swerved again. "No, no, no! Get down!"

Liza was pushing the seat all the way back and urging the greyhound down into the space already occupied by Bruiser. Liza pulled her legs up and moved farther back in her seat, moved higher.

The second shot pinged off the bumper and earned a deep bark from Yukon. "If he comes up here, too…"

"Get down, boy!" Liza reached back between the seats and grabbed Yukon's collar. "Get down!"

The third shot shattered the back window and Liza screamed. Holden ignored the sting of flying glass that peppered the back of his neck. "Are you hit? Liza, are you hit!"

"No! Yukon was already down on the seat. We're all good." She pushed herself up on one elbow on the console. "You're bleeding."

"They're just cuts." Holden pressed the accelerator all the way to the floor. "I've had enough of this bastard. Take the wheel."

"Are you kidding? We're flying!"

"Take the wheel!" He unhooked the Glock at his belt. "Come on, baby, this is what I do!"

"But it's not what I…"

By the time the next shot had taken off his right sideview mirror, Liza was steering. She straddled the console and stretched her left foot over onto the accelerator, while he rolled down the window and iced his nerves.

"Be careful. Oh, God."

Her prayer disappeared in the rush of wind that whipped past his head as he turned in the seat and stuck his gun out the window. He ducked back in as he caught a flash from the side of the vehicle behind them. The perp was shooting out his side window. Driving with one hand. Making steering corrections every time they hit a curve or he fired a shot.

"Make it easy for me, why don't you."

"Kincaid? I see the Lee's Summit lights up ahead. We're going to hit some traffic."

"Keep her steady, Parrish."

He crept out the window again, bracing his arms against the car frame to help keep the buffeting force of the wind from shaking his aim. Holden lined his eye up along the barrel, inhaled his breath and held it.

Headlight or driver? Couldn't get a clear sight on the driver. Headlight. No. Tire.

"Taking the shot."

Boom.

The car behind them jerked to the left and then flipped, rolling once, twice, a third time over the grassy median until it landed upright and skidded a good thirty feet, cutting up chunks of grass and dirt before it slammed to a stop on its fractured wheels.

Holden slid back into the car and holstered his gun. He took over driving but could hold Liza's arm and balance her while she climbed back over the seat and took her place between Cruiser and Bruiser in the back. He eased his foot off the accelerator and slowed them to a more normal speed.

But before he released Liza's arm, he pulled her back toward him. "Come here."

He turned his head and stole a sweet, deep, life-affirming kiss that left him as flushed and hot as the blush on her cheeks, before releasing her and turning his attention back to the road.

"Nice driving."

"Nice shooting." She pushed the dogs aside and finally fastened her seat belt. “You’re not going back to see if he’s all right?”

Holden arched an eyebrow in disbelief at the question. “I want as much distance between you and that bastard as I can get. Call 9-1-1 again. Give them the mile marker and notify them of the crash. Tell them I have Little Red, and I’m taking her to a secure location.”

CHAPTER NINE

LIZA WELCOMED HOLDEN's broad chest at her back and his strong arm looped around her waist as he rang his brother's doorbell. She was secure and sheltered, but there was an edginess radiating through his stiff muscles that made her wonder if she'd dreamed the caring man who'd held her while she slept.

He pounded on the frame beside the screen door. "Come on, Ed. Open up!"

Even though she hadn't seen a single car behind them once they turned off the highway and headed east through a little bedroom community and onto a gravel road that took them to this out-of-the-way acreage, Holden had insisted that she wait for him to escort her to the screened-in front porch of the gray stone house.

From the moment that first bullet had shattered her peaceful home, he'd gone into cop mode. Holden Kincaid was sexy and funny, one hell of a kisser, and he had a beautiful, mesmerizing voice whether he was crooning a lullaby or soothing her terrors with soft, meaningful words. She'd known he was a tough guy because of the guns and the uniform and the attitude, but she'd never truly seen the warrior in him until tonight.

He'd lost a good friend without shedding a tear. Shot to kill a man twice with an icy detachment. It had been downright scary to see the Jekyll-and-Hyde transformation between the man who'd put aside his own hurts to comfort her securely in his arms, and the man who stood behind her now with his gun drawn and his body positioned as a shield between her and whatever dangers still lurked in the predawn darkness.

The dogs were happy to be on solid ground and so was she. Her knees still felt more like gelatin than muscle and bone after the faceless home invasion and that wild car ride through the southeastern corner of Kansas City. But she felt as if she'd been to war, in her dreams and in her reality, and she was physically and emotionally drained.

Is that what Holden was feeling? Whatever risky, passionate emotions he'd shared in that last kiss while they were speeding down the highway, they were all bottled up inside him now. The loss of his smile and that edgy repartee that usually zinged between them added another layer of guilt onto the weight she already carried inside her soul.

Holden pulled her in tight as he knocked again. "Edward!"

The inside door swung open. Liza's breath caught in her throat and, no matter her reservations, she instinctively retreated against the wall of Holden's chest as Edward made a fantastical first impression right out of an English novel. The black screen of the storm door and the dim lighting inside intensified his brooding, unsmiling face, marked by scars and needing a shave. His hair was dark and unkempt, and his pale gray eyes glowed like a cat's in the shadows.

"You *are* on my hit list, little brother." His gravelly voice was quite unlike Holden's rich, seductive tones. He pushed open the screen door and stepped aside to let them enter. "Come on back to the kitchen. I made coffee."

She supposed she could overlook his morbid sense of humor if the man was going to offer them shelter for a few hours. Holden caught the door and nudged her in ahead of him while Cruiser, Bruiser and Yukon darted past and immediately set about investigating their new surroundings with their noses. "Thank you for letting us come."

Her effort at a cheery greeting fell on deaf ears. "Are those dogs?"

Um, yes. While Holden locked the front door, she evaluated his brother's expression and quickly decided that Edward Kincaid wasn't lacking any mental faculties, just some manners. "You don't like dogs?"

His gaze followed the dogs instead of looking at her. "My daughter always wanted a pet."

"Oh." This man had a daughter? A child lived in this remote, undecorated place? Surprise aside, some of Liza's trepidation about Edward dissipated. She'd been two years old when her parents had gotten the first pets she remembered—a calico cat named Purr, then an apricot poodle named Bobbi. She'd lived with something furry and four-legged ever since. "There are animals at shelters all over the city, waiting to be adopted. Some with dispositions that are perfect with children. At the clinic where I work, we even have this bull terrier who..."

Holden cleared his throat. When he caught her eye, he was shaking his head no, warning her to drop the subject.

Right. Not everyone appreciated a canine companion. "I can tie them up on the front porch if you want."

Edward finally looked her in the eye. She saw sadness in his, not aversion or disdain. "They're cool. Unless one of them stakes out my carpet."

"They won't." Being housebroken had always been rule one in her pack.

He nodded, resting both hands on his cane now, though she couldn't see any outward sign of injury like a cast or wrapped ankle beneath the hem of his dark jeans. "So you're the woman who saw my father's murder."

"Don't start, Edward." Holden stood beside her now, and even though he draped his arm behind her shoulders, she couldn't quite shake the chill that rippled down her spine. "It's been a long night."

Edward looked up at Holden, then studied Liza's face once more. His mouth crinkled into something she thought must be his effort at a smile. "Don't worry, Liza. My bark's a lot worse than my bite these days."

She had a feeling both could be equally dangerous. She stepped away from Holden's supportive, yet strangely cool touch. "I have partial amnesia regarding what I saw that night." She swallowed hard. This wasn't any easier to admit the second time around. "But I'm working on recovering my memories. I promise, I will do everything I can to help you. There were witnesses who stepped forward when my parents were killed. Because of them, the men responsible are now serving life in prison. I want to do the same for your family. When…when I can."

"You don't have anyone?"

She'd been braced for an entirely different question from that raspy voice—something more along the line of accusation or condemnation. Liza wasn't quite sure what he was asking. “I have my dogs.” She glanced up at Holden. “And your brother. For now.”

If Edward Kincaid had slapped her, she couldn’t have been more surprised when he stepped forward and wrapped one arm around her shoulder in a hug. There was some deeper meaning being communicated here that she wasn’t privy to. For some reason, she got the idea that this odd, unlikable man…liked her.

He tugged at the shoulder of the flak vest she still wore as he pulled away. “I think you can take this off while you’re in here.” When he’d released her entirely, he nodded at Holden. “He’ll do right by you.” He winked. “Or I’ll kick his ass.” The strange interchange ended and Edward limped toward the airy white kitchen at the back of the house. It appeared to be the only room where he’d turned on enough lights to see the decor. “I need coffee. Come on, little brother, let’s talk. You didn’t give me much to work with when you called, but I think I’ve got a plan.”

“Will you be okay, Liza?”

“Go on.”

But when she reached down to release the straps that held her flak vest in place, Holden’s fingers were already there. They brushed against each other and an electric current arced between them. Liza pulled away, an instinctive reaction to a nightmare’s touch, to the cold grasp of a dead man begging her to remember the truth. Or was it just a cautious reaction to a very warm, very real man who suddenly seemed like a stranger to her?

Holden’s hands stilled. “Is something wrong? Look, I know Edward comes across like the Grim Reaper at times, but inside he—”

"Hush." Liza pressed her fingers to his lips to stop the unnecessary apology. When his blue eyes unshuttered and locked on to hers, she slid her hand along his stubbled jaw to cup his cheek. "You're the one I'm worried about right now. I'm sorry about your friend. And I'm sorry Detective Grove got hurt. I know it doesn't mean much, but I *will* remember. If it takes me a lifetime, I promise I will tell you who killed your father and your friend."

Holden raised his large, nicked-up hand to cover hers, and she saw a glimpse of her Dr. Jekyll again in his wry smile. "It means everything."

She would have stretched up on tiptoe and kissed him then, or wrapped her arms around him and hugged him tight.

But Edward turned on a living room lamp. "The clock's ticking, brother. You coming?"

As the shadows left the room, she saw Kevin Grove's dried blood caked beneath her fingernails. "I guess I need to wash up."

Holden pointed to a convergence of three doors off to the side of the main room. "It's the one on the left."

She pulled off the flak vest and laid it on the couch beside his before turning toward the bathroom.

"Liza?" His soft voice stopped her. His hands on her shoulders turned her. His fingers threaded into her hair and pulled her up into a needy kiss. She wound her arms around his neck and held on, held her body as close to his as she could get. He kissed her lips, her cheeks, her eyes, and then he found her mouth and kissed her again. It was bruising and hot and grieving and assuring all at once. And when he pulled away, the Holden she knew—the Holden she loved—was there in his eyes again. "We'll be all right," he promised.

Liza nodded, then pushed him toward the kitchen and went in to scrub her hands.

He might not want the love that had blossomed in her heart and was growing with every passing minute. He might not even want the passion, after a time. But she wanted to ease his hurts and regain his trust and own it for a lifetime.

And the only way to do that was to one day be able to tell him who'd killed his father.

JUST OVER AN hour later, sunrise was creeping over the horizon as Holden closed the back hatch on Edward's Jeep. They'd packed a tent, sleeping bags, a fresh box of ammo for both his Glock and rifle, and a few day's worth of food and supplies for people and dogs alike.

"Here are the keys." Edward dropped a spare set into Holden's hand and patted the vehicle's fading green paint. "Try to bring it back in one piece. I'll take care of the Mustang."

Holden nodded his thanks. "You'll call Mom and tell her where I am? What's going on?"

"As vaguely as possible, but yes."

"She'll worry if I can't call her."

"I know."

A breathless laugh sparkled in the morning air, turning the brothers' attention to Liza, who was playing a rousing game of fetch in the side yard between a windbreak of trees and the house. Her hair was the same coppery color as the oak leaves, and the damp morning chill and the robust exercise had whipped her cheeks into a rosy color. She threw a big stick and Bruiser and

Yukon went charging after, while Cruiser was content to sniff the ground near Liza's feet.

It was a beautiful, normal—perfect—scene that Holden thought he could watch every morning of his life.

"I see what's to like." Edward hooked his cane over his wrist and leaned back against the vehicle, crossing his arms in front of him.

"Are you talking about the dogs or the woman?"

"Seems like they're a group package."

"They are."

Holden leaned against the side of the Jeep, matching Edward's stance. This was the brother he'd grown up with. The mentor and friend who'd taught him almost as much about being a man as their father had. He'd lost that friend on a tragic afternoon nearly two years ago—lost him to grief and the bottom of a bottle.

If there was any good thing that had come from their father's death, it might be that the loss of one good man had led to the rebirth of another. It might be a long time before Edward would ever risk his heart again—it might be never—but as far as Holden knew, since John Kincaid's funeral, Edward had stayed sober. Whether it was a testament to their father's memory, or Edward was truly beginning to heal, he didn't know. He was just glad to have some small bits of his brother back.

He only wished that the circumstances for their visit had been different, and that he could foresee more mornings like this one. But *this* was the only day he should be worrying about right now.

Holden pushed away from the Jeep and refocused his mind around the mission he had to accomplish—

keeping Liza alive. "If we leave now, we can be at the camping area by nightfall."

The plan he and Edward had discussed was to hide out for a day or two in the woods along the Black River in southeast Missouri where they used to go fishing with their father and Bill Caldwell. "Stick to the back roads," Edward advised. "You know them. Try to find a spot in or near Johnson Shut-Ins State Park." The park itself had been closed due to a break in the wall of the Taum Sauk Reservoir that flooded the Black River Valley. "They've got flood damage repairs made, but they won't officially reopen the park until spring or summer. So you won't have any tourists to contend with. And if it stays this chilly, you may not even have any locals. There's a sheriff down in that area I worked on a case with. I called and gave him the Jeep's license number—nobody will stop you or ask for ID or a park fee while you're down there."

Holden nodded. "Thanks, Ed. I'll let you know when we get there and call Grove in the morning to make sure Plan B is set before I bring her back in."

"Watch your back, little brother. And watch hers. She cares about other things more than she thinks about taking care of herself."

Was that what her promise and sympathetic touch had been about earlier? Some vow to take care of him, no matter what it cost her? An uneasy decision lurked along the edge of Holden's thoughts. Was Liza's eyewitness testimony worth the risk to her mental health or even her life? She'd sounded like she'd be willing to make that sacrifice.

But would he?

Would he be content with answers if something happened to Liza? Or would losing her cripple him the same way losing what Edward loved had crippled his brother?

Love. There was that word again. Right when he thought he'd cleared the emotions out of his head and could concentrate on the job he had to do.

"Yukon? Oh, damn. Yukon!"

These few days with Liza had moved at a supersonic pace. As the dog bounded off into the trees and Liza chased after him, Holden wondered if every day of her life moved this fast. He wondered if he could keep up. He wondered at just how badly he wanted to try.

"Here, boy!" she shouted. "Yukon! Hey, a little help?"

Holden stuck his tongue behind his teeth and let loose a shrill whistle. "Yukon! Come!"

The dog halted and turned. With a shake of his shoulders that reminded Holden of a shrug of resignation, the big malamute loped straight back to the Jeep and jumped into the backseat with the other two dogs.

"Show-off." Liza jogged up behind them, looking young and fresh and nothing like the tortured soul whose nightmares had left her in agony. She shot her fingers through her hair, fluffing the copper silk into irresistible disarray. "Thank goodness he answers to you. I thought I could trust him off his leash in the unfamiliar surroundings—that he'd be less likely to run off if he didn't know where his next meal would be coming from." Catching a deep breath, she pressed a hand to her chest and beamed a smile at Edward. "Thank you for all your help."

"Thanks for asking."

In two short hours, Liza had done for his brother what no one had been able to do for nearly two years—he smiled.

Just for a moment, and then it was gone.

If nothing more ever came of their relationship, Holden would always be grateful to her for that.

Edward? Maybe not so much. He was already heading back up to the porch and waving them away. "Now give a man some peace and get out of here."

MR. SMITH TILTED his face forward and looked into the mirror, inspecting the stitched-up gash in his shaved scalp.

With distinct injuries like the long bruise across his sternum, the slight scrapes from the air bag's deployment on his face—sure indicators of an automobile accident that would never be reported—an emergency room and full-fledged doctor had been out of the question. But this after-hours clinic offered a sufficient enough facility. And, more importantly, for the right amount of money, the staff who'd worked on him could be discreet.

"It's a good look on you." Long feminine fingers gleamed against starched black cotton as his employer helped him slip into the new shirt she'd brought him. She touched one French-tipped nail to the tiny tattoo—a Cyrillic *Z*—on his right shoulder blade, where he'd branded his allegiance to her. Her reflection smiled beside him. "It's another badge of honor for you."

"A badge of honor for failing his mission?" The boss paced in the background. Though Mr. Smith was savvy enough not to dismiss the boss's influence and experience, he could feel an air of desperation in the examination room. With the click of a remote, the television above Mr. Smith's unused bed was turned off. "This *job* is all over the news this morning. A car wreck on 291. A house in the suburbs shot up by rival gangs."

Mr. Smith pulled on a silver silk tie. "Is that the spin KCPD is putting on it?" Imagine that, the work of one man, trained in stealth, with an extensive arsenal at his disposal, being credited for the work of an entire gang.

The boss was less impressed. "What I see is a lot of damage, a lot of publicity—and no dead witness. Do I need to call in someone to assist you?"

Now *that* was insulting. "Mr. Smith" had been the code name for Z Group's top assassin for over thirty years. And he'd held the distinction longer than any of his predecessors. For one of his superiors to accuse him of losing his edge meant he was in danger of being stripped of his status. A *former* Mr. Smith had nowhere to go. Unless he moved up and became a boss.

Or he became dead.

Rich, number one and alive were all choices far better suited to his tastes.

He flicked a dimple into the perfect knot of his tie before turning to look the boss directly in the eye. "I will deal with Officer Kincaid myself. Without him, the redhead will be easy prey. Your secrets will be safe once more." And, his reputation as the best would be restored. "Did you get me the information I asked for?"

The boss nodded. "I've activated my contacts to see if we can narrow down the search. Until Kincaid calls in, we'll have to rely on deductive reasoning and track them."

A good hunt. He nearly licked his lips at the challenge. Securing a location for his assault on the safe house, including eliminating the one cop on patrol who'd seen his setup in the trees behind the neighbor's house, had been little more than a game to him. Kincaid's escape had upped the stakes and made the mission more suited to Mr. Smith's particular skills and talents.

Besides, the cop had jammed the firing pin of his favorite rifle with that crazy lucky shot from the house.

"Fine." The delay would give him a few hours to catch some shut-eye, put on a proper suit and clean his guns. "I'll need a new vehicle, as well."

"It's already in the parking lot out front. The keys are in your overnight bag." Side by side, the boss and his employer headed for the door, looking more like two business associates—or family, even—than the rivals they'd turned out to be.

Keep your friends close and your enemies closer.

Should he be concerned that the boss and his current employer could put aside their love-hate relationship and join together to turn him into the scapegoat for their dirty secrets and the dead bodies necessary to keep them?

Of course, he should. He'd put a contingency plan into place for that possibility as well.

The boss stopped at the door and turned. "Don't disappoint me."

Mr. Smith inclined his head with the slightest of nods and watched them leave. As he gathered his things and went outside to a new black SUV, he began to formulate his strategy. The redhead wasn't the issue anymore—though she was his paycheck and he would certainly get that job done. His seductive employer and powerful boss weren't even the issue. His personal mission now wasn't about Z Group or secret witnesses or covering their asses or any other damn thing.

This was personal. This was survival of the fittest.

Holden Kincaid's skills and resourcefulness had proved to be almost as good as his.

Almost.

There was only one Mr. Smith.

Kincaid was good. But he was better.

He had to be.

CHAPTER TEN

"PENNY FOR YOUR THOUGHTS." Liza strolled up beside Holden, who stood at the lip of the steep rocky bank of the Black River.

The moon was full, illuminating the path from their tent in the Ozarks, even through the canopy of tall, ancient pin oaks and evergreens. But it was cold in the moonlight, and away from the campfire, she huddled inside her sweater, wishing they'd had the time to pack winter coats. Of course, if they'd had that kind of time and opportunity, they wouldn't be roughing it like survivalists at a deserted off-season campground in the first place.

Holden was staring down into the water rushing past below their feet. Between the dark eddies and deeper currents, the water hit the big granite rocks, splashing up into the air and glittering like diamonds in the moonlight. It was a beautiful, rugged area, and she felt completely isolated from any vestige of civilization or danger.

So why was he still so quiet? "Hello? I staked the dogs out on their leashes and cleaned up all our trash. What are you doing?"

He breathed in deeply, stretching his shoulders against his sweater, and pulling his hands from the pockets of his jeans. "I'm thinking that it's too late to catch anything tonight."

Relieved by his answer, Liza laughed. "Come on, I already made a couple of mean turkey-and-Swiss sandwiches and even roasted marshmallows for those s'mores you ate. You are *not* thinking about fish."

"Canoeing, maybe? The river's deep enough here if you keep to the channel. Of course, when you get to the Shut-Ins," a unique formation of giant rocks that split the river into dozens of mini-waterfalls, "you'd have to carry the canoe quite a ways—"

"Wait a minute. You mean *you* in the generic sense, right? I am so not carrying your canoe for you."

That earned the beginnings of a familiar smile. "Well, we could put wheels on the bottom and hitch up Yukon. Make him do the work."

Liza shivered and hugged her arms around her middle. But she wasn't ready to walk away from this companionable exchange just to get warm. "Are there walking or biking trails around here? I bet this is beautiful earlier in the autumn, when the trees are just starting to turn. Or in the summer. All the shade would keep things fairly cool."

"It's a great place any time of year." She felt his gaze on her and Liza tilted her chin to meet his wistful expression. "My dad took us all over the state to camp and fish and hunt—"

"You shot Bambi's mother?"

He laughed. "I wondered when Dr. Animal Lover would figure that one out."

"Oh, from Day One, mister. I figured you were one of those outdoorsy tough guys. Intellectually, I understand about controlling animal populations and conservation, but I can't say it will ever be a hobby of mine." She crinkled up her face and made a confession. "I have to admit, though, that I love a good breaded catfish. My mom had a great recipe. Or some grilled walleye."

"You mean you're not a vegetarian?" He seemed properly aghast.

"Hello. I ate two of those turkey sandwiches, too." She swatted his shoulder playfully, then wound her arm through his and snuggled to his side. "Tell me about your dad and coming here."

His telling sigh quieted their laughter and brought them closer together. "Every weekend of every summer—unless one of us had a ball game or Scout camp—Dad would pack us up and take us somewhere. Mom came sometimes, but it wasn't her thing. Well, actually, I think she kind of enjoyed being outdoors, but she knew it was a guy thing for us."

"And you have three brothers, right?"

He nodded. "Sometimes, my dad's best friend from his fraternity and military days, Bill Caldwell, came with us. Man, did they have jokes and stories to tell that—" he cleared his throat "—I won't repeat."

"That good, huh?"

They stood together in the serenity of the moment for some time before Holden spoke again. "It was never about catching a fish or seeing who could build a fire without matches. It was about spending time with my dad. And my big brothers. It was about becoming a man."

"John must have been a wonderful father."

"The best. He taught us about integrity and character and loyalty. Taught us about love." She felt Holden grinning above her. "He taught me to sing, the best way to get back at Sawyer when he pulled a prank on me. He taught me to respect the land and appreciate the beauty of nature."

Holden leaned back from the link of their arms and reached down to tip her chin up. There was a drowsy longing in his expression that stirred an answering warmth inside her.

He studied her face long enough that she gave a nervous laugh. "What?"

"Thanks for listening. I miss him."

The laughter transformed into a liquid energy that filtered into her blood. "I know. I miss my folks, too. It's good to remember what was wonderful about them."

"Yeah."

"Yeah."

He drew his finger along the curve of her jaw. "Your skin's beautiful in the moonlight."

"Are you crazy? I'm a pale woman with freckles from head to toe."

"Seriously?" Within a heartbeat the mood between them changed from trading comforts to something much more intense. "You have freckles...everywhere?"

The look in his eyes changed from gentle longing to downright predatory. And daring.

Liza began a slow, knowing laugh and tried to back away. "Oh, no. No, no."

But Holden had a hold of her wrist. As she tugged away, he tugged back, pushing up the end of her sleeve. He touched his fingertip to the back of her hand. "One."

"You are not—"

"Two."

Liza tried to twist away, but he used the motion to spin her around and pull her back against his chest. With his arm pinning her waist, he brushed the hair from her temple and touched her cheek. "Three." He touched her again. "Four." And again. "Five."

She was laughing out loud by the time he dipped his mouth to the side of her neck. "Thirteen. Fourteen."

"Stop!" She wriggled against him, rubbing her bottom over the zipper of his jeans.

He moaned against her collarbone. "Fifteen."

"Kincaid!"

He palmed her belly, sliding his hand up beneath her sweater and undershirt to brand her cool skin. "I can only count the ones I can see. I wonder if I can feel them? Hmm." He tongued the sensitive skin at the juncture of her neck and shoulder. "Or taste them."

An instant heat followed the friction of his hand and mouth, filling Liza with desire as much as laughter. "You can't—" She made a token push against his arm, but his hand slipped higher. "You can't—"

His palm settled with a possessive heat over her bare breast and Liza cried out at the instant spear of fire that went straight to her core. "I feel *that,*" he whispered in a seductive caress against her ear. He caught the aching nipple between his thumb and forefinger and squeezed and tormented the pearling nub until she wasn't laughing at all, but whimpering with need. "Liza..."

His voice was low and urgent, and it fueled something urgent inside her, too. At some point in this seduction, Liza's hands had started moving, too. She reached behind her, digging her fingers into his corded thighs and anchoring her bottom against his growing need. The rush and splash of the river filled her ears and seemed to set the pace and the fury of the blood pumping through her veins. Something blindingly hot and ultra-feminine gathered in her tingling breasts and pooled between her thighs.

"We can't…here…it's…freezing…" It was a breathless protest, a beseeching request.

He pulled his hand from her breast and turned her, forcing her to retreat as he moved forward. He bent his head and kissed her. Took another step and obliged when she tilted her mouth to kiss him again. "Run."

"What?" She was mindless with fire and want, and didn't understand.

He kissed her one last time and slipped his hand into hers. "Race you."

"Oh, no, you don't." He pulled and she followed. Their steps were awkward at first, but then she found her balance and darted ahead. His long legs stretched and easily ate up the ground to surge in front of her. She pumped her legs faster and together they reached the tent, breathless and laughing, startling the dogs and on fire for each other.

Inside the tent Liza pulled off her sweater and shirt and toed off her running shoes as Holden zipped the tent flap shut. He unhooked his belt and gun and kicked off his boots while she skimmed his sweater over his head and arms, pausing only long enough to treat herself to a taste of taut male nipple nestled in a thatch of golden brown hair.

The race continued with a crazy, fumbling effort to zip the two sleeping bags together, lose their jeans and then climb inside the giant insulated bag before the brisk autumn temperature had a chance to chill their fire.

Holden squeezed her bottom and dragged her on top of him, finding her mouth and kissing her sweetly, deeply, thoroughly, kissing her until she thought she might burst from the conflagration of heat building inside her.

"What are you doing?" Liza asked when Holden reached outside the bag to retrieve a flashlight. Surely he wasn't having second thoughts. Had he heard something? "Kincaid?"

He turned on the light, grinning like a boy who'd just discovered a whole new jar of candy. "I lost count."

He rolled her off to the side and then dove inside the sleeping bag. "Kincaid?"

She felt the nip of his teeth on her bottom. "One."

By the time Holden got to ninety-three beneath the curve of her left breast, Liza was a feverish quiver of heat and desire. Breathing hard, feeling heavy, needing him, she begged him to finish the game. "Holden. Please."

He tossed the flashlight out of the sleeping bag and crawled squarely on top of her, propping himself up on his elbows and gently stroking the damp hair off her cheek. "Say it again."

"Please."

"Say my name. Not Kincaid. Say it."

She dragged her fingers down his slick back and squeezed the curve of his muscled backside. She grinned. "Holden."

He entered her once and retreated, teasing her. Entered her again and filled her up, letting her adjust to his size and shape. She'd concede the race if he'd only grant her what she needed.

"Now, Holden."

"Yes, Liza."

He captured her mouth and moved inside her and carried them both, winners, over the finish line together.

HOLDEN LAY AWAKE in the dark for some time after, his body blanketed by a beautiful naked woman, his soul replete with the kind of solace that could only come from a connection to another person that was as true and right as the link he felt to Liza Parrish.

He grieved for Dominic Molloy and his father. Railed against the injustice of having his father and best friend taken from his life by some bastard who thought they deserved to live and thrive while two good men were dead. He felt protective and possessive of, and totally humbled by the gifts this woman had given him.

Laughter. Hope. Healing.

Undeniable passion.

Unmistakable love.

They were fated to be together, meant to love—like that silly story about *Romeo and Juliet* she'd mentioned.

As he drew gentle circles across the smooth skin of her back, and the soft caress of her sleeping breath whispered across his chest, Holden vowed that their ending would be very different from the bard's version of that love story. They were going to survive this. They were going to marry and have kids—they'd have more dogs, at least. And they were going to live happily ever after.

Surely a fate that would deny him his father and best friend would not deny him this woman.

He raised his head to press a kiss to the crown of her soft copper hair. "I love you, Liza Parrish," he whispered. "I love you."

He was about to drift off to sleep himself when he felt the first jerk of her body. "Liza?"

"Shh, baby. Shush." Her words slurred against his skin.

Damn. The nightmare was taking her. He slid his fingers to the back of her neck and tried to coax her awake. "Come back to me, babe. Come back."

"Black Buick." She shifted in his arms but refused to wake. "See you." Her whole body was quaking now, reliving the murder and terror. "Tattooed. Pinstripe. Black man. No hair."

He gave her a gentle shake as her sleepy words began to ramble. "Liza. Come on, baby, wake up."

"No." She jerked. "I see… I see you."

"Liza?"

"Pinstripe. Woman. Don't get in."

"Liza." He said her name more firmly, shook her harder. But would she feel it as some kind of attack in her dreams?

"Who…? Thank you, Mr. Smith. No-o-o!"

Enough.

Holden palmed her head to his shoulder and held her tight as she screamed herself awake.

"Easy, baby. Easy." He peppered kisses over her face and hair, absorbing the lingering aftershocks of fear that vibrated through her body.

As her pulse evened out and her breathing relaxed, Holden tried to comfort her. "Liza—"

But she pushed away and sat up straight, pulling the sleeping bag and him up with her. "It was a woman!"

He reached for his sweater and pulled it over her head to keep her warm.

"What was a woman?" he asked, wanting to pull her back into the sleeping bag to keep warm.

Perhaps sensing his intentions, she pushed the voluminous sleeves up and shoved her bangs off her forehead, avoiding his grasp. "I remembered. Maybe not all of it yet. But I remember more of that night. Maybe enough to help."

"Hold on." He raised a calming hand. "You're telling me that all the sudden, you've gotten your memory back?"

She nodded, and crawled up to sit on her knees, pulling his sweater down to cover herself in the sexiest damn version of a mini-dress he'd ever seen. "It was a woman I saw wearing the pinstriped suit. A dark-haired woman who got into the backseat of the black SUV that night. She was the only person who came out of the warehouse after I heard the gunshots. She must have killed your father."

Holden was stunned. Liza could identify his father's killer? He had to believe her. Her skin was flushed with excitement, her eyes clear. "Why do you think you're remembering this now?"

"I don't know. Maybe, after six months feeling lost inside my own head, always looking over my shoulder and wondering if that person was the killer, or that one—and never even knowing who was a threat to me and who wasn't—maybe after all that..." She reached over to frame his face between gentle hands and smiled. "I think last night, for the first time in months, I finally felt completely safe. I knew I wasn't alone with my fear anymore."

He caught one hand beneath his and turned his head to kiss her palm. "You're not alone."

She pulled away, then lifted the top of the sleeping bag and climbed into his lap. Holden was more than happy to wrap his arms around her when she snuggled against his chest. "I can also tell you a little more about the men who were with her. There was that tattooed albino—all muscle—who was driving."

"Tony Fierro." Holden nodded. Atticus had uncovered Tony's identity earlier in the year. "He was murdered in his jail cell, after my brother Atticus investigated him. Fierro tried to recover some incriminating information my father had on the people Fierro worked for."

"So he is part of your father's murder investigation."

"Yeah."

He massaged the back of Liza's neck and urged her to go on. "What else do you remember?"

"The black man. Tall. Shaved head. Nice suit. Deep voice. The woman called him 'Mr. Smith.'"

"An alias, I'm assuming?"

"Yeah. It was like a nickname." Liza paused to take a steadying breath. "She said, 'The job is finished, Mr. Smith. I know what you mean about the satisfaction of seeing your victim's eyes before you pull the trigger.'"

"Oh, God." Holden's arms convulsed around Liza at the horrific image of what his father must have suffered.

Liza wound her arms around his neck and hugged him tight. "I'm sorry. I didn't mean to hurt you. I should have said that differently."

"No." Her caring eased some of the pain. His training as a cop helped him push the rest of it aside. For now. "I need to hear everything. Exactly as you remember it. No detail is too small. So a woman killed my father. She's friends with a hit man named Mr. Smith. And they took pleasure out of what they did to my father."

"There's something more I saw this time, Holden."

"Something more?"

She pulled away, but only far enough that he could

see the sorrow in her expression. "There was someone else in the car."

"A fourth person?" She'd never even hinted at that detail before.

"I couldn't get a good look at the face. But the dark-haired woman pulled something from her purse. It was a ring, I think."

Not his father's wedding ring—he'd had that on when they buried him. "Are you sure it was a ring?"

She held up her palm as if picturing exactly what she'd seen. "It was small and round and gold. She handed it to the person inside and said, 'John doesn't deserve to wear this anymore. His tattoo might say different, but he was really never one of us.'"

The slain members of Z Group had all had one thing in common—the tiny tattoo of a Cyrillic Z somewhere on their body.

"Is that important?" she asked softly.

"It could be. If we can find out who has that ring."

CHAPTER ELEVEN

HOLDEN STOPPED PLAYING with the curve of Liza's thigh where Kevin Grove had scratched his phone number onto her jeans. His senses buzzed on high alert. "What do you mean there was no body?" he asked into his cell phone. "I saw that car roll three times. If the crash didn't kill him, then he's in a hospital somewhere."

His disbelief reflected on Liza's face. "They can't find Mr. Smith?"

As the pieces of her mind began to fall back into place, there was no doubting that a professional hit man working for Z Group was after them.

Holden switched his cell phone to the other ear, forcing himself to turn away from the fearful uncertainty that made the skin beneath her freckles go pale. He wanted to pull her tight in his arms, wind the clock back seven months and pretend he had nothing to do but spend a lifetime of days like this one, sharing picnic lunches, getting better acquainted with her trim, taut body and the sassy mouth and sharp mind that went along with it.

But reality didn't work that way. He'd hoped that the people who'd murdered his father were taking some time to regroup and plan another strategy for silencing KCPD's star witness. But if the mysterious Mr. Smith was still alive, then they were out of time. If he had any connections at all, which Holden suspected he did, then he could already be tracking them. Danger and the death Mr. Smith promised could already be close by.

Holden gestured to Liza to start packing their lunch back into the cooler. She nodded and quickly went to work as he turned his attention back to the phone call. "Explain what happened."

While Grove gave him a report, Holden scanned a full 360 degrees for any sign of traffic on the park's gravel roads—or for any extra shadows moving among the trees. The detective sounded just as antsy about this whole turn of events as he was. "The air bags deployed. He was wearing his seat belt. Apparently, he walked away from the crash. I'll put Liza's description of Mr. Smith out over the wire, but…we lost him."

"Who the hell is this guy?"

"He's getting help from somewhere."

Holden's gaze was automatically drawn to the flash of Liza's copper-red hair. She was strong and sexy and savvy, compassionate to a fault and achingly vulnerable in a way that tugged at his heart and kindled an instinct to protect her that went far deeper than the badge tucked into the pocket of his jeans. Right now, *he* was the only help she had.

"Let's pack the rest of the gear," he instructed Liza.

Her gray eyes, brave but full of fear, connected with his. "He's coming, isn't he?"

He answered the rhetorical question by checking the Glock at his belt, then pulling up the right leg of his jeans to make sure the Smith & Wesson he wore in an ankle holster was loaded and ready to use. He picked up the cooler the instant she was finished and carried it to the back of the Jeep. "There's no need to panic, but we need to get moving. Grove and his men have lost track of Smith. I don't intend to make a stationary target for him."

"I'll get the dogs." Despite the sexy sway of her bottom as she jogged back to the tent, Liza was as game as any man he'd ever worked with. She might be scared—she should be—but she was keeping a level head and not allowing the emotion to cloud her thinking or question his orders.

Her cool head was a hell of a lot more conducive to survival than the irrational anger pumping through Holden's veins right now. Try as he might, the icy detachment he needed to ensure her safety just wouldn't come. This wasn't about protecting a witness any longer. Z Group had already denied him a father and a friend. He wasn't about to let them take this woman from his life. Not when he'd already opened up his heart and wedged her firmly inside.

"The press is all over this," Grove went on as Holden's gaze followed Liza's every step. "I keep directing them to the public liaison officer, but Hayley Resnick has already called me twice for a statement—about the gunfight at Liza's house and about your father's murder. She's not buying the cover that it was a gang-related shoot-out, and wants to know if I'm still working your father's case."

"Maybe she likes you." It was sarcasm meant to further the conversation.

"She's not my type."

"A gorgeous blonde isn't your type?" Holden returned to the tent, unzipped his gear bag and pulled out an extra ammo clip to tuck into his belt.

"You did get a look at my face, didn't you? Or were

you too busy watching Liza's backside to notice me? I think it's more that I'm not *her* type."

"You're pretty in my book, Grove."

"Bite me." Holden could hear a murmur of voices and other phones ringing in the background, and assumed Grove had set up a command center of sorts. "Look, I ran this by Major Taylor. I know you're hiding out someplace down south—"

"We're already on the move."

"Good. We want you to hit the road back to K.C. I'm working on arrangements to get you directly into a safe house. Are the dogs—?" Bruiser barked as Liza dumped his dog food back into the sack and carried it to the rear of the Jeep. "Ah, yes. Sounds like the kids are still with you. I'll make sure we can support them at the same location as well. I owe that little terrier my life. If he wants Fifi and caviar at the safe house, he'll get it."

Holden laughed. "I'm afraid you'll have to rescue your own pooch from the pound, Grove. I don't see Liza parting with any of these guys." Bruiser ran in circles around Liza's legs and continued to bark, getting Cruiser hopping and excited as she joined the parade. But hiding out from a hit man who refused to die made laughter impossible to hold on to. "Liza remembered more details last night."

"Yeah? Let me get my notepad. Go." By the time Holden had relayed Liza's account of the fourth person in the black Buick SUV the night of his father's murder, the mysterious gold ring in the dark-haired woman's hand and her comments about "John not deserving to wear it," the dogs had become truly agitated. "Is everything all right, Kincaid?"

Liza was kneeling down now, trying to calm them,

talking to the musketeers as though she expected them to understand every word she said. "What are you so fired up about? Did you see a squirrel? Come on, you two. I know this isn't our regular routine, but think of all the new smells and how much you like to ride in the car and..." Liza froze.

Like a call from his commanding officer, everything inside Holden went on alert. "What the hell?"

"Kincaid!" She grabbed the two dogs by their collars and dove for the ground as the passenger-side window of the Jeep shattered above her head.

Holden pulled his gun and ran. "We need backup! Now!"

"GET IN THE CAR! Get in the damn car!"

A second red dot of light danced through the brown grass on the ground beside her head and Liza rolled as the next shot tore up the dry leaves and dirt. "Where is that coming from?"

Why was this happening? Again. Please, God, not again!

Holden had pulled his gun and was firing blindly off into the trees to the north. Crouching low, he zigzagged back and forth, snatching Yukon by the collar and running up to her. "Move it, Parrish! Move!"

Keeping their unseen assailant pinned among the trees, he heaved the frantic-eyed malamute into the back of the Jeep.

"How did he find us?"

Holden slammed the back end shut and fired again. "Haul ass, Parrish. Talk later."

As he dashed around to start the engine, Liza obeyed, loading the other two dogs in. She was climbing up beside them when a slash of fire burned across her right arm. "Son of a—"

She grabbed her upper arm. For a split second she paused and stared in disbelief at the red stripe that grew thicker and wetter across the upper sleeve of her sweater.

"Liza!"

Holden's shout cut through her shock. As she shoved the dogs out of her way, he grabbed her uninjured arm and pulled her on in. Her feet were barely off the ground when he stomped on the gas. The Jeep rocked and spun and threw a wave of dirt and debris up behind it as the wheels dug deep into the earth for traction. Once the tires hit solid dirt, they shot off onto the gravel road. The momentum threw Liza into Holden's lap and slammed the door behind her. The dogs yelped as they were tossed from side to side across the backseat and floor.

"Stay down!"

Holden fired out her broken window, but the instant he stopped, a half dozen bullets pinged against the side of the Jeep. One thunked.

"How bad are you hurt?" The butt of his gun poked against her as he pressed his fingers into her back, checking her from side to side for injuries while her face bobbed atop his hard thigh. "Liza! How bad are you hurt?"

Bracing one hand against his denim-clad knee, she tried to right herself, tried to reassure him they were still in this chase together. "I'm okay. The bullet grazed me. It's a long gash, nothing more. I'll be fine."

Holden pushed her cheek back down to his thigh. "You're hit. That is *not* fine."

Another spray of bullets peppered the road behind them and took out the back window. She lurched inside her skin and Holden cursed. It was blue and pithy and only half of the fear and anger Liza was feeling right now. "How did he find us?"

"Pull the ammo clip from my belt," Holden ordered before answering. "I'm guessing the fourth person in that car you saw has something to do with it." Keeping her head down, Liza reached across Holden's lap and buckled him in before pulling the magazine of bullets from his waist. He did something to his gun and the spent magazine popped out onto the floorboards. He reloaded. "Can you buckle yourself in without raising up?"

Liza eased her death grip on Holden's leg and scooted backward to reach for the seat belt. Gritting her teeth against the ache that throbbed through her arm, she twisted around and secured the belt across her lap. "I'm good."

"You're doing great, babe. Just hang on to something." Holden eased a little more speed out of the racing Jeep as the sound of a powerful engine roared through the shattered windows. "Somebody has inside information. Those bastards knew where to find my dad on his Sunday morning run. Knew how to find the other Z Group members. They knew about Dad's journals."

"You mean somebody *we* trusted told him where we were hiding? Only Detective Grove and your brother Edward knew where we were, right?"

"Somebody eavesdropped or somebody told."

The growl of an engine and spit of gravel behind them grew louder. Liza grabbed the back of the seat, inching herself up to peer over the top. Black. Buick. SUV.

The driver's shaved head and dark skin were as familiar to her at sixty feet as they'd been a mere six feet away. The coldly intense expression chilled her just as deeply. "Mr. Smith. It's him—I remember him. Bald and big and—"

Holden pounded the steering wheel with his fist. "Hell!"

Liza ducked back down at Holden's curse. "What? That sounds bad. What's wrong?"

"He hit the gas tank. We're losing fuel fast. We won't make it to the highway." With a jerk of the wheel, Holden violently switched directions. The Jeep careened onto two wheels, throwing Liza into the door. They came down hard on the two airborne wheels and a terrier landed in her lap. "Here. Hold this."

Liza automatically wrapped her fingers around the gun Holden pushed into her hands. "I don't know how to—"

"Just don't shoot anything. Especially me."

His knuckles turned white as he fisted both hands around the wheel. Liza held on to both dog and gun as they left the road. Her stomach lurched as they vaulted down into the ditch and climbed up the rocks on the opposite side. "What are you doing?"

"Playing a hunch. Hoping like hell I'm right."

"About what?"

"Your Mr. Smith likes his nice suits and fancy cars? I'm guessing he's not a country boy."

"GO, GUYS! RUN! Run!"

Liza shoved the dogs away and they scattered into the trees and rocks, instinctively running away from the explosive pops of Holden's gun each time he turned to fire on the black man who pursued them.

"You're sure they'll be safe?"

"I can't guarantee anything right now, babe." He took her hand and helped her stand, leaning in to press a quick, strengthening kiss to her lips. "But we'll all make smaller, harder-to-hit targets if we split up."

She summoned a shaky smile. "I'm putting all my trust in you, Kincaid."

"Then I'll make sure I don't blow it. You ready to move out?"

Liza nodded.

They'd lost Mr. Smith and his SUV a few miles back. But the Jeep had run out of fuel and they'd been forced to move out on foot through the trees and giant rock formations that dotted the hills leading down toward the Black River. They'd paused long enough for Holden to tie his bandanna around her wound to staunch the seeping blood, and for Liza to check the dogs for injuries. Beyond a few nicks in Cruiser's hide, they were rattled by the stress of the unfamiliar situation, but basically unharmed.

She held tight to Holden's hand whenever she could and scrambled down the rocks leading toward the shut-ins and river below them. Sometimes she climbed, sometimes she slipped because the continuous splash of the water made the granite rocks mossy and slick. But always Holden was there to help her. To protect her. To keep her moving and alive.

Liza was a woman who was in excellent physical shape, but even she was panting from the endless descent and flat-out runs from tree to tree to rock to whatever hiding place Mother Nature offered them next.

Holden led her unerringly through twists and turns, over hard-packed dirt and through icy water.

After another five minutes, Liza realized the occasional scattershot of bullets had ceased. "Holden. Holden! Wait!" She tugged on his hand to get him to slow down and stop. The cold-eyed cop was back again, searching in every direction. They were both breathing hard, wet and nearing exhaustion. She snatched up a handful of his sweater and demanded he look at her. "I don't hear him behind us anymore. Can't we rest for a minute?"

He shook his head, barely sparing her a glance. "He's not that far behind us. Going off-road bought us some time, but not much. I feel him out there somewhere. Probably watching us right now." He touched her cheek, maybe saw something in her pale features or felt something in the chill of her skin. "I'm sorry, babe. Of course, we'll rest for a few minutes." He quickly glanced around them, looking for the best hiding place, no doubt. "Here. We'll..." He froze. "Son of a bitch."

"What? Kincaid, what?"

She followed his line of sight across to the far side of the river.

Despite the mud-stained suit and the gun cradled between his hands, Mr. Smith was smiling.

"Nice try, cowboy. Now who's the best?"

He fired.

THE BULLET RIPPED through Holden's shoulder before he could even raise his gun. He heard Liza scream as he wrapped his arms around her and tumbled down into the river. He felt every rock, every branch, every painful cry from Liza before they hit the icy water and plunged down into the swift-moving current.

He kicked them back to the surface, let Liza grab a deep breath, and then pushed her under the water again. The current buffeted them from rock to rock, threatening to crack a skull or break a bone. The water chilled, stole his strength as it carried them downstream toward the giant rocks and waterfalls of the shut-ins.

Plan B sucked. His Glock was long gone and the combination of blood loss and icy temperatures were rapidly depleting his strength. He needed a Plan C. And fast. Or he was going to die. And then Liza would be all alone against a living, breathing, deadly nightmare.

He didn't want her to be alone anymore.

As they bobbed to the surface again, he was vaguely aware of laughter, then cursing. Mr. Smith must have realized that his prey was only wounded, not dead.

Not yet.

The black man scrambled along the bank above them, firing into the water.

"Hold—" Liza's words bubbled as the river rushed into her mouth. She surfaced again beside him. "Spare gun! Your leg!"

Right. Damn. Idiot.

Thank God he'd fallen for a woman who could keep her head when the world was crumbling to bits all around her.

"I love you!"

He said the words and dove beneath the water to unstrap the Smith & Wesson at his ankle. Its power was limited, but his aim would compensate if he could keep a clear head and steady hand.

He hit the next boulder with his foot, slammed into

it with a bruising stop. The current pounded against his body, pinning him against the granite outcropping.

Guessing Holden's intent, Mr. Smith stopped on the bank above him, raised his weapon and trained the red laser dot center mass of Holden's chest.

Liza sailed on past as Holden raised the gun out of the water and lined the bastard up in his sights. Pain exploded in his side as he pulled the trigger.

LIZA TIED YUKON'S lead around Holden's wrist and commanded the dog to pull. "Come on, Yukon. Go! Pull, big guy. Pull!"

Yukon sat on the bank while she shivered. Liza was exhausted, too weak to pull Holden's unconscious body out of the water. He'd lost so much blood. In addition to being shot twice, he'd hit his head on one of the rocks when the kick of the gun had cost him his balance in the rushing water.

But Mr. Smith was dead, lodged in the rocks on the bank somewhere upstream.

She was free. She was safe.

But Liza was so tired. And Holden was so hurt.

"Damn it, dog. I saved your life. Don't you think you owe me one? Please."

Then Holden whistled. A shrill, loud, wonderful sound that hurt her ears and warmed her heart. "Move it!"

Obeying the voice she wanted to kiss with relief, the big malamute clawed at the mud and slipped back toward the river, but then his back paw hit solid rock and she felt a tug on the leash. "Come on, boy. Come on."

"Yukon, pull!" Holden's voice was stronger now.

Yukon leaned into his collar and pulled. And pulled.

Holden's arm came around Liza's waist as she found her footing and used what little strength she had left to help him.

When they were securely on dry land, Liza freed Holden's wrist. "Good boy. Good boy."

She wanted to hug the dog, but she was too exhausted to spare time for anything more than to press her hand to the wound in Holden's side. The movement of the water must have deflected Smith's shot to a less vulnerable region of the body, but she knew that a bullet could ricochet inside the body and do more damage than the entry wound itself.

"You're not going to die on me, are you, Kincaid? Kincaid?" Liza grunted with the strain of turning him, while Holden bit down on a moan. She probed and bent her ear to his chest and back to check his breathing, then checked his pulse. Finally, she pulled her shirt off from beneath her soggy sweater and created a makeshift bandage. When her shaking fingers and lack of medical supplies could do no more, she collapsed beside him on the riverbank. "Your shoulder wound just caught the flesh, nothing vital. It looks like the bullet is still inside. But your breathing is steady and I don't hear fluid inside the chest cavity, so I don't think it nicked a lung. The cold water might actually be a blessing. The temperature must have slowed your heart rate, so the bleeding isn't too severe. I'm used to treating dogs, not men, but I think if you don't move too much before I get you to an E.R., that—"

"I'll live." He pulled her into his arms and kissed her hard, then fell back to the ground to rest beside her. He snapped his fingers and Yukon ambled over to sit beside them.

"Lie down, you mutt." The dog lay down beside him, sharing the warmth of his body and finally offering his allegiance to the pack. "I'm sure my cell phone is shot. But there's a radio in the Jeep. If we can hike back to it, we should be able to call the local sheriff."

Hike? Liza's weary sigh came all the way from her freezing toes. "In a minute, okay?"

"Okay."

Bruiser and Cruiser joined them. Soon enough, they'd be rested and warm enough to think about doctoring wounds and making phone calls and living their lives.

Liza marveled at the way Holden had tamed Yukon, and the strong bond the two shared. She cuddled closer, understanding why the dog would want to bond with this man. "You just called my dog a mutt, Kincaid. And after he saved your life."

"*My* dog, Parrish. Yukon is *my* dog."

Yes, he was. And as they lay on the bank, warming in the sun, Liza rested her cheek against Holden's heart and hugged him as tight as her weary arms and his injuries would let her. "I'm yours, too."

CHAPTER TWELVE

HOLDEN KINCAID WASN'T the first gunshot victim the Truman Medical Center had ever treated, but he might well be the most popular. Even in the middle of the night, long after official visiting hours had ended, he sat up against a stack of pillows, winked at the nurse who'd come to change his IV drip and promised he intended to get some rest.

He'd survived a freezing river, a bullet in his gut, nearly losing Liza to a hit man, being life-flighted to Kansas City and surgery to remove said bullet and stitch him up inside and out. He was beat up, he was beat. But he could survive a few more minutes with his friends and family creating a hushed, friendly chaos around him.

And he could damn well survive until somebody let him see with his own eyes that Liza had survived her injuries as well, and was merely being kept overnight in the same hospital for observation. His mother sat on a chair beside his bed, and he squeezed her hand a little more tightly, just thinking about how much he missed Liza and how much he worried about how safe she really was when out of his sight.

Susan Kincaid squeezed right back. "Are you in pain, sweetie?"

"I'm okay." The tenderness of the surgery and bandages that held him together didn't ache too much unless he tried to move that side of his body. But even the sharp twinge that stabbed through his gut when he adjusted his position on the bed was nothing compared to the uncertainties about Liza roiling inside him.

"I'm yours," she'd said. But he'd been in and out of consciousness beside that river. Was she his for that moment? For as long as she was in danger and needed him? Was it forever? Or had he just dreamed what he wanted to hear?

It gave him a pretty clear understanding of the doubts and second-guessing Liza must have suffered through when her memory had been on the fritz. He didn't like not having the answers he needed. Didn't like it one damn bit.

Sensing his discomfort if not entirely understanding the cause of it, his mother pushed her chair back and stood, silencing the chatter in the room with a stern maternal look that could have commanded an entire police force. "Gentlemen? Visiting hours just ended. You can come back and see Holden in the morning. He needs to get some sleep."

"Yes, ma'am." With a flurry of similar responses, Holden's precinct commander, Mitch Taylor, and his S.W.A.T. team leader, Lieutenant Cutler—along with his buddies Rafe Delgado and Trip—left the room with handshakes, commiserations about Dominic Molloy, good wishes and gibes about getting out of work for a few weeks.

Bill Caldwell rose from his chair in the far corner and came to wrap an arm around Susan's shoulders. "Does that mean me, too?"

She reached up and patted his hand where it rested

alongside her neck. "You might as well, Bill. I'm going to stay the night and keep an eye on my baby boy."

"Mom…" Holden's token protest at being labeled the "baby" of the family when he towered over everyone but Sawyer quickly faded beneath the love and concern shining from her eyes. "Thanks for looking out for me."

"It's a mother's prerogative." Her wink made him smile.

Bill leaned in and kissed Susan's cheek. "Then I'll be going." He reached out to shake Holden's hand. "You feel better soon, son. I don't like seeing your mother get scared like she was today."

"Bill—"

"She might not show it. But you four boys are everything in the world to her." He kissed her again. "I'll see you in the morning for breakfast?"

A breakfast date? Susan nodded. "Good night."

But before Bill could open the door, all three of Holden's older brothers filed back into the room.

"Hang on a minute, Bill," Atticus said. "We need to talk."

The older gentleman laughed. "That sounds ominous."

There *was* something slightly ominous about the late night visit that made Holden grit his teeth against the pain in his gut and sit up straighter. Sawyer, Atticus and Edward—even with his cane to lean on—standing side by side at the foot of the bed created a daunting wall of don't-mess-with-me attitude. They were on to something. And the one thing that had united all four brothers—four different kinds of men, four different kinds of cops—and put them on a single mission was solving their father's murder.

"What's up, guys?" Holden prodded.

Sawyer circled the bed and wrapped Susan up in a bear hug and a kiss. "If you don't mind, Mom, we need to have a private conversation."

Once her feet were back flat on the floor, her narrowed gaze took in all four of her sons. "Man talk or police business?"

The grim looks meant police business.

"I see." She turned and smiled at Holden. "How about I go check on Liza Parrish. The doctor said her medical treatment in the field stabilized you enough to make it into surgery. I think I owe her a personal thank-you." She squeezed a hand or kissed a cheek of each man as she made her way to the door Atticus held open for her. "Behave yourselves. Holden needs his rest."

"Thanks, Mom."

Atticus didn't waste any time getting down to business as soon as the door closed. He pulled his reading glasses and cell phone from his suit jacket to read the information he'd stored there. "I got a message from Holly Masterson at the crime lab. She's doing an autopsy on your Mr. Smith to try to get an ID on him, and see if they can match him to anything at Dad's crime scene."

Sawyer had apparently been talking to Dr. Masterson as well. "Some of her lab files, including Dad's case, have been corrupted by a computer hacker—we suspect by one of the cons who escaped prison with Mel's ex-husband six months ago. At any rate, she's having her people retest the evidence they have on hand to rebuild the facts of the investigation."

Pulling off his glasses, Atticus continued. Apparently, while Holden had gone on the run with Liza, his brothers had been busy. "Dr. Masterson also told me that preliminary reports indicate the bullet they took out of you, little brother, is a disintegrator, matching the ones they took out of Dad, James McBride, and the Jane Doe at the dump I investigated earlier this year."

Edward had been silently hanging back until now. "Tell them about your hunch, A."

"I've asked Dr. Masterson to run a DNA comparison against my Brooke to see if the Jane Doe could be her mother, Irina Zorinsky Hansford." Holden remembered that Atticus and his fiancée, Brooke Hansford, had traveled to Sarajevo to move her parents' bodies back to the States from where they had been buried after a car wreck when she was still a baby. But the body in the mother's grave had turned out to be someone else. Had Brooke's mother, once a government agent who'd worked with John Kincaid, staged her own death? Or had someone moved the body to cover up a different crime?

Did the Jane Doe in the city dump or the dark-haired woman Liza had seen at the warehouse the night of John Kincaid's death have anything to do with missing mothers or the twisted cover-up that had prompted their father's murder?

But Bill Caldwell had picked up on a different oddity in the conversation.

"Disintegrating bullets?" he questioned skeptically. "Bullets composed of an alloy that breaks down in the body's tissues so that it can't be traced? That sounds like something we were developing in the test section of Caldwell Technologies. But there were only prototypes. They had no commercial value, so we halted production."

"No legitimate commercial value," Atticus pointed

out. “But an untraceable bullet would be a big seller on the black market.”

“Had any security leaks lately?” Holden’s sarcasm asked a very real question.

“No. None that I know of. And I know my company. I’ll still have my security team look into it ASAP, though.” Bill nervously twisted the ring on his finger as he looked from Holden to Sawyer, who’d moved in right beside him. But Caldwell hadn’t built himself a wealthy technology empire by backing away from suspicion or confrontation. The movement of his hands stilled and he pulled his shoulders back. “You’re not saying I had anything to do with your father’s murder, are you? He was the best friend I ever had. You four are like sons to me. And your mother is…becoming very special to me.”

Though Holden wasn’t completely comfortable with Bill’s growing relationship with their mother so soon after their father’s death, this conversation was about the case, not changing family ties.

Atticus tucked his glasses back inside his jacket. “You knew Irina Hansford, didn’t you?”

“Why would I know a woman from Yugoslavia? It’s not even a country anymore.”

Sawyer pushed further. “Thirty years ago, you and Dad weren’t just in the military together—you both worked for a covert agency called Z Group. Along with James McBride and Leo and Irina Hansford.”

Bill’s expression tightened into a poker-player’s mask. He held up his left hand to point out the gold fraternity ring he wore. “Your father and I were in the same fraternity in college. We went through ROTC—”

“Don’t lie to us,” Holden interrupted. He might not have been in on the discussion outside his room, but he knew where his brothers were going with this. "If Dad really was your best friend, you'll give us straight answers, even if you've been sworn to silence. Our father found out that Z Group was still in existence—thirty years after it was supposedly disbanded by the government. Only now they've turned into a bunch of arms and intelligence dealers. Somebody killed Dad—a woman, I believe—to keep the secret."

"You think John was murdered by a woman?" Bill's blank expression became a frown of confusion. "Then why am I under attack here? If someone in my company is responsible for supplying the weapons and ammunition that killed these people, then I'll look into it. I want to find John's killer as badly as the rest of you."

"KCPD can do that." Edward pushed Atticus aside to face Bill directly across Holden's bed. "We need you to drop the innocent facade and tell us everything you know about Z Group."

LIZA KNOCKED SOFTLY at Holden's door, bringing an abrupt end to the conversation on the other side.

"Come in."

The door jerked from her hand as a dark-haired gentleman with silver sideburns appeared in the opening. "Excuse me."

"Excuse..." But there was no need for her to apologize. His expression tense with an emotion that passed by too quickly to name, the man lengthened his stride and headed down the hall toward the elevators. Recovering from the startle, Liza pulled her hospital-issue robe together at the neck and snugged the tie belt at her waist. She swallowed hard, steeling her nerves and hoping that Susan Kincaid had been as accurate about her advice as she'd been sincere when she'd suggested that, since Liza was still awake herself, Holden would welcome a visit from her.

She stepped into the softly lit room. He already had three visitors—tall, dark-haired men—but her eyes were instantly drawn to the bruised face of the man sitting up in bed. Holden looked tired, pale against the crisp white sheets. His square jaw needed a shave. The faded hospital gown stretching from shoulder to shoulder seemed thin and insubstantial against the hospital's sterile, cool air. But that piercing blue gaze—blessedly clear and locked on to hers—made her insides knot up in a bundle of feminine awareness and heartfelt need. "Hey, Kincaid."

"Parrish."

She took another step into the room, glancing from one man to the next. "If I'm interrupting something important, I can come back in the morning."

"No." Holden's deep voice cracked, but his gaze never wavered from her. "They were just on their way out."

"But I thought we were going to compare our notes and—"

"Atticus." The biggest Kincaid brother, whom she'd learned was Sawyer, moved his gaze from the executive-looking one to Holden and back. "Think about it, smart guy. We can finish this tomorrow."

"Of course. I understand a man's priorities." After saying goodbye to Holden, Atticus turned to the door. He paused for a moment in front of Liza, then dipped his head and kissed her cheek. "Good to see you in one piece, Miss Parrish."

"Thanks. I—"

Sawyer picked her up and squeezed her in a hug before Atticus was out the door. He was warm and big and gentle as could be. "Glad I can finally do this." By the time he set her feet back on the floor she was too stunned to speak. "Keep my baby brother out of trouble, okay?"

"Liza." Edward nudged Sawyer out the door. His steely gray eyes lingered on her face for a moment before his chin dipped in a nod. Thanking? Approving? Of what? But he exited without saying another word.

As the door closed softly behind her, Liza thumbed over her shoulder and crossed to the foot of the bed. "What just happened?"

Holden's weary expression relaxed with a grin. "It's a Kincaid thing."

"Meaning?"

"Meaning they like you. Now get over here." He stretched out his hand toward her. "I'll probably rip some stitches if I leap out of bed at this point. I have something I want to talk to you about."

With a smile, Liza hurried to his side and clasped his hand between both of hers. "No leaping, okay? You've scared me enough for one day."

"The doc says I'm going to be okay," he reassured her. He stroked his thumb over the back of her knuckles, warming her entire body with the subtle gesture. "Who's watching the musketeers?"

"Believe it or not, Detective Grove volunteered to take them for the night. His apartment is going to be pretty crowded, but he seems to enjoy the company. In fact, I think he may be visiting our shelter to adopt a dog of his own soon." Liza turned her hands to halt the distracting caress of his thumb. She looked straight into his blue eyes and sought an answer. "What do your brothers know that I don't? Does it have to do with my testimony? I'm writing down everything I remember. And more and more details keep coming. My attending physician here gave me a list of reputable counselors I could talk to about memory loss. He thinks I'm at a point now where I'll remember all of it, eventually."

"That's great."

If not the murder investigation, then what had Holden and his brothers been discussing? And why wouldn't he look away? She began to feel a self-conscious blush creeping into her cheeks at his unblinking study of her. "You're not worried about me still, are you? Mr. Smith is dead and there are guards posted outside my room. You've got a trio of cops lurking outside of yours, too."

A plastic IV tube followed his hand as Holden reached out to brush a wisp of hair off her cheek. "I think I'm always going to worry about you."

Sweet. But he was stalling. "Spit it out already, Kincaid."

Holden looked deep into those silvery eyes. How could one woman be so beautiful, so brave, so stubborn and caring all at once? Freckles and copper hair, strength and sass, and a determination to do the right thing were proving to be an irresistible combination to him. Liza Parrish was a wake-up call to his heart and his life, and he always answered when he was called to a mission. "You love me, right? Because I'm 99.9 percent sure I'm in love with you."

Half a laugh and a wry smile made his heart pound faster. "Only 99.9, huh? So there's a tenth of a percent of you that's not sure?"

"No. I love you." The teasing came as naturally as

the need to touch her. He feathered his fingers into the silky copper at her temple. "But I don't want to come on too strong."

He detected a glitch in her smile. "We've only known each other for a few days," she said.

"Doesn't matter." He pulled her toward him, urging her to sit on the bed facing him. "My job requires me to turn off my emotions and pretend I don't feel a damn thing. But I haven't been able to do that with you. I tried to make protecting you part of the job, part of my dad's murder investigation. But I can't. What I feel for you—it's personal. It's real. And it's not going away. I know my family comes on like gangbusters, and you don't have anybody and you may be a little reticent to—"

She pressed her fingers to his lips. "Shut up, Kincaid. I'm not alone. I haven't been since I met you."

"Yeah, well I don't want you to confuse gratitude with…" The stern look in her expression eased the last of his doubts. They were going to be okay. His memory hadn't played tricks on him. "Shutting up now."

"I have Bruiser, Cruiser and Yukon—okay, so Yukon is a traitor and has adopted you instead of me." He kissed her fingertips as she pulled them away, then returned the favor by turning her warm lips into his palm where it rested against her cheek. "When I couldn't remember things, I didn't trust my own thoughts and feelings, much less allow myself to trust anyone else. But my dogs trust you. And they're the best judges of character I know. If they can believe in you, I can, too."

Holden wanted her closer. Wanted her in his arms, now. But he sensed that she needed to talk this out. "Coming from anybody else, that'd be a really cornball thing to say," he said. "But I know how you feel about the musketeers. I guess I've developed a soft spot for them, too. I'm glad I've earned everyone's trust."

"You've earned more than that." She inched a fraction closer and his pulse throbbed with hope. "I wasn't sure I wanted to give my heart to anybody ever again—I've been in tough-chick survival mode for a long time. But you didn't leave me any choice." She framed his jaw between her hands. *Say it, babe. Believe it.* "I love you, Holden. I'm in love with you."

"Works for me." The stitches in his side offered barely a twinge as he wrapped his arms around her and pulled her in for a long, leisurely, thorough kiss. When he finally came up for air, Liza was clinging to his neck, her faced flushed and smiling. Holden rested his forehead against hers. "So, if I want this connection we've made to go on forever, you'd be okay with that?"

"I'd be very okay with that."

"And say I wanted to marry you, would there be someone I should ask?"

"Besides me?"

"I know your parents are gone. Is there any other family…? Oh." She was grinning as she crawled beneath the covers with him, tenderly finding a spot where she could snuggle against his uninjured side. Holden wound his arms around her and tucked her healing, loving warmth even closer. "Fine. I'll talk to the dogs as soon as I'm out of here."

* * * * *

TAKEDOWN

For Norbert Wenzl. A true gentleman,
a fun guy, a kind soul. And my friend.

And for Cheryl Schuett. A smart, classy,
talented lady. Thank you for the immeasurable
positive influence you had on my son's life by
teaching him to read music. I'd work on a show
with you two any day. Thanks for reading my
books and loving theater.

PROLOGUE

Jillian—
Your smile and your laugh light up a room even on the darkest of days. The rose I sent made you smile, I know. Perhaps white, the color of purity, would have been a more fitting choice, but I know that red is your favorite color. You look stunning in red.

Sometimes, I don't know which I love more—your kick-ass body or that sweet personality. You can be one of the guys or the sexiest woman in the room with equal ease, and that always keeps me guessing—and wanting more of you.

Jilly, I know, too, that there's something deeper inside you that most people don't notice. Pain. Vulnerability. Need. I notice. I've felt those same things, too.

I want you to know just how much I care about you. I know where you've been—what you've had to overcome—the difficult path that lies ahead. I understand that we can show the world a strength we don't necessarily feel inside. I admire that about you—how you always keep fighting, even when it's tough—maybe especially when it's tough.

I just want you to know that you don't have to

keep fighting alone. I'm here for you. If you need anything, you don't even have to ask. I won't let anything—or anyone—hurt you ever again.

My heart will always be true to you.

I am forever,

Yours

While the letter printed off, he picked up the snapshot of her unwrapping the ribbon and plastic from around the flower he'd had delivered, and pressed a kiss to her adorably surprised expression. Then he dug a pin from the desk drawer and gently tacked the photo on the wall above the computer beside the collage of similar images hanging there.

His favorite picture was one in faded black-and-white newsprint, something from a state high school basketball tournament. But he knew Jilly's colors by heart. Long, dark brown hair. Eyes as bright and verdant as Celtic green.

And she was smiling. Right at him.

He smiled back and pulled the letter from the printer. Then, with clumsy gloved fingers, he pushed aside the gun and plastique, the ammo clips and clockwork devices, and cleared a spot on top of his desk to work. He folded the paper into three neat rectangles and stuffed it inside the matching envelope before rolling his chair away from the desk and heading out to deliver it.

Soon, she would know how much he had done for her, the risks he would take for her—all without complaint.

Soon, she would know how much he loved her.

CHAPTER ONE

"NICE SHOT, TROY!"

Jillian Masterson applauded as the basketball swished through the net.

Her young charge with the neat black braids pumped his fist in the air and whooped in victory. "Oh, yeah. I'm all that!"

"And a bag of chips," she cheered. He pushed his wheelchair beneath the basket to retrieve the ball while Jillian turned to her other patient and smiled. "Come on, Mike. Your turn."

"Basketball is lame," he groused.

Ignoring his ironic choice of words, she let his blue-eyed hatred for the world bounce off her skin and reached for his arms. Clamping one hand firmly around each wrist and bracing her feet in front of his, she pulled him out of his chair and balanced him against her shoulder while his leg braces locked into place. "Well, unless you want to plant some grass and turn this gym into an indoor football field, we're stuck with a basketball court. Let's try one from the free throw line."

"Why? It's not even a real court. Troy's baby brother could make a shot from that free throw line."

"You afraid you can't match up with an eighth grader?"

"I can do it," he argued. "I just don't want to."

"Show me."

"Jill…"

She stepped away, brushing the bangs from her eyes and shaking her ponytail down her back, forcing Mike Cutler, Jr.'s, reknit bones and weakened muscles to function on their own whether he liked it or not. She supposed the modified half-court in the university hospital's physical therapy center couldn't compete with the grass and fresh air and promise of the field where this high school athlete had once caught passes and run for touchdowns.

But she'd spare him the lucky-to-be-alive-get-over-yourself speech, knowing he wouldn't hear the words. She understood the black hole he was fighting to crawl out of. She'd lost her dreams when she was a teenager herself. Or rather, after her parents' tragic deaths in a plane crash, she'd single-handedly blown those dreams into smithereens, nearly ruining what was left of her older brother's and sister's lives as well as her own in the process.

Now, at twenty-eight, after rehab and long years of counseling and healing, she could look back objectively and see her mistakes, see that the love of her brother and sister, along with help and hope, had always been there for her. But Jillian would forever remember those dark days well enough to know that, at sixteen, Mike Cutler couldn't yet see beyond the fear, despair, anger and resentment that clouded his young life.

Instead of lecturing him, she stuck to the job she'd been trained to do—helping rebuild the bodies of accident victims and medical patients through physical therapy. And she was counting on the innate competitiveness of his sports-loving nature to help get the job done. Jillian reached down beside him to pick up the stainless steel cane from the polished wood floor beside him. Then she held out her arm and the cane, giving Mike the choice of which way he wanted to get himself to the free throw line eight feet away.

One of the advantages of standing five foot eleven herself was that she could look Young Mr. Attitude in the eye and not be intimidated by the width of his shoulders or the glare in his expression. "You gonna put your money where your mouth is and make the shot?"

"Do it, man." Troy Anthony put the ball in his lap and wheeled back over to their position. "If we don't play, then we'll have to go back to the weight room with the old farts and work out. I do *not* want to have Mrs. Hauser talking to me about her operation anymore. She smells like my great-grandmother used to. Creeps me out. And you know you don't want Old Man Wilkins talking to you about the Chiefs' off-season trades and recruitment again. That'd suck right down to your shorts."

Apparently willing to do anything to shut up his young compatriot, Mike snatched the cane from Jillian's hand. "Fine. I'll shoot the damn ball."

Jillian spared Troy a wink of thanks as Mike hobbled past her. She turned and studied the slight improvement in his jerky gait. A cataclysmic car crash had killed Mike's friend and shattered his legs. According to the medical reports Jillian had studied before writing up a therapy plan, it was a miracle that Mike Cutler was alive, much less walking. Several surgeries, steel pins and one determined father had gotten him to this point. But it would take a lot of patience—and convincing Mike to apply that stubborn attitude to his own recovery—to get him back to some semblance of normal life again.

"Here, bro." Once Mike had reached the free throw line and paused long enough to catch his breath, Troy shot him the ball.

Reading that split-second moment of terror in Mike's expression, Jillian reached around him and intercepted the straight-line pass. In one smooth movement that didn't allow either teen the time to feel embarrassment or regret, she tucked the ball against Mike's stomach, forcing him to steady it with his own hand. In the next second she took his cane, watching the muscles beneath his jeans and T-shirt clench and adjust to maintain his balance.

Good. Use what you've got, kid. You can do it.

Mike's athleticism would be as much a boon to his recovery as it had once been to her own. She'd remember to make good use of his natural balance and strength. Jillian bit down on the urge to cheer his success and pushed him a little further. "Dribble it."

An answering groan filled Mike's lungs with a deep, healthy breath. Jillian moved behind him, bracing his hips while he used different muscles and adjusted his equilibrium to control the bounce of the ball in front of him. She felt him tense his core muscles, stabilizing his body without any real help from her. *Excellent!* "Now shoot."

The normal bend of the knees to make such a shot couldn't yet happen, but the instincts were there. He raised the ball above his forehead, took sight of the net and pushed the ball off the tips of his long fingers. Jillian held her breath along with him as the ball arced through the air, hit the backboard and circled twice around the rim before dropping through the hoop.

"Yes!" She held up a hand and was rewarded with a high five. "Don't tell me basketball isn't your game."

Mike grinned. Stood a little taller. "Told you I could do it if I wanted to."

Uh-huh. Victory.

Troy rolled past him and the two teens touched fists. "Sweet, man."

Unexpected applause startled Jillian and drew their attention to the sidelines and the man standing in the doorway. "Nice shot, son."

Easy, girl. Flighty female had never been her style. She wasn't going to let her sick new pen pal turn her into a woman who jumped at the sound of a man's deep voice. Fixing a friendly smile on her face, Jillian calmed the startled leap of her pulse. "Captain Cutler."

Michael Cutler, Sr., filled the entrance to the gym, his square, muscular frame cutting an impressive figure in his KCPD uniform—black from shoulder to toe, save for the white S.W.A.T. logo emblazoned on his chest pocket and ball cap, and the brass captain's bars and KCPD badge pin tacked to his collar. His sturdy bicep was marked by a black armband, his long legs by the gun strapped to his thigh.

Talk about sweet.

"Jillian." He touched two fingers to the brim of his cap and acknowledged her with a slight nod.

Though she guessed he had only a couple or three inches on her in height, and was probably fifteen years her senior, Jillian couldn't stop the quiet little flutter of breath that seemed to catch in her throat each time the widowed cop came by to pick up his son after a therapy session. There was something overtly masculine about the military clip of his salt-and-pepper hair and the laser beam intensity of his dark blue eyes. Or maybe it was just the mature confidence of a man at ease inside his own skin, evident in every stride as he pulled off his cap and crossed the gym floor, that made Jillian's neglected feminine hormones stand up and take notice.

Objective appreciation, she told herself. An attractive man was an attractive man at any age—especially one who kept himself in as good a shape as Michael Cutler.

"Ow."

His son, Mike, Jr., pinched Jillian's shoulder in a painful squeeze, jerking her from her wandering thoughts. "I need to sit down," he whispered between gritted teeth. "Now."

"Of course." Jillian hid the blush warming her cheeks by helping Mike walk toward the chair. It was less embarrassment than guilt at being distracted from her job that had her sliding her shoulder beneath his arm and anchoring her hands at his waist to guide him to his seat. Mike's balance might not be rock steady yet, but he was doing the bulk of the work, moving as quickly as his clumsy legs would let him. Maybe something had seized up with a cramp.

"Are you in pain?" his father asked, instantly standing behind the wheelchair like a wall of black granite to keep it still while Mike turned and plopped onto the seat.

"I'm fine, Dad," Mike insisted, shrugging off his father's hand while Jillian knelt down to adjust the foot rests and position his feet. She glanced up into the teen's downturned expression. Just as she suspected. The only thing cramping was Mike's attitude.

His father must have sensed it, too. With a measured sigh, he moved away from the chair and turned to greet Troy. He shook the young man's hand. "Staying out of trouble?"

"Yes, sir."

"How's your brother? Dex, isn't it?"

"Yeah. He made the honor roll last semester."

"Good for him. Good that he's got a big brother like you in his corner. And your grandmother?"

"Working. Two jobs. Like always. I might be getting a job pretty soon, too. As soon as I get this thing all figured out." He spun his chair in a tight circle, proving that, physically, at any rate, he was closer to healing than Michael's son. "I'm trying to finish my GED, too, but the math sucks."

Michael inclined his head toward his son. "Mike's pretty fair with numbers. He's in geometry at William Chrisman this year. Maybe he can coach you."

"Dad!"

Troy shrugged off Mike, Jr.'s, shut-up-and-don't-volunteer-me-for-anything reprimand, his own tone growing a little more subdued. "I'll get it figured out."

"I like hearing that. Good luck to you."

"Thanks."

Jillian stayed down longer than necessary so that she wouldn't interrupt the man-to-man interchange that Troy got far too little of in his life. Even paralyzed below the waist and struggling to be the man in his family, Troy Anthony was still a big kid at heart. He beamed at the paternal approval in Captain Cutler's voice before wheeling over to Mike's side and thumping him on the arm. "Hey, will you be back on Monday, bro?"

Mike rolled his eyes, as if the Monday-Wednesday-

Friday sessions he'd been attending for the last month and a half since mid-February would go on forever and ever. "I dunno."

"Jillian said if enough of us got together, we could play some hoops. She says there's a whole wheelchair league in Kansas City."

Go, Troy. Jillian had hoped that pairing up her two youngest charges in therapy sessions would boost their mental outlooks as well as their physical training. "With that upper body strength and the hands you've got," she observed, "you'd be a natural."

If anything, Mike grew even more sullen at her compliment. "I told you I hate basketball."

"Mike—" his father scolded.

But Troy was back in can't-touch-this form. He knew how to push Mike's buttons. "You hate losing, too?" He spun his chair toward the exit and took off. "Last one to the machine buys the pop."

A beat of silence passed before Jillian coyly prodded Mike. "Didn't you buy the sodas last time?"

"Hey!" With a sudden burst of movement, Mike raced after the other teen, his hands gliding along the wheels of his chair. "Get back here, loser."

"I ain't the one in last place, loser."

"Shouldn't you be walk—"

Jillian grabbed Michael, Sr.'s, arm, stopping him from going after the boys. His forearm muscles bunched beneath her fingers before he swung his attention back to her. "Shouldn't he be walking to build up his leg strength instead of getting more used to that damn chair?"

Jillian drew her hand away from the crisp sleeve and the solid man inside the uniform before her curious fingers dug into that warm flex of muscle. "Let him have a little fun. He's already put in a decent workout session today. Physically, he's reached a plateau and I don't want to burn him out."

Michael Cutler's eyes, as blue and dark as a twilight sky, assessed the shrug of her shoulders before zeroing in on her expression. "He'll continue to improve, won't he?"

"His doctors seem to think so." Jillian reminded him of the good news without sugarcoating the bad. "Mike needs to build his self-confidence as much as anything right now. He needs to care about moving on to the next stage of his recovery before more strength and coordination training will do him much good."

Michael, Sr., rubbed his palm over the top of his hair, making the black and silver spikes spring up in the wake of his hand. "Sorry. It always comes down to the mental game, doesn't it?"

Jillian nodded.

"I just get frustrated that he's missing out on so much. He's still only sixteen."

"Think about his frustration."

"He won't even talk to me about the night of the accident. I had to read the details in a police report."

"Does he share with his trauma counselor?" Jillian's own sessions with Dr. Randolph, the psychologist who'd helped her through rehab at the Boatman Clinic eleven years ago, and who remained a friend and occasional father confessor to this day, had been invaluable to her mental recovery as a teenager.

"Not much. You seem to be the only person he opens up to." Captain Cutler worked the brim of his cap with long, strong fingers before everything about him went utterly still—as if he'd suddenly realized his emotions were showing and he'd shut them down. Such precision, such control. No wonder other cops snapped to his commands. *Stop noticing details about the man, already.* Jillian focused on what he was saying, made sure she was listening as he slid the cap into his hip pocket and continued. "He doesn't have to play football anymore, or go to Harvard or get rich. I'd just like him to leave his room once in a while and walk without those damn braces—meet girls and hang out with his buddies and be a teenager again."

"Trust me, it'll happen." Jillian went to retrieve the basketball Troy had left on the floor. She knew that damaged people healed at different speeds, and that not even a father's unflinching support could force the process to go any faster. "He just needs time."

"Well, I'm glad you have the patience to deal with him. You had him smiling and trading high fives before he knew I was here. Seems everything I say or do ends up in a shouting match or him closing the door and not saying anything at all."

Jillian opened the storage bin outside the equipment closet and dropped the ball in. "Just doing my job."

Michael Cutler was there to close the lid for her. His piercing eyes seemed to catch the light, even in the shadows from the stands and supports above them. "Working magic is more like it. He likes you. Likes coming here. It's just me at home since his mom passed away. Some nights, when he's shut up in his room and I can't figure out what he needs, it feels like he doesn't have anybody. I've thought about taking another leave of absence from work—like I did right after the accident—but then I think he prefers the time away from me."

"I'm sure that's not true."

"Don't count on it. I've negotiated with crazy people, talked kidnappers into releasing their hostages and convinced murderers to put down their guns. But I can't get my own son to open up to me. Pam—Mike's mother—she would have known how to talk to him, how to reach him."

A wistfulness briefly hushed his succinct tone at the mention of his late wife, making Jillian suspect that the father was missing the woman who'd been lost to cancer two years ago just as much as the son. Though she didn't know the details of Pam Cutler's death, Jillian knew the basics after discussions with Mike, Jr.'s, doctor when they'd been planning his physical therapy. And she understood down to her bones how the loss of loved ones could wreak havoc on the family left behind.

The urge to reach out and offer a comforting touch was powerful. But Jillian reminded herself that they were little more than friendly acquaintances—that it was this man's son she cared about—and stuffed her wayward fingers into the pockets of her khaki slacks, instead.

"Don't be so hard on yourself, Captain." She called the cops she knew by rank or nickname, the same way her brother, an investigator for the district attorney's office, her sister the M.E., her sister-in-law the police commissioner and her KCPD brother-in-law did. "I know how hard it can be on family to see someone you love hurt like that. You want to help him—make things right. But you can't. The reality is, accident or not—Mike's still a teenager. He's going to have moods. And he's going to have to figure out for himself how to make this work. In the end, the best thing you can do for him is love him."

Those blue eyes narrowed, silently asking a question. Yes, she was speaking from personal experience, but Mike's dad didn't need to know everything about her sordid past.

When she turned away to get her clipboard and wristband of keys, he followed her, letting her pretend she had no shameful secrets to keep. "He's got that. The love, I mean."

"Mike knows that, down inside. He may not remember it every day, but he knows you love him. Just the fact that you use your dinner break to bring him here to the clinic and pick him up means something to him." Jillian slipped the elastic key bracelet around her wrist and tucked the clipboard of treatment logs under her arm. Together, they headed toward the gym exit and the hallway beyond. "Look at Troy, on the other hand. He's fighting most of his recovery battle on his own. Ever since the shooting, his grandmother refuses to leave his brother, Dexter, alone. Either he's at school or she locks Troy in the apartment with him to keep an eye on him the evenings she works her second job."

"It can't be easy for her."

"I'm sure it's not—and I admire her for supporting her grandkids financially, but it's almost as if she's given up on saving Troy and is focusing all her energy on Dexter. If Troy wants to come to physical therapy he has to schedule the appointments himself and take the bus to get here. I've been giving him a ride home, at least, trying to give him a little extra attention and ease some of the burden."

"You're driving him home tonight?" The captain

stopped, checked his watch. It wasn't five o'clock yet, and she'd done it more than a dozen times. No big deal.

She turned at the doorway arch. "As soon as I log in these stats and sign out."

"Where does he live?"

Jillian named the street and apartment area just west of downtown Kansas City. His mouth thinned as he propped his hands on his hips. "At HQ we call that neighborhood No-Man's Land. It's not the safest place to be after dark."

"Clearly. Otherwise, Troy might not have been shot in the back by that stray bullet."

"I'm serious, Jillian."

Did he see her laughing? She knew about the dangers of No-Man's Land—more personally than Michael Cutler would probably imagine. If she could keep Troy from falling prey to them the way she once had by simply giving the kid a little extra time and offering him a ride, she would. "I don't take chances I don't have to. But I'm not going to let Troy shoulder his recovery all by himself, either. Somebody always knows when I leave and where I'm going."

"And when you get back?"

Jillian groaned. "It's just a car ride. I can handle it, Captain."

His low-pitched curse followed her into the hallway as she locked the gym door behind them. "I'm not your commanding officer, so why don't you call me Michael? That'd be a damn sight friendlier than 'ugh' or 'whatever,' which seems to be all I'm hearing from Mike these days."

Jillian relaxed enough to smile, glad his disapproval

of her efforts to help Troy had been short-lived. "Captain Ugh. I bet your men would love to call you that."

"My men wouldn't dare. Not to my face." Instead of heading past her door to get Mike from the break room, he followed her into her office. "Can you spare another minute?"

"Sure." Jillian hugged the clipboard to her chest and turned.

"I wanted to double-check the PT schedule. Mike's school is having their spring break next week. He's pretty bummed about making up extra class work while his classmates go on vacation, and since he seems to enjoy his time with you and Troy, I wanted to see if I could still bring him in for his regular sessions—give him a break from history and geometry and…me."

"I'll be here," Jillian promised. "Anything else I can do to help?"

"Yeah. Be careful driving through No-Man's Land. My son needs you." He pulled his S.W.A.T. cap from his back pocket and pulled it on over his head. The stern police captain had returned. "Keep your doors locked. If you feel threatened in any way, stay in your car and drive straight to the nearest police station. Run red lights if you have to. If you think someone is following you, stay in your car and honk the horn until an officer comes out to assist you."

"You know, I have a big brother to give me lectures like that. You don't have to."

"As long as you listen to one of us. I can give Troy a lift home on the days I'm off duty and don't have to get back to the precinct." He adjusted the brim of his cap to shade his eyes. "If riding with a cop wouldn't cramp his style."

"That's nice to offer. I'll ask him."

"Be careful. Mike's counting on you."

Look who was talking. She dropped her gaze to the sidearm holstered at his thigh. "You be careful."

"Always."

After he tipped his hat and left, Jillian watched him stride down the hallway. Yeah. Big-brotherly overprotection aside, fortysomething looked good on the police captain from this view, too.

Savoring the responding skitter of her pulse, Jillian turned to her desk. Her gaze landed on the droopy, fading flower in the glass vase there, and her heart rate kicked up another notch. Would it have killed the sender to include a note? Or even just a name?

Between friendly discussion and heated debates, she'd forgotten for a few minutes that not all men were as straightforward as Michael Cutler. Maybe she was only crushing on the older man because she was 99.9 percent certain he hadn't sent her that mysterious rose. As beautiful and blameless as the deep red flower might once have been, she'd lived with too many deceptions in her life already. The whole secret admirer thing had lost its charm long ago.

Dismissing the tiresome joke with a shake of her head, Jillian sat behind her desk, pulling up Mike's and Troy's files on her computer to chart the updates. But the rose kept taunting her from the corner of her eye.

It was the sort of apologetic gesture her ex-boyfriend, Blake Rivers, would have made to get himself out of trouble with her. She supposed breaking up with him after an attempt to rekindle a relationship—clean and sober style—had failed qualified as trouble. But she had no proof the flower had come from Blake. No reason to suspect him. She'd left him months ago. He'd moved on to some blonde reporter or red-haired heiress, according to the paper's society page. Jillian was old news.

And she intended to stay that way. As wealthy and handsome and devilishly clever as Blake might be, he had a reckless streak in him that had enabled her own addiction and nearly gotten them both killed. Jillian had promised her family, her therapist Dr. Randolph and herself that she was never going to go down that dangerous, self-destructive path again.

But if not Blake, then who had sent her the flower?

She supposed a phone call to Blake's office at Caldwell Technologies couldn't hurt. She didn't want to send any false signals to her ex, but a few words to put her mind at ease and set him straight on the romance-is-over message was worth the risk. And if the rose wasn't from Blake…?

Jillian was leaving a message on Blake's answering machine, reluctantly asking him to return her call, when Dylan Smith, another physical therapist who worked at the hospital's outpatient therapy clinic with her, knocked on her door. She waved him into the room as she hung up the phone. As usual, Dylan's dimpled cheeks and mischievous grin demanded she smile in return.

"What's cookin', Masterson?" He shoved his fingers through his muss of blond hair and sat down. "Makin' plans for a hot date?"

"I'm workin', Smith. Aren't you?"

"Hell, no. It's five o'clock, it's Friday and a bunch of us are going over to the Shamrock to hit happy hour. If you don't have plans, come with us."

The Shamrock Bar? Fun with her friends sounded tempting, but her drinking days were over. "Thanks for the invite, but I've got things to do at home this weekend."

"I helped you move into that apartment—up three flights of stairs, I might add—and everything looked neat and pretty and sitting in its place before we all left. Come."

Jillian grinned at his pitiful, boyish pout. "My bedroom is only half painted, and the dueling colors have been driving me nuts all week. We're supposed to have rain this weekend, and if I can't open the windows and work, I'll have to suffer through Pepto-Bismol pink and ice blue for another whole week. I need to get started on it tonight."

Dylan leaned forward, reached across the desk and laid his hand over the top of hers where it rested on the blotter. Every muscle in Jillian's fingers froze at the unexpected touch, though she managed to keep her smile in place.

"Just for an hour or two, Jilly? Please?" Dylan coaxed.

"I can't."

"I've got a bet with that new occupational therapist that I can eat an entire serving of the Shamrock's fried habaneros and win free drinks for a year. You can cheer me on."

"Or bring the stomach pump you'll need when you're done."

"Very funny. Where's the love?"

There was nothing secret about Dylan's harmless flirtations. If you were female, he flirted. Still, boyish charm aside, Jillian thought it wise to steer clear of romantic entanglements for now, and gently extricated her hand from his. "Sorry. Ask the O.T. to cheer you on. She's a hottie and it sounds like she might be interested in you. Share your habanero breath with her."

"You've got to have fun sometime." Dylan pushed to his feet, his grin firmly locked into place. He placed his hand over his heart and made a slight bow. "And I'm your man whenever you're ready. Oh, I forgot."

He reached inside the royal-blue polo shirt that matched her own clinic uniform, pulled out an envelope and set it on her desk.

"What's this?"

"Lulu at the front desk was on her way out. She asked me to deliver it to you."

Please, no. Jillian gingerly picked it up. No return address, and though the envelope had a stamp, it hadn't been canceled. But the name and clinic address clearly belonged to her. An uneasy feeling soured her lips into a frown. "I thought the mail already came."

Dylan plunged his hands into his pockets. "It must have dropped behind the counter or something."

Jillian shrugged off the perplexing mystery and slid her finger beneath the flap to open it. "Thanks."

He nodded toward the corner of her desk. "By the way, your flower needs some water."

"Don't you think it's a little late for that?" Enough with the torment. Jillian plucked the dead rose from the vase and dropped it into the trash. "I should have sent it over to the main hospital for a patient who'd take better care of it than I did. My bad."

His gaze seemed to fix on the fallen flower for a moment before the grin returned. "Not a green thumb, huh? I'll make a point to remember that next Valentine's Day."

"Bye, Dylan. Don't forget to take a gallon of milk and a fire extinguisher with you. Good luck, you idiot."

The blond charmer left with a laugh. Once she was alone, Jillian took a deep breath, pulled out the letter and leaned back in her chair to read it.

She slapped her hand over her mouth to keep from crying out.

MICHAEL HAD SEEN that look on the faces of parents waiting outside a school building locked down because of an armed intruder or bomb threat. He'd seen that look on a hostage-taker who'd gone off his meds and didn't understand why he'd been shot by one of Michael's S.W.A.T. team.

He hadn't expected to see it on Jillian Masterson's youthful face when he raised his hand to knock on her open office door.

Shock. Helplessness. Fear.

"Are you all right?"

Green eyes darted up to his and she jumped to her feet, sending her chair crashing back into the wall behind her desk. By the time she'd groused and righted the chair and spun around to face him, her cheeks were flushed a rosy color. He'd clearly startled her. Again.

"What…are you doing here?" she stammered.

His negotiator's instincts kept his voice calm, his movements slow and precise as he stepped into the room. Whatever was wrong here, he didn't want to aggravate the problem. "I forgot Mike's cane. The gym's locked. Are you all right?" he repeated.

Jillian wadded up the letter that was already half crushed in her fist and shot it into the trash can beside her desk. “I’m fine.”

And he was the tooth fairy. “Was that bad news?”

She swept aside a strand of coffee-colored hair that had fallen across her cheek and tucked it into the long, sleek ponytail at her nape. Then she was circling her desk, pulling the keys off her wrist, offering him a smile he didn’t believe. “It’s just one of those chain letters. You know, send it on to so many people and you’ll get a bunch of stuff in return. Annoying, aren’t they?”

He wouldn’t know. But he did recognize a load of B.S. when he heard it. “Jillian—”

“I need to sign out ASAP so I can get Troy home before dark. I’ll be right back so you don’t have to keep Mike waiting.”

Miles of long legs and the graceful athleticism of her walk quickly carried her down the hallway and around the corner. *Conversation over, old man. Take the hint.*

For a moment, Michael debated between trusting his instincts about people and minding his own business. But he’d spent too many years as a cop, training his mind and body to pay attention to the warning signs people gave him, to let her behavior go without an explanation. It was always easier to stop trouble before it got started.

Pretty, sassy, make-his-son-smile Jillian Masterson was in trouble.

Making sure he was alone in her office, he plucked the paper wad she’d tossed out of the trash can and unfolded it, smoothing it open against his thigh. He read it quickly. Read it again. Frowned.

A love letter.

One that made a healthy woman go pale, jump at his approach and toss the missive away with a flippant excuse before bolting from the room.

Right. Nothing suspicious about that.

CHAPTER TWO

"CAN YOU GET it, Troy?"

"Yeah, I'm good."

Jillian closed the passenger-side door of her dark blue SUV, pressed the automatic locks and turned a slow 360 to take note of the traffic, parked cars and local residents up and down both sides of the drab, run-down city block. There were patches of brightness and warmth here and there where hope and promise tried to shine through. A freshly painted window box waited for spring flowers to be planted. A trio of preteen girls sat on the stoop across the street, chattering in laughing voices under the rosy glow of the setting sun. Construction signs promised a condemned building was about to be razed and replaced by something clean and new.

But she was just as aware of the weary posture of the shopkeepers locking their doors and pulling down protective cages, the curious glances and quick dismissals from workers climbing off the bus at the corner and hurrying toward their respective homes before any kind of trouble found them. And she couldn't miss the homeless man, dragging a filthy backpack behind him as he turned into an alley and disappeared.

Thankfully, though, there were no pimps, no gang-bangers, no visible dealers she recognized from those lost days a decade ago when the dark corners and hidden secrets of this Kansas City neighborhood had offered her a false escape from the sorrows and stress of her teenage life. Of course, night hadn't fallen yet. Shadows and moonlight were usually the only invitation the cockroaches needed to come out of their holes.

A shiver of remembered nightmares rippled across her skin, leaving a sea of goose bumps in its wake.

You've moved beyond this place, she reminded herself with a mental nod, shaking off the sudden chill. She was older, wiser and ten years clean without a fix of coke. To her dying day, she'd atone for that wasted part of her life by helping youths like Troy Anthony move beyond the sucking trap of No-Man's Land the way she finally had. *So do it, already.*

"Wait up." Zipping the front of her sweatshirt jacket, Jillian hurried to catch up to Troy as he maneuvered his chair over the curb onto the sidewalk. She grabbed the handles and steered him up the concrete ramp that zigzagged beside the stairs leading to the apartment building's double doors. "I promised front door service, and that means apartment 517."

Troy turned his key in the lock of the inner lobby door. "Ain't nothing wrong with these magic hands. I can get up to the fifth floor by myself. You'd better head on home before dark."

"Is everybody my big brother today? This'll take like, what, five minutes max?" Jillian rolled him across the cracked tiles of the lobby floor, and waited while he pushed the elevator's call button. The numbers over the elevator doors didn't light up, but she could tell from the grinding of gears and cables that the car was descending inside the shaft. "I don't want your grandmother to worry about you getting home safely. She's got enough on her plate."

"You're sure you're not coming upstairs to snitch one of her chocolate chip cookies?"

"Hey, if somebody offers me homemade cookies and there's chocolate involved…" Jillian waved her arms out in a dramatic gesture. "Ahh!"

Their shared laughter ended abruptly when the light beside the super's door clicked on. Jillian clutched her fists back to her chest and she masked the catch in her throat with a cough. Great. Since when had she gotten so skittish?

Stupid letter. Stupid flower.

She smoothed her hair into her ponytail and tried to ease her paranoia by taking stock of her surroundings inside the lobby. She and Troy were alone. The super's light must be rigged with some kind of motion sensor that she had inadvertently set off, because no one else had entered the building behind them or come out of the apartment. She should be relieved the light had snapped on because it dispelled the evening gloom gathering in the lobby, although the corridor beyond the super's apartment remained in shadows. She *was* relieved. For a moment. Deliberately focusing her senses also gave her a whiff of a pungent odor that was decidedly less pleasant than the aroma of freshly baked cookies she imagined coming from Troy's apartment.

Jillian wrinkled up her nose. "What is that smell?"

"Probably Mrs. Chambers's cats in 102. She can't say no to a stray. You all right?"

"Yeah, I'm fine. I think somebody needs to change the litter box."

"You sure? You seem a little rattled."

"Just tired. It's been a long day." A final ding of the elevator gave her the perfect excuse to brush aside Troy's concerns. As the steel doors parted, she grabbed the handles on Troy's wheelchair. "The Jillian Masterson chauffeur service is ready to—"

"There you are. Where have you been? You're late. Way late." A sharp voice from inside the elevator greeted them before the tall, stout black woman braced the doors open with her thick, gnarled fingers.

"Grandma—"

"Don't you *Grandma* me."

Jillian pulled the chair back as LaKeytah Anthony stormed out. The older woman with the purplish-dyed hair reached out to her grandson to give him a tweak on his chin and a light cuff on his ear in one smooth motion. "Dex is upstairs by himself, doin' his homework. You were supposed to have him here forty minutes ago. Now I'll be late gettin' to my shift at the Winthrop Building."

"I'm sorry, Mrs. Anthony. I got held up at the office for a few minutes. Troy called."

"An hour ago!"

"It's rush hour," Troy defended. "Jillian drove as quick as she could. You know there's construction and stuff."

LaKeytah wouldn't hear it. "I thought the whole idea of you drivin' him was to get him home early. You know what I'm fearin' when I don't know where my boys are."

The *idea* was to get Troy to therapy, period. Saving the Anthonys time, money and concern was supposed to be the bonus. "It wasn't my intent to worry you."

"I can't get to work if he isn't here."

"Dex is fourteen," Troy argued. "He can be by himself for half an hour."

"How old were you when you got shot?"

"Mrs. Anthony!"

The older woman's fatigue was evident as she finally paused to catch her breath. "Maybe if I'd been here to walk you home that night…"

"Then maybe you'd have got shot, too."

Dismissing the sad logic of Troy's words, LaKeytah straightened and pointed a stern finger at him. "Dinner's in the microwave. Make sure Dex finishes his algebra." The accusatory finger swung toward Jillian. "I'm gonna be late to clean my offices now, thanks to you. If you want to help Troy, you get him home on time." With a grunt and a glare, LaKeytah stormed outside, letting the lobby's double doors slam shut behind her.

A beat of shocked silence passed before Troy leaned forward to open the elevator doors again. "Sorry about that."

Still feeling a sting of guilt, Jillian summoned a wry smile. LaKeytah Anthony worked two jobs, raised two teenagers and had plenty of reason to worry about her family in this neighborhood. Though she didn't appreciate being anyone's whipping post, Jillian thought she could understand the other woman's anger. "Your grandmother's stressed out about work, and like she said, she's concerned about you."

"She's concerned about Dexter." He rolled his eyes to punctuate his mocking acceptance that *he* was the grandson LaKeytah had already given up on. "She just wants me home so I can babysit."

"Troy." Jillian squeezed his shoulder. "It's more than that."

He shrugged off her offer of comfort. "She's got no cause to jump your case like that."

"Forget it." She wheeled him inside and let him position his chair while she pushed button number 5.

"I can get upstairs on my own."

"I know you can. But I promised to see you home, okay? Home's the fifth floor." The doors drifted shut. Let him be all tough and hide the hurt he must be feeling—Jillian was still going to care. "Besides, if anything happens to you between here and there, I don't want your grandmother chewing me another new one."

"I hear that." Troy grinned.

Jillian relaxed. He was going to be okay.

HE SILENTLY PULLED the door shut behind him and crept out of the shadowed hallway into the lobby, his senses finely tuned to the sweet scent of Jillian Masterson, despite the ammonia odor of soured kitty litter that left his eyes watering.

A terrible sense of right and wrong burned through his belly. What he'd just overheard had been wrong. All wrong.

He needed to make it right.

The old woman in apartment 102 had generously opened her door to give him directions to Troy Anthony's place. It had probably been more foolish than generous for the old cat freak to unlock her door to a stranger—but not as foolish as the woman who'd just reamed Jillian up one side and down the other for no good reason. Grandma Anthony's harsh words had upset Jillian, he could tell. She was worried about the boy, too.

She smiled and tried to apologize, even joked with the kid afterward, but he could tell.

Nobody upset his sweet Jillian.

And got away with it.

JILLIAN SWALLOWED THE last bite of the rich chocolate chip cookie and laughed as the two Anthony brothers dutifully closed the cookie jar and reached for their dinner plates to cut up their chicken. Dessert first had lightened Troy's mood, the sun was setting and it was time for Jillian to say her goodbyes and go home.

She plucked a stray cookie crumb from the sleeve of her jacket and popped it into her mouth before pushing her chair away from the kitchen table. "Don't forget to study for your GED, Troy." She winked at his younger brother. "You'll have to have Dex help you with the math."

Dexter laughed. "I will if you teach me how to dunk."

Troy rolled his eyes and put his big hand over Dexter's face, pushing the grin aside in a timeless gesture of brotherly annoyance.

Good. LaKeytah's lecture, the resulting guilt and the challenges of coping with his disability had all receded to manageable levels for Troy, and his attitude seemed fixed firmly back in the positive position. Jillian had trouble masking her own smile at his resiliency. Everything in Troy's apartment seemed clean, relatively clear of obstacles to his wheelchair and safe. He would be okay. "Call me if you need something. Otherwise, I'll see you Monday at the clinic."

"I'll get the door," Troy answered, angling his chair to follow her. "See ya."

Jillian waited to hear the door lock behind her before she went back to the elevator and pushed the call button. The doors opened immediately. She pulled her keys from her pocket and stepped into the empty car with a weary sigh. Short temper and paranoia aside, LaKeytah Anthony was to be commended for keeping her home in such good shape, and for putting square meals and a strong set of values on the table every day.

As she rode the elevator down, the musty odor of age and neglect screamed for some antiseptic and air freshener. But when she stepped out into the lobby, the smell turned more perfumey, more musky, like the scent of cologne on a man.

The subtle sweetness in the air was enough to pull Jillian up short and tighten her lips into a wary frown. She turned to her right, turned to her left—held her ground as the security light over the super's door blinked on again. "Hello?"

Her breathing quickened a notch. Of course, no one would answer. The elevator had still been on the fifth floor where she and Troy had gotten out. There was no one in this lobby, no sounds beyond the usual creaks and moans of the old building, no reason for that little shiver of awareness to creep along her spine.

Get over it, girl. No one is in here spying on you.

"Right," she agreed out loud, fighting to strengthen her resolve. Seeing nothing and no one, Jillian clutched her keys like claws between her fingers, pushed open the double glass doors and hurried straight down the steps.

Long shadows cast by the high-rise buildings cooled

the sidewalk as she lengthened her stride to reach her SUV. The chattering girls from the stoop across the street had gone inside. The bus stop was clear. Traffic had trickled down to a few cars. Still, that buzz of hyperawareness refused to dissipate.

She was being watched.

Whether it was idle curiosity, or something much more focused and sinister, didn't matter. Jillian tilted her head to check the windows of the apartments and businesses on either side of the street. Nothing but curtains and blinds and emptiness. It was more night than dusk now, yet she still peered into the alley across the way, looked through the windshields of the parked cars she passed. No one.

Those stupid letters had her rattled, that was all. Shivering, despite the decent warmth of the early spring evening, she jogged the last few steps to her car.

She'd just beeped the lock open when a beige Cadillac Escalade whipped around the corner and screeched to a stop beside her car, blocking her in. Instinctively on guard, Jillian drifted back a step. Had this guy been waiting for her to come out of the building?

The driver's-side window lowered and her shoulders stiffened with a flash of remembrance. And not a good one. Big black man. Shaved bald head. Muscular. Silent. Sure to be armed.

Known to her simply as Mr. Lynch.

As if she wanted to visit with a face from her past.

Get in the car!

Jillian turned and plowed right into the shoulder of a man she had even less desire to see.

"Easy, babe."

Isaac Rush.

As the whiskey-scented breath of one of Kansas City's most wily and successful drug dealers washed over her, Jillian swallowed a curse and backed away. His handsome, biracial face didn't make him charming. His tailored suit didn't make him sophisticated. The tight fingers that clamped around her elbow did make him dangerous, however.

She yanked her sleeve from his grip. "Don't call me that."

Now the big Cadillac with the armed chauffeur made sense. Jillian glanced over her shoulder and exchanged a silent nod with the big man. Lynch wasn't what she would call a friend, certainly not someone she would ever want to hang out with or run into in a dark alley, given that his job for Isaac involved guns and fists and breaking client's fingers. But, for whatever reason, the imposing, unsmiling brute had rescued her one night, a lifetime ago…from the very man who was sliding his fingers over Jillian's and the door handle right now.

But Lynch wasn't helping her tonight.

"Need something I can hook you up with, sugar?"

As if *sugar* was any better than *babe,* coming from this lowlife. Jillian snatched her hand away from the smarmy touch and stood tall. She'd be taller than Isaac if she'd been wearing heels instead of running shoes, but she doubted even that would intimidate him. "There's a reason you haven't seen me for ten years. I don't do that anymore. You have nothing I want. I was just giving a friend a ride home. Now if you'll excuse me."

Still, with money and Lynch and control of these streets to back him up, Isaac didn't give up easily. He leaned against the door, putting his body between her and getting in. "Somebody making trouble for you around here? Maybe I can help."

"You're the only trouble I see."

"Tough talk, Jilly. You know, I always liked you. And now that you're a full-grown woman, we can do something about it." *Liar!* Being seventeen hadn't stopped him from trying to *do something about* his attraction to her all those years ago. Maybe she should be grateful that his attempted rape had finally driven her to that lowest point where she could agree to entering rehab at the Boatman Clinic. But Isaac was still trying to make his role as her onetime supplier sound like something romantic had passed between them. He brushed his fingertips across the back of her knuckles. "I miss seeing you. We used to be the best of friends—"

With a silent scream pinging inside her ears, she grabbed his hand, twisted his wrist and pinched his nerve in a move her former cop brother, Eli, had taught her. Isaac yelped as his grip popped open and his knees buckled at the awkward position she'd put him in. Mr. Lynch's car door swung open, but Isaac put up his free hand to tell him to stay put.

"We were never friends." Jillian seethed between clenched teeth as she released her defensive grip and shoved him away. She pulled the SUV door open and climbed in.

"I like this new you. You've got spirit. It's hot."

With a groan at the unappreciated compliment, Jillian slammed the door shut. And locked it.

He was laughing as she started the engine. "You know where to find me if you change your mind. About anything."

Not bloody likely.

She leaned on the horn to get Lynch to move. The big black man might have saved her from some serious hurt once, had maybe even saved her life—and for that intervention she would always be grateful—but he seemed in no mood to go against his boss tonight. The time it took him to pull a cigar from his trench coat pocket and light it was the time Jillian needed to realize just how helpless she was at this moment. And just how annoyingly right Michael Cutler had been about the dangers of trespassing through No-Man's Land after dark.

Her breath caught in her throat and stuttered out on a mix of fear and adrenaline.

Locked doors couldn't keep Isaac and Lynch out if they wanted in. A bullet could pierce her windshield. They could march Troy and Dexter out here right now and threaten them, and she'd do whatever Isaac said to keep the boys safe. When she'd been high on coke or desperate for a fix, Jillian hadn't fully understood just how inescapably at the mercy of these two men she'd been.

She understood the threat now as clearly as the gun peeking from the holster inside Lynch's coat. *Get out of here!* She honked again. *Now!*

Isaac rapped on her window and grinned as she startled halfway out of her seat. "You come see me again sometime soon, babe. I'll have something real good for you, I promise. The first line will be on the house."

Then he raised his hand and signaled Lynch to move his car. The instant the Cadillac had pulled back enough for Jillian to squeeze her SUV out, she stomped on the accelerator, peeling away in a blind rush to freedom and safety, leaving Rush and Lynch and the tarnished memories from a past she couldn't quite escape behind her.

Her heart wasn't pounding so hard against her ribs that she couldn't feel the still watchful eyes glued to her every movement as she sped away.

CHAPTER THREE

"YOU DIDN'T HAVE to call me. I'm in my room. Homework's done. I'm fine."

Despite the reassurance of the actual words, Michael Cutler heard nothing but *Go away and leave me alone* in his son's voice. He tipped his cell phone up to his temple, shifted to a more comfortable position in the cab of his heavy-duty pickup truck and breathed out a steely sigh before pulling it back to his mouth and trying again. "You want me to get some food while I'm out? I can drive through and get you a couple of burgers on the way home."

"We ate dinner."

Technically, Mike, Jr., had pushed the stew around in his bowl, eaten half his grilled cheese sandwich and rolled away from the table as fast as his wheelchair would take him as soon as Michael had granted his request to be excused. "I don't mind running to—"

"Brett's waiting, Dad."

"I see." Brett was Mike's online gaming partner. They'd once been a trio of friends—before their classmate Steve had died in the crash that had shattered Mike's legs. Now the three caballeros were down to two and Michael didn't want to see his son isolate himself from any more of his former friends. "Well, tell Brett hi. You've got postapocalyptic worlds to save, I'm sure."

"I guess. Can I go now?"

"I'll be home in time to say good-night."

"Okay."

Click.

Michael downed the last dregs of his tepid coffee and crushed the paper cup in his hand. "That went well."

About as well as a standoff with a hostage-taker who refused to negotiate.

He shoved the empty cup back into the holder between the two front seats of his black pickup. Conversations like that one were a big reason he'd been sitting outside this particular brownstone for more than an hour already. This was one problem he thought he could fix. As soon as he'd clipped his phone onto his belt, Michael pushed up the sleeve of his pullover sweater and checked the time on his military-grade watch: 8:10 p.m.

"Where the hell are you?" he whispered, turning his attention from his taciturn son to the darkened windows of Jillian Masterson's apartment building. His watch had ticked away with the same ominous slowness the night Mike hadn't shown up by curfew and he'd finally gotten a call at 2:00 a.m. from a traffic cop to tell him his son was being airlifted from the scene of an accident. He wasn't jumping to any morbid conclusions yet, but he wasn't ready to dismiss his suspicions about Jillian being in some kind of trouble, either.

A quick perusal of the building's layout told him her apartment was on the front side, facing the street where he'd parked. And though several other residents of the south Kansas City neighborhood had pulled into the adjacent parking lot, unlocked the lobby's security door and lit their windows with the warm glow of activity inside, Jillian's third-floor windows remained dark, cold and empty.

Not that it was his job to watch over the leggy physical therapist's comings and goings. But with Mike shut up inside his bedroom with his headphones on and his attention glued to the epic zombie battle he and Brett were waging online, Michael had chosen to act on a concern he *could* do something about—finding out exactly what had put the fear into Jillian's green eyes when he'd found her reading that letter in her office.

Despite the promise she made that she'd do whatever was sensible to keep herself safe, Michael's gut and the excuses Jillian had come up with to dismiss her panicked reaction were giving him the same message. Something was very, very wrong in that woman's life. He'd worked too many domestic dispute calls with his team not to be suspicious about so-called loving relationships that invoked more terror than tenderness.

What she was doing for Troy Anthony was commendable and courageous, but not reporting in after a visit to a neighborhood where gangs and drugs and prostitutes often called the shots was worrisome enough. It was downright foolish if there was some kind of unwanted admirer in her life who could use the inherent dangers of Jillian's crusade against her—or who might even be a part of that world she was trying to help Troy leave behind.

She said she'd be safe at home before dark, damn it, and the sun had set an hour ago.

He needed her to help Mike unplug himself from his isolation and anger, and move on with his life. Selfish as it might be, Michael wouldn't let her efforts to help one young man jeopardize the recovery of his own son.

Squeezing the steering wheel in his fists, Michael eased out his frustration while keeping his senses focused and sharp. He'd felt these same pangs when Pam had been consumed with cancer and was dying. He'd wanted to protect her, too—wanted to do whatever it took to drive the uncertainty from her eyes and make her smile.

Maybe he couldn't fix Mike's problems, after all.

Maybe he couldn't help Jillian.

Maybe there wasn't a damn thing he could do to help any of the people who were most important in his life.

But he'd fought for Pam until the very end—until that last evening in the hospital when she'd finally told him to let her go. He'd promised his late wife that he'd fight just as hard for their son to live a long, happy life. Thus far it seemed Michael had had more failures than success. Mike had turned to the party life to cope with his grief. In his efforts to forget the pain of losing his mother, he'd lost even more—a good friend, football, the future he'd had planned.

It would take one hell of a fight to mend his son and reclaim the close-knit family they'd once had. And if Jillian Masterson was the key…

Giving up wasn't an option.

Michael scrubbed his palm over his jaw and tried to think this situation through. He liked Jillian well enough—better than a man his age probably should. No doubt there were plenty of young bucks in K.C. who'd noticed that long, sable-colored hair and those green Irish eyes, too. He was older, not dead. Jillian's endless legs, that beautiful mouth and the sharp remarks that came out of it awakened his masculine spirit in ways he thought had died two years ago with Pam. It was hard to look into her frightened expression and not want to touch her or hold her and drive away that fear.

Ultimately, however, his feelings were irrelevant. He just had to keep Jillian safe so that she, in turn, could continue to make the miracle of Mike, Jr.'s, recovery happen.

That meant thinking like a cop—like a veteran S.W.A.T. team commander. Fortunately, that was one thing Michael *could* do without any doubts.

Did he risk a call to her brother Eli—a former KCPD internal affairs officer who now ran investigations for the D.A.'s office? Did he call one of his own men, sharp-shooter Holden Kincaid, whose oldest brother, Edward, was married to Jillian's sister? In a roundabout way, he could ask if anyone had heard from her—if anyone knew of her particular plans for the evening. Did she have a meeting? A date?

"Why don't you panic the whole family and create some real chaos?" he muttered out loud. There'd be no more phone calls tonight. He knew better than that. One of the traits that made him the leader he was at KCPD was his ability to remain calm—his ability to rein in whatever he was feeling to keep his men focused and get the job done.

Michael's job tonight was simply to make sure that Jillian got home safely. Her personal life wasn't his responsibility. He just needed her in one piece and on the job Monday when he took Mike in for his therapy session. He needed Jillian to make his son smile. And laugh. And truly want to live again.

He'd ignore the stirrings in his blood teasing him that spending time with Jillian Masterson made *him* feel like living again, too.

JILLIAN STUFFED A French fry into her mouth and reached across the seat for another as she slowed her SUV and pulled into the parking lot of her building. She circled around once, looking for an empty spot, preferably one close to the door since the rest of her day had totally sucked and the idea of braving the long, lonely parking lot by herself was about as appealing as the sensation of having unseen eyes on her 24/7.

"Great," she muttered, reaching the end of the lot and circling around again. "Just great."

When she reached the entrance again, she pulled into the only empty spot she'd seen. It wasn't terribly close to the door, but at least it was close to a streetlamp and she'd have some light along most of the walk to help keep real and imagined shadows at bay. She doused the headlights, killed the engine and tried to psych herself up by telling herself that her long day—from Loverboy's letter to running into Isaac Rush after getting bawled out by Troy's grandmother, from lusting after Michael Cutler to the need for an N.A. meeting—was almost over.

The handful of fries she'd eaten since leaving the drive-through window at a fast food restaurant sat like rocks in her stomach. Still, all her training as an athlete, physical therapist and recovering addict demanded she get some kind of nourishment into her system, no matter how tired she was. So she grabbed the bag and climbed out. Greasy dinner, sleeping in a blue and pink bedroom and finally getting to a new day wasn't much, but it *was* something to look forward to.

The beep of her remote locking the car couldn't mask the slamming of a car door nearby. The instantaneous thump of her heart couldn't drown out the crunch of approaching footsteps, either.

Jillian spun around. Where was her company? Would she recognize a neighbor? Or was it *him?*

"Hey, Jilly," the male voice drawled, stopping her at the rear of her SUV. "I've been waitin' for you."

Seeing the familiar handsome face and spiked blond hair transformed her fear into irritation. "Blake. You scared the daylights out of me. What are you doing here? Didn't you get my message?"

"Didn't you get mine?" He loosened his tie and unhooked the collar of his striped shirt. "You stood me up tonight. I thought we were having drinks."

"I never said yes to a date. I never will."

"I love a woman who plays hard to get." He leaned in close, as if he intended to kiss her, and Jillian jerked away. He clamped his hand down on her wrist and she stomped on his instep. With a howl and a curse, he instantly released her. "Maybe not that hard, baby."

Another car door slammed. Could this night get any worse?

It could.

She saw the drop of dried blood at the corner of Blake's aquiline nose and realized there was a slur to his southern drawl. She shoved him away when he leaned in again. "Oh, my God, Blake—are you using?"

"Just a little. I don't know how many times I can let you break my heart without putting a stop to it. It dulls the pain."

"It dulls the brain. You're throwing your fortune away, maybe even your career. Don't blame me for your addiction. Good night."

He shifted his stance, blocking her path when she

tried to move around him. He laid his hand over his heart. "You hurt me, Jilly. Nobody's ever been able to take your place. I can get clean. I've done it before. Just give me a chance. Don't hurt me like this."

Fine. He wanted to talk pain?

"Did you send me a rose this week, Blake? Are you trying to rekindle something with me?"

"Hell, I'll buy you two whole dozen if it'll get you to come back to me."

"Did you send the flower?" She was beginning to think the answer was no, that the more expensive, dramatic gesture he'd just offered would be more his style. Still, she needed to be clear. "We are never getting together again. I told you that two Christmases ago when we tried to recapture the magic we once had."

Turned out it wasn't magic at all, but a curse. She had to have been high herself to think she'd ever been in love with a man like him.

"You need to go home, Blake, and sleep this off. In the morning, call Dr. Randolph at the Boatman Clinic. I've given you his number before. Get help. Please."

"Say you love me and I will."

MICHAEL STRETCHED HIS long legs out beneath the dashboard to control the restlessness inside him. Chances were, Jillian would show up safe and sound any minute now, and he was doing all this worrying for nothing.

Or not.

Hidden in the darkness of the truck's interior, he recognized her dark blue SUV as it zipped into the parking lot and circled around twice before she pulled into a space right next to the entrance and abruptly cut the engine and lights. In the circle of light cast by the streetlamp across from him, he could easily make out her jerky movements as she checked in every direction before grabbing a sack of takeout food from the passenger seat and locking the door behind her. Her long strides took her to the back of her SUV and she disappeared from sight.

And then he saw the blond man in the suit climb out of his Jaguar the next row over and stumble toward Jillian.

Michael's gaze narrowed. His pulse raced. "What the hell?"

He was out of his truck and dashing across the street when he heard the man shout out a curse. Michael slowed his steps, assessed the scene. Was Jillian in danger?

"Oh, my God, Blake—are you using?" Whatever was happening, Jillian seemed to be fighting the battle just fine on her own. Still, he'd seen such fear in her eyes that morning. If this was the guy responsible for putting it there...

Stepping into the grass to approach in stealth mode, Michael reached the hood of her SUV and identified each of their positions at the rear of the vehicle.

"Get help. Please."

"Say you love me and I will."

Michael circled around in time to see the blond man reach for Jillian. He snuck up behind the fool and had him in a headlock and on the ground before his fingers ever touched her.

"Michael!"

"What the hell?"

"KCPD, pal. Put your hands on your head and stay on the ground if you know what's good for you." He straightened to find Jillian staring at him, her soft mouth agape, her green eyes wide and confused. “You okay?”

“Where did you…? How did you…?” She blinked, and he read suspicion instead of gratitude there. “Are you following me?”

“This guy apparently is.” The *guy* squirmed, tried to get up. Michael put a boot squarely in his back and pushed him back down to the asphalt. He still needed an answer. “Did he hurt you?”

“No. He’s an old boyfriend. He wouldn’t…” She hugged the sack she carried up to her chest and glanced down at the man on the ground. “His name’s Blake Rivers. I just wanted him to leave me alone.”

Blake Rivers tried to turn his face up to Michael. “Who are you, old man? You can’t be her daddy, ’cause he’s dead.”

Jillian gasped. Michael knew enough of her history to know that that had been a cruel, tactless thing to say. “I’m a friend. One who’s going to do whatever the lady tells me to do. Get the hint?”

He didn’t. “Jilly and I have history.”

“History’s in the past. I’m talking about right now.” Michael pressed a little harder with his boot. “Jillian, do you want this man around?”

The sack took a beating from her wringing fingers. “Blake, I told you I can’t see you anymore. I just wanted to know if you had sent me a rose last week.”

“Baby, I told you to your face how I feel.”

“You *can’t* have me back. Ever. I don’t know how many different ways I can say it—you’re not good for me. Now go home.”

“Why? So you can bang this old fart?”

“Michael isn’t—”

"Michael can handle himself just fine." Proving he was as good as his word, Michael hauled Blake to his feet and escorted him back to his car. "The lady said goodbye. You're leaving." He stopped long enough to open the car door and look him straight in the eye. "You sober enough to drive, pal?"

Blake sputtered for a moment, blinked his vision clear and then climbed into his Jaguar and started the engine. Michael was already calling in the name, plate and location to alert traffic patrol as the car pulled out and sped away.

Hopefully, he'd get home without incident. Hopefully, Michael had done enough to keep him away from Jillian.

But if he'd been expecting gratitude, or even a friendly hello, from her, he'd been mistaken.

As he rejoined her at her SUV, he didn't bother asking if she'd been rattled by the encounter with her ex. Jillian stood tall and strong. And she was spitting mad.

"Did you follow me uptown to Troy's apartment, too?"

He pointed to his pickup across the street. "No, I've been waiting over there."

Anger twisted into confusion. "That wasn't you watching me?"

"No, that jackass in the Jaguar…" She wasn't talking about now. His gaze narrowed in on the tight lines of strain bracketing her mouth and every muscle in him tensed, instantly on guard. It wasn't anger that had her so tense. "Watching? Explain."

"Never mind, Captain." She turned away.

They were back to *Captain?*

"Jillian, did something else happen?" He reached for her arm, touched the soft fleece of her sleeve.

She whirled around and smacked his hand away. "Don't touch me!"

As instantly apologetic as she'd been quick to attack, Jillian reached out and patted his chest. She smoothed imaginary wrinkles in his sweater and blood surged to the point of contact. "I'm sorry. Long day. I..." Her gaze following her shaky fingers, she brushed her fingertips over the brass and blue enamel badge clipped to his belt. If she was worried about assaulting a police officer, or muttered one word about not respecting her elders... But she curled her fingers into her palm and the explanation died in her upturned eyes. "Thank you for coming to my rescue. Sorry I hit you."

He was a man. He was a cop. He was here. He could handle whatever she had to say. Michael softened his voice, taking the authoritative clip from his tone. "Don't apologize. Just talk to me."

"I can't." Shaking her head, she wrapped both hands around the crumpled takeout sack. "You're not here to solve my problems." A tiny frown dimpled the smooth, tanned skin of her forehead. "Why are you here, anyway? Is Mike okay?"

"Mike's fine. He's holed up in his room and won't have a civil conversation with me, but I know he's safe. You? I'm not so sure."

"Just don't give up on Mike—keep trying to connect, no matter how rude or sullen he gets. You never know when the message is going to kick in. If he keeps hearing the words and seeing the actions, he'll understand that you love him, and that he's not in his fight all alone.

Well, if you don't need anything else..." She held up the fast food sack. "Dinner's getting cold."

"Sage advice, Obi-Wan. But like I said, you're the one I'm worried about right now."

"I'm okay." With a smile he didn't buy, Jillian bade him good-night and headed down the walk toward the front door again. She was on the first step when she turned to face him. A deep, ragged breath lifted her shoulders. "Who am I kidding? Would you do me a favor? If you're not on duty—of course you're not on duty, you're not in uniform—but if you don't have to be anywhere—"

"What is it?" He was already closing the distance between them. Michael stopped on the step below her, tilting his chin ever so slightly to look up into her eyes.

"Would you..." Her fingertips danced just above his chest again, as if he needed to be soothed before she could ask him the favor. His pulse seemed to pick up the same jumpy rhythm. "Would you walk me up to my apartment, Captain? Just make sure it's clear to go inside. I've had some weird things happen lately, and I'm getting a little paranoid."

More weird than that letter? "What did Blake Rivers say to you?"

"You know I used to be like him. I suppose now I'm just sober enough to know that something isn't right."

He knew she didn't talk about her past life much, but she'd shared enough. He'd have done his homework on the woman responsible for his son's recovery, anyway. And besides, Mike's response to her was so strong, it didn't make a difference. "You don't deserve this harassment. You beat your addiction, Jillian. You made something of your life."

"Not enough, it seems." Or else she wouldn't have some creep making her startle at a man's unexpected touch? "You sure you still want to help me?"

Michael simply nodded, stepping up behind her to shield her from unseen eyes she thought were *watching* as she unlocked the door and led him inside. When she hesitated at the open elevator doors, Michael touched the small of her back and guided her inside. When the doors closed behind them and she didn't move away, he let his fingers slide beneath her jacket to rest just above her belt in an even more protective gesture. The sinuous curve of her hip beneath her knit top told him she was as firm and fit as she looked.

But the pulsing heat that warmed his fingers even at that innocent contact warned him that his interest in helping Jillian might not be as paternal and altruistic as he might have thought. He quickly drew his hand away as if he'd crossed a forbidden line of friendship and tucked his errant fingers into the front pockets of his jeans.

She'd asked the KCPD *captain* to escort her upstairs, not the red-blooded forty-four-year-old who couldn't seem to keep his hormones in check tonight.

He peered down the third-floor hallway before he let her exit the elevator. Clear. The muffled sounds of television shows and lively conversations filtered through his ears as they passed by her neighbors. Nothing unusual there. Once they reached Jillian's door, Michael put a hand on her shoulder to hold her back so he could enter her apartment first.

"No sign of forced entry," he stated as she pulled out her key. Still… Michael pressed Jillian back against the wall beside the door frame and looked her straight in the eye. “Stay put. I don’t want to mistake your movement for something or someone else.”

Jillian looked straight back and nodded.

Unhooking the cover on the holster at his waist, Michael rested his hand on the butt of his Glock and crossed the tiny dining area to see what was on the other side of the counter that divided the open kitchen area. A few dirty dishes in the sink, a wireless phone on the wall with a blinking red light indicating four messages. But nothing seemed out of place. He checked the window that opened onto the fire escape off the kitchen. New lock. State-of-the-art. “Have you had a recent break-in?” he questioned.

“No. I asked Eli to replace the old lock for me. The metal had rusted.”

Beefing up the locks—evidence of a woman who lived alone in the city showing common sense? Or did Jillian have a more specific reason for not feeling secure in her own home? How many *love* letters did a woman have to receive before she felt compelled to change the locks and have a cop walk through her place?

Scanning quickly and thoroughly from left to right, he moved through each of the remaining rooms. Living room clear. Bathroom clear. Her bedroom was a little messy—the smell of fresh paint tinged the air, and the bed was still rumpled from where she’d lain among the sheets and quilt. The window, inaccessible from outside without a fire engine ladder or rappelling rope, was cracked open to help disperse the paint fumes, but the room and closets were clear.

“I don’t see anything out of place.” Michael secured his gun and came back into the living room.

“Thank you.” Jillian’s shoulders sagged with genuine relief before a bolt of internal energy fired through her. She opened the door and flashed him a smile that surely meant goodbye. "You won't tell Eli or my sister that I'm losing it, will you? They worry enough about me living on my own. Now I can tell them that the finest of Kansas City's finest said there was nothing to worry about."

That wasn't what he'd said, and Michael wasn't ready to be dismissed just yet. He braced his hands on his hips and stood his ground. "Does this paranoia of yours have anything to do with that love letter you threw away this afternoon?"

Boom. Smile gone. The door drifted shut as she stormed across the apartment to meet him in the kitchen. "You went through my trash?"

Michael shrugged off the accusation. "Didn't need a warrant to do it. Something was…*is* clearly bugging you. And don't tell me it's my imagination. I know what brave people who are trying to hide how scared they are look like. Is it an abusive boyfriend? That Rivers guy who won't take no for an answer?"

She tossed the sack onto the counter and planted herself in front of him, matching his stance and nearly matching his height. "One, I don't have a boyfriend, and two, what business is it of yours who follows me or sends me things I don't want?"

Whoa. "You were followed tonight? I told you to drive straight to a police station—"

"You're twisting my words around—"

"*You're* the one who asked me to check out your apartment." One beat of silence passed. Then another. Michael's burst of temper squeezed into something much more controlled, much more concise. "You're being stalked, aren't you?"

The flush of defensive anger drained from her face, leaving Jillian's smooth skin an alarming shade of pale. *Swift negotiating tactic, Cutler.*

When her gaze dropped to the middle of his chest and her head bobbed with a reluctant nod, it wasn't victory at finally getting a straight answer he was feeling. The nagging burn in his gut that had told him something was wrong wasn't eased one bit by the truth.

"Jillian..." Michael reached out to brush aside the strand of hair that had fallen across her cheek. He gently tucked it behind her ear, then cupped his hand against her jaw. The cool velvet of her skin, the warm beat of her pulse throbbing beneath his fingertips—*they* eased the guilt and worry in his gut. He tipped her face back up to his and drifted half a step closer. "You jump every time I enter the room, and you go on the attack every time I even suggest that you might be in danger. Sure signs you're hiding something. This isn't something you can fight on your own. You shouldn't have to."

Her nostrils flared as she took a deep breath. Her eyes locked on to his. Her hands curled into tight fists and rested against him. "I don't know what to do. I don't know how to make it stop."

Michael stroked the side of her neck, dipping his fingertips into the coffee silk of her hair. Her pulse was quick but steady. "Have you reported him to the police?"

She tapped at his chest. "And tell them what? He hasn't threatened me in any way. He just...*loves* me."

"Does it feel like love?"

Her answer was to walk straight into his chest. She clutched a fistful of the sweater she'd smoothed so meticulously earlier, and buried her face at the juncture of his neck and shoulder. She was shaking.

Michael was much more than a cop standing there in Jillian's kitchen as he wrapped his arms around her and hugged her tight against his body, trading solace for the tactile reassurance of her warmth and trust. He turned his mouth to the delicate shell of her ear. "Now tell me who this bastard is—and why he's got you so spooked."

CHAPTER FOUR

JILLIAN BURROWED INTO Michael's unyielding strength, drawing in deep breaths of the clean, musky scent that clung to his skin and the white T-shirt that peeked out above the neckline of his sweater. The overwhelming onslaught of frustration and helplessness, loosed by Michael's unexpected tenderness, calmed as the strong, steady rhythm of his heart drummed beneath her hand.

His fingers tunneled beneath her ponytail, gently massaging the tension at her nape. He slipped his arm beneath her jacket to catch her more closely around the waist, creating an intimate rustle of denim against khaki as his sturdy thighs rubbed against hers. The hardness of his gun and badge poked into her belly, but she had no desire to adjust her stance for fear the slightest movement would end the embrace.

"Have you reported this?" he whispered against her hair.

"No." She didn't want to talk. She simply wanted to breathe easy for a few moments while his strong arms and soft, deep voice shut out the chaotic events and irrational fears of the past few weeks. She just wanted to feel…safe.

And for the first time in weeks, she did.

But Michael Cutler had KCPD running through his blood, and the respite couldn't last. He wanted answers and demanded action. Tucking a finger beneath her chin, he nudged her face up to meet his probing gaze. "Your brother is married to the commissioner. Your sister is married to a homicide detective. Have you told any of them what's going on?"

Reluctantly, Jillian pushed away and hugged her arms in front of her, trying to hold on to some of his warmth. "You want me to embarrass all of them by sounding like a whack job?"

"Besides the fact that they're family and I know they care about your well-being—what if this creep has something to do with their position in the department, or a case one of them has worked on? It wouldn't be the first time a criminal has targeted a family member out of retribution. You know you should report a stalker. They'd want to know that."

Jillian shrugged, knowing just how foolish she'd sound if her story made it onto a police blotter. *Former juvenile delinquent who nearly ruined her family eleven years ago is at it again. Can't the commissioner's husband and KCPD's assistant medical examiner keep their little sister out of trouble?* "There haven't been any threats. Certainly nothing specific against my family. All I have are a handful of letters and a dead rose—"

"And the feeling that someone's following you."

"And what do I say? Hey, Eli and Holly—this guy says he loves me." Jillian picked up her cold sack of dinner and tossed it into the trash beneath the sink. What little appetite she'd had was long gone. "He might need to have his head examined, but you can't arrest a man for that."

She was beginning to wonder if the connection she'd felt with Michael—the shared heat, the need, the attraction that was growing more difficult to ignore by the minute—had all been the ruse of a skilled S.W.A.T. negotiator, to get her to drop her guard and lure her into talking. Because he was keeping his distance and the questions kept coming. "You don't know who sent that letter today?"

"I don't know who sent any of them."

"Plural?"

Why not? Whatever his reasons might be, Michael Cutler wanted to hear her story. And she'd reached the point where she needed to tell it.

"Here." Jillian crossed into the living room and pulled out a manila envelope from the desk behind the sofa. As he'd followed her, she only had to turn around to hand him the package. "There are eight of them. They started coming about a month ago. Kansas City postmark, no return address, no name. I don't know what they'll prove, but when you've grown up around cops—"

"You hold on to potential evidence." He unhooked the flap and used the hem of his sweater sleeve to pull the first one out. "Self-gummed envelopes and stamps, so no DNA. No handwriting to trace. Probably no fingerprints, either, if he's being that careful, but I'll pull in a favor at the lab and ask them to run these for trace, anyway." His stern expression never wavered as he skimmed through the contents of each message. "Anything about the wording sound like someone you know?"

"Not really. He keeps everything pretty generic." Just personal enough to send a chill down her spine. Jillian stuck her hands into the pockets of her sweatshirt jacket and wondered if she was ever going to feel warm on her own again. “Compliments. Poetry. Promises. I call him Loverboy, but trust me, it’s not an endearing nickname. I needed something tangible where I could focus my…” Fear? Loathing? Terror? Jillian shrugged. “If I knew the guy, I might think the messages were dorky, but flattering.”

“Like a kid with a crush?”

“Like a sicko with a grand, idealized notion of what I’m looking for in a relationship.”

“He’s put you on a pedestal.” Michael tucked the letters carefully back into the envelope. “I’m guessing it’s someone you know, even peripherally, someone from your present or past. You’ve smiled at him or spoken to him or done something for him that he interprets as you having feelings for him.”

“Believe me, I don’t.” Jillian paced back into the kitchen and filled the kettle on the stove to fix some hot tea. There had to be a way to shake the chill that filled every pore.

Michael followed. “I’ve answered more calls than I’d care to count because a man doesn’t have a good grasp on what the reality of loving a woman is.”

She froze with the box of tea bags in her hands. “Calls? As in S.W.A.T. team calls? You think it could escalate into something that serious?”

“I’m not willing to treat this as a joke. And even if you think this could be a harmless prank that would end up embarrassing your family, my years of experience tell me to consider this guy a serious threat until he proves otherwise.”

Jillian turned off the stove and sank into one of the chairs at her kitchen table. Hot tea wasn’t going to help. “Now you’re really scaring me. What if he tries something when I'm with a patient? Or he hurts someone here in my apartment building?"

"Look, I hope I'm wrong, but in my job you're better prepared if you understand the worst that could happen. I just want you to see this in a sensible way, and take the precautions necessary to keep yourself safe. Telling me is the first step." He laid the envelope on the table and pulled out the chair beside her. When he rested his calloused fingers over hers, Jillian turned her hand and latched on to the comfort he provided. "Things could be escalating already. First, he's merely sending you notes. Now he's watching you—getting closer to actually interacting with you? What made you think he followed you tonight?"

"A movement out of the corner of my eye or a scent or I don't know what made me think I had somebody's attention when I was in Troy's neighborhood." Isaac Rush and his lieutenant, Mr. Lynch, might have topped the list as an in-her-face danger, but Isaac was hardly the love letter type—not when he could use bribery or blackmail or brute force to get what he wanted from a woman. No, this had been something more secret—more sinister—because it lived in the shadows. "I… ran across some people I knew…when I was younger."

"What people?"

My former supplier and the enforcer who saved me from being raped by said dealer one night.

Jillian's fingers twitched with the self-conscious shame she still carried with her. Michael Cutler didn't know what she'd done as a teen, who she'd been. Since she'd been a juvenile at the time, her court appearances as both the accused and accuser had been sealed. Her journey back to sobriety was her business—news that she'd once been a coke addict would probably end this conversation and his concern right now—and jeopardize Michael's willingness to let her work with his son. She chose her words carefully. "Blake is an old boyfriend, who got me into the party scene when I was in high school. I rebelled big time after my parents died. Some of those parties ended up in No-Man's Land."

She sought out his dark blue eyes, wondering if he could piece together the truth, wondering if she'd see judgment there. Nothing. No pity, no condemnation—no understanding or forgiveness, either. Just a cop with an unreadable expression.

Her fingers twitched inside his grasp. "That was my old life, Cap…Michael. I swear I'm not that person I was in high school anymore."

"Maybe this guy doesn't know that. Can you get me a list of all the men you've ever dated? Starting with those party boys in high school?" He squeezed her hand before releasing her and pulling out his wallet. When he pushed to his feet and handed her his KCPD business card, Jillian wondered if this was his answer to her vague confession. He wasn't the kind of man to be attracted to a rebellious wild child. But he would be kind and professional to anyone who needed his help—even a handful of past and potential trouble like her. "Call me if you think of anything else, or you feel like you're being followed again, whatever—day or night, you call. If anything else happens, we're making an official report. I'm not afraid to look like a fool if it turns out to be nothing."

Yeah, but he had a stellar reputation to back him up. No one would dare question Michael Cutler's sensibility or fire up the rumor mill about a past life coming back to give him just what he deserved.

With his card in hand, Jillian followed him to the door. She hated to see him go, but had no grounds to ask him to stay. "I only wanted you to check my apartment for goblins and perverts. I wasn't asking you to launch a full-blown investigation."

Michael paused in the open doorway and turned. "I only wanted you to help my son walk again. I didn't realize I'd be asking you to heal his spirit as well. It's the most important job in the world right now, as far as I'm concerned. If I can help my go-to woman get the job done with Mike, then I intend to."

Go-to woman. She liked that. She wasn't about to let him down. "I don't mind. Mike's a cool kid."

"That he is." His gaze skimmed over her lips, and Jillian felt the brief but focused interest as intimately as a caress. "I like it when you smile. I like it a hell of a lot better than..." He blinked, and when he opened his eyes, his attention had shifted and the heat had vanished. "I don't want you distracted by this guy, Jillian. And I sure as hell don't want you hurt. Mike lost his mom, lost a friend—nearly lost his own life—in a span of two years. I don't think he could handle another blow like losing you right now."

With that charge reminding her that Jillian's mission was to help the son and not lust after the father, she pulled her shoulders back and reassured him—reassured herself. "This guy will lose interest, and it will all blow over soon, I'm sure. Mike won't have to worry about anything. I'll be there for him."

"And I'll be here for you." He held up the manila envelope, firmly dismissing any lingering misconception that some sort of personal bond between them had been acknowledged and awakened tonight. "I'll call you if I find out anything about Loverboy."

"Good night, Michael. And thanks."

After she locked the door and hooked the security chain, Jillian headed back to the kitchen. Her stomach growled in protest at being forgotten since her lunch break at noon, but she was so drained by the assault on her emotions tonight that she lacked the energy to do more than grab a slice of cheese and a bottle of water from the fridge. Once the provolone had been gobbled down, she pressed the button on the answering machine and let the messages play while she peeled off her jacket, untucked her top and made her way back to her bedroom.

She shook her head as Dylan Smith's voice gasped about failing the hot pepper test, and took note of her brother, Eli, informing her that he'd be out of town for a few days while he traveled to Illinois to interview a prisoner for one of the D.A.'s cases. Yes, she had his cell number. Yes, she had Holly and Edward's number if she needed something while he was away. She cringed as Blake Rivers invited her to meet him for drinks at nine to discuss why she didn't want to see him anymore, and smiled as Dr. Randolph called to see if everything was all right. No doubt he'd gotten word that she'd stopped off at the clinic to attend a Narcotics Anonymous meeting this evening. After the unsettling letters and a run-in with Rush and Lynch, she'd needed a dose of support and a reminder that she had the power to cope with the stress in her life.

She turned on the light, tossed her jacket onto the bed and froze.

"Michael?" She mouthed the word like a prayer.

She was surrounded by cool, icy blue. There was no hot-pink wall left for her to finish this weekend. Every wall had been freshly painted, neatly trimmed. But not by her.

"Michael?" Sense. Security.

Fear tried to jump-start her feet into backing out of the room, but her eyes were drawn with morbid fascination to the mussed-up bed and dented pillow. The same bed she meticulously made every morning of her life, the way she'd been trained to do in rehab.

Her water bottle bounced across the carpet. "Michael!"

Jillian ran through her apartment, unlocked the door, cursed the chain that refused to cooperate with her jerky fingers. "Michael!" she screamed.

Once she slid the chain out of its slot, she threw open the door and sprinted down the hallway.

"Michael! Michael!"

"Jillian?" Michael's voice boomed from the stairwell. Footsteps pounded each step. "Jillian!"

"Michael!"

Seconds later he materialized at the end of the hall. Tall. He took the last flight of stairs in three strides. Dark. The expression on his face meant serious business. Dangerous. Gun drawn, charging straight ahead.

Jillian flew into his arms and clung tight around his neck. "He was in my apartment. He was in my bed."

"YOU'RE CERTAIN IT was the same guy who did this?" Detective Edward Kincaid scribbled a detail on his notepad. The paint roller was conveniently missing and the paint can in her closet had been pristinely cleaned.

Jillian hugged her arms hard around her waist, still feeling a creepy sense of violation just standing in the doorway to her bedroom. “Unless you or Eli came in and worked, and then lay down on my bed for a nap, I’m sure there’s no one else who would have painted this today.”

“Easy, kiddo. I’m pretty sure my partner will alibi me for today.” He braced his hand on his knee and pushed to his feet.

“You know I wasn’t accusing you.”

“I know.” Jillian’s brother-in-law was a big, scarred-up man, a little on the quiet side unless he had something important to say—and he took very seriously his role as stand-in big brother while Eli was out of town.

After pocketing his notepad and pen, he turned Jillian away from her bedroom and, limping ever so slightly beside her on his rebuilt knee, walked her back into the living room. “So what do I tell Holly about this Cutler guy?”

“I thought you were here to take my statement.”

He scrubbed a hand over his scarred chin and jaw while she took a seat on the sofa. “Not grill you on your personal life?”

Jillian’s gaze darted over to Michael, speaking in a hushed, articulate tone on his cell in her kitchen. He was probably on the phone to Mike, Jr., explaining why he was so late coming home. “Captain Cutler isn’t part of my personal life. I work with his son at the clinic.”

The cushion beside her sank as it took Edward’s weight. “Uh-huh.” He closed his hand over both of hers where they rested in her lap. “And that’s why you were holding on to him so hard when I showed up. Cutler’s lucky he's got any hands left the way you were wringing on his."

"Edward."

"Look, you know I've got your best interests at heart. Holly's going to freak when I tell her you had a break-in at your place. Imagine what she'll do when she finds out there's a new boyfriend in the picture, too."

"He's not a boy."

"Interesting distinction to make." He waved aside any attempt to reword her protest. "Kiddo, you've got the oldest soul of anybody I know—except me, maybe. And we all know what a jackass your last date, Blake Rivers, turned out to be. I get why you'd be drawn to a mature man like Cutler."

"You make him sound like he's over-the-hill." Despite the shards of silver in his hair, she knew from very personal contact that Michael Cutler was fit and firm and strong in every way a man should be. With his badge out to warn curious neighbors back into their apartments, he'd carried her all the way down the hallway to her apartment with one arm around her waist. And he hadn't let go until she'd buzzed Edward into the building forty-five minutes ago. "He's not."

Edward squeezed her hands. "Hey, I'm not judging your taste in men. Your sister fell for a beat-up piece of work like me, and I thank God every day she did. I just don't want to see you have any more hurt in your life."

"Holly fell for you because you were there for her when she needed a hero. Michael's just a friend who wants me to help his son. I've got a stupid crush on him, that's all."

"Whatever you say." Edward leaned in and teased,

"He breaks your heart, I break his legs. Even if he does outrank me."

"Edward!" Jillian smacked his shoulder with a sisterly jab and laughed.

"I haven't heard that sound for a while." Michael flipped his phone shut as he joined them. Good grief! Jillian's cheeks burned at the idea he might have overheard exactly what they'd been discussing. But if he had, he politely overlooked her misguided feelings and stuck to cop speak with Edward. "Investigating's not my specialty, but I do know a thing or two about surveillance and protection. I called in some members of my team who'll take shifts to keep an eye on the apartment building so we can start documenting who comes and goes, maybe have a chat with anyone who doesn't belong. I'll see if I can arrange regular drive-bys at the physical therapy clinic next week, too."

"I'll get the ball rolling from my end, then—get the history we have so far documented in the system. At the very least we've got a crackpot with no respect for personal space, and at the worst..."

He didn't need to finish that sentence. Jillian knew her brother-in-law had seen the worst life had to offer. She knew her sister's love had brought him back from the brink of losing himself to an addiction the same way she had. He squeezed her shoulder before standing. "The first order of business is changing your locks. There are no signs of forced entry, so that means somebody has a key."

"But Holly and Eli are the only ones I gave a key to."

Michael splayed his fingers at his hips, his gun and badge and guarded stance reflecting something more than the warrior-like persona she was used to seeing in the other men in her life. "It's easy enough to make a copy if someone can get his hands on the key."

That something extra was an air of command that even big, bad Edward deferred to. "The building super will be my first stop on the way out." He glanced down at Jillian. "Who else might have access to your keys?"

It was rare for Jillian to feel short and small, but being flanked by the twin towers of testosterone was a little disquieting. So she asserted her own strength and stood. "I wear them on my wrist at work, or since I don't usually carry a purse, I stuff them in my pocket. I think they're still in my jacket."

"Get them so I can have the lab check for tool marks or any other signs of tampering—and pack a bag with whatever else you might need. You can stay out at our place tonight. I'll make sure the lock gets rekeyed first thing tomorrow morning." He flicked a glance over to Michael, then came back to read her face as well. "If you haven't already made other plans?"

Michael's dark blue eyes were already locked on to hers when she lifted her gaze to his. That look made her feel important, protected. *He* made her feel safe. Not new locks. Not the entire force at KCPD seemingly now at her disposal with these two cops reporting the break-in. A ridiculously idealistic thought crossed her mind. Wrapped up in Michael's arms, breathing in the scent and strength that was uniquely his—*that's* where she felt safe. For a woman who had guarded her heart and denied the impulses of her own feminine needs for so long, the urge to reach out to Michael and get closer to him in whatever way she could was suddenly so potent within her that her fingers drummed nervously together and she had to shove her hands into her pockets to keep them at her side.

Michael had a teenage son at home that he wouldn't want to endanger. Besides, they were friends. *Just friends.* She couldn't ask him to do any more for her than he already had. She blinked, and the needy spell was broken. "No, I haven't made plans."

Michael's eyes shuttered and he circled around her to shake Edward's hand. "You'll get those letters to the lab?"

Edward nodded. "I'm glad you were here, Captain. If that bastard had still been in here when she got home…"

"I'd have taken him out," Michael stated matter-of-factly, releasing his hand. "You keep her safe."

"Yes, sir."

Michael had his hand on the doorknob when he stopped, turned and strode back across the room. Edward must have discreetly stepped aside, because suddenly Michael Cutler was in Jillian's space, his dark eyes narrowed as he skimmed every nuance of her startled, hopeful expression. With just his fingertips, he brushed her hair off her face and tucked it behind her ear. Leaving his fingers tangled in her hair, he shaped his hand to cup her jaw. And then he leaned in, his lips aiming for her cheek, but hovering just short of making contact.

Jillian held her breath as his chest expanded and contracted with a weary sigh that tickled across her skin. With the subtle pressure of his fingers, he angled her face, lowered his head and covered her mouth with his own.

The kiss was hard, unapologetic, and achingly abrupt with everything she sensed he was holding back. Jillian's blood heated in an instant response and her lips softened, parted, wanted. She leaned in.

But the kiss was over and Michael was leaving before she'd barely braced her hand against his chest.

He pulled away, walked away, opened the door. "I'll see you Monday at the clinic."

Her brother-in-law's voice startled her from her prolonged stare at the door Michael had closed behind him. "You sure what you're feeling is one-sided?"

Jillian was no longer sure of anything tonight. "I'll go pack my bag."

THE ELEVATOR BUTTON DINGED.

Ignoring her broken moans the way he'd ignored her wasted pleas, he pulled the old woman out of the shadows and dragged her onto the elevator. He pressed the number 5 button, then stepped over her and walked out of the building into the night. The unscrewed bulb over the super's door had never once given him away.

After climbing into his vehicle, he pulled out a handkerchief, wiped the blood off the brass knuckles he wore and stuffed them both back into his coat pocket. Once he was out of the neighborhood, he peeled off his gloves and tossed them into the first trash can he drove past.

His message had been clear. The old woman would never make *that* mistake again. Jillian would be safe.

He pulled down the visor above the steering wheel and smiled at the picture there. Pressing a kiss to his fingers, he reached up to stroke her dark brown hair.

"I love you, Jilly."

In every way that mattered, he would always take care of her.

CHAPTER FIVE

THE WEEKEND PASSED and Monday morning dawned without further incident. No letters, no break-ins, no kissing, no Michael. Jillian wouldn't have thought the KCPD commander to be the impulsive type, but how else could she explain that kiss?

It hadn't been any paternal peck on the cheek or kind reassurance. It hadn't been a clumsy, inexperienced attempt to show off who the big man was in the room, either.

Michael's kiss had felt passionate, like a man staking his claim. Like a man hungry for something he couldn't quite put into words. His kiss had slipped past barriers and cracked open the door on something unnamed and unspoken deep inside Jillian, too.

But they were *just friends*.

Her mission was to help Mike, Jr., heal—not help herself to Mike's father. She'd done too many selfish, hurtful things back when she'd been using, and there was a lifelong penance to pay because of it. Mike Cutler, Jr., needed her, and that's where her thoughts should be focused. Michael, Sr., was everything she hadn't fully realized she wanted in a man until now. But he was off-limits.

That kiss had been a onetime thing—an aberration her bruised heart couldn't afford to repeat.

She spent the weekend building up her confidence again and locking her protective emotional armor back into place. She let Holly pamper her with hot chocolate and late night sister-to-sister talks about everything important and nothing in particular at their rustic country home on the outskirts of Kansas City. With Edward watching over her shoulder, Jillian herself had supervised the installation of a new door lock and dead bolt for her apartment. She answered Eli's worried phone call and assured him that there was no need to cut his trip short and have the D.A. send a replacement to conduct the prisoner interview.

She didn't want her family worrying over her and curtailing their own lives the way they had when she'd been using and on and off the streets. She was an adult now. She carried a ten-year sobriety pin on her key chain. She had a master's degree and a professional career. Edward and KCPD had an investigation into the letters and break-in well under way. And she was getting to know the members of KCPD's S.W.A.T. Team 1—Michael's team—by name.

Holden Kincaid.

Rafe Delgado.

Trip Jones.

Alex Taylor.

They introduced themselves when they parked outside her building; she brought them coffee. There couldn't be a better guarded woman in all of Kansas City. Loverboy didn't stand a chance.

So why had it been impossible to sleep in her own bed last night and spend any more time than was absolutely necessary at her apartment this morning?

Jillian pressed her fingers to her neck and marked

off her pulse against her watch as she started her last lap around the hospital complex. She'd gotten in early enough before the PT clinic opened to put in two miles before hitting the showers and getting ready for her first patient. What she couldn't forget about the weekend she hoped she could beat back into the recesses of her mind with a good, hard workout.

She waved to Alex Taylor, a young Latino cop who was the newest and youngest member of Michael's team. Poor guy. Low man on the totem pole got stuck with dawn patrol. He sat in the hospital parking lot in his beat-up Jeep, drinking a super-size cup of coffee and wolfing down some sort of breakfast wrap. He gave her a salute and a smile and was unwrapping a second breakfast item by the time she'd rounded the corner of the building beyond the parking lot.

Jillian was running along the exercise pathway lined with elm trees, just beginning to bud out with their leaves, when she saw that she'd have company on the last leg of her run. "Hey, Smith! So how did those hot peppers work out for you Friday?" she teased, pulling up beside her coworker and matching his pace. "Did you make the bet?"

"Morning, Masterson." Uh-oh. That didn't sound too positive.

Dylan's blond curls were sticking to the perspiration dotting his forehead and temple, indicating he, too, had been running for some time. Their positions on the exercise path must have been staggered just right for her not to notice him until now. "So, are you slowing down or am I catching up?" she asked between breaths.

"It has to be me," he drawled. "I'm still hurtin' from Friday. I did great on the first five habaneros. With my glass of milk, I thought I was going to get through all twelve. Then I sprouted a fever. My eyes watered. My toenails were sweating. By the eighth one, I was done." He buzzed his lips with a cranky sigh. "They've been burning through me ever since."

Jillian couldn't stop the grin that split her face. "I knew that was a sucker's bet."

"Hey, no laughing," Dylan whined.

"Did you get your date with Miss Hottie in Occupational Therapy?"

"Yeah, but I had to put it off until next weekend, I felt so crummy. How about you? Did you get your paint job done?"

Smile gone. Laughter forgotten. Jillian pretended the uncharacteristic hitch in her step was due to uneven pavement rather than any creepy memory of a stranger violating her apartment. Ignoring Dylan's question, she kicked her stride into a higher gear and challenged him to beat her to the finish line. "We'd better get those peppers out of your system and get you back in shape if you've got a date. Last one to the clinic cleans the stinky towels out of the locker room."

"You wish!"

She barely beat Dylan around the hospital grounds. She couldn't run fast enough to outpace her own fears.

"That's not good." Jillian slowed her steps to a jog when she spotted Alex Taylor on his cell phone, pacing outside the PT Clinic's glass doors.

"What's the scoop, Masterson?" She'd been running so hard, trying to blank out her thoughts, that she'd almost forgotten Dylan Smith had been running the path behind her. She felt his fingers sliding down the length of her ponytail until he caught a handful of her shirt and pulled her back to a cautious pace beside him. "Is he wearing a gun?"

"He's a cop." A twinge caught in Jillian's side as she abruptly stopped and sucked in deep gasps of air to catch her breath. "Officer Taylor?"

Alex cut his phone call short and moved toward her, his dark eyes fixed with a menacing light on the blond man running up behind her. "Everything cool here, ma'am?"

Did he think Dylan had been chasing her? Jillian pinched one hand at her side and held up the other to warn him off. "Friendly race, Officer," she assured him between breaths. "Dylan Smith. He works with me."

"We got a call from Dispatch, ma'am. I've got to suit up and run." Alex Taylor was barely her height and no older than she was. Still, he conveyed a pointed look over her shoulder, silently warning Dylan that everything had better be friendly between them. "But I want to make sure everything is all right before I go."

"A call?" As in something that required guns and body armor and outthinking bad guys who didn't want to surrender? "With Captain Cutler?"

"Yes, ma'am. He'll run the team and coordinate with Bomb Squad on this."

Bomb squad? Oh, Lordy. *That* little stitch in her side had nothing to do with her vigorous run. She understood cops, understood the danger they had to face—but this morning, the true meaning of that danger hit her square in the gut. Men like Michael Cutler, like her brother, like Alex Taylor, were true warriors. They had bigger enemies to take on than her overattentive fan. The men and women of KCPD were well trained for situations just like this. Michael didn't need to be distracted by her problems. He needed to focus on the job he had to do, and gather his team around him. Now.

Feeling as if she'd already wasted too much of Alex's precious time, she waved him away toward his Jeep. "I'm fine. Go."

"I'm sure the captain will have one of us back at your place tonight." Alex was already backing toward his car. "Just use your common sense. Try to stay with people you know. Call if you need anything."

"I will. Don't worry about me." She was a little rattled, a little winded, but more than determined to send him on his way. "Now go. Save the day. Kansas City needs you."

And watch Michael's back.

Once Alex sped away in his Jeep, Dylan laid his hand on Jillian's shoulder. "Did he say *bomb?* Why are you talking to a cop? Are you okay, Jilly? Are *we?*"

She straightened at Dylan's frantic tone. "It's nothing here. Don't worry. He's, um…doing some security work for the father of one of my patients." *Smooth way to skew the truth, girl.* She pulled her keys from the pocket of her shorts and unlocked the door ahead of Dylan. She was ready to end this conversation and get going on something useful that wouldn't give her time to worry about the dangers of Michael's job and would prove to him that she wasn't a distraction *he* needed to worry about.

Loverboy had already created enough havoc in her life. She didn't need to complicate it any further by adding her own misguided feelings about Michael Cutler into the mix.

"I've got my first patient in twenty minutes. I need to hit the showers. Stinky towels are on you, Smith."

"MIKE?" JILLIAN HALTED in the PT Clinic lobby after taking her last patient back to her room in the geriatric wing of the main hospital. Lulu had company at the front desk. "What are you doing here? I wasn't expecting you until three o'clock."

After back-to-back sessions all morning, her stomach had been set on a sandwich from the cafeteria, her mind set on catching up on some paperwork. A blue-eyed teenager with doom and gloom stamped all over his downturned features hadn't been part of the plan.

"There's no school."

Spring break, right. Most kids would be celebrating.

"And you're so bored out of your mind that you came to see me?"

That taunt earned an eye roll. Good. At least now he was looking at her as she walked up to his chair to continue the conversation. "Did your friend Brett drop you off?"

"No. He's on the school trip to D.C."

For one fleeting moment, Jillian scanned the lobby and even peeked through the glass doors into the parking lot out front to see if she could get a glimpse of his father. But there was no tall, dark man in uniform, no familiar black pickup parked outside.

Mike must have sensed where her thoughts had turned. "Dad's at work. His team got called in early this morning."

"So I heard."

"Some guy's trying to rob a bank." Was Mike worried about his dad? His blasé tone said no. But then stoicism seemed to be a family trait, and Mike, Jr., was a hard son of a gun to read at the best of times. She understood how time alone at home could give a body more time to think about things he or she didn't want to think about. Maybe he was worried, and showing up for his appointment two and a half hours early was his way of showing it. Wasn't being trapped with her thoughts and fears the reason she'd gotten up at 5:00 a.m. to go running?

"Any word on what's happening?" *Whether or not anyone's been hurt?* A knot of dread soured the idea of lunch in her stomach.

"There hasn't been anything on the TV yet," Mike answered. "That's usually a good sign."

"TV is your barometer to tell how well the police are doing?"

"Hey, if Dad's not on a special news bulletin, then that means he's got it all under control."

If that wasn't the answer a cop's son would give, she didn't know what was. For both their sakes, Jillian had to laugh. And change the subject to one that wasn't quite so disquieting. "So, how did you get here? You didn't drive, did you? You know you're not allowed to do that with those braces, right?"

"If Troy can figure out the bus, so can I. I didn't know I'd get here so freaking early. You're not going to send me home and make me come back again, are you?"

Instead of teasing him about miscalculating time or the efficiency of Kansas City's public transit system, she complimented his resourcefulness. "Sounds to me like you're getting around a lot more independently than you give yourself credit for."

"Can't we just do the session now?"

"Well, you're welcome to come hang out with me anytime." A sudden inspiration twisted her thoughts into something a little more devilish. "But I've got work to do. If you're going to be here, then I'm going to put you to work, too."

"Work?" He smacked at the velcro brace on his thigh. "What can I do?"

"You'd be surprised, big guy. Come on." She unhooked the brakes on his wheelchair and turned him toward the hallway leading to the gym, workout rooms and their offices. "First things, first, though. Have you had lunch? That's where I was headed. I'll even show you the shortcut I use to get from the PT wing to the main building."

"I'm not hungry."

"I thought guys your age ate 24/7. Unless you're sleeping, of course." She nudged him a step closer into polite sociability. "My treat."

"Just a couple of cheeseburgers, I guess. I suppose eating will kill a little time."

"You sweet talker you. Is that how you charm all your dates?"

"Date? Jeez, Jillian, you're old enough to be, well, not my date. I came for a stupid PT session, that's all."

Over the hill at twenty-eight, hmm? But Jillian took no offense. Mike's blushing cheekbones indicated a healthy burst of circulation, and sitting up straighter in his chair meant he was tightening those core muscles. Jillian smiled behind his coal-black head. Score one for the PT today.

She bypassed the gym entrance and pushed Mike around the corner toward the recreation lounge, chatting away as they passed the windows and locked door of her office. "There are all kinds of hidden corridors in this complex. In some places, they built a new addition adjacent to an older part of the building, leaving these open passageways between them. Did you bring your cane?"

"I forgot." Probably on purpose. As if she'd let him sit on his duff for an entire afternoon, cane or not.

"Then I guess we're limited to wherever the chair can go. But there is this one cool place off the lounge where, if you were mobile on two feet, you could walk through without anyone knowing you're even there. It opens up in the back of the storage closet next to the pop machine and leads straight to the equipment closet off the gym. Of course, you have to have keys to get into the closets in the first place, but it's cool if I get really thirsty to just buzz from closet to closet, get a soda and sneak back in without anyone ever knowing I left."

Mike seemed intrigued by the possibilities. He pointed to the storage closet behind the tables and chairs as soon as they entered the lounge. "It'd be a sweet way to sneak up on someone and scare the crap out of 'em."

"Hadn't thought of that. I bet Lulu would jump a mile if you opened up the closet door and yelled 'Boo' while she was taking her coffee break."

"Can I look?"

"Yeah, but you can't go in with that chair." Jillian pulled her keys off her wrist and unlocked the door. Then she turned on the overhead light and picked her way through crates of soda pop cans and vending machine snacks. She pushed open the panel at the back of the closet. "See? Would you rather go exploring? Or help me clean equipment and file my reports?"

"I know what you're doing, Jillian."

She winked. "It usually works, doesn't it? Want to check it out?"

He grabbed his wheels and neatly spun himself away

from the closet. "I'm hungry. Let's go get cheeseburgers."

Quickly catching up to him, Jillian guided his chair through the patio doors and along the walkway that led across a garden courtyard to the cafeteria wing on the opposite side. "Okay. But trust me, filing reports is pretty boring stuff."

Thirty minutes and three cheeseburgers later, Jillian was pushing his chair back through the lounge and down the hallway to her office. "Okay, Mike, last chance. You can choose alphabetizing files behind door number one or dishpan hands from washing the jump ropes and wiping down the free weights." She paused to unlock and push open her door, giving Mike plenty of room to roll past her into the room. "I know. There is a third option. You can put that smiling face to good use and help Lulu greet patients at the check-in desk."

His answering glare was spot-on.

"Files it is." But when Jillian would have laughed, she choked on a muffled scream instead. "What now?"

In a heartbeat, the world around her shrank down to the bouquet of twelve crimson carnations sitting in a vase on her desk. Her pulse thundered in her ears. She squeezed her keys so tightly in her fist that she nearly pierced the skin of her palm. Locked. The damn door had been locked!

Defiant curiosity drove her feet across the room for a closer look, but the fear that oozed out her pores and crept across her skin kept her from touching anything. Unlike the rose she'd received last week, this bouquet had a card attached. An unsigned card that simply read *You're welcome.*

For what? "You think I'm grateful for your help, you sick son of a—"

"Jillian? Are you talking to me?"

Mike. She wasn't alone. She whirled around, zeroed in on dark blue eyes.

"Where's your dad?" She patted her pockets, looking for the business card Michael had given her on Friday. Maybe it was in her jacket. She pulled her running jacket off the coat stand beside the door and rummaged through the pockets. Empty. She tossed it on a hook. "Do you know your dad's number?"

"Yeah, but he's at work. It's for, you know, emergencies. You can leave a voice mail. Is something wrong? Do you need me to leave?"

She was still a bit too dazed by the violation of this latest message to know much beyond one thing right now. "I need to call Michael."

She needed to hear that deep voice and feel his calming, strengthening touch right now.

With the misfortune of impeccable timing, Dylan Smith chose that moment to show up at her door, knock and waltz right past her to her desk. He touched one bloodred flower and leaned over to sniff it. "Nice. Somebody must have been paying attention to the fact you don't like roses. You gonna let these die, too, Masterson?" He straightened and glanced over his shoulder. "That's hard on a man's ego, you know, to see how little you care about his gifts."

"I don't care about..." His teasing transformed her shock into suspicion. She wedged herself between him and the desk and, standing nose to nose, backed him up a step. "How did you know about the flowers?"

He pointed his thumb over his shoulder. “Um, passing by? Door open?”

“Did you put the bouquet in here?”

“I just got back from lunch.”

She advanced. “Answer my question.”

He retreated. “I saw them at the front desk and—”

“Did you put the flowers in here?” She poked him in the chest and nudged him back another step. “Do you have a key to my office?”

“No! Chill.” His raised hands and irritated frown indicated she’d gone past curious interrogation. “Jeez, Jilly. I was just saying, I saw the flowers at the front desk when I went to lunch. Who put the burr up your butt today?”

“Hey, buddy, just leave her alone, okay?” Mike edged the wheel of his chair between her and Dylan.

Dylan arched a golden brow and glared at the teen. “And you are?”

“A patient, Dylan,” Jillian defended. Apparently one with a protective streak that echoed his father’s. She shoved her bangs off her forehead and inhaled a calming breath. Remembering that she was the adult here, she rested her hand on Mike’s shoulder, thanking him and reassuring him at the same time. “I’m sorry I jumped down your throat like that, Smith. But Mike isn’t the problem here. Did I tell you someone broke into my apartment on Friday?”

Dylan swore beneath his breath and was instantly contrite. “No. Did they take anything?”

“They didn’t steal anything. Whoever it was got in and painted my bedroom.”

“Painted…? Is that a crime?” Dylan asked.

"Someone broke in?" Mike repeated, perhaps better understanding her sense of violation. "Are you okay?"

"I'm fine. I'm just a little paranoid about my space and my things now. I don't like knowing someone was in here while I was out. I don't want these. Here." She picked up the vase and thrust it into Dylan's hands, shooing the flowers away as though they disgusted her. Bright, beautiful blooms aside, they did. At the last moment, she snatched the card from the bouquet and stuffed it into her slacks. "Would you take those down to the hospital wing for me? Maybe give them to Mrs. Carter. She was here this morning."

"That's a nice gesture, but they're so pretty…they must mean something special."

"My allergies have been acting up."

"Okay. To the hospital they go." Dylan squeezed her arm and offered a sympathetic smile. "No worries. You take care."

After Dylan had gone, Mike frowned. "You have allergies?"

"No." Jillian circled her desk. She tossed a stack of folders into Mike's lap. "Why don't you start by alphabetizing these?"

Then she pulled out the hospital directory and sat down to dial the number for Maintenance.

She'd be changing the lock on her office door, too.

CHAPTER SIX

"THINK, CUTLER."

Michael muffled his helmet mike beneath his gloved hand and leaned back against the brown S.W.A.T. van where he'd set up his command post. Dale "Buck" Buckner had hung up on him again, sticking by his promise to *blow away* his ex-girlfriend and detonate the bomb he claimed to have rigged to explode the instant her limp thumb came off the detonator's trigger. What a hell of a way to terrorize someone he supposedly cared about. Her weeping pleas hadn't moved him any more than Michael's logic had.

This morning's bank robbery hadn't turned out to be about money at all. This six-hour standoff was about *love,* loss and a sheaf full of violated restraining orders.

Greedy gunmen were a cinch to negotiate with compared to a call like this one. Thieves might be desperate, but they wanted something. Michael could give them what they wanted—at least long enough for his men to take them down and put them in cuffs.

But a guy like Buckner had nothing to lose. He didn't care about his freedom. He didn't care about his life or the lives of his ex-girlfriend's coworkers. He sure as hell didn't care about material things. He just wanted his woman back. And if that didn't happen, he'd make sure that no one else could have her, either. And he'd take out anyone who tried to keep them apart—Michael, her boss at the bank, the Jackson County judicial system, pretty much anyone who made his ex laugh or smiled at her or even looked her direction. Buck thought he could force Daphne to love him and walk out of that bank a free man.

Michael knew better. This was going to end badly. Daphne Mullins was going to wind up dead and Buck would kill himself, and anyone else who happened to get in his way, so that he wouldn't have to live without her.

The waste of it all squeezed like a fist in Michael's gut. He was getting too old for this kind of crap. Too old for fighting and trying and people still dying.

God, he wanted to be young again. He wanted to feel strong and invincible, the way he had when Jillian Masterson had walked into his arms and held on to him as though he just might have the answers she needed. He wanted to feel the hope pounding through his cynical veins again. See the trust shining in her sweet green eyes. He wanted to kiss her and touch her and come alive again, in ways he seemed to have forgotten since his wife's death and Mike's accident. The stubborn brunette with her risky do-gooding and miracle smile had turned to him as though she believed he could save the day. And for that brief moment when she kissed him back, he believed he could.

But after six hours, with only one hostage released, Michael didn't have any more answers in him. He wasn't the hero Jillian needed any more than he was the man getting the job done here.

Tuning out the chatter on the radio inside his helmet, as well as the doubts settling inside his heart, Michael tipped his chin up to the sunshine. He needed to forget about what he was feeling and clear his head. He needed options, short of storming the bank and taking out innocent hostages and maybe even losing his men in the process. Perfect blue sky. Perfect spring weather—sunny, but not too hot, even suited up in the layers of protective and communications gear and weaponry he wore. What a lousy, lousy day.

The streets outside the Drury State Bank looked as if the army were gearing up for another D-day invasion. Police cruisers, the bomb squad robot and its armored command center, uniformed cops, off-duty officers, detectives, snipers, bomb squad techs—all waited for his word to launch their attack and take out the SOB who'd walked into the bank that morning with a military duffel bag and a suicidal attitude.

Michael had tried every trick in the book. But giving up wasn't an option. His men were depending on him for guidance. Kansas City was depending on him for protection. Daphne Mullins was depending on him for her very life. He needed to calm himself, get creative, think beyond the pages of any training manual.

And then his upturned eyes zeroed in on the roof of the bank. Could that be the new trick he needed? Standard bank security had every entrance sealed tight, and Buckner wasn't about to let anyone on the bank staff override the lockdown. But what if there was a way in that didn't involve doors or windows?

Michael pushed away from the van, energized by the chancy idea that just might work if his men lived up to the speed, accuracy and resourcefulness of their training.

He tapped the microphone in his helmet and summoned his men while he organized his plan. "I need a sit rep. Who's got eyes on our perp?"

"Shades are still drawn on the front windows, boss," Holden Kincaid answered from his position on the rooftop across the street. The deep voice of Michael's number-one sharpshooter crackled through the static in his ear. "I do not have a shot at this guy. I repeat, I do not have a shot."

Alex Taylor, the young patrol officer whom Michael had handpicked to replace Dominic Malloy, the funny man who'd been gunned down in a shoot-out at a safe house, added his observations from his position at Kincaid's side. His job was to protect Kincaid and keep an ongoing assessment of potential casualties in the area so that the sharpshooter could concentrate on making his shot and taking out the perp on a moment's notice. "I've got two thermal images on the monitor on the other side of those blinds."

"But there's no way to tell which one is Buckner and which is the woman," Kincaid pointed out.

Malloy had been Holden Kincaid's best bud and a damn good scout. Taylor had some big shoes to fill, and the rest of Michael's men didn't hesitate to point that out. But to his credit, Alex Taylor didn't seem to be backing down, either. "What I was saying is that none of the other hostages are showing up on the thermal. Could be he's moved them to a separate room or into the vault."

That meant there might be a way to get them out. The brain cells were ticking.

"Trip?" Michael spoke into the mike again, summoning their big man, Joseph Jones, Jr.—Triple J or

Trip, as the men liked to call him. "You still on the roof of the bank?"

"Yes, sir."

"How fast can you open the AC vent up there with the tools you've got on you?"

He heard the hesitation in Trip's voice. "The fans are still running inside. Anyone who goes through there would be chopped to bits unless we kill the power, and that would alert Buckner for sure. There's no clear path."

"How fast?" Michael repeated. If Trip could jerry-rig a truck to run on parts scavenged from a lawn mower engine, a feat he'd accomplished on a survival training mission, he could make this happen.

"I'm on it, sir." He heard the scuff of boots or a rifle being laid on the roof as the big man went to work. "I'm assuming you want me to figure out a way to stop the fans, too?"

"You're reading my mind, Trip." Michael was back at his post now, sighting each of his men and the other KCPD men and women who were keeping curiosity seekers and the press at bay.

He spotted Rafe Delgado, charming a pretty blonde reporter into staying inside her news van beyond the cordon tape. "Delgado. Get me something to talk to Buck about. I'm going to call him back and keep him distracted while Trip's working."

Rafe secured his rifle on his hip, tapped the news van and signaled the driver to move farther away from the potential blast area. Then he was on the horn again, a reliable source of information, as usual. "The heart attack victim Buckner released is en route to Truman Hospital. Looks like he'll make it. I've got the name on Buckner's cell mate at Leavenworth, where he served his time before the army discharged him. The warden says he's a phone call away if we need him. His civilian parole officer is on the scene with me, but says he doubts Buckner will listen to him. No luck getting a hold of his mother, either. Looks like you're going to have to sweet-talk him out all by yourself, boss."

"You know what a charmer I can be." He allowed his men their moment of stress-relieving laughter, then got dead serious again. "Let's make this happen, men. Let's get these hostages out. That's priority one." He picked up the phone to make the call. "Trip? Tell me you've got a way in through the roof, big guy."

"Almost there, sir. Running silent is slowing me down. Just about… Oh, hell."

Michael stopped dialing. *Oh, hell* was not part of the plan. "Trip—explain."

"Little man, I need you up here."

Alex Taylor was nearly a foot shorter than Trip. "I know you are not talking to me."

"Get up here, Shrimp. My shoulders won't fit through here. I can't cut it open any further without going electric, and Buckner would be sure to hear the saw."

Taylor groaned. "You got this?"

Holden answered his new partner. "I'm good. If he cracks those blinds, I'm taking him out."

"Belay that wish, Kincaid. Wait for my signal," Michael ordered. His goal was to prevent *any* casualties, and until he knew the setup of the bomb inside, that meant getting as many innocents out of there as possible before risking the final solution. "Taylor, I want you on the roof now. I need you inside in five minutes. Preferably in one piece."

"Yes, sir."

"Delgado—I want you to rig a minicharge that will bring down that window. Then join Kincaid to back him up. That'll be your best sight line. Trip, I want you ready to go in the instant Taylor can get an access door open for you, and help him get those hostages out. I need eyes on this guy, people. I need eyes."

Michael punched in the last number and waited for Buckner to pick up on his end.

It rang twice before the man with the bomb and the gun picked up. "Yeah? What do you want now, Cutler?"

Daphne Mullins's labored breathing tore at Michael's conscience. But he tuned out her distress and focused on the job at hand. "Buck. I've got an old friend of yours here. Your P.O. He says you won't talk to him. You want to tell me why?"

Five minutes later, the answers Michael needed to hear reported in with succinct, whispered tones in his earphone. The bomb trigger taped to Daphne Mullins's thumb was a dud. The so-called explosives in Buckner's bag were nothing more than wires and laundry, according to Taylor and Trip. But the .40-caliber S & W and 9mm Glock he carried were real enough.

Ten minutes later, Buck was still haranguing away about the unfairness of a world that would keep him and Daphne apart while Alex and Trip were silently moving the hostages to the rear exit.

"Captain? The alarm's going to sound as soon as I open this back door," Trip whispered.

Michael had already pulled the phone away from his mike. "Understood. Holden? You and Delgado ready up there?"

"Yes, sir."

"On my mark, take out the window, get the hostages

out the back, and Holden, take this guy down." He inhaled a deep breath for all of them. "Now."

MICHAEL ESCORTED THE two D.B.'s to the medical examiner's van himself while his men packed up the S.W.A.T. truck.

His team had saved nine lives today. Even the banker who'd suffered a heart attack at the beginning of the hostage crisis—when Michael had negotiated his release and begun to think that they might get through this day unscathed—was going to pull through just fine. But it was hard to think of this mission as a success.

Yes, the charge Delgado planted had shattered the bank's front window and ripped apart the blinds. A split second later, Kincaid's shot had dropped Buck like a stone.

But not before Dale Buckner had put his Smith & Wesson to his girlfriend's heart and taken her life with him. Not before he'd pointed his gun out the window and fired a wild second shot.

Daphne Mullins had spent the last few hours of her life living in terror. They'd done everything they could to save her. But in the end, it wasn't enough. Nobody should have to live in fear of another person like that. They should never have to be afraid of someone who claimed to love them. Not Daphne. Not Jillian.

Michael's fingers teased the cell phone in his pocket as the M.E.'s van slipped away with its police escort. He should call Jillian, make sure she was all right. Find out if the lock had been fixed on her apartment, if she'd had any more disturbing contacts from Loverboy, if he'd been on her mind even half as much this weekend as she'd been on his.

But she was at work and he was in a mood. No telling what raw, needy thing might come out of his mouth right now. Besides, if he didn't get his butt in gear and make his report to the commissioner who'd arrived on the scene, then the press would be hounding him and his men for their take on what had happened today.

KCPD commissioner Shauna Cartwright-Masterson was a far better spokesperson for the department than he could possibly be right now. His men were professionals, well trained. They'd risen to every challenge he'd put in front of them today. But it wasn't their job to handle PR right now. They needed time to themselves to work through their emotions. Taking a life was no easy thing. Losing a life was even tougher. They didn't need the media in their faces.

They all needed to blow off some steam. Holden would go home to his wife, probably go for a run with their pack of dogs and then do the things Michael remembered newlyweds doing. The other three bachelors needed to get back to headquarters, hit the showers, maybe find some friends and get something to eat or drink. Or they should go down to the Shamrock, pick up some pretty thing and get busy.

Michael needed… An image of long, coffee-colored hair and a beautiful smile flashed through his mind. Ah, hell. He tugged at the Kevlar vest he still wore, aching for some sort of release that he'd kept in check for days now. But just because he was on fire for a woman fifteen years his junior didn't mean that Jillian Masterson was feeling the same randy, needy, want-to-be-a-part-of-her-life impulses for an old warhorse like him.

"Captain Cutler?" The lady commissioner's voice cut through his thoughts, forcing him to forget about his own needs for the time being, and concentrate on making his report.

"Commissioner." Michael fell in step beside her as they moved away from the crowd to the relative privacy of the S.W.A.T. van.

"Good work, Captain."

He wasn't about to mince words. "Two people are dead, ma'am."

"Mr. Buckner?"

"Yes, ma'am."

"Any of ours?"

"No." Once she and her uniformed escort were out of sight behind the van, he turned to face her. "But the girlfriend didn't make it."

She tucked a swath of silvery blond hair behind her ear and nodded. "It could have been a lot worse, Michael. S.W.A.T. Team One secured the scene and rescued nine hostages. You kept who knows how many innocent bystanders from being hurt."

But he'd lost the girl. The commissioner could probably sense that her reassurances, while true and important to the safety of the community, hadn't tapped into his gut and eased the sense of failure he felt. Michael's gaze slid over to his men, silently stowing their gear at the back of the van. "What do I tell them to make this right?"

"This was a tough one, I know, and speculating just how much worse the result could have been if you and your men hadn't been here doesn't help right now. I'll speak to the victims' families and keep the press out of your hair. Take your men out for a drink tonight, Captain. Then go home and spend time with your son and anyone else you care about. Do something normal. Celebrate that they're safe."

Michael breathed a little easier. "Sounds like a plan."

"I understand you've been seeing my sister-in-law, Jillian."

Huh? The conversation took a sharp left and drove right into a place he wasn't ready to acknowledge yet. He propped his hand at his hip and straightened. "Jillian works with my son. I've seen her at the physical therapy clinic for several weeks now."

The commissioner's sharp eyes indicated she knew there was more to the story than that. "Jillian can handle it if you want to talk about today."

"I'm fine."

"You're trained to listen, Michael. You're trained to keep it all inside so that there's always someone who can keep a cool head in a crisis." She reached up and patted his shoulder. "Sometimes, even the best of us have to let it out with someone we trust. Today's events might break her heart, but they wouldn't shock her. Jillian may be the baby of the family, but she's been through a lot more than you know." Probably more than Shauna knew, too, since Jillian hadn't told anyone about Loverboy's gifts and letters until he'd forced the information out of her on Friday.

"I'll be fine, ma'am," Michael reiterated.

She dropped her voice to a whisper. "Look, I promised Eli I'd keep an eye on her while he was out of town. But I won't invite her over for dinner if she has...other plans, with you."

"Don't you think I'm a little old for her? I bet her brother would."

"That card doesn't play with me, Captain. I'm ten

years older than my husband." Shauna pulled back, her tone and posture dismissing him. "The heart doesn't see age when it finds what it wants."

Was Jillian what he wanted? Or did he just want to keep someone so important to his son's life safe?

Damn. He pulled back his sleeve and looked at the time. He needed to book it out of here if he wanted to get Mike over to the clinic for his afternoon session. Michael pulled out his personal phone and turned it on. "I'll be seeing her this evening. I'll give her your message."

"If you want." The commissioner laid out one last order. "Debrief at the station, but the paperwork can wait until tomorrow. Get your men out of uniform and out on the town."

"Yes, ma'am."

As the commissioner and her escort headed for the lights and microphones and waiting cameras, Michael jogged around to the back of the truck and made a quick inspection. His men were nearly ready to roll.

"Yo, Delgado." His second in command caught the helmet Michael tossed him. And while Rafe stowed it for him, Michael turned away to call Mike.

His son's cell rang and rang. What the heck? Michael tried not to remember that the last time Mike hadn't answered, he'd been lying unconscious in a mangled-up car. When it switched over to voice mail, his message was short and sweet. "It's Dad. Call me." He tried their home phone and ended up leaving a "Where are you?" on the machine there.

Michael unknowingly began to pace as he searched through his voice mail messages. Work. Work. Nothing from Mike. But there was a message from the physical therapy clinic, and another from a number he didn't recognize. He played the first.

"Michael? It's Jillian. I didn't want you to worry if you called home and no one answered. Mike's with me—has been since lunch. That clever son of a gun isn't as handicapped as he likes to claim he is. He got himself here for his therapy session. Since he was so early and there's no school to worry about, I had him stay and put him to work. You'll just need to pick him up at five when we're done." His son needed a reminder about the rule to always let him know where he was going, but Jillian's words made him smile. His go-to woman had come through for Mike again. "Oh." Her voice hushed, putting him on alert. "He sent me flowers. And a card."

Michael stopped in his tracks. The hesitant waver in her tone told him exactly which *he* she was talking about. He squeezed his eyes shut as a vivid aural memory of Daphne Mullins's sobs played in his ear. No way was he going to let that sicko Loverboy terrorize Jillian until a violent death was the only outcome left for her.

He didn't buy the false cheer in her "See you at five," nor was he waiting until the end of the day to get to her.

He smacked the driver's-side door by Rafe Delgado and signaled him to start the engine. "Let's get this show on the road."

Michael was buckled in and they were on their way to the KCPD downtown headquarters building by the time the unidentified message began to play.

"Michael?" Jillian again. He read off the number to Alex Taylor, strapped himself into the seat behind him and ordered him to track down the source. "I've got Mike at the hospital."

Everything in him tensed. *Mike?*

"Sorry, that didn't come out right. Don't worry, he's not hurt." But now Michael worried that *she* was. *Talk to me, sweetheart.* "It's, um, Troy Anthony. We were worried when he didn't show up at three, so Mike called him. Someone assaulted Troy's grandmother early this morning."

Alex Taylor interrupted. "The number's a public phone at Truman Medical Center, sir."

All eyes in the van were on their rock-still leader as the message continued. "Mike's been super with Troy—I think those two have a real bond. I'm skipping the therapy session because this is more important. We're hanging out in room 1312 at Truman Medical Center, so you can find us here when you're ready to pick him up." As proud as Michael was of his son, as hopeful as he'd been in months, there was something wrong. He heard it in the sudden hush of Jillian's voice, as if she was turning away so no one would overhear. "Michael, I…um, I think Mrs. Anthony was hurt because of me. I think *he* did it. Because she yelled at me. He told me I was welcome, as if he'd done me a favor. Maybe it's just the paint, but the things she said about her attacker… This is my fault."

No. No way.

"I saw you on the news." As if she needed something else to worry about. "Mike says that's not good. You looked tired, but okay. I hope you are. I'm so sorry about that woman. Take your time. I'll keep Mike with me as long as you need me to. Bye."

Michael saved the message. Tapped his phone against his temple. Stared at the yellow lines zipping past the center median on the road.

"Everything all right, Captain?" Delgado asked.

"Yeah." Who was he kidding? He turned to Delgado, raised his voice to be heard all the way to Trip in the back of the van. "No. I planned on taking you guys to the Shamrock tonight. Drinks on me. But you'll have to give me a rain check."

"No sweat."

"Forget it."

"We can handle it."

"Is it Mikey?"

He'd absolutely picked the best men for his team. And not just because they were each solid, skilled cops. "Mike's okay. It's a friend. Take a detour, Rafe."

The glib sergeant had already turned the van south toward the Truman Medical Center.

CHAPTER SEVEN

JILLIAN RUBBED HER HANDS up and down her arms, feeling a chill that went far beyond the hospital's air-conditioning, as LaKeytah Anthony repeated her story to her brother-in-law, Detective Edward Kincaid. Edward seemed skeptical that the attack on Troy's grandmother had anything to do with her, but Jillian knew. Beyond any kind of logic or circumstantial evidence, she knew.

An aunt and cousin had come to pick up Dexter to stay the night with them, but said their home was too small to accommodate Troy's wheelchair. Troy had covered the slight by insisting he wanted to stay at his grandmother's side. He claimed he was old enough and independent enough to stay on his own.

At sixteen? In the same building where LaKeytah had been given a concussion, along with a broken arm and jaw? Nobody should be alone when his family had come under attack like that.

But her compassion for Troy didn't make it any easier to stand here in the dimly lit room and listen to LaKeytah Anthony's story.

With LaKeytah's jaw wired shut and her body sedated to ease the pain, her words slurred and her eyes kept drifting out of focus. But the older woman seemed perfectly clear on the details. "He hit me from behind. And then I don't know much of anything. I never saw his face—only know it was a man by the pitch of his voice. He said it was a warning, that the world was an ugly place for a lot of people, and that I didn't have the right to take out my anger and frustration on anyone else and add to their burden."

Which was exactly what she'd done to Jillian the evening she'd gotten Troy home late.

"He said…" a tear leaked from beneath LaKeytah's closed eyelid, and Jillian nearly wept with her "…there would be no second chance…to keep my mouth shut."

Jillian shivered in the doorway and suddenly felt a hand nudging hers away from her arm and giving it a squeeze.

Mike's young face was creased with concern. "You okay?"

No, she wasn't. She squeezed back and smiled. "Will you stay with Troy? I don't think he should be alone right now. I need to get some fresh air."

He nodded and Jillian slipped into the hallway. She leaned back against the wall just outside the door and shuddered with a weary, wary breath. Was this her fault? Did Loverboy think this was what she wanted? Was this his twisted way of taking care of her? And how did he know LaKeytah Anthony had reamed her out in the first place?

Did he live in Troy's building? His neighborhood? Isaac Rush and Mr. Lynch instantly came to mind. She knew Isaac to be violent, but dishing out vigilante justice if there was no profit to be made? And Mr. Lynch was certainly big enough and powerful enough to have carried out the attack LaKeytah described. But what was his motive? If defending her truly was the reason for the assault, it made no sense. They'd only ever really talked that one night. The night he'd pulled her out of Isaac's bed and sent her to the police station to file charges of attempted rape. No. He had nothing to do with her life.

So did that mean Loverboy had followed her to Troy's building? Was his attention about more than letters and flowers? Her skin crawled at the notion that he could be watching her, even now. "Oh, God."

Jillian swept the hallway with her gaze. Was that him? The orderly with the cart? The bleary-eyed intern? She thought she was going to be sick.

Needing something, anything, to do besides stand here and suspect every man she saw—doctor, visitor, patient—she spotted the water fountain near the floor's main desk and made a beeline for it. She splashed a palmful of cool water on her cheeks and neck and then leaned over to get a drink.

A hand brushed her shoulder. "Jilly? What are you doing here?"

"Don't touch—" The solicitous voice startled her and she spun around, spraying the man in the white lab coat with the water drops that clung to her hair. "Dr. Randolph." She pressed her fingers to her lips, embarrassed to wear her fears so close to the surface and have greeted an old friend so rudely. "Sorry. I didn't realize it was you."

Bushy brows that matched his short, silvering hair arched behind his glasses. "Are you all right? Is someone in your family hurt?"

"Oh, no. No, no. Holly and her husband, Eli and his wife, they're all fine."

"I'm relieved to hear that." He hunched his lanky

shoulders and looked straight into her eyes. "You're not…?"

She knew that look—had hated it when she'd been seventeen and sitting through her first group therapy sessions at the Boatman Rehabilitation Clinic. There was something strengthening about being able to dismiss his concern. "I'm not looking for a meeting." Reaching into her pocket, Jillian pulled out her keys and dangled her ten-year sobriety key fob for him to see. "I'm still being good."

A kind eye winked as he straightened. "Glad to hear it."

She shouldn't have been surprised to run into Wayne Randolph at the medical center. Though she knew him from rehab and private counseling sessions over the years since, Dr. Randolph also practiced psychology at the hospital, assessing patients and directing them into various mental health programs that complemented the physical care the medical staff provided.

He put those assessing skills to good use. "You never answered my question. Why are you here?"

She linked her hand through his arm and walked him a few steps away from the fountain to give the next person in line the chance to get a drink without eavesdropping on their conversation. "The guardian of one of my patients was assaulted."

"Was she hurt badly?"

"Badly enough to be hospitalized for a few days. A lot of weird things have been happening lately. This is the worst of it so far."

"So far?" He rested his hand over hers on his arm and gave it a fatherly pat. "My goodness, dear. Are you in trouble? Can I help? Do you need to talk?"

"Always the therapist, aren't you?" Jillian shook her head. "You know, sometimes I think..."

"What?"

Why not? Dr. Randolph would understand this more than anyone she knew. "Do you think horrible things like this happen around me because of the destructive choices I used to make back in high school? Are other people paying for my mistakes?"

"You mean like cosmic retribution for a misspent youth?" Dr. Randolph turned her in his arms and pulled her in for a hug. "No. Sometimes, bad things just happen." He patted her hair and rocked her like a little girl. "You were one of the strongest young women I ever worked with, Jilly. I always knew you would turn your life around. And now you've gone on to do good things for so many other people. If anything, you've learned from your mistakes, and are making the world a better place because of it."

Trading one last hug around his waist, Jillian pulled away, appreciating the kind words if not fully believing them. "It is good to see a friendly face, Doc. I'd better get back to my friends. See if I can help."

"All right. Remember to call my office for an appointment if you decide you need to talk about anything."

"I will. Thanks."

Feeling marginally better, and slightly less paranoid, she headed back to LaKeytah Anthony's room. A nurse went in before Jillian could reach it and shooed out all her visitors. Troy came out first, looking more subdued than she'd ever seen him. Mike wheeled his chair out behind him.

"Maybe I'm not good for anything anymore," Troy

muttered, as if repeating words he'd just heard. Jillian's heart twisted in her chest. "I can't blame her for puttin' her heart and soul into Dexter now."

"She's doped up on pain meds, man." Mike nudged his friend in the arm. "You remember what that was like. She doesn't know what she's saying. She didn't mean it."

"I should have done something," Troy insisted. "I'm the man of the house." Displaying a rare burst of temper, Troy smacked the arm of his chair. "If I wasn't in this damn wheelchair..."

Mike didn't have a good answer for that one and looked equally dejected. Jillian hastened her steps, intending to intervene, but Mike came up with an alternate strategy of his own. "Hey, dude, you hungry?"

Troy shrugged. "Whatever."

"I know a shortcut to the cafeteria."

"Okay."

As the two teens rolled around the corner, Jillian shook her head, marveling at the resiliency of youth. Underneath all that attitude, Mike Cutler was a natural. Compassionate. Intuitive. He had so much to offer the world if he'd give himself half a chance.

Edward came out of the room next, softly closing the door behind him. He draped an arm around her shoulders. "I've gotten all I can get from Mrs. Anthony right now. The nurse says she needs her rest."

"What I said makes sense, right? I feel like I should apologize to her."

"You'll do no such thing." Edward's tone was adamant. "I get the idea from Troy that his grandmother yells a lot. There's no evidence to prove you had anything to do with the motive for her attack, beyond freaky coincidence. I've got my notes and the card from the flowers you gave me to add to your file, and I'll keep in touch with the detective assigned to Mrs. Anthony's case. But right now, unless the lab comes up with something concrete to tie it all together, we just have to sit and wait and keep a close eye on you." He hugged her close and pressed a kiss to temple. "Love you, kiddo. Call if you need anything."

"I will." Jillian shivered when he released her and automatically hugged her arms around her middle.

The scar on his jaw throbbed with concern. "You gonna be okay?"

"As long as that whack job is out there terrorizing me and hurting others in the name of love?" She shook her head. "I don't think I'm ever going to feel okay."

"I do." Edward was looking over her shoulder. "Turn around."

Frowning at the odd request, Jillian turned. Her breath caught in her chest, then rushed out in easier, quicker gasps.

Michael Cutler was striding down the hallway. Tall, intent, black hair rumpled. Wearing his uniform and needing a shave. Walking straight toward her.

"See ya, kiddo."

Jillian barely heard Edward's goodbye. She was already rushing forward, her eyes locked on to the mesmerizing strength of midnight blue. "Michael? Are you all right?"

She didn't pause, she didn't ask—she zoomed right up to Michael, locked her arms around his waist and turned her ear to his starched shirt and the strong beat of his heart underneath.

He braced his feet to catch her and wrapped his arms

around her, burying his nose against her hair. "I'm okay. Are you safe?"

"But the news about the hostages at the bank, I saw—"

"Damn it, woman, I'm worried about *you.*" He leaned back, caught her face between his hands. He smoothed her hair off her cheek and tucked the loose strands behind her ears. He read every nuance of her upturned eyes, every catch or gasp of breath. He brushed the rough pads of his fingers across her brows, her cheeks, her jaw, her mouth. He pressed his thumb against the swell of her bottom lip and went still. "I don't scare easily, sweetheart, but your messages…"

"I'm okay." Her whispered words transformed the touch of his fingers into a caress against her lips. "Better, now that you're here. But I'm okay."

Instead of giving a verbal response to her mushy confession, his gaze darted to the right and the left. Then he grabbed her by the hand and led her down the hall to an empty patient room. "Is Mike around?"

He pulled her inside. "He took Troy to the cafeteria to eat."

"Neither one's hurt? Upset?" The door closed.

"A little shaken, but they'll be fine." He took her by the shoulders and pushed her back against the wall beside the door. "Michael?"

He kissed her.

An almost angry stamp on her lips at first. And then he cupped her face and angled her mouth and covered her mouth in a kiss that was as gentle as it was hungry, as thorough as it was needy. Winding her fingers into the collar of his shirt, Jillian parted her lips and kissed him back.

She quickly realized it was pent-up desire and fear

and confusion and want, not anger that made the kiss so powerful, so crazy. Because Jillian was feeling it, too.

The tension between them had simmered for months, excused as latent attraction to a handsome, healthy man. She rose on tiptoe and wound her arms around Michael's neck, her palms tingling at the contrast between his starchy uniform and his short, silky hair.

The fears she felt—for her own safety, for his—had brought that tension to the surface, made it harder and harder to filter her feelings through polite decorum. He had a hang-up about their difference in ages; they both wanted to put his son before whatever it was they were feeling.

Michael's tongue slid between her lips and rubbed against hers, creating friction and heat and the desire to conduct her own exploration. She stroked smooth, firm lips, delighted at the rasp of beard stubble against her softer skin, tasted coffee on his tongue. Oh, yeah. They were way more than *just friends*.

He pulled her away from the wall into the hardness of his chest. His hand slid down her back to squeeze her bottom and lift right into the swelling evidence of his desire for her. Jillian moaned as her body absorbed and reacted to sensation after sensation. Her small breasts felt tight and womanly, rubbing against him. Her lips felt swollen, feverish, sexy. Her heart pounded against her ribs and she felt hot, heavy, farther down.

"Michael…" She peppered kisses along his neck, his jaw, his chin—anything he'd let her reach as he turned his attentions to the rapid pulse beating along the side of her neck.

It was an emotional release, a catharsis for them both.

"So pretty. So strong. So hot. So good. I need…" He

breathed against her ear. His arms tightened around her, shook.

"What do you need, Michael? Please tell me what you need."

He pulled the band from her hair, sifted his fingers through its length, buried his nose in a handful of it and breathed deeply. "God, I need..."

At this moment, in this room, she'd give him whatever he wanted.

Instead, Jillian's toes touched the floor. Then she was standing flat-footed. And then she was leaning back against the wall for support, panting as Michael scrubbed his palm over his face and backed away.

Breathing just as hard, he shot his fingers through his short, ruffed hair and held out his hand, as though warding away temptation itself. "This can't happen. This shouldn't happen."

"Why? If I want it, too?" She pushed away from the wall.

He retreated a step. "I won't take advantage of your vulnerable state just because I had a lousy day and I'm freaking out of control!"

She'd never heard him raise his voice before, and though the force of it stung, she suspected it wasn't directed at her. His shoulders lifted with a deep breath and heartbeat by heartbeat, she saw the invisible armor of his captain's uniform slide back into place. "I'll get it together. I promise." He paced across the room and came back a different man than the passionate, open one who had nearly seduced her a moment ago. "Explain the situation to me. Tell me what we need to do."

Angered that he was taking the blame for what had happened, hurt that he thought she wasn't old enough or sensible enough or experienced enough to know her own desires, Jillian retrieved the rubber band from beneath the nearest bed and tugged her hair back into a messy ponytail. "For one thing, don't be so hard on yourself. It took the two of us to make that kiss happen."

"I'm talking about the messages, the attack on Mrs. Anthony. I'm talking about Troy and Mike and their welfare."

"I know what you're talking about." She was raw and achy and mad as hell that he refused to acknowledge the connection between them. "You're talking about being a cop. You're talking about being a father. But I don't think you're comfortable talking about being a man. Not one who feels things and wants things. Not one who might need something for himself. At least, not around me."

A pulse beat in the tight clench of his chiseled jaw, as he threw every bit of his considerable authority into the stiffness of his posture. But the steeliness wavered in his dark blue eyes and Jillian's anger immediately dissipated.

"I'm sorry. That wasn't fair to say. I know we each have a lot on our plates right now, things that take priority over…a relationship."

He braced his hands at his hips, relaxing a fraction. "So you see why a…relationship…shouldn't happen between us?"

"No." She pressed her hand to his chest to silence his argument. "But I see why it shouldn't happen right now."

She turned and pulled open the door.

"Jillian…"

"Troy needs a place to stay," she stated without

looking back. "I'd take him home with me but I don't know if the clinic would think that was appropriate. Besides…" She felt Michael's heat, coming up behind her. She saw his hand on the door above hers. "I don't know if it would be safe for him there."

"Troy has a place to stay. He'll come home with Mike and me. The house is completely handicap-accessible. It would probably do them both some good to spend more time together."

Finally, Jillian turned to face him. "You'll take Troy in?"

"If he accepts the invitation."

"Thank you." Couldn't he see what a great team they made? How could Michael deny this bond between them? Maybe he just wanted to deny he'd discovered it with *her*. A recovering addict with a stalker in pursuit probably wouldn't be any man's first choice for a mate, no matter what attraction sizzled between them. And she was especially unsuitable for a man of Michael's responsibilities and reputation. Acceptance had always been a big part of moving on with her life. "We're still friends, right?"

After a moment, Michael nodded. "Friends."

Despite the iron fist of reality crushing her heart, Jillian stretched up to press a kiss to his jaw. "Thank you."

CHAPTER EIGHT

ANYONE JILLIAN MIGHT want to see on the street in front of Troy's apartment building was smart enough to be safely locked up inside their homes at this time of night. Chattering girls. Decent working folk. Shopkeepers trying to make an honest profit. There wasn't a one of them in sight as Michael steered his extended-cab pickup into a parking place across the street.

Instead, there were hookers and junkies and other souls that she'd just as soon would stay in the shadows where they lurked. Even the trio of homeless men hanging back in the alley, standing around the trash can fire they'd built, knew enough to stay off the streets of No-Man's Land after dark.

Michael shifted the truck into Park and left the engine idling as he scanned the sidewalks and parked cars around them. Jillian clutched the dashboard, her own trepidation growing as he leaned against the window and looked up at the apartments across the street. She knew he was seeing and evaluating every potential danger.

"I see a lot of lights on the fifth floor," Michael observed. "That means the neighbors are still up. Yours is the one on the end, right, Troy?"

"Yes, sir."

Michael had taken the time at the police station to

change into his civvies when she'd driven him over from the hospital to pick up his truck. But he still wore his gun and badge in plain view on his belt. He was expecting trouble, and because Michael did, Jillian expected it, too.

He braced his arm on the back of the seat and turned to the teenage boys seated behind them. "You ready? We'll go up to your apartment, pack whatever you need and get on the road to our house ASAP. All right?"

Even though this was the place Troy called home, she could see he wasn't particularly comforted about being here. "If it's all the same to you, Mr. Cutler, I'd rather not go in. I don't know if the super's got Grandma's blood cleaned out of the elevator yet." Jillian's breath stuttered right along with his at the sickening image. "I don't think I can go in there again if he hasn't. Here are the keys."

Michael took the keys and closed them in his fist. "All right. I'll go." He looked across the front seat to Jillian. "I want you to slide over here behind the wheel. Be ready to drive off if anybody who shouldn't approaches the truck."

"It'll be quicker if I do it," Jillian suggested. "I've been in the apartment before and know where things are. Then we can all get out of here sooner."

"I'm not letting you go in there by yourself. That was the whole point of me driving."

"You're not coming with me and leaving these boys alone here." Jillian reached for the door handle. "I'll go."

"I'd rather call for backup."

"And wait even longer? These boys shouldn't be here."

"*You* shouldn't be here," he insisted. He slipped his

hand across the seat until it rested next to hers. "Jillian, is this about what happened at the hospital? Are we going to fight about everything now?"

"What happened at the hospital?" Mike asked from the backseat.

"Nothing." They answered in unison, showing the boys that there was a new kind of tension simmering between the adults in the front seat.

Jillian took a stab at offering an honest explanation. "We had a disagreement about…how to proceed with—"

"Events that have happened today," Michael finished, discreetly leaving out any mention of kisses and confessions and decisions that a relationship with Michael Cutler was out of the question.

"I just asked." Mike crossed his arms and sank back into his seat.

"Son, I'm sorry. I've got a lot on my mind right now. I'll try to explain it better later."

"Whatever."

With the air inside the truck thick enough to slice, someone needed to break the tension. Jillian volunteered. She moved her left hand to let her fingers slide over Michael's. "I'm picking up clothes, a toothbrush and Troy's meds. Once I'm inside the lobby, the doors will lock behind me and the security light will come on. Right, Troy?"

"Yeah."

Michael spread his fingers to capture hers between them. "Mrs. Anthony was attacked in the lobby," he pointed out.

"Fine. If I see or hear anything suspicious, I'll come right back out. When I get into the apartment, I'll turn the light on so you'll know I'm there. I'll turn it off when I leave. I'll lock every door as soon as I'm through it." She was trying to come up with a reasonable plan. "Give me ten minutes—fifteen tops. If I'm not back, you lock these boys in and come get me."

He turned their hands, pressing the keys into her palm and curling her fingers around them. "I'll give you ten."

Jillian felt three sets of eyes on her every step of the way across the street and into the building. When she was secured inside the glass double doors, the light came on and she turned and waved to show she was safe. Michael answered by pointing his finger and insisting she get a move on.

Keeping her eyes and ears tuned to any sign of movement, she pushed the elevator button and waited as its gears churned into action. Hopefully, if others had been using the elevator, that meant Troy's fears had been unfounded and the elevator had been cleaned of all signs of the attack.

But waiting meant she had time on her hands—only seconds, perhaps, but time enough to think. Time enough to *feel* every detail around her and take notice of the subtle warnings she should be paying attention to. The super's light kept the lobby brightly lit, but made it difficult to see down the first-floor hallway. And from this angle, the light reflected off the glass doors, creating a visual barrier between her and the reassuring sight of the black pickup parked across the street.

Jillian tucked her ponytail inside her jacket and zipped it up to the collar of her polo. No sense giving a perp something easy to grab on to. Just where had LaKeytah's attacker been hiding? In that corner? In that one? She arranged the fleece-lined hood around her neck, easing the prickle of awareness that raised the delicate hairs along her nape. The elevator dinged on a floor above her, meaning it had stopped for someone else to get in. Did she want to wait to see who might walk out, or worse, who might decide to share a ride back up with her?

Pulling her cell phone from her pocket, Jillian scrolled through her numbers until she found Michael's. She centered it on the screen and rested her thumb on Send in case she needed to speed-dial him for help. One by one, she slipped Troy's keys between the fingers of her right hand, giving herself at least some kind of weapon to defend herself with if necessary.

The longer she waited, the more her thoughts took hold.

She couldn't smell the ammonia odor from the apartment with all the cats, but she could detect the hint of something else in the air. A hint of musk, like men's cologne. The scent seemed familiar but Jillian couldn't place it. And delicate as it was, as though the man wearing the cologne had walked through the lobby some time ago, or was standing at a great distance, the air around her suddenly grew cloying.

As if the scent was closing in on her.

As if the man who belonged to that scent was closing in.

Who was she kidding? She was done waiting here.

Five flights of stairs was an easy climb for a woman who ran wind sprints or jogged nearly every day of her life. The concrete and steel stairs had a light on each landing and were blessedly devoid of company and perfumey smells. The physical exertion also worked some magic at toning down her paranoia. *Just keep moving. Don't think.* Jillian was barely breathing hard by the time she reached the fifth floor and opened the service door. She quickly got inside the Anthonys' apartment and locked the door behind her.

Light on. Grab gym bag from Troy's closet. Pack clothes, pack underwear. Pack iPod and ear buds—no teen should be without his music. Move to bathroom for toothbrush, into kitchen for pill bottles in cabinet. Snatch family photo off refrigerator and stuff into bag. Zip it shut. Check time. Smile. She'd make ten minutes with time to spare. Light off. Lock door.

Jillian didn't even bother with the elevator. Slinging the bag over her shoulder, she headed straight for the stairs. But the descent didn't go quickly or smoothly.

She had her foot on the first step off the fourth-floor landing when she smelled it and stopped. She sniffed the air. Not that sick cologne scent. Something acrid. Chemical.

Something burning.

Clutching the railing, she moved down several steps, bringing herself closer to identifying the sour stench. She stopped again. Not a fire, but something long forgotten and all too familiar.

Someone in the stairwell was smoking crack.

"Oh, jeez," she whispered as a shiver rippled down her spine. It wasn't temptation she was feeling, but shame. She squeezed her eyes shut against a flashback of familiarity. Crack might not have been her drug of choice, but this had once been her world. Hiding out in empty stairwells and abandoned rooms, escaping reality, losing herself. Why had she ever let herself become a part of this?

How could she ever really leave it behind and be the strong, worthy, loving—loved—woman she fought every day to be when this was still so very real for her?

"Stop it." Jillian tried to shake the thoughts out of her head. Those were just the kind of debilitating mind games Dr. Randolph had worked so hard with her on to overcome. Under his guidance, she'd learned how to turn her experience into knowledge that could help others. She'd learned to use her talents as therapy, and turn her weaknesses into strength. She could overcome grief, she could overcome drugs, she could overcome anything—just as long as *she* believed she could do it. She'd kicked her addiction. She'd gotten healthy. She was making a difference in the world now.

She could damn well pack a bag and get back down these stairs.

At the third-floor landing, she was close enough to hear the voices.

"I never thought I'd see this day, Rivers."

Rivers? Blake?

Jillian inched around the corner, her heart crying with concern for a friend who hadn't been able to find his way out of the past the way she had.

"Hey!" She jerked back at the sound of a thud and a grunt, hating that she recognized Blake's slurred southern drawl. "I wasn't dealin', man. We were sharing. I wouldn't step on your turf, Isaac. You know I wouldn't do that."

Her own stomach muscles clenched at the next thud and breathless curse. She reached into her pocket for her phone. And Michael.

"Then where'd you get the money?" Isaac Rush's voice was crystal clear.

"It's mine. I earned it."

"Selling this? She's *my* customer."

Thud.

Blake gasped for breath. "Hell, man. I've got money. I buy from you. You know I've always been good—" Another punch. A fit of coughing.

Jillian felt every blow with him.

"You can't sell what I give you without giving me a cut of the profit. You understand?" A moment of silence. Footsteps heading down the stairs. "I don't think he does."

"That's my cash!" Blake protested.

And then the beat-down started in earnest.

Jillian pressed Send and ran down the stairs. "Stop it. Stop it!"

She stepped over the pipe and the passed-out woman on the stairs and rounded the corner in time to see Mr. Lynch throw Blake up against the wall of the second-floor landing. The black man's coat swung around him like a cape as he pulled his gloved fist back to strike another blow. Blake put up his hands and staggered, begging for mercy. But with his puffy eye and bleeding lip, Jillian didn't wait to see if he'd crumple to the floor or suffer another punch.

"Stop!" She dropped the bag and ran straight down to Blake, putting herself between him and Lynch.

"Mr. Rush?" Lynch's dark eyes fixed on her upturned face as he called down to his boss. For a split second, his big fist hovered in the air, but he stayed his hand. He pulled back the front of his coat, needlessly reminding her of the gun he carried. "Don't do this, girl," he warned. "Get out of the way."

Blake's clumsy hands clamped down on Jillian's

shoulders and her knees nearly buckled as he leaned his weight against her in an effort to stay on his feet. "I traded tit for tat with her. I didn't do anything wrong," he spat beside Jillian's ear.

"That's not how Mr. Rush sees it."

"He sees what he wants. Takes what he wants."

"Blake, shut up." She turned and slid beneath his arm, propping him up as she tugged at his waist. "Let's just go."

"Jilly." Isaac Rush turned the corner, blocking their slim escape route around Lynch's broad shoulders. "You decided to take me up on my offer, after all."

"No." When he reached for her hand, Jillian jumped back, knocking Blake back into the wall, accidentally jabbing her elbow into his ribs. "I'm helping out a friend. We just want to leave."

Blake cursed, too blinded by pain and the drug in his system to understand the danger they faced. "You tell him, baby."

Isaac sneered. "Is this what you ended up with, sugar? A man who pays to get laid? I was first class with you all the way. I can hook you up with something good, I promise. Nothing cut-rate like Loverboy here."

Loverboy?

The unfortunate choice of words pierced the bubble of adrenaline that had sent her charging down these stairs and fueled her defiance. Now she could see the folly of trying to rescue anyone.

Out of bravado, but not out of hope, she turned a pleading eye up to Mr. Lynch. "Let us go. Please. The same way you let me go that night. I know you remember."

The hand on the gun never wavered. "I remember."

"What's she talking about, Lynch?" Isaac didn't sound pleased.

"You don't belong here, girl."

"Neither does he. Please let us go." She thought she detected a subtle shift in Lynch's position, screening Isaac from direct view. Jillian didn't wait for a better opportunity to escape. She tugged. "Come with me, Blake."

But the idiot still had enough ego in him to keep his mouth going. "You've gone soft, Lynch. You're not so tough against both of us, are you?"

Lynch made a growling sound and lunged at Blake.

Blake yanked Jillian in front of him like a shield. Their feet tangled and Blake fell, pulling her with him.

Glass shattered. Men shouted. Someone cursed.

"Jillian!"

She heard her name, but her chin clipped the railing, and her skull rang with the impact, distorting the voices around her. Blake came down on top of her and her knee cracked against a step, shooting pain all the way down to her toes. She curled into a ball as much as she could and tumbled down to the next landing where she landed with a jolt on top of Blake.

"Jillian!"

"KCPD. On the ground. Now."

"Back off!"

"Easy, pal. Don't move."

"I'll take that."

Hands were on her, pulling her off Blake's chest, lifting her from harm's way. Her head throbbed. Her leg ached. Every movement seemed to reveal another bruise.

"Careful," a deep voice snapped beside her ear. "Cover him."

"He's clean, boss."

Twin steel bands caught her behind her back and legs, and her cheek lolled against solid, encompassing warmth. The pure, clean scent of soap filled her nose and nubby wool tickled her skin. She was sinking into a cozy heat until a jolt of pressure stabbed her chin. "Ow!"

Her eyes blinked open. Her foggy brain began to clear.

"Jillian?" Long, sure fingers were unzipping her jacket. "I need your sweatshirt, okay, sweetheart?"

She nodded, trusting the voice if not fully comprehending the words. Jillian sat up and lifted her arms when requested. The long fingers were red and wet with blood. She looked down and watched it drip onto her polo shirt. Her blood. "Oh. Did I…?"

"Are you hurt anywhere else? Twist anything?"

"I bumped my knee."

A firm hand probed her leg and she winced when it found the swelling around her kneecap.

"Nothing broken."

"She okay, boss?"

The last of the fog drifted away and Jillian realized she was sitting in Michael Cutler's lap at the bottom of the stairs. She was hurt, but he was here, pressing her wadded-up jacket against her chin to stanch her wound. She was safe. With him around, she would always be safe. "Michael?"

Dark blue eyes locked on to hers, searching for something. And then he nodded. "She'll be okay. Delgado?"

"This one's out cold. But he's still breathing."

"Taylor?"

"The girl's coming around, but she's pretty mellow."

Delgado? Taylor? She knew those names. Jillian lifted her gaze to follow the angle of Michael's commands.

The stairwell was swarming with cops—three of them, at any rate. Alex Taylor came from upstairs, his badge hanging from a chain around his neck over the football jersey he wore. He guided the blank-eyed hooker onto the step beside Isaac Rush, who sat glaring into space, his hands bound together by his own necktie. Michael tossed a pair of handcuffs to the blond she recognized as Holden Kincaid in the lobby. He wore his badge clipped to the front pocket of his jeans and a gun tucked into the back of his belt. A second gun he held in his hand never moved away from the supine form of Mr. Lynch, even as he locked the cuffs around the black man's wrists. A third cop, Rafe Delgado, with blue-black hair and olive skin, knelt over Blake's body on the landing above her.

Blake's body? Jillian jerked in Michael's lap, trying to scramble to her feet.

"Easy," Michael warned, looping his arm around her waist and anchoring her into place.

"Is he…?"

"He's alive, ma'am," Delgado answered. "But we need to get him to a hospital."

"Lucky bastard," Isaac whined. "He was willing to sacrifice Jilly to get out of here in one piece."

"Enough." The short cop in the football jersey pulled his gun and urged Isaac to be silent.

"Holster that, Taylor," Michael ordered. "These are too tight quarters and somebody might get hurt."

"Yeah, Taylor," Isaac mimicked, "put that gun away before you hurt the boss's lady."

Jillian felt the tension that stiffened Michael's body, but his steady gaze never blinked as it shifted to Isaac. "Put a muzzle on it."

Isaac shrugged. "Hey, we were trying to keep the lady safe, too. Jilly and I are old friends. Mr. Lynch and I were trying to convince her to leave when Rivers there went nutso on us."

Old friends? The gulf between Michael and Jillian widened. It didn't matter what she felt for him—that she was falling in love with him. A veteran cop who commanded men like these and a former teen addict who'd run the streets and spent time with the likes of Isaac Rush? Yeah. That was a relationship that was gonna happen. Try introducing her as Mike's stepmom or taking her to a dinner with his departmental colleagues. Whatever Michael felt for her, he didn't *want* to feel. He was just a good cop. A good man. Doing the right thing. He'd protect her. He'd be her friend.

But love her?

Maybe her heart should set its sights a little lower. Maybe she should focus on her work and her patients and forget about a happily-ever-after with this man.

Suddenly, the shelter of Michael's body felt like a trap, one she was embarrassed to be caught in. Jillian pushed against the arm at her waist and struggled to get to her feet.

Instead of freeing herself, she wound up clinging to Michael's shoulders as he shifted his hold on her and stood with her in his arms. "Rafe, you have things under control here?"

"Yes, sir. Bus is en route for this guy. Perps are secure."

"Good. Wait for the local boys to get here and make the arrests. I don't want to step on anybody's toes. I'm taking Jillian out to my truck."

"Put me down." Jillian flattened her palm against his chest and tried to push away. "It's just some bruises and a cut on my chin. I can walk."

"Humor me." He strode across the lobby, his boots crunching over shattered glass from around the door lock. "Seems the only way I can know you're safe is to hold on to you."

"I was only trying to help."

"Just keep that cloth on the wound. I think you'll need stitches."

Resigning herself to the humiliation of causing this man more trouble than she was worth, Jillian dutifully wound her arm around his neck and wedged her jacket beneath her chin. "Kincaid," he snapped. "Get the doors and take that bag out to my truck. I'm driving her to the E.R. myself."

"Yes, sir."

The few curiosity-seekers who'd gathered to see what the crookedly parked vehicles and flashing red and white lights were all about moved in to get a closer look at the tall man with the black-and-silver hair carrying the injured woman with the pale resignation on her face across the street. They cleared a path for him, and scattered entirely when a man built like a tank got out of the cab of Michael's truck and circled around to open the passenger-side door. Another cop?

Michael finally set her down on the passenger seat and secured her safety belt over her lap. "Thanks, Trip."

He dismissed the off-duty officer who'd stayed outside to protect Troy and Mike. "Better get across the street and keep these people from contaminating the scene until backup gets here."

"Yes, sir." He tipped the brim of the KCPD ball cap he wore. "Ma'am."

As soon as Michael closed the door and opened a bin in the back of his truck to secure the bag and pull out something else, Mike and Troy scooted forward.

"Jillian?"

"You okay?"

With the combination of blood and being carried out, the boys were understandably concerned.

She reached over the back of the seat to squeeze their hands. "Cuts on the head and face bleed a lot because the blood vessels are so close to the surface. It probably looks worse than it is."

"It looks sick to me." Troy pointed to her chin. The driver's door opened and Michael climbed in. "Did that guy attack you? Did you see his face? Did the cops arrest him?"

"The police have everything under control, Troy," Michael stated, turning the key in the ignition. "We're all safe." Except maybe Jillian, judging by the death ray of don't-you-ever-scare-me-like-that-again shining from his eyes. "Everybody buckle up. Here."

He reached across her to pull a first-aid kit from the glove compartment. With swift, sure fingers that were still marked by her blood, he unwrapped a wad of gauze and ripped open some adhesive tape. He tossed her ruined jacket to the floor at her feet and replaced it with a more sanitary wrap.

His movements were precise, yet gentle, as he shook

out his black insulated KCPD jacket and tucked it around her like a blanket. “Don’t you go into shock on me.” He tapped the crude bandage on her chin. “Keep the pressure on that.”

Mike reached over the seat and rested a hand on Jillian’s shoulder. “I’ll make sure she does.”

Touched by the maturity of his concern for her, Jillian covered his hand with hers and held on.

Michael flashed his lights, honked his horn and pulled out. With some hard turns, he wove his way through the parked vehicles his team had left in the middle of the street and stepped on the accelerator.

“Did I get hit on the head, or did the cavalry just come to my rescue?”

Mike squeezed her shoulder. “Dad called his team as soon as you left the truck.”

Michael slowed to take a corner. “Fortunately, they were all in one place. The Shamrock’s not that far away.”

“The Shamrock Bar?” Jillian asked.

“You know it?”

“A lot of the PTs and hospital staff go there for happy hour.”

“A lot of cops do, too.”

They fell into a long, awkward silence as Michael sped through lights and zipped through downtown Kansas City to get her to the Truman Medical Center.

The bright lights marking the emergency room’s canopied entrance were in sight when she spoke again. “I was just trying to help a friend.”

“I know. You’re always out to save somebody, no matter what the risk is to yourself.” He pulled into the parking lot and found a space close to the entrance. After he shut off the engine, he turned to her. “Did you ever consider that maybe one of those *friends* is particularly grateful for what you've done for them?"

"You mean the letters?" She patted the air, silently asking him to drop the subject in front of the boys.

"What letters?" Troy asked.

But Captain Cutler was nothing if not thorough. "I mean the letters, the flowers, the watching, the favors you don't want, the making you afraid."

"A friend wouldn't do that to me."

"A friend wouldn't use you as a shield in the middle of a fight, either."

"Blake didn't…he wouldn't."

"He did." He pulled his phone from his belt and held it up in his fist. "I heard every damn word."

"Dad!" The crackle of worry in Mike's voice shushed the debate. "Scaring Jillian won't help right now. You didn't lose her. We…didn't lose her. Just get her inside and make sure she's okay."

Michael's face betrayed pain when he looked back at his son. Then he scrubbed his hand over his jaw, taking the emotions with it. "Smart kid." He reached back and cupped Mike's cheek. "Damn smart kid. I guess I'm the one who's scared."

He gave Mike a fatherly pat and then got out. When he opened Jillian's door, she'd turned to climb down, but Michael blocked her path. He cupped her face in the same tender gesture he'd used on his son, only there was no good-ol'-boy pat on the cheek. "You've touched a lot of lives, Jillian—ours included. I think you *know* the man who is sending you those letters. He's around you somewhere in your life, a lot closer than you might think. He doesn't care about the good you put into the world. That's what scares me."

And then he kissed her. In front of his son, in front of Troy, in front of the waiting E.R. attendant with a wheelchair. No subtle touch, no secret room. He kissed her softly, gently, thoroughly. Jillian snuggled inside the heat and scent of Michael's jacket around her and leaned into the kiss. His lips cherished hers, his calloused fingers soothed her feverish skin. Inside, she was melting, wanting, weeping at the poignancy of his tender kiss.

There was no more falling in love with this man. She was there. She wasn't sure how the two of them together could ever work beyond moments like this, but there was no doubt in her heart that she loved him.

Perhaps succumbing to the "whoa" and "Go, Captain" and nervous laughs from the backseat, Michael broke off the kiss with an aching sigh, picked her up and set her down in the waiting wheelchair himself.

But out of earshot of the boys, he had one more sobering warning to whisper against her hair as he pushed her inside the hospital. And a promise. "Tonight we were lucky. My men were close by. But I'm not going to trust that will happen the next time. When I take Troy home with us tonight, you're coming, too."

CHAPTER NINE

"I'D HAVE BET good money that two sixteen-year-olds with pizza, pop and no school to worry about would have been pulling an all-nighter." Michael opened the door to what had once been Mike's bedroom before the leg braces and wheelchair had forced him to move down to the first floor. He raised his voice so that Jillian could still hear him in the bathroom across the hall as he tossed a set of sheets onto the bare mattress and started making up the bed. "Mike and Troy are both zonked out downstairs. I turned off the game they were playing and covered them up."

"It's awfully late, even for night owls."

Michael turned at the breathy voice in the doorway behind him—in time to catch Jillian in the middle of a yawn that stretched her freshly washed face. After a couple of hours in the E.R., getting stitches in her chin and an X-ray of her knee to ensure that nothing was broken, the hot shower had gone a long way to wash away the memory of seeing her dazed and bleeding at the bottom of a stairwell with an armed Goliath, a known drug dealer and that weasel of an ex-boyfriend all trying to get their paws on her.

Now he wished he'd thought to offer her some fresh clothes to replace the ones she'd put back on. Her sweat-shirt jacket and royal-blue polo had been stained with blood and grime, and disposed of at the hospital. That left her in a white tank top and her torn khaki pants—and the black KCPD jacket she'd adopted since he'd covered her with it in No-Man's Land. With the insulated sleeves rolled above her wrists and the collar turned up around her neck, it seemed as though she'd turned his working jacket into a robe.

The shoulders were too big for her, and her slim, athletic frame swam inside the girth of it. But he decided he liked the way it looked on her. It was probably some male instinct dating back to Neanderthals, seeing the woman he cared about wrapped up in something that belonged to him. As if the woman inside belonged to him, too. His weary body hummed with an electric response at just how feminine and delicate she seemed inside those ordinary, masculine clothes. Barefoot. No makeup to hide her smooth skin and wide, full mouth. Sleek, long hair glistening like the richest cup of coffee.

Yeah. He probably liked her in that shapeless black jacket a lot more than he should.

Shaking his head, Michael tucked in the corner of the fitted sheet near the headboard. It had been a helluva long day for him, too, to let some primitive, emotional reaction to her appearance lead his thoughts off track like that. "I take it you're not a night owl?"

"I prefer the morning sun." She was plaiting her damp hair into a loose braid and he had to force himself to look away from the unintentionally sensual display. "Too many memories of late nights and wasted days."

"I can't imagine coming back from the place where you were, Jillian."

She flicked the braid behind her back and crossed to the opposite side of the bed. "You make it sound like

I did an amazing thing. I got into the party scene and used cocaine because I was so freaked out that my parents had died on their way to see me play an exhibition game. It's a wonder I ever graduated from high school."

He shot a pillow at her across the bed, which she deftly caught and set into place. "Yet you *did* graduate. You got a college degree and a master's in physical therapy. And you've been sober, what, ten years?"

"Eleven."

"I'd say helping others, especially the ones who are most needy, is your drug of choice now."

She grabbed the edge of the bright red top sheet and folded a neat hospital corner. "I would have said running and shootin' hoops was my regular fix. But I guess saving the world one person at a time keeps me out of trouble." Her relaxed, graceful movements stuttered to a halt as her green-eyed gaze darted over to his. "Well, sort of."

She hurried around the bed to complete the other corner, and plucked the bedspread out of his hands. "I'm just kind of going through a bad spell right now, with…Loverboy and Blake and Troy and…" She hugged the cover to her chest and laughed, but he couldn't detect any real humor. "I'm sorry that my problems have turned your life upside down, Michael. Sometimes I wish you never would have found that letter. I never meant to get you or Mike or Troy or anyone else hurt."

Michael pulled the cover right back and tossed it onto the bed. Something closer to the Neanderthal in him pushed aside rational thought. He snatched the front of the jacket she wore, an edge of the collar in each hand, and pulled her right to him. Close enough for toes to touch. Close enough for breaths to mingle. Far enough away that he could see deep into the expressive kaleidoscope of moss, jade and emerald in the irises of her eyes.

"I can't imagine you dealing with that bastard on your own. His actions are already escalating, and I've seen firsthand where that kind of diseased relationship leads." He smoothed the damp silk of her hair off her cheek. "No woman should be at any man's mercy like that."

"Michael, is this…?" She slid her hands around his wrists, eliciting sparks of heat against his skin. Those Irish eyes were so vivid, so vulnerable. "Is that the cop talking? Or the man? Because I really don't want to misread what's going on here."

He traced the edge of the bandage on her chin, carefully avoiding the neat row of stitches underneath. "I always thought we were the same guy. I want to protect you for Mike's sake. He needs you." He pressed his thumb against the soft pink swell of her lips and the desire to claim those beautiful lips throbbed inside him. "Sweetheart, I'm fifteen years older than you. But I'm sure not feeling like a daddy watching out for his little girl."

"I sure don't feel like a little girl around you." She smiled beneath his touch. "You're not who I would have thought I'd want. But I do. I can't help it. I do."

"You're good for my ego, Miss Legs." He stroked his thumb across her lips, denying himself the pleasure of touching them with his own. He needed to think here, not just react. This was more than lust he was feeling for Jillian, more than duty that had him making a bed for her under his roof. "But I never thought there'd be another woman in my life after Pam died. I don't know what to make of whatever's going on between us."

A tug on his wrist pulled his thumb away from its distracting exploration. "Do you feel like you're betraying her by feeling something for me?"

"No," he answered honestly. "I know that chapter of my life is over. I'll never forget her—she gave me my son and fifteen beautiful years of marriage—but I don't know what it is I feel for you. I don't want to get it wrong. You've got enough to cope with—hell, we both do. I don't want to complicate things more than they already are. I thought I was done with relationships, that I would be a cop and a dad for the rest of my life—and I was fine with that. But then you come smiling in and waking things up and making me think I'm not quite so—"

"Don't you dare say…" her face crinkled up in an adorable attempt to hide another yawn "…over the hill. See? You are in the prime of your life, Captain. I'm the one who can't keep up."

"It's two in the morning. Some old…" He saw the eyebrow of reprimand arch up and smiled. "Some *wise* man I am. Keeping you up talking when you need your rest." Fisting the jacket collar in both hands, he pulled her forward and pressed a kiss to her forehead. His lips lingered against her smooth, cool skin as he fought the magnetic desire to pull her body into his, to feel her supple curves aligning with his harder angles, to feel her generous spirit consume his closed-off heart and breathe life into it again. He kissed her again and pulled away, because that was what *she* needed right now. "I'm at the end of the hall if you need anything."

She wrapped her arms around her waist in a posture he was beginning to recognize as a tell for when she was feeling vulnerable. And it made every instinct in him want to hold on tight and shield her from whatever made her afraid or unsure. But she needed protection right now, a chance to recuperate. And as long as his head wasn't in the right place, he wouldn't be any good to her.

"I want to finish this conversation, Michael. I think it could be very important…" another yawn "…for both of us."

He felt disjointed, incomplete, keeping his distance like this. He was a grown man—his body could simmer with want and he could walk away and deal with it. But his brain was a different thing. He needed to think. He needed to understand what he was feeling before he could give her the answers she needed. "When we're rested and thinking clearly. I promise. Good night, Jillian."

"Good night."

Walking away from that wounded, worried face was one of the hardest things Michael had ever done.

SHE HADN'T HAD the nightmare for a long time. Try as she might to wake herself, Jillian's body and mind were too tired, her emotions too raw and unsettled, to will it away.

Jillian couldn't think clearly as she tumbled through the doorway and landed in a heap on the floor. The room was dark, the smell was foul. Too much cologne couldn't mask the body odor and incense that reeked throughout the apartment.

The slam of a door jerked her to her senses. The hand on her arm jerked her to her feet. "Did you and your boyfriend help yourself to my stash?"

"No!"

Isaac Rush's hard fingers pinched her arms. His pockmarked face twisted with contempt. "He didn't pay, sugar. You're gonna have to."

"I don't have any money."

He picked her up and tossed her onto the bed like so much trash. "You think I'm giving it away for free here?"

"Isaac, no." Jillian scrambled to get away when he sat at the foot of the bed and kicked his shoes off. Her arms and legs tangled in the covers and she fought to free herself. "I don't do that. Blake said he paid you. I want to see Blake."

"Blake's already gone, sugar. Left you to take care of the bill." He reached out and touched her foot. She jerked it away and backed against the headboard. Isaac laughed as he crawled farther onto the bed. "That's not how a man takes care of his lady." Striking as quick as a snake, he grabbed her ankle and dragged her back down on the bed. She kicked with her free foot, but he got hold of that ankle, too. And then she was flat on her back and he was on top of her. "I could set you up for life, baby, if you'd just spread those long legs and be with me."

"I don't... I don't want to." She shoved his face away from hers, kicked at his legs, twisted her knee.

Her shoe clipped his shin and he swore. He slapped her across the cheek. "Everybody pays!" The blow rang through her skull and brought tears to her eyes, killing the fight long enough for him to unzip her jeans. "One way or the other, everybody pays."

"Stop." She smacked at his shoulders and tried to roll him off her. She was vaguely aware of a door opening, of someone else entering the room.

"Sugar, we've got something special. You know we do."

She was more aware of his hand tugging down her pants. Jillian clawed at his wrists. "Stop!"

A shadow loomed up behind Isaac, and suddenly he flew across the room and she was free. Blinded by tears and panic and darkness, she could only hear the scuffle, the grunts and protests as she scrambled off the bed and fastened her jeans. Her rescuer grabbed a syringe from the nightstand and followed Isaac into the corner. It had never been this bad before. She'd never been this terrified.

Before she could even think to run, the black man who'd gotten rid of Isaac was back. Mr. Lynch. Oh, God. Did he want something from her, too? He grabbed her arm, but Jillian's scream was quickly muffled by the clamp of his hand over her mouth.

He'd dragged her all the way to the lobby doors before he let her speak again. "What are you doing? Where are you taking me? Where's Blake?"

"That pig of a boyfriend got you into this mess. I'm gettin' you out." He threw open the door and pulled her onto the front stoop. "I never believed it was right to pay like that. You ain't even legal age yet. You're too good for this life. Too young." He shoved her away and turned for the door. "Go home, girl."

Jillian ran back. "I won't leave without Blake. Isaac will hurt him when he finds out I took a hit and didn't pay."

"You're not paying that way." He caught her by the arm and hauled her all the way down the stairs. "Your boyfriend's long gone. Isaac's my problem. You don't ever come back here."

"But—"

"You don't belong here, girl." When she didn't move, he pushed her away. "Get out of here!"

Once Jillian found her feet, she ran. She ended up on her brother Eli's doorstep.

The next day she was in court, her skin crawling with a terrible need.

Then she was in her small room at the Boatman Clinic, going through withdrawal. In Dr. Randolph's office for meeting after meeting, and talking and hugging and healing.

For a moment, Jillian breathed fresh air. Her body relaxed. She rolled over in the bed.

And then the merciless talons from her past dug into her mind and sucked her back down into the nightmare.

She couldn't escape. Not ever. Not really. The fear was the same, the helplessness real.

Red carnations were raining down all around her, stinging her sinuses with their perfumey scent. The horrible sound of fists pounding on bruised and broken flesh spasmed through her body. A man's voice whispered disturbing, indistinct words in her ears about love and need and being his. Then he just said her name.

Over and over again.

"Stop it." Jillian thrashed from side to side, bound by the words, tortured by the promise behind them. "Stop it!"

And then she was running. Pushing her way through the sea of flowers and running through the darkness. The voice pursued her.

Jillian. Jillian.

"No!" she cried out. A light flashed on, searing through her retinas and bringing her pain. "Please, no."

With light came a new scene, more grisly and frightening and confining than the last.

She was trapped on an elevator now, the walls and floor red with blood, not flowers. A dark figure lay slumped in the corner, its moans of pain matching Jillian's own mewling cries.

This was her. Her fate. Her punishment.

Jillian. Jillian.

"Leave me alone!"

The elevator doors opened, but there was no place to run, nowhere to hide. A faceless man walked in, carrying a bouquet of bright red flowers. "You're not alone. I want you. I love you."

"No." She backed into the corner, raised her hands to fight.

"I love you." The flowers had vanished and his hands were on her now.

"No."

"I love you, Jillian." His hands crept around her throat.

She struck out at his featureless face. "No!"

He raised his fist into the air. "Love me."

"No."

She felt his rage like a fist in her gut. "Love me!"

"No!"

"Love me!"

"Jillian!" Hands were truly on her now, battling with her flying fists and twisting body as her screams tore through her. "Jillian, wake up!"

"No!" Jillian panted for breath. Sweat beaded between her breasts and at the small of her back.

Her eyes focused on the light from the lamp on the bedside table. Then coal-black hair with sprinkles of silver registered. Her wrists were bound against her pillows, her body pinned in a spread-eagle position. She saw broad shoulders, an unshaven chin and midnight-blue eyes.

"Michael?"

"Are you with me?" Those piercing eyes scanned every nuance of her changing expression as she found her way back to the football-themed bedroom in Michael Cutler's house.

As she found her way back to the blessed security of Michael watching over her. "Michael!"

He released her as soon as he knew she was herself. As he pulled away the covers that wreathed her body, she pushed herself up and threw her arms around his neck.

"Michael, it was awful."

"Shh." He absorbed her momentum, catching her around the waist and falling backward onto the bed, pulling her to rest on top of him. He smoothed the sticky hair away from her temple and pressed a kiss there. "It was a bad dream. Just a dream. You're safe."

She shifted her ear to the reassuring thump of his heart and turned her nose into a crisp mat of sooty curls and the clean, familiar scent of his warm skin underneath. He loosened her hair and sifted his fingers through it, then slipped his hand beneath the weight of it to palm the nape of her neck. Jillian wasn't sure how long they lay together that way, with Michael gently rocking her back and forth, feathering kisses against her hair and neck and down across the jut of her shoulder.

When she finally sighed an unfettered breath and wiped the remnants of tears from her swollen, hot eyes, he shifted his grip to frame her face and tilt her eyes up to meet his. A hint of a smile played on his lips. "You gonna clock me again?"

"Did I really hit you?" He tapped the edge of his jaw and her gaze flew to the spot. A red mark. She felt her own cheeks turn a similar color. "Oh, no. I'm sorry."

She made a graceless attempt to find a place to put her knees and climb off him. But he foiled her escape by simply smiling and rolling onto his side, dumping her onto the bed beside him and throwing his leg over both of hers to let her know he had no interest in breaking the contact between them.

And there was plenty of contact. Lots and lots of places where their bodies touched or the thin barrier of her tank top and panties, and his black boxer shorts left little to the imagination. Jillian let Michael's deep, drowsy voice mesmerize her while her body took note of all the glorious, intimate contrasts between them.

"That's why I held you down. Hope I didn't scare you. Just protecting myself." The crisp texture of hair along his muscular thigh and calf tickled her smoother skin like the soft lick of a cat's tongue. His left hand had settled with a possessive claim around her bottom, trapping her soft feminine center between the heat of his palm and the unyielding hardness of his body. "You scared me plenty enough for both of us. Your screams woke me. You were really fighting a demon of some kind. Do you need to talk about it?"

"I haven't had the nightmares for a long time," she admitted, feeling the dark shadows of memory and imagination being chased back into the corners of her mind by her own growing response to the heat and strength of the man holding her. Jillian rubbed her palms across the angles of his neck, chest, shoulders and arms, waking a primal feminine power inside her to feel his muscles jump and bunch beneath each stroke of her hand.

"You were exhausted. That doesn't help." He shifted his position slightly, perhaps to hide the growing evidence of his arousal nudging against her thigh. His blue eyes demanded her attention and she willingly tilted her face to read the promise shining there. "Were you thinking about what happened tonight with Rush and Lynch? They're both in jail tonight. Rivers is in the hospital, with a guard watching him. They can't hurt you."

"I know." Her breathing quickened when his gaze dropped to her lips and his eyes dilated and darkened. "It was just some of the horrors of my past getting mixed up with everything that's going on now. Tonight. The letters. Mrs. Anthony. What you said about things getting worse."

"I shouldn't have scared you like that." He blinked, moved his hands to a more neutral position, which turned out not to be very neutral at all because his chest brushed against the pearls of her tight nipples, sending a burst of electric energy from that point of contact straight down to her womb, making every point of contact suddenly several degrees hotter. "I can be…" he swallowed hard and she watched the movement all the way down the column of his throat to see that his chest was rising and falling in an unsteady rhythm, too "…pretty harsh about making a point."

"No. I want to be smart about this—how I handle things." Jillian squeezed her eyes shut, fighting to control the warring impulses inside her. Fear and comfort. Nightmares and light. Past and present. Patience and desire. Following the lonely existence her choices had sentenced her to and following her heart.

"Jillian." He sensed it, too. The hand at her waist squeezed almost to the point of pain as he struggled to maintain control. "I haven't wanted anything like this for a long time. But I'm smart enough to know it can't just be something physical. I don't want to get this any more complicated. I don't want to make it worse for you."

"You can't." She stretched up to kiss his lips, feeling both hope and fear as he caught hers and tried to cling to them as she pulled away. "At the hospital, you said you needed something from me. I need something, too. I need to feel. I need to know that I'm okay, that some part of me is still normal. For a little while, anyway. Michael." She rubbed her palm across his prickly jaw and begged him to understand. "Please."

"Yeah." He dipped his head to reclaim her lips. Once. Twice. Again. "I need that, too." His dark eyes told her the truth. "I need you."

And then there were no more words. He framed her face between his hands and took her mouth in a deep, fiery kiss. Jillian ran her fingers behind his neck and over his hair, opening herself to him in every way possible. What he wanted, she bestowed. What she needed, he gave.

When he skimmed her tank top off over her head, she gasped in delight at every sure sweep of his hand against her feverish skin. When he laved his tongue around the pebbled tip of her breast, she moaned at the frictional caress. When he opened his hot, wet mouth over its aching mate, she bucked beneath him.

His hands were in her hair, at her hips, on her thighs and in the swollen, needy thatch between.

With every touch, an ember was born inside her. With every kiss, it burst into flame. She was molten, fluid, alive with Michael Cutler.

When he moved on top of her, pressing her body into the mattress beneath the good, masculine weight of his, Jillian welcomed him as he slipped inside. Michael propped himself up on his elbows so he could soothe the waiting sparks with a kiss on her panting, parted lips. Jillian wrapped her long legs around his hips and locked them together. She wrapped her arms around his shoulders to hold on for the ride. She wrapped herself up in the power of that deep midnight gaze and let him see the flames of need and gratitude and love shining in her own eyes.

She pulled him down to her when he began to move inside her. He thrust his fingers into her hair, burying his nose against her neck as he plunged into her throbbing heat.

Jillian came and cried out and cried out again as the fire exploded deep inside and radiated through her in wave after wave of heat. A moment later, Michael's hands fisted in her hair and he poured out his own release deep inside her.

Sometime later, while Jillian dozed on the pillow of Michael's shoulder, he picked her up and carried her down the hall to his own bedroom and tucked her into the four-poster bed. She murmured a drowsy protest that her own legs were working and he shushed her with a kiss.

He climbed into the bed behind her and spooned his body to hers, pulling the covers up over them both.

"Sleep, sweetheart." Brushing her tangled hair off her face, he whispered a promise against her ear. "You're safe."

Jillian sank into a deep, decadent sleep. Together, they'd burned the nightmares out of her system and replaced them with the sweet dreams and fierce gift of Michael Cutler's healing touch.

MICHAEL TOOK THE STAIRS two at a time, carrying a tray filled with two mugs of coffee and a package of chocolate fudge toaster pastries. Clearly, he was going to have to hit the grocery store if he was going to be keeping two teenage boys in his house.

But when he opened the bedroom door—and quickly closed it behind him again—food was no longer the first thing on his mind.

Jillian was standing in front of the bathroom mirror, wrapped in nothing but a towel. She had her long brown ponytail draped over one shoulder and was using his comb to smooth the tangles of their late-night tussle from her hair. "Good morning."

Obviously, she'd opened the door to let the steam from her shower escape—not to give him a midmorning peep show that revved up his energy more than that first cup of coffee he'd already drunk. So he made a valiant effort to turn his head from each stroke of her hand and carry on a normal conversation. "Good morning. Coffee?"

"Please."

He set the tray on the dresser and brought her a mug and one of the pastries. "Sorry. Breakfast pickings are pretty slim today. The boys have already wolfed down the cold pizza and grazed through whatever they could find in the cabinets."

She laughed as she set down the comb and picked up the steaming mug. Her sniff and sip and resulting "mmm" were a little like heaven for him, too. "That's good. Thanks."

Tactical error. In addition to miles of smooth, tanned skin stretching over sleek curves, the humid air in the smaller room was heavy with the scent of soap and Jillian herself. But he could handle this morning-after awkwardness if he didn't look directly at her or her reflection in the mirror.

But his effort to avoid her eyes left him staring at the long purplish bruise that adorned her collarbone this morning. He reached out and touched it gently with his forefinger, and then touched another bruise on her arm, and another. He bit back the furious desire to count each of the marks on her arms and legs, and who knew where else, from her tumble down the stairs with Blake Rivers last night.

She seemed to think the risks she took were some kind of penance she owed for a rebellious youth. But no woman, especially a warrior as brave and stubborn and giving as Jillian Masterson, deserved to be hurt by the very scum of the world she tried so hard to help.

Something about the stillness of his posture, or his inability to move his gaze from the black-and-blue swelling at her knee, must have betrayed him. She cupped the side of his clean-shaven jaw and turned him to face her. "Michael."

"Do they hurt much?"

"I'm okay. My chin's a little tender," she admitted,

"but I'm okay. I'm better inside, too, now. Thanks to you."

He caught her hand and pressed a kiss to her palm before pulling away. *Lighten the mood, Mr. Gloom and Doom.*

Turning to rest his hip on the vanity beside her, Michael pulled out the slick material that he'd stuffed into the back pocket of his jeans. "Here." He handed her the pair of basketball shorts that Mike had picked out for her. "I thought you might like to wear something besides those blood-spattered khakis today."

Mention blood. Right. That's how to move beyond that raw feeling of wanting to do some damage to the people who'd threatened and hurt her.

He'd have to learn to count on Jillian's resiliency. "Mike doesn't mind me wearing them?"

"He offered."

"I'll have to thank him." She pulled the shorts on beneath her towel, hiding a few more inches of leg, and tilted her mouth into a frown. "You're still going to take me back to my apartment to get my own things, right? I called Lulu at work, and she said she'd get Dylan to cover for me until lunch. But I can't wear these when I do show up."

"Relax. I'm off the clock today. I'll take you."

"And I'd like to get my own wheels back."

"Your SUV will be safe enough on the KCPD lot." She propped a hand on her hip and turned to argue, but he didn't give her the chance. "Besides, I'm not letting you go anywhere without an armed escort. Today, I'm your man. I'll take you home, take you to work, take you to wherever. But I am not letting you out of my sight until we, *a,* have a better idea of who Loverboy might be and what his intentions are, and, *b,* I know you're not going to run off and put yourself in unnecessary danger again trying to help someone else."

The frown curved into a wry smile. "That's awfully bossy of you."

Michael sat back on the vanity top and crossed his arms over the front of his black T-shirt. "I like being in charge."

"So I gather." She rested a gentle hand on his forearm. "That's an awful lot of responsibility, Michael."

"I can handle it."

"You probably can," she agreed. "But that doesn't mean you have to be in control all the time. Cut yourself some slack."

Right. When Michael Cutler lost his focus, he got off his game. And that's when people got tossed down a flight of stairs. Or shot by an obsessive ex-boyfriend.

As if he was going to let any of that happen again.

"Get dressed."

She arched a rebellious eyebrow. "Yes, sir."

When Jillian turned to pull on her bra and tank top and lose the towel altogether, Michael went back into the bedroom to retrieve his own cup of coffee and try to get his head firmly back into cop mode, which meant putting some distance between them.

He took a bite of cold pastry and chewed while he slid his holster and badge onto his belt and secured his Glock. Maybe he needed his uniform and body armor on to get last night and the memory of Jillian's sexy, fragrant hair and supple body flying apart all around him out of his head. When Jillian padded out of the bathroom and went straight for the black KCPD jacket he'd loaned her last night, and shrugged it around her shoulders, he knew he was never going to be able to completely separate his thirst for the fire Jillian brought into his life from his need to protect her.

But he'd find a way to get the job done. "I got the boys up without any problem and got their day started," he reported.

"I could have helped with that."

"You needed your sleep."

"And you didn't?"

She was tying on her tennis shoes now. Her sporty attire and lack of makeup made her look even younger. But the legs? His jacket? His Neanderthal hormones were kicking in again. Nope. He wasn't tired at all.

He gave up on the idea of breakfast and keeping his distance and crossed to where she was sitting on the edge of the bed. Pulling her to her feet, Michael wrapped her in his arms and covered her mouth with a kiss. He teased her lips and taunted and tasted, and then got dead serious about claiming all of the eager response she offered when she stretched up on tiptoe and wound her arms around his neck, running her hands along his nape and hair in that needy, graspy way that had ripped away the last of his defenses last night.

When he felt the bedpost at her back, he realized he'd been shamelessly driving his hips against her, and finally tore his mouth from hers. His heart was pounding, his breathing was ragged, his jeans were tight. But he rested his forehead against hers and pulled back, desperately needing the cool air that flowed between them.

Apparently, the only way he was going to know peace with this woman was to hold her in his arms 24/7. But his peace of mind wasn't her problem. He looked down into her upturned eyes, thinking she knew exactly just how far out of his control his life was spinning since he'd invited her into it.

But that wasn't a fact he was ready to admit. Not when he needed to keep it all together to protect her from Loverboy.

He turned away from those knowing green eyes and swatted her bottom before heading for the door. "Say good morning to the boys. I'll meet you out front in my truck."

HIS CLOTHES WERE WRINKLED and a little ripe after his long night. A bite of lunch would be nice. But he wasn't leaving his parking place until he knew Jillian had come home and seen the gift he'd left for her.

He knew the policeman had taken her to the hospital, that she'd be cleaned up and cared for there. He'd wanted to be at the medical center this morning to see for himself that she hadn't been seriously injured, but he'd been unavoidably detained.

What happened last night couldn't be allowed to happen again. Sweet, brave Jillian in the wrong part of town, outnumbered and outgunned. She was fortunate that her injuries hadn't been life threatening. A tumble down those old stairs could have broken her neck. She could have been hit, strangled, or shot by a desperate man so full of himself that he didn't care about the danger he put others in.

But *he* cared. He cared that Jillian was safe. That she wouldn't be hurt like that again. He'd seen to it personally that that bastard would never hurt her again.

She'd be so pleased. It was the least he could do for the woman he loved. It was just a taste of all he was willing to do for her.

He pulled down the visor over the steering wheel and touched the picture of her he'd clipped there. "I'll take care of you, Jilly. Whenever you need me, I'll be here for you. One day you'll understand just how much I love—"

A black pickup truck passed him on the road and turned into the parking lot of Jillian's apartment building. He'd been concerned that he hadn't seen her dark blue SUV in the lot, but now it looked as though the officer who'd driven her to the hospital last night had also picked her up this morning.

He didn't like that. Didn't like other men doing favors for her. Last night, he'd allowed it. It was quicker than getting an ambulance to her, and he'd had no other choice but to let her go. But today…

Suspicion and loathing burned a hole in his empty belly. He kissed his fingertip, then shook it in reprimand at the smiling image looking back at him, before closing the visor and starting the engine. She shouldn't be trying his patience like this, not when he'd been so worried for her. Not when he'd done so much.

After the black pickup pulled into a parking place, he turned into the lot himself and slowly circled around, keeping an eye on Jillian. When the driver got out, he tapped on the brake and laughed at his foolishness. It was that old cop, the one with gray in his hair. He never should have suspected Jillian of betraying him. Naturally, she'd feel safe with a father figure like that. Considering where she'd come from, all she'd endured and overcome, she probably found great comfort in the paternal asexuality of Graybeard there.

He waited and watched as the senior cop opened her door and walked her around to the back of his truck.

And then he saw that they were holding hands. They

laughed. She tugged on the man's hand and he turned. Jillian touched the side of the old man's face and drew him down for a kiss.

He sat up straight. His blood boiled in his veins.

The tramp! Giving her lovin' out for free to every man she met when he'd been faithful and true to her for longer than she deserved. He loved her because she was sweet and innocent and his.

"I love you, Jillian." He shifted his foot to the accelerator. "*I* love you."

CHAPTER TEN

JILLIAN HAD HER keys out of her pocket as soon as Michael turned the truck into the parking lot of her apartment building. But she wasn't about to let this conversation end with him claiming that he was perfectly fine—that there were no lingering regrets about the outcome of the hostage crisis at the bank yesterday, that he wasn't as perplexed by the yin and yang of their relationship as she was, and that everything was peachy keen and under control in his world.

"I know it's hard." She reached across the seat and tugged at the sleeve of the pullover sweater he wore, wanting to offer comfort as well as understanding. "But acceptance does come. With enough time."

He took his hand off the wheel long enough to squeeze her hand. "Have you moved past feeling guilty about the things you did all those years ago in No-Man's Land?" When she pulled away at the uncomfortable change of topic, he let her. "I know you understand guilt and regret the way I do, Jillian. Have you really moved on and left all that behind you?"

"Most of the time."

"And when you can't?"

"Like with you and the shooting yesterday?" Uh-huh. She could tell by the tension in his knuckles around the steering wheel that the incident was still weighing heavily on him. "I'm blessed with family. And a good therapist who still listens to me every now and then when I need him."

"I tell my men to talk to the police psychologist when they need to." Michael pulled into a parking space and turned off the engine, turning in his seat to face her. "Pam used to do that for me. Just listen. Before she got sick. I wouldn't dump on her after that. And I won't unload on Mike."

Had he talked to anyone beyond a grief counselor since his wife's death? Pam Cutler had been blessed to have such a stalwart man by her side as she succumbed to cancer. But maintaining control of his emotions didn't necessarily mean Michael was dealing with them. "Maybe you should try opening up with Mike a little. He's sixteen. He's trying to be a man. But he's been through a lot. Maybe if he sees you opening up about some of your fears and frustrations, he will, too."

"Damn, if that doesn't make sense." His eyes narrowed as if he couldn't quite believe what he'd heard. Or couldn't believe he was actually considering taking her advice. With a shake of his head he got out of the truck and circled around to meet her. He took her hand and walked her toward the building. "How'd you get so wise for someone so young?"

Jillian halted at the back of his truck and tugged on his hand to turn him. "I'm twenty-eight, Michael, not a child."

"Don't I know it. This might be a hell of a lot easier if you were."

With a smile, she cupped his strong jaw and rewarded his open-mindedness with a kiss. She didn't intend to make it easy for him to dismiss her very real, very grown-up love for him. "You can dump on me anytime," she whispered. "And keep talking to Mike. Give him a chance. Give yourself—"

She heard the whine of tires spinning to find traction.

"Jillian!" A powerful engine roared in her ears an instant before Michael's arm clamped down like a vise around her waist and they went flying through the air. A green monster barreled past in a rush of wind, spitting gravel that nipped at her skin a split second before they hit the ground and skidded across the asphalt. Michael tucked her head against his chest and they rolled until the front wheel of his truck slammed them to a stop.

"Stay down!" Michael scrambled to his feet, gun drawn, and ran after the speeding car.

"Michael, no!"

Ignoring new bumps and dizziness and shock, Jillian sat up, curling her knees to her chest and huddling next to the wheel as she braced for the sound of a gunshot. Tires screeched. She cringed. Horns honked. Michael cursed. No shots. Thank God. And then the only sounds she heard were her heart pounding against her ribs and the crunch of footsteps hurrying back toward her.

"This is Captain Cutler, S.W.A.T. Team One."

As soon as she saw him turn the corner between his truck and the car beside it, Jillian pushed to her feet. His gun was back in its holster and his cop face was on as he tipped his cell phone away from his mouth and took her hand to help her stand. "You're bleeding." He nodded down at her knee. "You okay?"

"Good enough." She stooped over to brush the debris from her skinned-up knee and idly noted she had a matching pair of bum knees now, not unlike her childhood as a tomboy. From this angle she also noted the tear in the sleeve of Michael's sweater and the scrape along his elbow underneath. "You?"

"I'll live." He hugged her right into his chest, blocking her between the vehicles, as he turned his attention back to the dispatcher on his cell phone. "I know *green* and *car* isn't much to go on. Run the partial plate to see what you get. Keep me posted if traffic patrol pulls over anyone that matches. Cutler out."

He clipped his phone back on his belt. Keeping her tucked against his side, Michael headed across the lawn, making a beeline for the front door even as his eyes scouted in every direction around them. "Let's get you inside in case he decides to come back for round two."

Jillian had no problem hanging on and picking up the pace. "Do you think that was him? Loverboy?"

"Oh, I know it was."

"Did you see his face?"

Michael stood at her back while she unlocked the security door and led him inside. "I was too busy trying not to get hit. We almost had a head-on collision at the entrance. He was gone by the time I got the other car clear."

"No one else was hurt?"

"Not this time." Despite her nightmare, they went straight for the elevator. Once inside, he continued to hold her and Jillian rested her head against his shoulder, feeling the adrenaline of fear and danger starting to wane. "A few days ago, you said you felt like someone was watching you. Maybe he's been around here all along and I was too blind to see it. Did you recognize the car? Do you think you may have seen it before?"

She waited for the doors to open on the third floor before she answered. "I didn't get that good of a look—

just a blur of green as it flew past us. It was a lighter color. Almost mossy. I'm trying to think of anyone I know who has a car that color..." She saw the envelope tacked to her door at the end of the hallway. "Michael."

Dread rooted her to the spot for one moment. Outrage sent her running down the hall the next.

But Michael was there, snatching her wrist out of the way as she reached for it. "Don't touch it. I want to know how he got inside the building. Do you have gloves inside?" She nodded. "Get 'em."

Under Michael's careful eye, she took the envelope inside her apartment. Self-adhesive seal. No stamp. No postmark. Just her name typed across the front.

While Michael paced from window to locked door and back to the sink to wet down some paper towels, Jillian opened the envelope. A strip of pressed gold and nickel slipped out and clunked onto the kitchen table. She flipped it over to see the *R* engraved on the opposite side. A money clip. Was it another unwanted gift? It wasn't her initial and she didn't want it any more than she'd wanted those flowers. Was it something she was supposed to recognize? She unfolded the letter. Maybe she'd find answers there.

My dearest Jillian,

Are you safe? Are you well? You've changed the lock and now I can't get in to help you. It's all right, my love. I know you're afraid. I forgive you.

I was frightened myself last night. For you. It broke my heart to see how brave you were. You don't belong in Isaac Rush's world. You never did. To know that you would risk your life to help someone who doesn't appreciate you the way I do sickens me. You have a noble, beautiful spirit that I've come to know so well, and I admire your dedication to helping others. But please, please, please—don't let your past destroy you. It would kill me to see you hurt by another man.

The blood drained down to her toes and she sank into the nearest chair as she read on.

I love you. More than my own life. More than my own freedom. And I know you have feelings for me, too, that we can never express. You don't have to say you love me. Because of your brave heart and generous spirit, I know you care.

I will treasure the beautiful gift you are every day, even when we're apart. I will honor that gift. And I will protect the love you have for me inside you.

I have always been there for you, Jilly. I'm here for you now. Here is proof of my love for you. I've seen to it personally that the man who hurt you last night will never hurt you again.

I'm keeping you safe from the horrors of your life. I will always keep you safe. I know that some day when we are together, in this world or the next, you will thank me.

Until then I am forever,

Yours

"What has he done now?" Jillian swiped at the tears burning her eyes and looked down to the man kneeling beside her, cleaning her scraped-up knee. "I don't understand."

Michael set aside the towels and quickly read the note. "He was there last night. In No-Man's Land. He must have seen what happened to you in Troy's building."

"But what does he mean, 'never hurt you again'? Who does that freak think he's protecting me from?" *Oh, no.* She picked up the money clip on the table and traced the *R* with her gloved finger. *R. Rivers.* He'd used her as a shield to escape from Isaac and had pulled her down the stairs with him in his haste to get away. "Blake." She leaped to her feet, ignoring the pain of the sudden movement. "We have to get to the hospital. We have to help Blake."

"Jillian. Jillian!"

But she was already out the door. Already afraid she was too late.

MICHAEL'S PHONE CALLS to the Truman Medical Center and then to Edward Kincaid had given him the grim news long before he and Jillian arrived at the hospital. Not that she'd take his word and let him spare her the trip. She had to see it for herself.

Blake Rivers was dead.

The hospital room was about as cold and pristine as the anger beating in Michael's heart. He didn't care one whit about Rivers, but he cared a great deal about the stony-faced woman wrapped up in his jacket and hugging herself beside him.

Jillian shouldn't have to be here. She shouldn't have to see this. It wasn't the most disturbing D.B. Michael had ever dealt with. But the body was still in rigor mortis, indicating how violently and helplessly Blake Rivers had suffered right before his death earlier that morning.

Edward had gotten there first, to cordon off the room and take statements from the staff, who hadn't noticed anyone or anything out of the ordinary until Blake's monitors had stopped and signaled them at the floor desk. Edward hadn't been able to convince Jillian to wait out in the corridor to let them work. His wife, Dr. Holly Masterson-Kincaid, was the medical examiner in charge of the initial analysis of the body. She hadn't been able to convince her sister to leave the potential crime scene, either.

What chance did Michael think he had to get her out of here without upsetting her even further?

"Sweetheart..."

She jumped when he spoke and huddled even deeper inside the collar of his jacket. But her feet wouldn't budge. In the end, Michael opted to simply hold on to her.

"And you can rule out accidental death?" Edward asked his wife, taking Michael's cue to stand at the end of the bed to block the worst of the scene from Jillian's view. "He did have a head injury."

"Not a life-threatening one, according to his charts." Though not as tall as her younger sister, Holly Masterson-Kincaid had the same leggy figure and dark hair that Jillian had, as well as that familiar twist to her mouth when she was deep in thought. Like now, as she bent over Rivers's hospital bed with her flashlight and inspected the body. "The facial petechiae indicate suffocation, but there are no ligature marks or other bruising around his neck." She studied the fingernails on one hand before carefully sliding a protective paper bag over the hand. "There's trace here. And some of these bruises are newer than the others. He struggled against something. Or someone."

Energized by a sudden discovery, Holly circled behind her husband and approached the body from the opposite side. With a steady balance between flashlight and plastic tweezers, she plucked a tiny filament from Rivers's mouth and held it up. "Probably the person who held a pillow over his face."

After sliding the filament into a tiny envelope, Holly walked across the room. She hugged Jillian around the shoulders, and held on even tighter when she tried to shrug off her supportive touch. "I'm sorry, hon. It's definitely murder."

"I knew it."

Thank God she was responding to someone. A tear trickled down Jillian's cheek as she turned her eyes to her sister.

"Now can I get you out of here?" Holly asked.

With a nod, Jillian allowed Holly to lead her into the hallway and down to a row of seats. Michael followed and sat on the opposite side, wishing Jillian would hold on to his hand the same way she'd latched on to her sister's.

After a drink of water from Edward and a chance to compose herself, Jillian turned to Holly. "This is my fault."

"How do you figure that? Edward told me about the letters and the break-in. I would have thought Blake was a prime suspect—he never did seem to get over you breaking up with him."

"Can't say I'm sorry to see the SOB go." Edward sat on the arm of Holly's chair, resting his palm on her shoulder and taking her hand when she reached up to find his. "Do you know how many possession charges he's had over the years? They were all pled out or dismissed. He was spoiled and selfish and never good enough for you, kiddo."

"It doesn't matter who Blake was. Don't you get it? *I'm* the reason he's dead. First Troy Anthony's grandmother. Now this? Nobody look cross-eyed at me—he'll probably come after you, too." She turned to Michael, digging her fingers into the sleeve of his sweater, begging him to understand. "What if Mike throws a temper tantrum during a therapy session? Or you…" She reached up to cup his face and the tremors he felt in her normally confident touch nearly broke his heart.

"Jillian." He spread his hand over hers, warming her, comforting her, wishing he could tell her everything would be all right.

"I couldn't handle it if something happened to you or Mike." She turned to Holly and Edward, including them in her plea. "To any of you."

When she faced Michael again, she sat up straight and breathed in deeply. The tears had dried, the shaking had stopped. All good signs that she was feeling more like her old self again after the triple shock of the attempt on her life, the letter and Blake's death. Still, an uneasy feeling stirred in Michael's gut. He knew that determined glint in her eye. He wasn't going to like what she had to say.

"I want to meet this guy."

"Absolutely not."

"Bad idea," Edward echoed.

"Jilly, no."

"Three votes to one." Michael pushed aside his gut reaction of stark, crazy fear for her, and stated the facts in his most authoritative tone. "That bastard tried to kill you today. Everything he's done has gotten more dangerous and more personal. You are not going to seek this guy out. You are not going to contact him. You are not going to set yourself up as some kind of bait to smoke him out. We'll get him. Without putting you in more danger. I promise."

"I don't want to wind up like Daphne Mullins. She was a victim. I won't be. I want to meet this guy and tell him to his face he has no idea what…love is." Her gaze drifted away to a nebulous point beyond his shoulder, then snapped back into focus. "Jilly."

"What is it?" Michael asked, sensing something very important had just clicked together in her brain. And it had nothing to do with his warnings to keep her safe.

"He calls me Jilly." She turned to her sister. "Sorry, Holly, but it's not my favorite nickname. Mom and Dad used to call me that. It makes me feel like a kid."

"So…?"

She raised her gaze to Michael. He understood. She was already zeroing in on this Loverboy bastard, and he couldn't do a damn thing to stop her.

"I'm making a list of everyone who calls me Jilly."

"SHE CAN'T BE left alone. Ever. That's all there is to it."

Michael paced in his office at home, listening to the grim recording Edward Kincaid had brought over after he and Holly had gone back to Jillian's apartment to pack a bag of her things.

The messages recorded on Jillian's answering machine had started with a relatively benign "I'm so worried. Are you okay?" and had progressed to the definite threat of "You freaking tramp! After all I've done for you, you aren't even the least bit grateful?"

"How many messages did you say he left?" Michael asked.

"Lucky thirteen. The frequency of calls is harassment enough." Edward's expression looked as murderously grim as Michael felt. "Holly's already called Eli. He's on a flight back to K.C. first thing in the morning. I can get my brothers to help keep an eye on her when they're off the clock."

"My team will, too."

"But this is Jillian Masterson we're talking about. Stubborn as they come," Edward pointed out. "Unless you know some sweet-talk trick that I never learned, sir, she's not going to hole up in your house indefinitely while we try to ID the guy."

Michael tuned out the next "Jilly, I'm sorry. You know I love you. I didn't mean..." recording and sat in the leather chair behind his desk, leaning forward to where Edward sat on the opposite side. He might outrank Edward at KCPD, but there were familial concerns he needed to respect. "Are you and Holly okay with her staying here?"

Edward scratched at the late night stubble lining his scarred jaw before he nodded. "Like I said, stubborn. If this is where Jillian feels safe, then this is where we want her to stay. Your experience with witness protection and running special weapons and tactics means you're probably the best man for the job, anyway. But you know she's going after this guy. She wants to maintain her regular routine so that we don't scare him off. She thinks she's protecting us."

Yeah. That had been a pointless argument that had lasted all the way home from the hospital. The only way to truly make Jillian and the people around her safe was to move faster and think smarter than Loverboy. "Any suspects we can bring in for questioning?"

"Isaac Rush and his man Lynch both posted bond this morning. I vote for one of them as the perp in the car with the death wish. They both had history with Blake Rivers." Michael liked Edward's methodical approach to discussing a case, and wondered what his secret was for detaching his emotions from an investigation that hit so close to home. "Could be one of them had another reason for silencing Rivers, and is using this stalking thing to cover up the real motive. We're trying to trace their movements since their release from lockup this morning."

"You think terrorizing Jillian has been a setup to mask the motive for Rivers's murder?" Michael didn't like that scenario any better. "Are Rush and Lynch smart enough to plan out a hit that far in advance?"

"I'm just throwing possibilities out there. Holly told me that Lynch *rescued* Jillian back when she was a teenager—kept her from being assaulted by Rush. Maybe he's got some kind of savior complex with her. In his eyes he's taking care of her still."

"That would fit with what I overheard in the stairwell at Troy Anthony's building. She was pleading with Lynch to let her go *again*."

"Of course, if Rush was the one attacking her—"

"He doesn't have feelings for her." A drug dealer who still had a thing for the woman he'd gone after when she was an underaged teen? The idea curdled Michael's stomach. "He's a businessman."

"One who'd take Rivers out if he thought Blake was conducting business on his turf. He's not above using Jillian, or anyone else, to maintain his power." Another message from the answering machine tape began to play. "That son of a bitch."

"...death is the only way. My love for you is pure and lasting. I can't allow you to mock my feelings for you again. I won't abide that kind of cruelty. I'm ready to give you the opportunity to show me that your love runs just as deep." And if it didn't? Michael's hands curled into fists at his sides. "I'm forever yours, Jilly. Forever."

So Edward Kincaid wasn't any more inured to the vile filth Loverboy was spouting about Jillian than he was. Every curse Edward uttered resonated deep inside his bones as Michael walked over to the tape player and shut it off. "She doesn't hear this tape, understood?"

Edward caught the cassette when Michael tossed it to him. He tucked the tape inside his jacket pocket and stood. "What if she can identify the voice?"

Michael shook his head. "It's raspy and distorted on the tape. Either he's pretty inebriated or he's intentionally masking it. I won't put her through listening to those for no reason."

"There's no sense dumping the numbers on her cell phone, either. They're easier to trace. He'd be too smart to leave a number there. And we haven't had any luck narrowing down an ID on the green car, either. This guy has *anonymous* down to an art."

How did they trip up a guy that clever? One who knew enough about Jillian—where she worked, where she lived, where she went to help her patients like Troy Anthony—to avoid showing up on the radar anywhere? Michael splayed his hands, racking his brain for answers. "How do we get this guy to show himself? What's his weakness?"

With a soft knock at the door, he had his answer.

Jillian walked in.

Michael's heart flip-flopped inside his chest. He'd already lost Pam. He'd nearly lost his son. Both, to events beyond his control. And he'd been powerless.

He couldn't lose anyone else he loved on his watch. He couldn't do it. It almost hurt his eyes to look at Jillian and feel this way.

Bait.

"I'm ready to give you the opportunity to show me that your feelings run just as deep."

Death.

How could he ever risk Jillian's life? Even if that was the only way they could draw Loverboy out and shut him down for good, how could he risk losing her?

Jillian's green eyes narrowed as they met his across the room. She sensed something—something Michael couldn't yet put into words—and he turned away to needlessly straighten the items on his desk.

But when her sister came in behind her, the two women laughed. "I don't know about you, but I'm ready to drop." Holly went straight to her husband and wound her arms around his waist. "After the day we've had, I vote for a good night's sleep for everybody. We'll tackle everything fresh in the morning."

"Troy talked with his grandmother," Jillian added, getting Michael and Edward up to speed on what had been going on outside of this protection brainstorming session. "His aunt agreed to let Dexter stay with her family indefinitely, and the hospital is keeping LaKeytah until arrangements for home health care assistance can be arranged. And guess who's going to be doing physical therapy with her on her wrist and hand? As long as it doesn't interfere with her insurance coverage,

I figured doing some pro bono work was the best way I could make up for the attack."

Michael bit back the urge to point out that *she* wasn't responsible for any attack. Loverboy's skewed logic and growing penchant for violence were the only cause to blame. But Jillian couldn't be swayed from accepting some of the guilt.

"Then we got Troy and Mike to bed after teaching them Hearts and letting them beat us."

"Hey, I wasn't letting anyone win," Holly protested with a smile. "Those boys are sharp. You put them together as a team and they're unstoppable."

Michael appreciated the compliment about his son, even managed to generate a smile as he turned back to the group. "That's a testament to all the progress Jillian's made with them. Before Mike started physical therapy with her, I could barely get him to come out of his room. Now she's got him kicking ass and taking names."

"That's the Jillian brand of magic," Holly concurred. "She's always had a way of bringing out the best in people."

No one said the words, but judging by the sudden pall in the room, Michael suspected they were all thinking the same thing. Jillian's big heart had unknowingly touched Loverboy's, and brought out the absolute worst in the man.

Holly quickly went over and hugged her sister. "I'm sorry, sweetie. I've been trying to keep your mind off him all night."

"That's impossible." Jillian hugged back just as tightly. "I love you for trying, though. And for listening."

Holly pulled away and brushed a wayward strand of hair off Jillian's face. "You know, if the stress of all this gets to be too overwhelming—"

"Don't worry." Jillian pulled away and mimicked her sister's tender gesture, tucking one of Holly's dark curls behind her ear. "I'm not going to go off the deep end and start looking for a fix."

"What I was going to say, smarty-pants, is that you can call me anytime if you need to talk. Or see if Dr. Randolph is available. I know you haven't used for years and I know you're a grown woman now." Edward stepped forward, draping his arm around Holly's shoulder and backing up the message. "But that doesn't mean you have to cope with everything yourself."

"I won't."

"You don't have to take care of anybody but you right now."

"Yes, ma'am."

Holly ignored the teasing sarcasm and turned to Michael. "I asked her if she wanted to come home with us. She said she wants to stay here."

"That's fine with me." It was the only way Michael wanted it right now.

"Don't let her run off on any wild-goose chases," Holly cautioned. "She'll try."

Michael had already learned as much. "I know."

"I'll be good," Jillian promised, hugging Holly and Edward both and ushering them toward the front door of the house. "I'll let KCPD handle the investigation into Blake's murder. Now go. I need everyone well rested and on their A game tomorrow if you're going to be solving murders."

There was another round of trading hugs and shaking hands and saying good-night. Once Edward and Holly had driven away, Michael made a quick check of the house and grounds before bolting the door and turning out the lights. The boys were asleep. The house was secure. His gun had never left his side.

He found Jillian back in his office, staring out the window into the overcast night, hugging her arms around her middle. She'd changed into a pair of jeans and a long-sleeve T-shirt, hiding all of her injuries except for the stitches and bruise on her chin beneath her clothes and long hair. But he knew they were there. She stood tall and strong, but he knew how fragile she was inside. And when she turned to face him, he didn't buy the brittle smile on her lips.

"So did you and Edward decide my fate?"

He wasn't going to answer that loaded question. Instead, he held out his hand and hoped that Jillian would take it. "Holly was right. It's been a long, exhausting day. We both need our rest."

Though she took his hand and let him lead her upstairs to his bedroom, weary or not, Jillian made it clear she hadn't changed her resolve about finding Loverboy. "I promised to let you guys work on Blake's murder. But if there's anything I can do to make that rat come out of the woodwork, I'm going to. Of course, I'm hoping you or Edward or Eli will be there to catch him when he does."

Michael peeled off his torn sweater and tossed it into the trash can. "And how are you going to do that? Go through that list of yours and ask every man who has ever called you Jilly whether or not he tried to kill you today?"

"If I have to."

He carefully laid his gun and badge on the lamp table beside the bed, replaying in his head each of the threats from that tape. He'd heard that kind of sick rhetoric before and had seen firsthand where that kind of obsession could lead—and how little he could really do to stop it.

"Jillian." He circled around the foot of the bed and stopped her in the middle of changing into the T-shirt she slept in, taking her by the shoulders and giving her a slight shake. "I can't live through you becoming another Daphne Mullins. What if I'm not there when this guy shows up again? What if I can't save you?"

"Do you want to live with that kind of fear and doubt the rest of your life?" Green eyes, devoid of the hope and humor he'd once seen there, looked into his. "I don't think I can."

With that, Michael released her. He let her have the bathroom first and then quickly brushed his teeth, turned off the lights and slipped under the covers. She lay on the far side of the bed, curled into a ball, facing away from him. Not exactly an invitation to cuddle or try to make his point one last time.

Maybe he'd been foolish to ever consider a future with Jillian Masterson. Not because of the age difference that had once worried him. Not because he wanted her focus to be on Mike's continuing recovery. Not because she was headstrong and compassionate and driven to get involved helping others, even when it meant putting herself at risk.

He'd be a fool to plan a future with Jillian. Because he'd loved and lost before. And he wasn't sure he was strong enough to love and lose again.

Still, when the nightmare snuck into her dreams again, Michael was there to wake her and hold her and wipe away her tears. When she asked him to remind her what it was like to be cared for by a man she could trust, Michael stripped them both naked and made love to her in the most tender, beautiful way he knew how. And afterward, when she fell asleep in his arms, skin to skin, his fingers in her hair, her hand over his heart, Michael knew it was too late to save himself from the heartache of loving Jillian.

He loved her. Period.

He'd never been in control of falling for her at all.

CHAPTER ELEVEN

"ELI, YOU LOOK AWFUL." Jillian planted herself in her big brother's path to stop him from wearing a rut in the carpet outside Wayne Randolph's office at Truman Medical Center. Though little could diminish his tall, lanky, chiseled good looks, the fatigue that deepened the taut lines beside his eyes and mouth was marked enough to raise the concern of any sister worth her salt.

"Thanks, champ. You're a ray of sunshine yourself."

She reached up to straighten the knot of his tie and smooth his rumpled lapel. "Sit down and relax before you fall over. I know you were up all night finishing up your case so you could get here this morning."

"Champ, if I stop moving and fall asleep, I won't be any good to you. Your friend Michael had to report to work today. Edward is following up on a lead on that green car. So it's my turn for baby-sister sitting." He leaned over to kiss the top of her head. But she read equal parts chastisement and love in his dark eyes as he straightened. "You should have told me on day one when you started having trouble with this bastard."

"There wasn't anything I couldn't handle at first." His baby-sister remark told her she'd been right to believe that he'd yet to outgrow his overprotective genes with her. "And I wasn't about to give you a reason to shortchange your work at the D.A.'s office or lose sleep over me."

Eli arched a dark eyebrow. "For your information, I completed the job that D.A. Powers sent me to do in Illinois. And the only reason I ever lose sleep over you is that, unfortunately, I taught you everything you know about being hardheaded." His gaze slipped past her to the table behind the receptionist's counter. "Hey, is that coffee?"

She grinned as her brother chased down his favorite drink, though the guilt she felt at causing him worry and taking him away from a reunion with his wife, Shauna, didn't diminish. That guilt was one of the reasons she was here this morning. The other reason? It was the first of several long shots she intended to disprove.

"Jilly?" She turned as Wayne Randolph strolled into the reception area, his short hair slicked down by the spring rain falling outside. He set down his briefcase and opened his arms to greet her with a hug. No bad vibe there. Dr. Randolph felt too much like family for her to resist, and she walked into his arms and hugged him back. "To what do I owe the pleasure?" he asked, pulling away.

"Well, your receptionist said you didn't have any appointments until nine, and that if I got here early, maybe you could spare me a few minutes before your first patient? I hope that's okay."

"Heavens, yes." He picked up his briefcase and ushered her over to his office. "You don't need an appointment to come talk to me. Eli. Good to see you again."

He stopped when her brother approached and extended his hand. "Dr. Randolph."

The psychologist shifted his position so that his hand

rested lightly at the back of Jillian's waist as he faced the not-so-subtle head-to-toe inspection from big brother. "Will you be joining us? Is this a social visit?"

"No."

Jillian touched her brother's wrist and silently urged him to lighten up a tad. She had a feeling every man was suspect in his book until proven otherwise, and she fully intended to prove that the man who'd turned her life around in rehab was no suspect. Even if, after eleven years, he still called her Jilly. "I have a couple of things I wanted to get some advice on, Doc, if you don't mind listening. And a favor to ask."

Dr. Randolph nodded. "Sometimes you just need to talk things through with an objective listener. Eli, make yourself at home. Jilly, come on inside."

Jillian settled into a familiar tweed chair while Dr. Randolph shrugged into the white lab coat he wore over his shirt and tie. He paused for a moment to clean his glasses before crossing to the desk. He tucked his briefcase underneath beside his feet and leaned forward, propping his elbows on the blotter and steepling his fingers together. "So what's troubling you? Something with your brother? I remember having lots of conversations about him being strict and overbearing."

"That was my teenage perspective. He was pretty young himself when Mom and Dad died and he took on the task of raising Holly and me. We've worked through all that." For a moment, Jillian felt like kicking off her shoes and curling her legs beneath her in the chair the way she'd sat so many times in Dr. Randolph's company in the past. But she was older now, stronger, too, she hoped. And since he was giving up his time for her, she'd skip the reminiscing and get down to business. "No, I'm having a little trouble with a different relationship."

"What kind of relationship?" Even though this was an informal session, he pulled a mechanical pencil from his pocket and began jotting notes.

"The girl-boy kind."

He raised a bushy eyebrow. "You want dating advice? Not exactly my area of expertise."

"Maybe not. But you always did have a way of helping me think more clearly. After these past few weeks, I find myself second-guessing everything I do or say."

He sat back in his chair, tapping his pencil against his chin. "Because of this boy?"

"Man, Doc," she corrected. "This guy is definitely a man." She smiled at the vivid image of Michael Cutler's tall, whipcord body and piercing blue eyes. True, there might be some silver sprinkled in with the coal-black hair on his head and chest, but that only added some interest to the mix. His age didn't make him a mature man. It was more about his patience and caring and determination. His confidence. His skills as a protector—and a lover. No, there was nothing boyish at all about Michael Cutler. "With everything I've been through, I don't think I could be interested in anyone who had too much little boy in him."

"I've never known you to have a relationship before." Dr. Randolph adjusted his glasses to gauge her reactions to his words. "I know you've dated—I'd be surprised if a beautiful young woman like you didn't. But I always thought your trust issues kept you from committing to a relationship."

"Oh, I trust him." Michael was the first person she'd told about Loverboy—okay, so he'd discovered that letter and forced her to tell. But they'd shared so much this past week—heated arguments, quiet conversations. Fear. Laughter. She'd given him her body. She'd given him her heart. None of that could have happened without trusting Michael.

"I meant trusting yourself to make the right choices." Dr. Randolph was leaning forward again, probing for deeper answers. "You used to talk about the bad choices you made when you were young. I don't think you'd be talking to me if you believed you'd chosen the right man."

Jillian scooted to the edge of her chair. Perhaps she hadn't explained the problem clearly enough. "My feelings aren't the problem, Doc. Convincing him that we belong together—that we could really make it work—that's where I'm running into problems."

"Why is that?"

"Because he's older than me. We share a physical attraction. But sometimes I think…"

"What?"

Here came the second-guessing. "He thinks that I'm too young to know my own heart. Or that it'll change if someone else comes along." She gripped the arms of the chair, transferring her frustration into the nubby tweed upholstery. "It won't. He's the finest man I know. He's been there for me when I needed him the most. I've never felt this way about another man."

"Are you in love with him?"

Something fragile, yet hopeful, unfurled inside her. "Yeah. I love him. It even feels right to say it out loud. But how do I convince him?"

Dr. Randolph took the time to jot something more on his notepad. But when he looked up, he offered Jillian a paternal smile. "Be patient. He'll figure it out. Sometimes, when a man is older and set in his ways, it can be hard to believe that love has finally found him."

"Found him again," Jillian clarified. "He's a widower."

"Oh?"

Jillian was feeling better. The doc was right. Look at the patience it had taken to coax Mike, Jr., out of his wary shell. If she hadn't been so hung up with her paranoia about Loverboy's intentions, she might have been able to see that caution was a Cutler family trait. "Do you think I should say something to his son? I don't want Mike to think he's any less important to me just because I'm in love with his dad."

Dr. Randolph's pencil ripped through the top page of his pad. "Damn." He tore out the page and wadded it into a ball. When he tossed it toward the trash can and it deflected off the rim and rolled across the carpet, Jillian jumped to her feet to retrieve it for him. But Wayne Randolph was already out of his chair. He picked up the trash and dropped it into the pocket of his lab coat before Jillian could reach it. "He has a son?"

Jillian straightened when he did, sensing an irritation about him that wasn't there before. She was probably eating up too much of his time. "If it doesn't work out with his dad and me, I want Mike to understand that my feelings for him won't change."

He pulled back his sleeve and glanced at his watch.

"That's the right thing to do, isn't it?"

"Sounds to me like it's something you should discuss with this old man of yours."

"Old*er*," she corrected. "Trust me, there's nothing *old* about this guy."

"Hey, um..." Dr. Randolph pulled down his sleeve and turned to Jillian with an apologetic smile. "Sorry to cut this short, but I really do have to prep for my nine o'clock. You said you needed a favor?"

"I'm the one who should apologize for using up your time." She went with him when he headed for the door. "Do you remember anyone else from my rehab days who called me Jilly instead of Jillian? I know Isaac Rush did—still does."

The doc halted abruptly and caught Jillian by the hand, demanding she look up to see the concern etched on his features. "You're not having anything to do with that street thug again, are you? I thought you were smart enough to stay away from him."

"It wasn't intentional. But I ran into him when I was helping one of my patients. Needless to say, it wasn't a happy reunion." Jillian extracted her fingers from his grip and stuck her hands into the pockets of her running jacket. There was no easy way to confess this when he was probably already thinking the worst by her mention of Isaac Rush. "I've been getting some crank calls and letters addressed to 'Jilly.'"

"And you think Rush is behind it?"

"I don't know. I'm just trying to find out every possibility."

"'Jilly,' hmm? You know I won't be able to give you patient names."

"I know. But maybe someone who works there? Or used to? Anything you can remember would be helpful."

"I'll think on it." His concern eased back into a familiar smile and he drew Jillian in for a hug. "Be careful, Jilly."

"*You* be careful, Doc," she replied, pulling away and

opening the door. "I can't tell you how dangerous this guy is. I don't want to see anyone else I care about get hurt."

HE DIDN'T KNOW if he wanted to love her or punish her for betraying him.

His eyes burned as he lifted his head from his work and stared at all the images watching over him. He reached up and touched the worn spot on the photograph of Jillian running laps around the hospital complex. The early morning sun shimmered in the dark mane of hair that flew out behind her. So beautiful.

He curled his gloved fingers into a fist and drew them back to his lips, breathing deeply to ease the acrid bile of frustration and disappointment that churned in his stomach. An image might be beautiful to look at. But it couldn't compare to the warmth and softness he'd felt touching her real hair.

All of these captured faces couldn't match the real thing smiling back at him. And he'd made her smile often. That had always been his gift to her—to offer her a glimpse of hope when she needed it, to make her laugh. He'd done so many things for her—made her smile, helped her with work, eased her stress, kept her safe. He'd killed for Jillian Masterson. He was ready to kill again.

And that was how she repaid him?

He swept his fist through the air, pure rage clearing a path off his desk. Papers flew. Glass shattered. Tools bounced across the floor.

That image was burned into his head more clearly than any of the others he'd collected. His sweet, innocent Jilly touching another man's face. Pulling another man close for a kiss. Sticking her tongue down another man's throat.

Smiling and kissing and holding tight to another man.

She'd probably done other things to him, too. He'd seen where she'd spent the last two nights.

He'd loved her first. He'd loved her even when Jilly hadn't loved herself. He'd given her every opportunity to see that. His love was pure and everlasting, and she was destroying it with her foolish actions.

Her adolescent lust for that other man would pass. He would forgive her the transgression. His loyalty to her would always be true.

He deserved her love.

He deserved her.

No one else could have her.

She just needed his help one more time to understand that.

His resolve firmly in place, his outrage firmly in check, he picked through the debris on his desk and lifted the sealed envelope. He brushed off the bits of glass and slipped it inside the pocket of his coat. He slipped the freshly packed magazine of bullets into his gun and tucked it into its holster.

Then he stood and fastened the front of his coat over the bulk of the special gift he wore around his chest. His stint in the army had taught him several things. How to handle a gun. How to be silent and listen. How to do the tough job when necessity called for it.

And how to protect what was rightfully his.

"HE SHOOTS. HE SCORES!" Jillian cheered as Troy's shot swished through the net. She rebounded the ball and dribbled down the free throw lane out beyond the three-point line as he spun his chair and gave chase.

A little two-on-one ball at the end of the day seemed to be the ticket for lightening everyone's mood as they waited for Michael to come pick them up at the end of Troy and Mike's PT session. Not that Mike and Troy had given her much to complain about. During a set of arm curls in the weight room, Mike had even opened up a bit about his late friend Steve. He'd been the one into lifting weights and bulking up for the football team. While both boys had enjoyed working out and working hard during football camps, Steve had been the health nut. Because of that, Steve hadn't been drinking the night of the accident that had claimed his life. He'd volunteered to be the designated driver at the underage party where Mike had tried his first beers.

It had been an offhand comment between one weight machine and the next. But the confession gave Jillian a bit more insight into Mike's emotional state during his recovery. He wasn't just crushed over losing a friend and his ability to play football. He was probably feeling guilty about having survived the crash at all while his more responsible friend had died.

It was a discovery she'd mention to Michael. If he ever got there. Jillian's watch read 5:15. She prayed that Michael's unusual tardiness was the result of something as benign as rush-hour traffic, and not because his team had been called out to another dangerous situation. She wondered if Mike ever watched the clock that closely or worried this much about his father's late arrival.

Not at the moment, judging by the way he pushed his chair back and forth, trying to keep her away from the basket.

"Oh, no, buddy," she taunted, squaring off to shoot. "If you want to block my three-pointer, you're going to have to be taller than that."

"Masterson."

Jillian pulled up short midjump and turned to the gym's open doorway. Dylan stood there, his jacket zipped, his expression annoyed. She propped the basketball on her hip and jogged over to him. "Yeah, Smith?"

"Everyone's gone home. Are you okay to lock up or do you want me to stay until your cop friend shows up?"

"I'm good." She nodded over her shoulder, indicating the two teenagers behind her. "I won't be alone. Are you heading over to the Shamrock?"

"Not tonight." He patted his stomach, reminding her of the consequences of his last visit to the bar. "What do you want me to tell the cop sitting out front?"

"You noticed him, huh?"

"Kind of hard to miss the armed guards that have been hanging around the clinic the past few days. It makes some of my patients nervous. Hell, it makes me nervous." He pointed to his own face to indicate the bandage on her chin. "Are you sure you're ready to be back at work?"

"I'm fine." She summoned a smile. "I hope they haven't cramped your style too much." The tightness around his mouth never left his expression. "Dylan, is something wrong?"

"Nah." He shoved his hands into the pockets of his khakis and shrugged. "I guess I've got to stop hitting on you now. You and that cop are the real thing, hmm?"

"I hope so," she answered honestly. She had to shrug, too. "I know you tried. And I'm flattered. But, um, it just never clicked with me. And besides, there's the whole romance between coworkers thing that can get—"

"Pretty awkward. Yeah, I know."

Jillian extended her hand and an apology. "I hope we can still be friends."

After a momentary hesitation, Dylan took her hand and held on a little longer than what felt comfortable. "I'll get over it." When he finally let go, Jillian quickly returned her hands to the ball and retreated a half step. "I'll tell the officer outside you're still in here with the boys and lock the front door on my way out. The hospital corridor entrance and patio exit off the lounge are already locked. You should be safe. Good night, Jilly."

"Good…night."

Jilly? Everything inside her tensed and she hugged the ball to her stomach. No. Not Dylan. She couldn't have worked side by side with the man for this long and not have known, not have suspected.

She didn't take another full breath until he was out the door. She pressed the back of her hand to each cheek, feeling feverish and unsettled. *Idiot.*

A lot of people called her Jilly. Didn't make them all stalkers and killers. Dylan's mood could be chalked up to spicy peppers and a bruised ego. If he had wanted to hurt her, he'd have had more opportunity than most, given all the hours they worked together. His was one more name she could scratch off her list.

"Hey, Jillian," Troy called. "Are we playin' or what?"

Concentrate on the task at hand and let Edward run his investigation to track down Loverboy. Michael would be here soon enough and then her world would right itself again.

She pulled her ponytail away from the perspiration

at the back of her neck and spun around to face her opponents. "Definitely playing."

She ran the ball past Troy, then dribbled a circle around Mike's chair. When she turned to the basket to shoot, she had a wall of Mike Cutler, Jr., in her face.

He was on his feet, his leg braces locked, his hand in the air, positioned to block her shot. Jillian rocked back on her heels, beaming with a double dose of pride and awe. "Wow. Look at you. Standing on your own. Balancing yourself."

Despite the obvious clench of his jaw as he struggled to maintain his upright posture, Mike wore a bit of a devilish grin himself. "You said I needed to be taller."

"I thought basketball was lame." She quoted him from an earlier session.

"It is." He pulled the ball from her hands and sat back in his chair with a wicked grin. "But losing's worse."

With a round of cheers from Troy, he wheeled to the basket and banked a shot off the backboard. Jillian couldn't help it. She absolutely couldn't help herself. As soon as Mike and Troy were done butting fists and trading celebratory gibes, she reached around Mike's shoulders and hugged him. "I am so proud of you, big guy."

He patted her arm where it crossed his chest and tilted his ear against hers in a cool teenage guy version of a hug. "Thanks."

Pulling away before she embarrassed Mike, Jillian traded high fives with both boys. "Great workout today, guys. I think this rates a call to your dad to tell him the good news."

Mike's cheeks were pink. "All I did was stand up."

She leaned over and pressed a kiss to one of those pink cheeks and watched it redden. "Mike, what you did today is as big as the first day I left rehab and faced the world on my own.

"My phone's in my office. I'm calling your dad." She pulled her keys from the pocket of her slacks. She'd truly feel like celebrating if she knew Michael was on his way. Maybe surrounded by father and son and friend, she could actually push aside her fears about Loverboy for a little while. "Hey, guys?" As long as they were feeling good, she'd keep Mike and Troy moving. Hurrying over to the corner of the gym, she unlocked the storage closet and rolled out the ball bin. "Will you two gather up the basketballs and put them in the storage closet for me?"

"Will do."

"Thanks, guys."

With a buoyancy to her stride that belied her beat-up knees, Jillian headed out of the gym and down the corridor to her office. She tried to focus on the joy she felt at Mike's small victory instead of noticing the stillness of the clinic without patients and staff to create the normal buzz of noise that filled the rooms. She tried to imagine how thrilled Michael would be when she told him that Mike had made significant progress in his attitude toward rehabilitation today instead of imagining the curious eyes watching her from darkened offices and shadowed corners.

But when she rounded the corner to her office, Jillian quickly pulled back and flattened herself against the wall. She pressed her fingers against her lips to stifle the urge to call out or gasp with surprise.

Ever so slowly, she held her breath and peeked around the corner again. *Oh, no. Please no.*

She pulled back against the wall again and clutched

at the wallpaper behind her, willing her knees not to buckle.

There was a man at her door with a ring of keys, jerking on the knob and cursing beneath his breath. "Changed the damn lock here, too. Ah, Jilly, Jilly. What am I going to do with you?"

It could be coincidence—it could be lousy timing that he was here at this moment trying to break in. But Jillian knew. After all this time. After all the letters, the professions of love—after fear and murder had changed her life—she knew.

It was him. He was here.

With feet and heart like lead, she crept back along the corridor, barely daring to breathe as the man she'd known for so many years damned her and praised her with every other sentence.

Jillian's first intention was to get outside to the cop assigned to watch her until Michael showed up to relieve him. But he'd hear the door opening. A phone call from the front desk would make even more noise.

And then she remembered the boys.

She remembered LaKeytah Anthony's battered body and Blake Rivers's frozen dead face.

Training her ear to any sign that Loverboy was following her, she dashed into the gym. Her expression alone must have told the boys that something was wrong.

Mike pulled the ball he'd been about to shoot into the storage bin back into his lap. "What is it?"

Jillian grabbed Troy's chair and pushed him inside the closet. "Not a word. Either of you," she warned.

"What's wrong?" Troy asked.

"Shh."

Mike was already following them in. She plucked the basketball from his grasp and turned him so that both wheelchairs would fit. "If either of you has your cell phone, set it to silent and text 9-1-1."

Troy pulled out his phone.

"Jillian?" Mike caught her wrist as she climbed over his legs.

She had every intention of pulling the door shut and hiding in the closet with them. But then she heard the footsteps and knew she couldn't risk discovery and anyone else being hurt. She twisted free and squeezed his hand. "Text your father. Tell him Loverboy is here. He'll know what to do. And please, not one sound."

Without another backward look, she shut the door behind her. At the first tiny clank of chair wheels tangling with each other, Jillian started dribbling the ball. She made as much noise as she could, charging the basket and making a perfect layup, drawing attention away from the closet.

She never got the chance to make a second shot.

"Hello, Jilly. I suppose this meeting was inevitable. I'm glad I can finally tell you the truth."

Jillian turned around and looked straight into the barrel of Wayne Randolph's gun.

CHAPTER TWELVE

"I NEED EYES on this guy. Somebody tell me they've got a way into the gym."

Michael Cutler had been a cop for too many years to see this day. An emergency text message from his own son at the same time he got a 9-1-1 call from Dispatch? Both telling him Mike and Troy were trapped inside the medical center's physical therapy clinic with a guy who claimed to have a bomb, and that said bastard was holding the woman he loved at gunpoint.

Edward Kincaid had finally gotten the break they needed, following up on fifty-one green cars in the Kansas City area until he tracked down the only owner with a connection to Jillian.

Dr. Wayne Randolph.

Mild-mannered miracle worker from the Boatman Rehabilitation Clinic. Jillian's mentor. Father figure.

Loverboy.

Eli Masterson had gone through Randolph's office with a fine-tooth comb and found a wadded-up ball of torn paper with the word *Jilly* scribbled on it over and over. With Kincaid obtaining a search warrant, Michael's own team had been in the process of conducting a raid on Randolph's home when Mike's text message had come.

Dad
Trub at PTC
J taken
Gun/Bomb/Help

In Randolph's basement office, they'd found .45-caliber bullets, materials to make a pipe bomb, a set of copied keys and the sickest display of obsession Michael had ever seen. Pictures of Jillian tacked to a bulletin board. A newspaper photo from her high school basketball championship game. A handwritten thank-you card that credited Randolph with saving her life in rehab. Candid shots of Jillian—from the clinic, at her apartment building, hurrying down 10th Street near Troy's apartment building in No-Man's Land.

Maybe Randolph had sensed they were closing in. Maybe something Jillian had shared in their session this morning had set him off. Whatever his motives, whatever his reasoning, Randolph had Jillian locked inside a windowless half-court gymnasium, carrying a pistol and a bomb.

Night was here. Rain was falling.

Mike and Troy were missing, presumably also in harm's way.

It was the worst-case scenario of Michael's life.

And S.W.A.T. Team 1 had gotten the call.

He rubbed at his chest through the Kevlar vest he wore. The protective armor was supposed to protect the vital organs inside his body. Yet he was already suffering from the emotional bullet that had pierced his heart.

It was impossible to shut down the fear and anger he felt. He'd promised to keep Jillian safe. And now he might lose her before he ever had the chance to make things right between them.

The emotional barrage might have incapacitated a different man. But Michael Cutler had twenty-two years of experience and the best training KCPD could provide running through his veins. He spoke into the radio at the command center they'd set up in the clinic parking lot and asked for a situation report. "I need a sit rep now."

One by one, his men reported in.

Holden Kincaid was on the roof. "Negative, sir."

Trip Jones had secured the clinic's main entrance. "Negative."

Alex Taylor was on his belly outside the gym's locked doors. "I've got two thermal signatures in the center of the gym, but I'm blind here."

Michael waited a few seconds more for his sergeant to report in. "Delgado?"

"I'm checking out some mice in the wall."

"Come again?"

Rafe Delgado's voice dropped to a whisper. "I'm coming in through the patio entrance. I heard something I want to check out. But no visual yet, sir."

"Keep me posted."

Tossing the handheld radio back into the gear box at the back of the S.W.A.T. van, Michael turned to Edward Kincaid. "At least tell me we've got the rest of the clinic evacuated and a perimeter set up."

Edward nodded. "Your men's room-to-room check hasn't turned up anything. The hospital staff and patients in the connecting corridor area have been moved to the far end of the complex. Uniformed officers have the immediate blast area cordoned off and Bomb Squad is ready to go in on your order."

Everything about their response thus far had gone by the book. "So why don't I feel any better about this?"

"Because Jillian's the one trapped inside." Edward pulled back the front of his jacket and propped his hands at his waist. "I won't feel good about any of this until I see her out here in one piece."

Michael fingered the phone that usually served him so well. But a call to Wayne Randolph's phone had ended up at an answering service that said he wasn't responding, and a call to Jillian's phone went straight to voice mail. He couldn't negotiate with a hostage taker if he couldn't reach him.

And standing here, supervising reports that told him nothing, wasn't getting him any closer to having Jillian safely in his arms again. He needed inside that gymnasium. He needed to look Wayne Randolph in the eye and tell that murdering SOB exactly what he could do with his style of loving.

The radio crackled to life as Rafe Delgado buzzed in. Michael's senses all leaped to attention. "Captain? You're going to want to see this."

"MIKE?"

Rafe Delgado stood by the counter in the clinic lounge with his rifle on his hip and his eyes peeled as Michael swallowed his son up in a hug.

"Dad."

"Thank God you're safe." It almost didn't register that Mike was standing on his feet, hugging him back. He pulled back long enough to drop a spare Kevlar over Mike's head and closed the straps on either side of his torso. Then he palmed the side of his son's flushed face, trying to distinguish panic from excitement in his expression. "Where's your chair?"

"I had to leave it behind. Once I got the braces locked, I could move okay. It's the getting up and down that's tough."

Michael nodded. He'd want details later. For now, it was enough to know he was okay. "Rafe, let's get him out of here."

"No." Mike snatched at his arm, his balance wavering a bit at the sudden movement. "Troy's in there. So is Jillian and some creep with a gun."

"I know, son." Michael stiffened his arm to give Mike something sturdier to hold on to as he took a small step toward the patio exit where he'd come in. "As soon as my men can find a way into that gym, we're getting her out. We'll get them both out."

Mike pulled away and tottered back toward the storage closet where Rafe had discovered him. He shook off Michael's efforts to steer him back toward the patio. "I know a way in."

"How?"

Michael followed him into the closet and watched Mike push open a small door in the back. "The same way I got out."

"YOU LIED TO ME. All these years you've been lying to me."

The duct tape that bound Jillian's wrists together pricked at her skin and bruised her with every twist and pull as she tried to free herself. The desperate movements stopped abruptly when Dr. Randolph turned and walked toward her again. As far as he knew, she was sitting in the middle of the gym floor beside the leather briefcase with the pipe bomb inside, listening in rapt attention to his wandering diatribe about love and loyalty and loss.

She hoped.

He scratched his temple with the tip of his black steel pistol, dislodging his glasses and forcing him to stop and set them back into place before continuing.

Dr. Randolph had proudly shown her the bomb. Like a professor leading a classroom lecture, he'd patiently described in detail how he'd created it, how he'd learned to be a fairly decent shot in the army and how he wouldn't hesitate to use either skill if she didn't do exactly as he said.

"I taught you in rehab that you should never lie to me. I thought you'd learned your lesson." He pulled the gun from his temple and glanced at it as though surprised to discover he'd pointed it at his own head. But he didn't seem to have any qualm about pointing the gun directly at hers. Jillian jumped inside her skin, but she had no place to run, no way to fight him as long as her hands were bound like this.

All she had were her words. "I never lied to you, Doc. Maybe those first few weeks in the clinic when you asked me about how long I'd been doing drugs or what was the craziest thing I'd done to get my hands on some coke. But once I was healthy, once you helped me heal, I never told you another lie."

He shook the gun at her. "You loved me."

"I never said that."

The same mouth that had recited a sonnet to her a few minutes ago now spat nothing but contempt. "You loved me!"

When he knelt down beside her, Jillian scooted away.

But he caught her by the elbow and jerked her back, peeling off a layer of skin at her wrists. She bit her lip to hide her yelp of pain. But the same lip trembled with fear when he pressed the gun to her forehead and used it to brush her bangs out of her eyes.

"You sent me cards, pictures, letters over the years. Sharing your life with me. Thanking me."

She couldn't look into his eyes. She could only follow the gun as he continued to caress her with it. "I was grateful. Your patience and caring turned my life around. I always thought of you as a friend. Maybe the closest thing I had to a father since losing my dad. I'm sure you had other patients who felt the same—"

"A father figure?" He pushed to his feet and paced away again. Jillian instantly raised her wrists to her teeth and tried to cut through the tape that way. "No. It was love. I saw the way you smiled at me each time we met."

A scuffling noise from the storage closet diverted her attention from the tape. *No!* She'd warned the boys to stay quiet. If Randolph knew they had an audience now…

"I *do* love you." She said the first thing that came to mind, praying she was loud enough to mask any noises the boys made. It might have been true, up until a couple of hours ago when she'd seen him trying to break into her office. "Just not in that way. I loved you…" She swallowed hard so she could speak the lie. "I love you like a friend, Doc. Maybe even like family. But the flowers and the love letters… I never loved you in that way."

"Lies, Jilly!" The gun swung her way again as he stalked toward her. "All lies!"

He knelt beside her again, but this time to pull the pipe bomb from inside his briefcase and lay it across her lap. Every muscle constricted, trying to draw her body away from the lethal pipe. But there was no escape. The heaviness and instability of the weapon weighed her down, rendered her immobile, trapped her in place next to the man who was running his fingers through the length of her ponytail and pressing kisses to strand after strand as he spoke.

"I was content to love you from a distance because I knew you weren't ready to be loved. That was always one of the hardest lessons for you to accept, Jilly, dear." He paused to inhale the scent of her hair and Jillian's stomach clenched against the urge to gag. "You've always questioned your own worth. How many conversations have we had over the years about you feeling like you didn't deserve to have good things happen to you? You were barely more than a child when you lost your parents. That's more than most adults can cope with. Yes, you made some bad choices, got involved with Rivers and Rush and other men who never had your best interests at heart. But that doesn't mean you have to pay for those mistakes the rest of your life."

Jillian sucked in a shuddering breath and he rewarded her by running his fingers through her hair again.

"So beautiful. Inside and out." He stopped playing with her hair long enough to curl the fuse connected to the bomb around his finger and then pull it straight and smooth it out against her thigh. "You should be proud of everything you've accomplished, Jilly. I am. You deserve to be happy. You deserve to be loved. I was only waiting for you to be ready to accept me. I waited until you were old enough, until you were confident enough. Then I began to woo you. And how do you repay me?"

He waited until she tilted her tear-filled eyes up to him to answer.

"You gave your love to another man."

Michael. Yes, she loved him. In his skewed view of reality, Wayne Randolph was exactly right. For years, Jillian always believed she had a debt to pay society before she could love and be loved. He'd helped her finally learn that lesson.

She loved Michael Cutler. And if she ever, ever got out of this gym alive, she would do whatever was necessary to earn his love in return.

"I taught you how to love," Wayne continued. "I thought our ages would be the thing to keep us apart. And then I see you kissing another older man. *We're* supposed to be together. You're supposed to love *me*."

"What are you going to do, Doc?" Jillian asked. "Are you going to kill me for disappointing you?"

"For betraying me, you mean?"

Why had she ever thought the eyes behind those glasses had been kind? "I don't love you, Wayne."

"What?"

"I don't love you."

The shock of her quietly rebellious words must have distracted Wayne from the sound of a door opening and closing softly behind her.

"Randolph."

The doctor jumped to his feet, his gun swinging toward that beloved, deep voice at the back of the gym. "You! Get out of here!"

"Easy, Randolph." Jillian turned her head just enough to see Michael holding up his left hand in surrender as he slowly pulled his gun from his thigh holster and set it on the floor. "I'm just here to talk. I'm Michael Cutler, KCPD. My men and I needed to see what the situation was like in here. See if there was anything we could do to help. Jillian, you all right?"

She didn't know whether to weep with relief or yell at him to run and get as far away from her as he could. "I have a bomb in my lap."

"It'll be all right, sweetheart. Bomb Squad's outside, waiting for my signal."

"Sweetheart?" Dr. Randolph took a step toward the unarmed cop. "So you're the one. You couldn't keep your hands off her, could you? You couldn't keep your hands off my Jilly."

Michael kept his hands in the air, a gesture meant to show he posed no threat, though the uniform and S.W.A.T. vest and focused eyes said something different. "I'm a negotiator, Randolph. Like I said, I'm just here to talk. Now I can reassure my men that everything is under control in here."

"Liar." Wayne advanced another step. "I'm surrounded by liars. You're here to get your tramp back." And another. "You can't have her!"

"Why don't you put the gun down and we'll discuss this?"

"There's nothing to discuss. Jilly is mine. She loves *me*. We will be together one way or another."

"Put the gun down, Randolph."

He was too close to Michael. Even a lousy shot couldn't miss at that range. "Michael. Please just leave. I don't want anyone else to get hurt. Please."

"I'm not leaving you."

"Get. Out." Wayne wrapped both hands around the gun and took aim.

"Put the gun down or I'll take it from you."

"Michael!"

"Get out!" Wayne pulled the trigger and Jillian screamed.

"No!"

Michael jerked back against the gym wall and sank to the floor.

"No!" She tried to turn, tried to steady the bomb on her thighs and get to him to help. "Michael!"

Randolph came back and grabbed her ponytail, spinning her around to face him. A million pinpricks of pain stabbed across her scalp, and burned her eyes with tears. "I hate you, Wayne! I hate you!"

He ignored her kicks, ignored her screams, ignored her pain. He pulled a lighter from his pocket and reached for the fuse. "It's you and me, Jilly. Forever."

"Randolph! Get away from her!"

"What?"

"Michael?"

Wayne picked up his gun, took aim as Jillian whirled around.

"Drop it!"

Michael already had a bead on Wayne when the doctor fired.

Jillian jerked at each gunshot. Held her breath.

She watched the circle of blood bloom across the front of Wayne Randolph's jacket as his knees buckled and he collapsed to the floor. Dead.

"Jillian?" Michael was at her side in an instant, his boot on Randolph's gun, taking no chances as he slid it from his lifeless grasp and tucked it into the back of his uniform. "Sweetheart, you're not hit, are you?"

Then he was on his knees beside her, carefully lifting the pipe bomb and placing it back inside the briefcase. "Jillian, are you hurt?"

His hands were on her face now, running along her arms and down her legs. The shock of the last few seconds hadn't entirely worn off as she pushed aside his assessing hands and caught his face between her own bound hands. He stilled long enough for her to see the clear, focused strength shining in those dark blue eyes. She shook her head in disbelief. "He shot you."

"That's what the body armor's for." Michael leaned in and covered her lips in a quick, hard, life-affirming kiss. Then he drew a wicked-looking knife from his belt and sliced through the tape at her wrists, freeing her.

He pulled those same wrists around his neck and scooped her off the floor and into his arms. "I'm not hurt. I can walk."

"Humor me, okay, sweetheart?"

Jillian tightened her arms around his neck and smiled. "Okay."

"And do me a favor. Press the button on that radio on my shoulder." She pushed the button and Michael turned his chin to his shoulder, carrying her back to the closet where she hoped the boys were still safely hidden, snapping orders all the way. "Taylor? Take down that door and get the bomb squad in here now. Trip, I need evac assistance with a wheelchair-bound hostage in the gym. Kincaid? Make sure the ambulance is ready. Delgado? Tell Mike his plan worked. We're coming out."

"I UNDERSTAND SURVIVOR'S GUILT, SON."

Michael couldn't remember the last time he'd had this long or this meaningful a conversation with Mike.

Certainly not since the accident and Pam's death. Sitting together on the back step of the S.W.A.T. van while Edward Kincaid supervised the debriefing of everyone in the aftermath of a hostage crisis wasn't how he'd pictured this breakthrough moment. But Michael wouldn't have changed the drippy weather or beehive of official activity for anything. His son was finally talking to him.

"You don't think I would have died in your mother's place?" he explained. "I'm the tough guy—the one with the dangerous job. She was kind, gentle, loving—smarter than I'll ever be. There's not a day that goes by that I don't think it should have been me."

Mike swiped at the tears in his eyes and nodded. "Steve was the good one. He was being responsible by not drinking. He was being a good friend by taking me home when I'd had too much. I worked hard in the classes I liked and blew off the others. But Steve… he worked hard at everything. He wanted to be a firefighter like his dad. He had something useful to give the world. I was just going to play football. It should have been me who died in that crash."

Michael wrapped his arm around his shoulders and hugged him to his side. "I'll argue with you on that one. Grief is a lousy thing to deal with. For months after your mom died, I was just going through the motions. I shut down inside. But then you got hurt, and I kind of woke up from that guilty haze I'd been living in. I realized I had a job to do—the most important one in the world."

"Being a cop?"

"Being your father." He loosened his grip, and was heartened when Mike didn't immediately slide away. "You know what else I realized? That I was dishonoring your mother. No, I couldn't save her. Nobody could.

God's got her now because He probably needed somebody to get His books in order."

Mike's mouth tilted with half a grin. "Yeah, she was a freak about organizing stuff, wasn't she? Classroom parties. Little League fundraisers. The football parents' booster club."

"She was a pro, wasn't she?"

"Yeah."

Michael caught his son's last tear with his knuckle and flicked it away. "I finally got my act together and realized mourning your mom, feeling guilty about her death—just going through the motions of living—would really tick her off. Your mom would have wanted me, wanted *us,* to really live. To make a difference in the world. To do our jobs well. Set goals—achieve them. Make friends. Feel things."

"Sounds a lot like the way Jillian lives."

"Yeah." That was an admission to make. "She's a pretty gung-ho lady, isn't she?"

"I was thinking I could do some of that, too. You know, setting goals, making a difference?" Mike locked his braces into place and pushed to his feet. Michael stood, too, intending to help him, but it was pretty clear that moving from a seat into his wheelchair wasn't a big deal anymore. Another reason to thank Jillian. "I thought about majoring in physical therapy in college, or becoming a sports trainer or coach. Troy and I even talked about how we could open some kind of training center together."

"Get through high school first." Michael did his fatherly duty and reminded Mike to keep those priorities in the right order. "I don't think I've ever been prouder of you, son, than I am of you tonight. I love you."

"Love you, too, Dad." When Michael started to lean in for another hug, Mike put up one hand and turned his chair with another. Okay. Real world. Enough mush for one night.

And that was when they discovered they weren't alone. Having answered all of Edward's preliminary questions, Jillian was standing a few feet away, hugging her arms around her middle. The sprinkle of rain still falling couldn't mask the tears running down her face.

Michael felt a tug on his sleeve and bent down to hear Mike whisper, "Now go give her the same speech. Mom would like her. *I* like her. Don't screw it up."

With a nod and a wave, Mike rolled past her and joined Troy under the awning of the PT clinic's entrance, where Trip and Delgado were regaling the boys with stories that earned them lots of high fives and laughs. A weight had lifted from his heart tonight, and Michael decided to take his son's advice.

He reached inside the back of the van and pulled out his black KCPD jacket as Jillian approached.

She smiled. "Mike's my hero tonight, finding a way to get you inside the gym so you could save me. He's a good kid."

"He's a great kid." Michael draped the jacket around her shoulders and all kinds of primitive, possessive, perfect feelings started drumming through his blood.

"I was scared I was going to lose both of you tonight."

"I love you."

He said it bluntly, startling her. As those beautiful green eyes returned to their normal size, he startled her again by fisting his hands around the collar of the jacket and pulling her up into his kiss. He took his own sweet time easing the surprise from her lips, then tracing the seam with his tongue and urging them to part so that he could slip inside and taste the essence of Jillian herself. He was pretty well kissed himself by the time he came up for air and rested his forehead against hers with a contented sigh.

"I feel young and strong when I'm with you. You gave me back my son." He covered her hands where they clung to the collar of his uniform with his own. "You make me give a damn about living again."

"I love you, Michael." The words sounded right. Felt right. Were right. "I love your son. And I'm damn lucky that you feel something for me, too."

"Not just 'something,' sweetheart. Love. I feel love."

"So what are we going to do?" She wound her arms around his neck and pulled herself closer. "Do you think we can make a relationship work?"

He slipped his hands beneath the jacket she wore and sealed the embrace. "Are you still going to go on your crusades to save kids who've been through hell?"

"After I take a bit of a break to rest up, yes. Are you still going to be a S.W.A.T. cop?"

"Yeah. I think I may have the knack for it." She smiled and the moment was complete. "I'm still going to be a father and I'm hoping I'm going to be a husband again, as well."

"A husband?"

"Yeah. To you." He was dead serious now. In that controlled, I'm-the-boss way that he normally did so well. "Mike told me not to screw this up, so I thought I'd better put it out there before you get away from me—or I lose you to some other man."

But Jillian saw right through the tough guy facade

to the man who would forever be vulnerable to a tall, leggy woman with sweet green eyes and coffee-colored hair. She gently cupped his jaw. "You are never going to lose me, Michael Cutler. I love you. And it would be the greatest honor of my life to be your wife."

"And that's a firm yes?"

"Haven't you figured it out yet, Captain? I didn't slow my steps because of your age. I was just waiting for you to catch me."

"When did you ever slow down for me?"

Her lips curved into a sly grin. "Just kiss me."

* * * * *

Read on for an excerpt from
MIDNIGHT RIDER
The latest installment in the
***BIG "D" DADS: THE DALTONS** series*
by Joanna Wayne

When her search for a killer leads to danger and bull rider Cannon Dalton, homicide detective Brittany Garner will face her toughest case yet: catch her long-lost twin's killer, and try not to fall for the man who might be her infant niece's father…

"The woman in Greenleaf Bar was you?"

"You don't remember?"

"Vaguely."

He struggled to put things in perspective. That had been a hell of a night. He'd stopped at the first bar he'd come to after leaving the rodeo. A blonde had sat down next to him. As best he remembered, he'd given her an earful about the rodeo, life and death as he'd become more and more inebriated.

She must have offered him a ride back to his hotel since his truck had still been at the bar when he'd gone looking for it the next morning. If Brit was telling the truth, the woman must have gone into the motel with him and they'd ended up doing the deed.

If so, he'd been a total jerk. She'd been as drunk as him and driven or she'd willingly taken a huge risk.

Hard to imagine the woman staring at him now ever

HIEXP69806R

being that careless or impulsive.

"Is that your normal pattern, Mr. Dalton?" Brit asked. "Use a woman to satisfy your physical needs and then ride off to the next rodeo?"

"That's a little like the armadillo calling the squirrel roadkill, isn't it? I'm sure I didn't coerce you into my bed if I was so drunk I can't remember the experience."

"I can assure you that you're nowhere near that irresistible. I have never been in your bed."

"Whew. That's a relief. I'd have probably died of frostbite."

"This isn't a joking matter."

"I'm well aware. But I'm not the enemy here, so you can quit talking to me like I just climbed out from under a slimy rock. If you're not Kimmie's mother, who is?"

"My twin sister, Sylvie Hamm."

Twin sisters. That explained Brit's attitude. Probably considered her sister a victim of the drunken sex urges he didn't remember. It also explained why Brit Garner looked familiar.

"So why is it I'm not having this conversation with Sylvie?"

"She's dead."

Find out what happens next in
MIDNIGHT RIDER
by Joanna Wayne,
available January 2015 wherever
Harlequin Intrigue® books and ebooks are sold.

HIEXP69806R

Read on for an excerpt from
THE SHERIFF
The first installment in the
***WEST TEXAS WATCHMEN** series*
by Angi Morgan

Mysterious lights, a missing woman, a life-long secret revealed…all under a star-studded West Texas sky. Sheriff Pete Morrison must protect a gorgeous witness, Andrea Allen, from gun smugglers and…herself.

"We've got to get you out of here."

"I am not helpless, Pete. I've been in self-defense courses my entire life. And I know how to shoot. My gun's in the bag we left outside."

Good to know, but he wasn't letting her near that bag. He dropped the key ring on the floor near her hands. "Find one that looks like it's to a regular inside door. Like a broom closet. I'm going to lock you inside."

"Are you sure they're still out there?"

"The chopper's on the ground. The blades are still rotating. No telling how many were already here ready to ambush us." He watched two shadows cross the patio. "Let's move. Next to the snack bar, there's a maintenance door. Run. I'll lay down cover if we need it."

They ran. He could see the shadows but no one followed. Hopefully they didn't have eyes on him or Andrea. He heard the keys and a couple of curses behind him, then a door swung open enough for his charge to squeeze through.

He saw the glint of sun off a mirror outside. They were watching.

"Can you lock the door? Will it lock without the key?"

"I think so."

"Keep the keys with you. I don't need them. Less risky." Bullets could work as a key to unlock, but they might not risk injuring Andrea. He was counting on that.

"But, Pete—"

"Let me do my job, Andrea. Once you're inside, see if you can get into the crawl space. They just saw you open the door. Hide till the cavalry arrives."

"You mean the navy. He won't let us down," she said from the other side of the door. "This is his thing, after all."

Pete had done all he could do to hide her. Now he needed to protect her.

Find out what happens next in
THE SHERIFF
by Angi Morgan,
available January 2015 wherever
Harlequin Intrigue® books and ebooks are sold.

HIEXP69808